It's Like CANDY

Also by Erick S. Gray

Nasty Girls

Money Power Respect

Ghetto Heaven

Booty Call

It's Like CANDY

AN URBAN NOVEL

ERICK S. GRAY

ST. MARTIN'S GRIFFIN
NEW YORK

Published in the United States by St. Martin's Griffin, an imprint of St. Martin's Publishing Group

IT'S LIKE CANDY. Copyright © 2007 by Erick S. Gray. All rights reserved. Printed in the United States of America. For information, address St. Martin's Publishing Group, 120 Broadway, New York, NY 10271.

www.stmartins.com

The Library of Congress has cataloged the first St. Martin's Griffin edition as follows:

Gray, Erick S.
    It's like candy : an urban novel / Erick S. Gray.—1st St. Martin's Griffin ed.
    p. cm.
    ISBN-13: 978-0-312-34997-4
    ISBN-10: 0-312-34997-1
    1. Sisters—Fiction.   2. Queens (New York, N.Y.)—Fiction.   3. Criminals—Fiction.   4. Prostitutes—Fiction.   5. Ex-convicts—Fiction.   6. African American women—Fiction.   7. City and town life—Fiction.   I. Title.

PS3607.R389I87 2007
813'.6—dc22   2006050598

ISBN 978-1-250-80584-3 (trade paperback)

Our books may be purchased in bulk for promotional, educational, or business use. Please contact your local bookseller or the Macmillan Corporate and Premium Sales Department at 1-800-221-7945, extension 5442, or by email at MacmillanSpecialMarkets@macmillan.com.

Second St. Martin's Griffin Edition: 2021

10   9   8   7   6   5   4   3   2

*I dedicate this book to my family, my friends,
and to those who have lost a loved one to violence,
drugs, and abuse.*

ACKNOWLEDGMENTS

I want to say that, despite my ups and my downs, I still feel blessed. I thank God every day for my talents, my family, my daughter, and the people who have come in and out of my life. Some folks are here to stay, and some were meant to leave—never hold or force yourself onto something that wasn't meant to stay in the first place. Numerous people have influenced my life, in both positive and negative ways. I've fallen many times, but I refuse to stay down. I just dust myself off and keep it moving. Trials and tribulations have made me stronger, and brought me closer to God.

And before I end this, I have to say one more thing. . . . Someone once told me that our lives are simply a reflection of our actions. If we want more love in the world, then we must create more love in our hearts. Life will give you back everything you put into it. It's a reflection of you. Enjoy it, cherish it, and never stop believing in yourself.

It's Like
CANDY

"You lookin' for a date, luv?" River asked, staring into the burgundy Benz, focusing on the Caucasian driver.

"Excuse me?" the driver asked. He was a bit confused by her question.

River stepped closer to the car. She leaned into the passenger window and repeated, "I said, is you lookin' for a date?"

"How much?" he asked. He was clad in his usual day-to-day business attire; white shirt, black tie, and cheap shoes, being the average-looking Joe. He had just gotten off from work, and wanted a quick blow job before he went home to his wife. He knew about the track in South Jamaica, Queens, and knew what went on there. It was no secret to the man in the Benz that this was where the action was. Where pussy was up for sale at a reasonable price.

"You a cop?" River asked.

"No. I'm just looking for some fun."

"You want your dick sucked, that's fifty," River told him, staring him down and waiting for an answer with her hands resting on the passenger door.

The middle-aged accountant, who'd just put in three hours of overtime at his firm, couldn't resist River's beauty. He was dazzled by her sinuous, long, jet-black hair, her petite figure, scantily clad in a short denim skirt and a revealing halter top, seductive dark bedroom eyes, and her beautiful long soft legs stretched out in a pair of three-inch stilettos. Her peanut-butter complexion and glossy lips caused the man to get a slight bulge in his jeans.

"You dating or what?" River exclaimed, snapping him out of his lustful daydream.

"Huh? Um . . . yeah, get in," he said. He leaned over and opened the passenger door.

River glanced around briefly and then quickly jumped into the Benz. Her date, who introduced himself as Ronny, politely shook her hand and asked where to.

"I know a spot. It's quiet, and hardly any cars come around. You ain't got to worry about anyone bothering us," River said.

"Just lead the way." Ronny put the Benz in drive and drove off.

As Ronny drove, he couldn't help but constantly glance down at River's gleaming long legs. He was horny, and even though he'd been married to his wife for ten years, Ronny occasionally loved the company of a prostitute, preferably black. He loved the sisters from head to toe, but had married a white woman, because he knew that his family would hate him if he ever brought a black woman home. So he drove the extra twenty minutes into Queens and prowled around the risky neighborhood for a quick fix of pussy.

"Turn here," River instructed, and Ronny made a quick right.

He couldn't help himself, River was beautiful, and he yearned for her. He wanted to touch her all over, grope her luscious figure and get it started immediately.

"You're beautiful," he told River.

"Thanks," River said, being short with him.

"You got on any panties under that skirt?" he asked, glancing down at her legs for the umpteenth time that night.

River displayed a counterfeit smile and kept her mouth shut. She just wanted to get it over with. He was lanky and nerdy-looking, and she knew that if it wasn't for the money, she would have nothing to do with him.

"Can I touch you?" Ronny asked, already stretching his free hand out and gently brushing his fingers against her crossed legs.

River looked at him, and replied, "I do have on panties."

"What color?"

"Blue."

"That's my favorite color. Can I see 'em?"

River sighed, and thought, *Here we go wit' another fuckin' perverted asshole.* She lifted her hips, her ass hovering over the plush leather seat, and pulled up her denim skirt, exposing the blue thong underneath.

Ronny smiled. "You really got a nice body."

"Turn here," she said.

Ronny made another right.

"Ayyite, pull up in this alley."

He parked his car in an isolated industrial area where there was nothing but empty tractor trailers, parked trucks, and buildings and warehouses vacant for the night.

"My money, please," River said. "No treasure, no pleasure."

He went into his pocket and pulled out two twenties and a ten. "I want you to suck my dick nice and hard. I want you to play with my balls too," he told River, looking like an eager child.

"Ayyite, pay up first and then we can get this party started."

He passed her the money, and River stuffed the cash into her tiny purse.

"Take 'em off, white boy. We ain't got all night. You got fifteen minutes to come." She looked at the clock on the dashboard.

He quickly unbuckled his khakis, pulling his pants and his white briefs down to his ankles. His pale white dick became exposed, and River had to stop herself from laughing as she looked down at his small pink raw sausage and thought, *Damn, where's the rest of it?*

"I want you to jerk me off, too," he said, getting excited.

River pulled out a condom, and before anything, she started to jerk his little shriveled penis. She always thought that white men were so corny. Only a few were worth her time, and Ronny wasn't one of the few. If anything, she wished she could castrate him and save him the trouble and the embarrassment.

"Oooh, yeah . . . do that. Beat my dick. Beat my dick," Ronny gasped, feeling River's warm hand moving rapidly up and down his slight erection.

As River jerked him off, she glanced out the back window. It was dark all around, and she knew she had to keep an eye out for the boys and the stickup kids that lurked in the night. Ronny was so enthralled with the hand job he was receiving that he had his eyes closed, forgetting that he was parked in the wrong hood.

"You ready for me?" River said seductively.

"Yeah, suck my dick, you black bitch!" Ronny moaned.

River didn't argue or curse him out. She gave him a bitter look, but she let the racial slur slide. She had other plans.

"Suck my dick before you make me cum, bitch. Do what I paid you to do."

"You got ten minutes, baby. I'm gonna do you real good. You gonna enjoy me," River said.

"I want my money's worth."

Ronny reclined his seat and River slowly rolled down the condom on his white little dick. It didn't have that far to go. Then River glanced out the back window again, and noticed a car creeping toward them with the headlights off.

If Ronny had been street smart, he would have known that River was hesitating. But his hormones and lust for an exotic black woman made him weak and dumb. He'd been doing this for so long, coming into a Queens hood and picking up black prostitutes, that he felt he was safe out there. He was a client loyal to the track and his money was green just like everybody else's.

With the doors still unlocked and the windows rolled down, he was definitely an easy target. River glanced back again, and saw two men creeping toward them. But she went on as if everything was cool.

"Bitch, suck my—"

"Get the fuck out the car, niggah!" A loud and shattering voice suddenly pierced the air as a large black figure violently grabbed Ronny from the driver's-side window and pulled him out of the car, dropping him to the ground.

Ronny was terrified and wide-eyed as he stared up at his attacker. He was on his hands and knees with a loaded 9-mm pointed at him.

"What's going on?" he asked in a horrified voice, looking like he was about to piss on himself, with his pants still around his ankles. A slimmer second man came into view, and he too gripped a 9-mm. Both men wore black ski masks.

"Niggah, shut the fuck up and fork over that cash, muthafucka, before I blow a hole in your white ass!"

"My money's in my wallet," Ronny fearfully explained.

"Give it up, then, niggah!"

He slowly tried to reach for his pants pocket, but his pants were down too far around his ankles.

"I got that," River said, coming from around the passenger side, and pulling off his pants completely.

Ronny didn't fight. He let River reach for his pants, pulling them off and leaving him bare-assed. River extracted his wallet, another set of keys, and a small picture of his wife and kids.

"You married, got kids and shit, and you out here trying to get your little dick sucked while your wife and kids wait at home for your trifling ass," River said.

"Please, don't kill me. I'm sorry."

"Damn right, you're sorry," River replied, shaking her head.

"Yo, get in the car," the stout man dressed in all black said, referring to River. "We takin' his shit."

"No, please . . . take my money, but please, not my car. I just started making payments on it," he cried out.

"Fuck you!" the slimmer black male shouted, with his gun trained at Ronny's head. "You having a bad night, muthafucka!"

Suddenly, the larger man went up to Ronny and brutally began striking him in the head with the butt of his gun. He continued to hit his victim until his face was bloodred, and the man was nearly unconscious.

"That's enough!" River cried out as she looked on in shock.

"Let that be a lesson to him. He needs to stay his white ass where he came from. Ain't no need for this cracker to come around here and mess wit' our women."

Ronny lay unconscious, sprawled out on the ground, with his dick still exposed. River still had his pants in her hands.

"I think he's dead, Red," River said, panic showing on her face.

"Fuck that cracker! Get in the car, River," Red shouted.

River didn't hesitate on getting in the car with her accomplice. His partner jumped into Ronny's Benz and drove off behind Red and River.

"Why you do that, Red?" River shouted. "We had his money and keys already. You didn't have to beat him like that."

"Yeah, I did, cuz I bet you his white ass will never come around here again," he stated. "He touched you too. I hate it when men touch you, River."

"I'm not your property, Red, remember that," River stated angrily.

Red glanced at her, but didn't respond. He got jealous easily.

River sighed and sat back in her seat, gazing out the window as the car raced down Rockaway Boulevard toward Far Rockaway to a nearby chop shop to get money for the stolen Benz.

River had been scheming in the streets of southeast Queens with Big Red and Twinkie for a year now. She had known both men for a while. They met at the club, and she figured that they were career criminals, getting involved in anything from major drug sales to grand larceny.

Big Red approached her one day at a strip club on Jamaica Avenue. He watched her dance naked onstage for a moment, then wanted to talk to her after her set. He bought her a drink, flaunted a handful of money, and told River that he had a very lucrative proposition for her to get easy money. River was listening. When Red told her what he wanted her to do, she was very reluctant at first. But dancing was getting tiresome for her, and she wanted something new for herself. Thinking it over, and even knowing that becoming a pawn to entrap men for a stick-up crew would be consequently dangerous for her, she still accepted the job.

River did her first holdup in Brooklyn, helping Big Red and Twinkie stick up two drug-dealing brothers who were eagerly willing to take River back to their two-bedroom condo in Canarsie for a night of a lusty threesome.

River discreetly disclosed their information to Red, and an hour later, he had both brothers bound and gagged in their condo and robbed them of everything they had.

Two months later, River was becoming a pro at luring men to her without even saying one word to them. Instantly they came to her, willing to wine and dine her and take her away on vacations. Only later would they find out it was a dire mistake.

"Take me home!" River said, becoming more and more frustrated that Red had beaten that white boy in the alley so severely.

"What?"

"Take me home, Red!" River sternly repeated herself.

"Yo, you still upset over that white boy?" Big Red asked, glancing at River. "It was a job."

"You didn't have to beat him like that. He had a family, Red."

"Oh, like you gave a fuck about his family when you was setting him up," Red countered.

"Take me home now or I'm out," she threatened.

"You can't be serious."

River kept quiet. Her look said it all to Red.

"You a piece of work, River . . . fuckin' fo' real. Bitch suddenly wants to have a fuckin' conscience," Red cried out, making a sudden U-turn in the middle of the street.

River remained quiet until Big Red dropped her off at her place one block off Hillside Avenue.

"I'll talk to you later, Red," River said dryly as she jumped out of Red's car and walked to her front door. Red quickly drove off, followed by Twinkie in the stolen Benz.

River shared a basement apartment with a female roommate named Tah-Tah, who was a stripper at Day Dreamz, a Queens strip club on Hillside Avenue.

Tah-Tah was beautiful, but a gold-digging chickenhead who only cared about money and herself.

"You home early," Tah-Tah said, sitting on the couch and doing her own pedicure in her underwear.

"I thought you would be at the club already," River said, walking past her and not wanting to talk to her.

"'Kay picking me up around one. You know a bitch can't miss a night tryin' to get my money," Tah-Tah said.

"Whateva!" River said, not being in the mood.

River went into her bedroom and closed the door behind her. She didn't know why she flipped out on Red. She didn't really care for the white boy he'd beaten, but she felt that this game they were playing was getting old for her and too risky. And it didn't help her mood that tonight she had her period. For her, it seemed like going from stripping to becoming a stickup kid, it was one endless hustle after another.

2

"Yo, E... you did' your thang tonight," Rah shouted, a bit tipsy. He was having a really good time at the celebration Eric was giving for his niggah Rah, who was getting married next week. Rah held a cup filled with Hennessy in one hand and a chocolate big-booty sistah with the other.

Eric stood off to the side, watching his niggahs have a good time with the strippers he brought for them—ten butt-naked beautiful hoes who were all willing to pull no punches when it came to treating the men right and giving them whatever they wanted, as long as they were paying—VIP lap dances and whatever. If they had the right cash, then it was on.

Eric rented out a Brooklyn basement with three available rooms for VIPs and a spacious open living room, where the girls got naked and did their thang on the carpeted floor. Dildos and all kinds of sex toys came into play, and that's when the big bills started coming out. Tens, twenties, and fifties were spread out across the floor and that definitely inspired the girls to go on and freak each other.

There were about twenty-five men in attendance and they tipped the girls generously, got drunk on Alizé, Hennessy, Coronas, and

E&J, felt on some titties and ass, and listened to constant rap and R&B playing on CDs.

The atmosphere was calm, no drama and no problems. Everybody in the room knew each other, and the girls Eric brought in were frisky, freaky, flirtatious, cute, and down for whatever.

"Yo, E . . . how much you charging for a room?" Raheem asked, a brown-skinned thick-booty bitch with platinum hair clutched under his arm.

"Twenty, my niggah," Eric responded.

"Damn, niggah . . . twenty. And she charging me sixty to fuck. Yo, y'all tryin' to break my pockets. . . . shit, I thought we were peoples, E," Raheem spoke in a tipsy and joking manner.

"We are, that's why I'm charging you twenty up front, because the liquor's free."

Raheem laughed. "You my niggah, E . . . fo' real." He gave Eric dap.

"I'm worth it, baby. You don't wanna tap this phat ass. My pussy gonna do you right," the platinum-headed stripper proclaimed, turning around and slapping her ass.

"Damn, look at that shit jiggle. A niggah could surf on that ass," Raheem joked. "Yo, here's your twenty, E. Yo, a niggah gotta do him tonight. Baby-moms upstate and shit. Pussy went on vacation."

Eric chuckled, collecting Raheem's twenty, and letting him and his big-booty VIP pass through to the narrow hallway, where three available rooms awaited them.

So far, Eric had profited about three hundred for the night, collecting cash at the door and collecting twenty apiece for the rooms used to fuck in.

He couldn't believe Rah was getting married. They'd known each other since the ninth grade, and Rah was always the light-skinned guy with pretty eyes, a playboy who had a woman for each day of the week. But he guessed Rah finally found that certain individual piece of pussy that was able to keep him happy at nights, and probably for the rest of his life.

Eric knew he had to throw Rah the bomb bachelor party and still make his money too. He charged fifteen at the door, having his man Donald hold down the door and make sure the men paid to get in. Donald was six foot three, 275 pounds, and you could test him if you wanted, but guaranteed if you did you'd be losing three or four teeth before the end of the night. Donald, he didn't play, he was a cool dude, but he loved fighting and smashing people's heads in whenever they caused him or any of his boys trouble. He used his size to his advantage, and he was strong as an ox.

The bachelor party went off big, the girls were right, and the money was continually flowing. None of the strippers were complaining to Eric about folks being cheap. Each of the ten girls had made about two hundred for the night so far. Of course, out of the ten ladies, eight of them were doing VIPs and sexing men for that little extra cash down their G-strings.

R. Kelly blared out of the speakers, and Eric watched a trio about to go down in the center of the room. Two dark-skinned strippers, who were completely naked with tits and ass for days, slowly took off Rah's clothes, and had him lying on the carpet naked, with his dick hard in the air, and being encircled by friends who cheered him on with alcoholic drinks clutched in their hands.

Eric knew what was about to go down. The husband-to-be was about to get his freak on for the last time. And he had the right two women to go out with. Bambi and Hershey were no joke—two curvaceous, voluptuous, black sistahs, with long black hair, and asses that J.Lo couldn't even compete with. They were cute, and they were quick to fuck and suck a man for the right amount. But since Rah was getting married next week, they were willing to satisfy him sexually for free—and it didn't hurt the ladies that he was cute, too.

Rah smiled, showing niggahs that he wasn't ashamed to get

naked in front of a crowd and show the ladies what he was working with. He was cocky, as he was working with nine inches.

"Yeah, niggahs . . . y'all thought I had a small dick, huh?" Rah boasted, smiling.

"Ain't nobody worrying about your ugly-ass horse dick. We lookin' at the bitches," a man in the crowd replied.

Everybody laughed, and the women prepared to get down to business, making some fellows envy Rah.

Hershey started it off. She clutched Rah's hard erection in her grip and slowly leaned forward, engulfing his big dick in her warm, sensuous big lips. Rah groaned, feeling blessed.

Bambi hovered her phat ass over Rah's mouth and slowly came down against his jaw, and Rah started to eat out Bambi as she lay pressed against his face.

"Rah, you wilding right now . . . but damn, yo . . . that shit lookin' good as fuck," Rah's best man, Mel, shouted out. He looked on wide-eyed as he watched Bambi straddling Rah's face, with her pussy deep in Rah's mouth.

"Shit!" Mel muttered.

Eric stood off to the side, shaking his head. He had to laugh. He knew when Rah, Mel, Donald, him, and the rest of these crazy people from Queens got together that it was going to be one hell of a party. And tonight was no disappointment.

"Yo okay, E?" Sparkle asked. She was this petite, Hispanic Mariah Carey–looking stripper who was sexy as fuck.

"I'm good, Sparkle," Eric returned, not really looking at her, but paying more attention to the action ahead of him.

"Your friends are crazy," Sparkle said.

"Yeah. I know."

Sparkle was one of the two strippers who weren't doing VIP at the party. She believed in making her money just by taking off her clothes and entertaining the fellows. She really despised the hoes that had to fuck just for an extra buck, because they made it bad for her.

About five men had already asked her if she did VIP, and she politely told them no. Some persisted, telling her that there was more money in it, but she held her ground, and if they got too rude, she would then walk away and pay that one no mind all night.

She was doing all right for the night, had made herself about $180 just by dancing and grinding. She strutted around in leather knee-high boots, red-laced thong, and a very short scanty pink T-shirt that barely covered her nipples.

"You good?" Eric asked.

"Yeah, I'm makin' my ends."

"Pardon me, luv . . ." a slim male interrupted as he approached Eric with a well-rounded young woman by his side. "I need a room."

"Twenty, Jay," Eric told him.

Jay reached into his wallet and passed him a twenty, and then happily strutted down the hallway to the nearest room.

Sparkle quickly exchanged glares with Jay's date for the night. She thought that Jay's date was a nasty bitch with no respect for herself, just some cheap whore who'd fuck anyone for a Happy Meal. And the shorty that Jay was about to fuck, who went by the name Mousey, thought Sparkle was a stuck-up, stupid, light-skinned bitch who believed she was better than everybody else. It was well known that the two didn't like each other.

Sparkle remained by Eric's side. It was clear that she had a small crush on him. But Eric was about business, and he never mixed business with pleasure. So he looked on Sparkle as a friend, nothing else. Even though many of his friends called Eric crazy, and constantly beat in his ear, "You need to hit that, son . . . do you . . . Yo, Sparkle, I know her shit is good."

Some of Eric's friends would have loved to find out how good that pussy was, but Sparkle didn't fuck, no matter how much cash they threw at her. It wasn't happening.

The episode with Rah, Bambi, and Hershey got even crazier as

Bambi straddled Rah's waist, and started to ride his long big dick, clutching his chest, and Hershey took her turn in pressing her damp pussy down on Rah's face, straddling his face tightly, as she panted, feeling Rah's tongue swim around in her.

Eric smiled and Sparkle muttered, "Them some nasty bitches."

Suddenly Eric's cell phone started vibrating against his hip. He quickly reached for it, flipped open the case and saw that it was his niggah Critter calling.

He answered the call, but had to step outside to hear Critter clearly because the noise and music were deafeningly.

"Critter, what's good?" Eric asked. "I thought you were coming through?"

"Yo, E, I need your help," Critter said.

"What the fuck you do?" Eric asked, knowing Critter was always into some shit.

"I got this bitch at my place, and she won't leave yo."

"What? You can't kick the bitch out of your own place?"

"Yo, come talk to her for me. I'm 'bout ready to smack this hoe, but you know a niggah on probation. And I ain't tryin' to get locked up over this silly bitch."

Eric sighed and returned with, "Ayyite, Critter, I'll be over there in a minute. Just don't do no stupid shit."

"Good lookin', E," Critter said, hanging up.

Eric went back into the party and informed a few of his peoples that he had to leave and handle something. He told Donald to take over and call him if there were any problems. But with Donald, he knew that there wouldn't be any problems.

"Fuck you, Critter! Why you tryin' to fuckin' play me? You stupid, Critter. You stupid!" Starr shouted from the locked bathroom door, gripping the cordless in her hand and threatening to dial 911.

"Starr, why you being a fuckin' bitch? Just open the fuckin' door. I just wanna talk to you," Critter shouted.

"No. I want my money. I'm gonna call the cops on your stupid ass if you don't give me my money," Starr shouted back.

"Yo, ain't no need to call police to this, bitch. Bitch, you know I'm on probation."

"Exactly!"

Critter sighed. At that point, he wanted to kick the bathroom door down and strangle Starr. "Yo, Starr, all I got on me is twenty dollars."

"Then we got a problem, Critter. I want all of my fuckin' money. Don't be tryin' to fuckin' play me, niggah! What I look like to you?!"

Critter wanted to answer cleverly and sarcastically, but he knew it wouldn't be wise. He heard the doorbell, and walked to the front door, peeped outside, and saw Eric. He sighed in relief and quickly opened the door.

"E, thanks for coming."

"What shit you got into now?" Eric asked, cutting him off.

"Yo, I got this bitch who locked herself in my bathroom, and she ain't tryin' to leave, E. This hoe tryin' to extort a niggah," Critter explained.

"Extort?"

"Yeah, the bitch talkin' about she want money from me and shit."

Eric laughed. "Damn, Critter."

"I know, man," Critter responded.

Critter was blacker than Wesley Snipes and Whoopi put together, looking like a moonless night. He was about five feet eleven, and was slim, weighing no more than a wet dog. Critter had a bad history with women. He was sex-starved, the kind who'd stick his dick into anything with a pulse and a phat ass. Critter had no taste and no class, he was just searching for pussy continually, and thinking with his dick. Bitches always got Critter into trouble. He had four kids, and his baby-mamas—none of them were pretty but their bodies were tight.

Critter was always telling Eric, whenever E joked about the women he fucked with, "Pussy ain't got no face."

To Critter, pussy was all the same to him, no matter the shape, look, or size of a woman. And Eric knew that no matter what, Critter was always gonna be Critter. They had grown up together and Eric was always looking out for Critter.

Eric followed Critter to the back bedroom, and he saw clothes sprawled out all over the place, food was spilled across the floor, empty condom wrappers lying around, and the room stank of a strange odor.

"Damn, Critter," Eric said, screwing up his face from the smell.

"Yeah, niggah . . . I know. I was gonna clean up, but you know, things kinda got out of hand."

"Who that in there wit' you, Critter?" Starr shouted from the bathroom.

"Come out and see," Critter shouted back.

"I know you ain't bring niggahs in here to jump me. You know I still got the phone up in here wit' me. And I'll call the cops on your sorry ass," Starr threatened again.

"Fuck you, Starr! I'm tired of your shit!" Critter cursed, getting irate.

"Critter, calm down," Eric said. "Let me handle this."

Eric approached the door and knocked on it gently.

"What the fuck you want?" Starr said heatedly.

"Yo, luv . . . I'm just here to talk," Eric casually explained.

"So talk that dumb-ass niggah into giving me my fuckin' money," she barked.

"How much does he owe you?"

"A hundred."

"Damn."

"Your boy, Critter, he a cheap-ass bastard. Fuck him!"

Eric smiled, glancing over at Critter, who stood a few feet away looking pathetic clad in blue-and-white boxer shorts and a wifebeater.

"Yo, luv . . . you sound young. How old are you?" Eric asked.

"Sixteen."

"What?" Eric was shocked.

"Yeah, niggah, I'm sixteen. And if I call the cops on this phone, and tell 'em how Critter was up in his apartment fuckin' a minor, that niggah goin' to jail. So he better give me my fuckin' money. I ain't playin' wit that niggah no more."

"Sixteen!" Eric mouthed over to Critter, who shrugged his shoulders. Eric was appalled. Critter was a grown man, damn near thirty in three years and he had a sixteen-year-old girl in his apartment. Eric wanted to beat the shit out of Critter himself.

"Ayyite, luv . . . Critter's wrong for that, but there ain't no need in involving the police," Eric told her.

"Yeah there is, if he don't pay me my money."

"Why do he owe you a hundred dollars in the first place?"

"Because it's what I charge," she stated.

Eric tittered. He couldn't believe what he was hearing. Critter was paying a minor to have sex with him. *This niggah is losing his fuckin' mind*, Eric thought. All that pussy he had down at Rah's bachelor party, and Critter was up here fuckin' minors and getting caught up in stupid situations. Eric wanted to bounce and let Critter handle his own problems, but that was his boy, and he couldn't leave him hanging out to dry like this.

Eric knew Critter was broke. But if Critter thought that he was going to fuck Starr and get his nut off, and then easily swindle shorty out of the money he owed her, then he was wrong. Starr was up on her game, and she knew how to use her age to extort men. If they didn't pay, then she called the police, and they went to jail. She'd gotten away with this hustle many times, especially with horny older men, and then afterward Starr would beat them over the head for an outrageous price sometimes, depending on the individual. Once she conned a police captain for a thousand dollars. She had him by the balls and he willingly paid. He could have fought it, but he knew the exposure of his having sex with a sixteen-year-old girl would not have been good for his reputation.

Eric looked over at Critter in disappointment and he knew that there was only one way to handle this situation. "Ayyite, luv, what's your name?"

"Starr."

"Ayyite, Starr, listen. I'll pay you the hundred. You good wit' that?"

"As long as I get paid, I'm good."

"Okay."

"First slip the money under the door," Starr demanded. "I want the money in my hands first, and then I open this door."

Eric shook his head. Shorty was definitely on point. He had to respect her game. Eric reluctantly went into his pocket, pulled out his bankroll, peeled off a crisp hundred-dollar bill, and slid it under the bathroom door as told.

Starr quickly yanked the money free from his hand. A few minutes later, the bathroom door opened, and Eric stepped back, waiting to see this Starr who had a serious attitude and knew how to hustle a niggah.

Into Eric's view came a cute, brown-skinned, thick, curvy young girl who was clad only in her panties and bra, and sported braids that went straight back. Her tits filled the bra completely and her young thighs were tight and firm.

"Damn, you only sixteen?" Eric said, surprised by Starr's physical appearance.

"She's a conniving bitch, that's what she is!" Critter spat.

"Fuck you, niggah!" Starr said.

"Yo, chill, Critter," Eric said.

"Niggahs be tryin' to play me like I'm stupid," Starr proclaimed, staring over at Critter with an annoyed look plastered across her cute face.

"Yeah, whatever . . . go ahead wit' that shit. You still a bitch!" Critter countered.

"Niggah, it ain't never too late to get back on that phone and call police," Starr threatened.

"Nah. Ain't no need for that, Starr. Critter's gonna start behaving himself, right, Critter?"

Critter sighed, staring over at Eric. "Yeah, whatever!" He waved him off.

"Starr, get dressed. You got your money," Eric said. "So, we good?"

"Yeah, we good," Starr answered, pulling up her tight jeans against her skin. "Last time I do business wit' a cheap niggah like Critter."

"Bitch, I ain't cheap!" Critter said, "you just ain't worth the hundred."

"Niggah, whatever. You saw all this and had to be all up in it. Do me a favor, Critter. Next time your ugly ass see me, keep your fuckin' mouth shut and keep fuckin' walking. I ain't tryin' to deal wit' your ugly ass!"

"Bitch, who you callin' ugly?" Critter snapped.

"I call it like I see it," Starr quipped back.

"Children, children," Eric said, "let's be adults in this room, or try, at least."

"Umm, only adult I see in this room is you," Starr said, looking at Eric.

Starr continued to get dressed. She was scantily clad in tight jeans, a close-fitting white T-shirt that accentuated her big breasts, and adorned stilettos, looking like a prostitute from the track. She then stuffed the hundred-dollar bill down her pocket, collected the rest of her things, and walked out the door.

Eric couldn't help but admire her assets from behind. For a young girl, Starr had a body, and she looked older than sixteen. But once she opened her mouth, that young age came out, and he wondered how Critter got involved in that.

When Starr was gone, Eric turned to Critter, and said, "Sixteen, Critter. Damn, pussy that hard to get?"

"Yo, my bad, E . . . but that bitch got a body for days, you know what I'm sayin'? I just got caught up."

"Niggah, you always gettin' caught up when it comes to your dick. Yo, you owe me a hundred."

"I know, good lookin' out, E. You know I got you when I get paid again."

"Niggah, you better," Eric said. "Shit, I got all this pussy down at Rah's bachelor party and you out here tryin' to fuck young girls, Critter. What the fuck is wrong wit' you?"

Critter snickered. "Man, them stuck-up strippers. Shit, they be tryin' to beat a niggah in the head wit' them prices. I ain't got it like that."

"So you're tryin' to swindle sixteen-year-old girls now. That's how it is, now, Critter? You promising them money that you ain't got?"

"Yo, I'm just tryin' to do me, that's all. A niggah tryin' to live."

"Whatever, niggah. C'mon, I'm heading back down to Rah's party. You coming. I see I can't leave you here by yourself. You don't know how to act," Eric said.

"Yeah, let me change first."

"Put on sumthin' nice, Critter. I don't want you scaring off the ladies wit' your stankin' ass."

"Ha, ha, you funny, niggah."

3

Starr stood on the corner of South Road and 150th Street hoping to make herself some quick cash by doing what she knew best, selling pussy. It was twenty minutes past midnight, and she stood on the track dressed in tight blue jeans that highlighted her thick young hips, stilettos that gave her a three-inch boost, and a denim jacket, with nothing underneath but a bra. She teased drivers as they drove by, waving them down and flashing open her jacket so they got a quick glance of her scantily covered breasts.

Men couldn't believe that such a raving young beauty was turning tricks. She made dozens of cars slow down and some came to a stop, asking, "Yo, how much?"

Starr was one of three girls working the track on a warm spring night, and she loved it because it was quiet, and there was no competition. The majority of the girls couldn't compete with Starr. She was young, and drop-dead beautiful, and willing to let anyone fuck her in the ass for the right price. For a sixteen-year-old girl, she had the body of a woman.

She made a quick hundred in a half hour by fucking a fifty-year-old man in the front seat of his car. It was really fast money for her, because she was in and out like lightning. As soon as he parked his

Lincoln in a desolate area so they could have some privacy, Starr got paid first, then quickly unbuckled his khakis, jerked him off for a few minutes to get him hard, and then put a condom on his small erection. She got out of her jeans, showing her eager male trick that she had no panties on, and slowly straddled him in the front seat. She came down on his dick bit by bit, clamping her love muscles around his erection, and let out a counterfeit moan. She swayed her hips back and forth, causing her trick to grab at her long graceful hair and shout, "I'm coming!"

In less than five minutes he came, praising Starr for her skills. "I wanna see you again," he said, watching Starr pull up her jeans.

"You got another hundred dollars?" Starr asked, not even glancing at him as she focused on getting herself proper again to go back out on the track.

"I got fifty," her trick replied.

"Fifty gets you a blow job. You wanna fuck me again, you need fifty more," she sternly explained.

Starr glanced at him, and thought, *Damn, old man, you had trouble getting it up the first time, take a time out. I don't wanna kill you out here.*

The man nodded and looked heartbroken. He'd never had pussy like that before. He was definitely enthralled by Starr.

"Can I get your number?" he asked.

"No problem," Starr said. She quickly gave him her cell phone number, and he promised to call again for another date with her. And they always did.

Ten minutes later he dropped Starr off where he had picked her up. Starr quickly got out, told him thank you, and looked for the next car to get into.

Five minutes after she was dropped off, a green Altima pulled to the curb, the driver lustfully gazed at Starr, and shouted, "Your name Starr, right?"

"Yeah. You lookin' for a date?"

"Hells, yeah. You don't remember me? I fucked you last week, and you was off the hook," he said.

Starr smiled, but she didn't remember him, faces came and went in her line of work. She didn't have time to remember names and faces, only making them Benjamins. Starr got into the Altima, and the driver pulled off, ready for round two. Starr was a celebrity when it came to selling pussy on the track. Dozens of men asked for her despite her age. When it came to sex, Starr held nothing back, giving all of her dates a 100 percent of the wildest and freakiest time that they would ever have. She knew how to please a man in every way, from stroking their egos to their dicks, fucking her tricks as if she really loved them. And she owed her subtle sexual skills to her mother, even though she resented her mother bitterly.

As Starr was getting fucked doggy style in the backseat of an Altima, something her trick said to her triggered sudden thoughts and emotions about her mother.

"Your pussy is gonna make you rich, Starr," her trick stated gripping her naked hips, sweating profusely, and thrusting in and out of her as she panted.

Your pussy is gonna make you rich, Starr was something her mother had continually told her when she was young.

Starr remembered her mother's words as if it was yesterday. She had been only twelve years old when she lost her virginity.

She grew up in Brooklyn, Bed-Stuy, in a brownstone on Albany Avenue one block off Fulton Street. Her older sister, who was sixteen at the time, had left home a year ago, leaving Starr alone with her mother. Her sister couldn't handle the abuse that came down endlessly from her mother, so she packed her bags and was willing to try her luck out in the world on her own.

Their father, Henry, had left home when both of his daughters were very young. He just couldn't handle his wife's constant and brazen infidelity. He always thought that maybe she would stop and love him as a wife should. But like a fool, he gave his wife chance after chance to change. Men would call his home and ask for his wife with no respect for him, and he'd curse them out and warn them not to call his home ever again. His wife, Sheryl, would be out all night constantly, leaving him alone with two small children. But his boiling point came when he returned home from work early one afternoon and found his wife engaged in a threesome with two men, while his younger daughter, Starr, lay sleep in the bed next to them.

Sheryl was getting fucked doggy style, while she had the second man's erection deep down her throat. Shocked, Henry began attacking one of the men and beating on him. But his friend quickly jumped in, pulling Henry off his pal, and they began stomping and kicking Henry while he lay in a fetal position on the floor.

Sheryl screamed for them to stop, and after a moment more of beating Henry up and waking his daughter, Starr, in the process, both men finally stopped.

They taunted him and raved about how good his wife's pussy was, and how good a fuck she was. Henry continued to lie on the bare floor crying, watching both men get dressed and leave.

Sheryl went up to her weeping husband and tried to show some comfort by wrapping her arms around him and saying, "Henry, I'm sorry!" But Henry angrily pushed her away, and shouted, "Get away from me, you stupid cunt bitch! You do this in front of our daughter?! Don't you care?"

At that moment, Henry felt as though he could kill her as he seethed with jealousy and rage. But he glanced over at his tearful daughter and stopped himself from making the biggest mistake of his life.

He was humiliated and no longer felt he could be a man or father to his two daughters. The thugs had beaten it out of him that day. He felt ashamed. He cried alone every night. And when he couldn't take the pain and the abuse anymore, he left two weeks later, without leaving so much as a good-bye letter to his wife and kids.

After her father and her sister left, the abuse trickled down to Starr. Starr remembered one night when she was alone in her room watching TV, and she started hearing moaning coming from her mother's bedroom. Curiosity got the best of her, so she went toward her mother's room to investigate. The door was ajar, and she slowly stared into her mother's room, only to see her mother on her knees giving a man a blow job.

The man that her mother was giving sexual pleasure to was tall and very dark. He was naked, and sported a well-kept afro. He was also well built, and very well endowed. Starr gazed at his dick, having never seen anything like it. She watched her mother suck on his dick as if it was a candy bar.

"Ummm . . . deep-throat that shit, Sheryl," she heard the man say. And Starr continued to watch her mother swallow up his big dick as though her mouth was an endless black hole. It disappeared into her mouth like some magic trick.

Starr watched and made the mistake of putting her hand against the door too much, pushing it more open suddenly as the door creaked.

Her mother turned and saw Starr standing there with a frightened gaze.

"That's your daughter?" the man asked.

"Yes. Starr, I thought you was asleep," her mother said.

"I can't sleep, Mama," Starr said, her voice soft and innocent, as she tried not to look at the stranger in front of her.

"I'm glad you're up anyway. Were you watching us?" Sheryl asked.

"No, Mama," she lied.

Her mother gripped her lover's dick in her hand and asked, "Starr, do you know what this is?"

Starr quickly shook her head no, lying. She knew what a dick looked like. The male students in her class used to flash her and some of the other girls their little peckers when the teacher wasn't around.

Some of the girls would stare and giggle, while others would turn their heads quickly, and cry out, "Ill!"

Starr continued to stand nervously in front of her mother. The large man intimidated her as he stood stark naked in front of her with her mother's hand gripped around his dick, stroking him gently.

"You wanna learn how to suck a dick, Starr?" her mother asked. "You need to. You gotta know how to please a man if you want to keep a man around. The more you please a man, the longer he'll stay around."

Starr continued to stand there. She wanted to leave and go back into her room and finish watching TV. But her mother prevented that by saying, "C'mere, Starr, hold him in your hand and get the feel of it."

"No, Mama, I don't want to," Starr said.

"Girl, don't be silly, you ain't a baby anymore. It's time you learn how to start pleasing a man if you want to have a man," her mother stated.

"But, I don't want to," she repeated.

The sudden look on her mother's face told Starr that she was in trouble. Her mother got up off her knees and approached Starr vigorously and grabbed her daughter aggressively by her nightgown, and shouted, "You're my daughter and you do what I say! Now stop being a little bitch, and grab that big dick in your hand. It won't hurt you."

"But Mama—" Starr tried to speak, but her mother raised her hand and gave her daughter a stinging slap across her face.

Starr started to cry, looking up at her mother in horror.

"You go over there and become a woman!" her mother ranted.

Reluctantly, Starr went over to the man, who just stood there smirking down at Starr. It was even bigger for her up close. Starr got down on her knees as tears trickled down her cheeks, and slowly reached up and gripped the man's nine-and-half-inch dick in her hand. Her mother stood over her too, and began talking her through the episode.

"Now slowly move your hand up and down his penis, Starr. They love it when you take your time and show that you ain't scared of it," her mother instructed.

Reluctantly following her mother's orders, Starr slowly moved her small hand up and down his hard shaft. The touch of it was strange for her; it was hard, but so warm, and began pulsating in her hand.

The man let out a slight moan watching Starr slowly jerk him off.

"Good, Starr . . . now do it a little faster," her mother said proudly.

Starr moved her hand up and down his large penis as fast as she could. It felt as if the more she jerked him off, the harder it got in her hand.

Her hand action went on for five minutes until she heard her mother say, "Okay, Starr, now here's where you get a man to really love you. I want you to put his dick into your mouth and suck it."

Starr gave her mother a dreadful look. She didn't want to. She was twelve, and she thought about boys, but her mother was taking her to a whole new level.

"Starr, I'm not gonna tell you again. A real woman should know how to suck a man's dick. There's nothing to be afraid of. You take his dick and put in between your lips and move your jaw up and down."

Starr continued to cry, becoming even more hesitant. But her impatient mother suddenly grabbed Starr by the back of her head and pushed her face against his testicles. "Suck his dick like you love him!" she shouted.

Starr unwillingly opened up her mouth and slowly pressed her lips against the tip of his dick with her mother's hand still clutched around the back of her head.

"Suck it!"

Starr swallowed him inch by inch, coughing and gagging at each inch that went into her mouth. The man moaned, standing over Starr with his hands on his hips. Starr was able to take on six inches before she gagged even harder and removed his dick from her mouth.

"Mama, please, I can't do it anymore," Starr pleaded. But her mother grabbed a handful of Starr's hair and pushed her face back against his testicles, shouting, "Open your got damn mouth and please him!"

With her eyes drenched with tears, Starr reluctantly continued to suck his dick as her mother forced more down her throat by pushing the back of her head. Suddenly Starr started to gag even harder and quickly threw up on her mother's man.

"Shit!" he shouted, jumping back from her puke and spit.

"Starr, what the fuck is wrong with you? You'll never become a woman if you can't handle something so simple," Sheryl yelled.

Starr got up and quickly ran to her room and cried all night.

But that incident was just the beginning of more unspeakable things to come for Starr. A week later, as Starr lay in bed asleep, her mother came into her room unexpectedly with a tall stranger.

"Starr, wake up," her mother said accosting her out of her sleep.

Starr looked up at her mother, disoriented. She glanced over at the man in her bedroom and became extremely nervous.

"I have a friend who wants to meet you," her mother said, walking over to her night lamp and turning it on.

The light shimmered over Starr's innocent, soft brown, petite body, and the man smiled. He peered down at the beautiful Starr sprawled on her bed in a long white nightgown and licked his lips.

"You say she's a virgin?" the man asked Sheryl.

"Never been touched," her mother replied.

"Mama," Starr cried out. Her heart began to beat rapidly, and she tried to hold back her tears, becoming aware of what her mother was up to.

"You say five hundred?" the man asked.

"Not a penny less," Sheryl said, with her hand outstretched.

The man went into his pocket, pulled out his wallet, and removed five crisp hundred-dollar bills and put the money in Sheryl's hand.

Sheryl quickly counted the money, and then said, "She's all yours. Have fun."

"I will."

With that, Sheryl walked out her daughter's bedroom, leaving her daughter alone in the room with the man. The door closed behind her, but not before she heard her daughter cry out, "Mama, no! Mama, come back! Mama, please, come back. . . ."

She ignored her daughter's cry for help and stuffed the folded cash down into her bra. Unbeknownst to Starr, her mother had a growing crack addiction, and saw more money coming in faster by not just selling her own body for sex but her daughter's too.

Inside the bedroom, the man climbed onto the bed with Starr, who was backing away from him, crying. He ripped her nightgown off her, and tore off her panties. Starr tried to resist, but he was too strong.

"I paid for this, so relax!" he scolded. He began unzipping his pants. He stared at Starr's developing breasts, and moved his hand in between her bare thighs, and his dick got hard just by the touch of her.

"Mama!" Starr cried out, but to no avail.

She was quickly forced on her back; her legs forcefully spread open, and she felt him climbing between her naked thighs. He wasn't as big as the man from last week, but it was still scary for her.

Suddenly, she felt the man thrust his six-inch hard-on into her without any concern for her being young and a virgin; the abrupt pain of her vagina being torn open caused Starr to scream. Tears trickled down her face.

The man continued to thrust into her while he grunted and panted, sweating freely over her body. Blood oozed down Starr's bare thighs, and she had never felt so disgusted. The man who pounded his dick repeatedly into her for ten minutes had to be in his late forties.

"Damn, you so tight. I never had it so tight," he proclaimed as he huffed. He clutched her bedsheet tightly and shouted, "I'm coming!"

Moments later he pulled out his dick and ejaculated across her stomach.

There was a loud knock at the door. "Baby, your time is almost up!" Sheryl shouted. "You got five more minutes."

"I'm already done," he said.

When Sheryl walked into the room, he was already fastening his pants. She saw Starr still lying in bed with the sheets pulled over her head and she was sobbing uncontrollably.

The man looked at Sheryl with beads of sweat still across his forehead, and stated, "Best piece of pussy that I ever paid for. She was definitely worth the five hundred."

"You wanna fuck me next?" she asked.

"Nah, I gotta go. But next time I'll take you up on your offer." He walked by Sheryl and strutted down the stairs and quickly made his way out the door.

Sheryl turned to look at Starr, who was still lying with the sheets over her head.

"Starr, baby, get up," Sheryl said. "It wasn't that bad. You became a woman tonight. We made some good money, too."

Starr didn't respond. Her crying was loud and pained.

Sheryl went over to the bed and took a seat by her daughter's side. She began rubbing her daughter's ankle and said to her, "Starr, everything's gonna be okay. Believe me, Starr, your pussy is gonna make you rich one day. Sometimes, what we got between our legs is all we need to get by. These niggahs out here will continue to pay for some pussy until the day they die. You use that to get ahead. A woman should never be broke in this world. Now suck it up, and get over it. The worst is finally over. You know what dick feels like, so get used to it. We gonna get paid."

Starr suffered sexual abuse from her mother for two years until, like her father and her older sister before her, she finally reached her boiling point, too.

She had been fourteen at the time, and it had been a hot spring day. Starr was hardly in school anymore, because her mother had her turning tricks twenty-four/seven, and her mother saw school as getting in the way of business.

Sheryl had dropped out of school when she was fifteen, and she had so many men supporting her since a young age, that it became normal for her. She couldn't see living life any other way, for herself or her daughters.

Starr was in the kitchen making lunch when she heard her mother call out for her. She knew her mother was in her bedroom with a date because she heard them from the kitchen panting and raving. She grimaced at the thought of the man her mother was fucking. He was obese, bald, with nasty razor bumps and looked like his breath stank.

Starr ran to her mother's bedroom, where she saw her mother lying down naked on her bed. Her mother was still beautiful, even with a crack addiction. Her hair was no longer lengthy and graceful, but she'd become thinner during the past two years.

Starr looked over at the man who was in white shorts and a wifebeater. His skin was very hairy, and he was very unattractive. Just the sight of him made Starr's skin itch and her stomach turn. She knew her mother had fucked him, because the room reeked of sex.

"Now how much are you willing to pay?" her mother asked the man.

"Mother, no," Starr said, fearing that her mother wanted her to fuck him.

"Starr, relax, it's not what you think," she replied.

"For me to see that . . . I'll give you a thousand dollars right now," the man said.

Sheryl smiled, and said, "Let me see the cash."

The man went over to his pants and pulled out a large amount of money rolled together in a rubber band. "I got four grand here; this shows I'm good for it."

Sheryl smiled generously, and removed herself from the bed. She went up to her daughter, and said, "Take your clothes off."

"What?"

"Starr, I said take your clothes off. And I'm not gonna tell you twice," her mother chided.

Fearing her mother's wrath, Starr reluctantly began to get undressed. For fourteen, she was filling out beautifully in all the right areas. The chubby man lustfully gazed at her naked body and touched himself.

He stared at both mother and daughter standing stark naked in front of him and couldn't believe his eyes.

"You sure she's only fourteen?" he inquired.

"Yes," Sheryl said. "Now pay up."

He passed Sheryl the cash, and shortly afterward, she started to do the unthinkable. She pushed her daughter onto the bed, down on her back.

"Starr, spread your legs," she instructed.

"Mama, are you serious? No!" Starr became defiant. But a hard slap across her face changed her sudden attitude.

"Bitch, he's paying us good money to see this. Now shut the fuck up and do as you're told," her mother said.

Starr clutched the side of her face, teary-eyed. She felt her mother opening her legs. She tried to resist, but her mother struck her again, harder this time, drawing blood from her mouth. From the look in her mother's eyes, Starr knew she was high.

"Open your legs, Starr, before I beat the shit out of you," she threatened.

As she sobbed, believing her mother's threats, Starr reluctantly opened her legs and lay down on her back. She felt her mother's hand run down her thighs, and she cried harder. Her legs quivered, she wanted to close them, but her mother was a madwoman.

Then she felt her mother's tongue enter her slowly, and felt her tongue swimming around in her. She cried out louder. She couldn't believe that this was happening. It was wrong. Immoral. But for a thousand dollars, her mother didn't care. For this much cash, her mother had no limits.

Starr continued to lie there motionless with a river of tears rolling down her face. She looked up at the man who was paying to see this, and thought, *What kind of monster are you? How can you pay to see this? I hate you. I want you to die.*

He smiled and gripped his four-inch dick in his hand and masturbated slowly as he looked on.

"Damn, I wish I had a camera," he said.

Sheryl ate her daughter out with no remorse. It was as if she was with a stranger. Money was her only concern.

For ten dreadful minutes, Starr remained frozen, crying during the duration of the sexual act. When her mother was finally done, she just lay there, the pillow beneath her head soaked with tears. She couldn't move. She didn't want to move. She wanted to die.

"Starr, get up. We got paid," her mother said, donning a blue robe.

But Starr heard nothing, just silence and pain aching in her heart. She couldn't believe the ordeal she'd just gone through.

"Fine, then, lay there all day if you want. I got a thousand dollars on me and I'm gonna have me some fun," her mother said, leaving the bedroom.

That was Starr's breaking point, and a week later, like her sister before her, she packed her bags and left home, never to return again.

"I'm coming!" her trick shouted while he continued to thrust into Starr. "Shit, you got some good fuckin' pussy."

Starr clutched the headrest to the front seat, and her other hand landed against the backseat, as she panted, snapping out of her daydream.

"Come for me, baby," she said.

"Aaaaaahhh, shit . . . damn . . . damn . . . shit!" he cried out, trembling as he came in Starr, then he fell back against the backseat, very well satisfied.

"You good?" Starr asked, pulling up her jeans.

"Hells, yeah. Yo, fo' real, Starr, your pussy is gonna make you a rich woman one day."

"Please don't say that," Starr said, suddenly offended.

"What? It's the truth. You definitely got some good shit. I'm gonna put your pussy up on Ebay and shit, make millions," he joked.

"Would you shut up already?"

"Damn, what's your problem? I'm giving you a compliment."

"Just don't!"

"Shit, you got the bomb pussy, and I'm being nice, and you actin' like a bitch about it. Your moms blessed you wit' a hell of a body. So what the fuck is your problem?"

"You know what . . . fuck you!" Starr cursed. She grabbed her things, quickly got out of the car, and strutted up the street. Her date looked on in surprise at her sudden reaction, shrugged it off, and went about his business.

As Starr made her way back to South Road, tears began to form in her eyes. It had been two years since she left home, and at sixteen she was doing what her mother taught her best, *how to use what you got to get what you want out of life*.

4

"River, how much doe you got?" Big Red asked. They were hidden away in Big Red's basement in East New York, where Red planted his thuggish ass every night after he came back from being out in the streets. It was one of the many safe houses for Red and Twinkie.

"I got two hundred," River said, holding a bunch of wrinkled tens and twenties in her hand.

"What about you, Twinkie?" Big Red asked.

"I got a hundred," Twinkie replied.

Big Red frowned. "Fuck this! We need to step this shit up. We only made about six hundred over the weekend. We're slippin' on makin' this money. Some of these dealers are gettin' wiser."

Twinkie agreed. Between the three of them, that was two hundred apiece. And River couldn't deal with that. She didn't mind that Big Red and Twinkie were using her as bait to reel in these horny, lustful men who were drawn to her out on the track. But it needed to pay off, and the men they were going after barely had fifty dollars in their pockets. Red and Twinkie had to lay off the drug dealers for a minute and come up with a different game plan. So they targeted the tricks on the track.

Without River, Big Red and Twinkie's scam wouldn't exist. And she knew it, too, which was why she wanted more money, because she was taking all the risk by getting in the car with the strangers and allowing them to see her face, while Red and Twinkie always wore masks.

But she knew that her time would come. She'd settle for the two hundred now, an even split between the three partners. But in the future, it was going to be different for her. She wanted more money or she was out.

"River, you my girl, fo' real. You be hookin' these niggahs in lovely. Yo, that white boy, I thought money was gonna shit on himself," Big Red stated. "But yo, we need to step up our game a little, y'all feel me?"

"I feel you," Twinkie agreed.

"Yo, some niggahs out on the track are getting hipped to our thang, and these pimp niggahs, they strapping up. But I ain't worry about that," Red said. Big Red was huge, with a bald head and a dangerous mystique about him. He'd also had a crush on River for the longest time. They called him Big Red because of the small freckles that were plastered across his face.

"So what you thinkin' about?" Twinkie asked. Twinkie was Red's partner, his right hand, a ride-and-die hood niggah. They worked really well together. Twinkie, dark-skinned and with long braids, was a clean-shaven thug with piercing dark eyes and a constant scowl on his face. He owned many guns, and knew how to use them accurately if there was ever a problem to solve. A lot of men tried to tease him about his name, given to him by his deceased grandmother because her grandson had loved Twinkies so much when he was a kid. But Twinkie had shot at many who came at him about his name.

"Yo, River, I was thinkin', you a dime-ass bitch fo' real. You be havin' niggahs' nose wide opened and shit. You the baddest hoe on the track," Red said. River didn't know whether to take that as a compliment or what. But she sat there and listened.

"But yo, we can take you and get at these niggahs wit' the real money, I'm talking about hundreds of thousands and shit. You be a front, get to a niggah and make him trust you and shit. I'm mean, we gonna take our time wit' this, instead of rushing to get paid for a quick dollar. We gonna study your marks and find out where they live, what kind of cars they drive, and shit. You know what I'm sayin'? You fuck wit' the niggah and get the rundown on him and shit, his house, cars, how much he's banking in his account, shit like that. You know what I'm sayin'? Word, River, you know a niggah gonna spend doe on you. You know that pussy sells. You know what I'm sayin'?"

"Yo, I feel ya on that one, Red . . . fo' real," Twinkie agreed. "That's what I'm talkin' about. That platinum money."

"So, you ready to step up, River?" Red asked.

"Niggah, whatever." River replied dryly.

"Yo, girl, you gotta be excited 'bout this, you know what I'm sayin'? I mean, you gotta show interest in a niggah, make him believe you like him and shit. You gotta be believable that you wanna fuck a niggah. Shit, if it comes down to it, fuck the niggah to make it real."

River sighed.

"I'm tryin' to get this money, make this shit long-term and shit. I ain't tryin' to live like some broke niggah. Y'all feel me?"

"That's what's up," Twinkie uttered.

"So, when we gonna start this?" River asked.

"Shit, this week. I already know a niggah we can hit right now," Big Red informed them.

"Who?" Twinkie asked.

"Some cornball niggah, who likes to floss and thinkin' he a big baller. I been watchin' him. But I know he stacking paper. I used to go to school wit' the niggah. He hustling, but I know pussy is his weakness."

"Let's get this money," Twinkie shouted, rising and giving Red dap.

River's beeper went off, catching her attention. She glanced at the number, and then said, "I gotta go." She raised herself up out of her seat and headed for the door.

Big Red jumped up and followed her upstairs. "River, hold up," he called out.

"You know I was just kidding about you having to fuck a niggah, right?" Big Red asked, looking more concerned now.

"Yeah, I know," River said.

"But I want us to step up. Too many niggahs getting money out here, and I wanna be one of them niggahs eatin' lovely, too."

"Ayyite, Red." River said, with her main focus on leaving Red's place.

"You okay?"

"Yeah."

"So, what you doin' tonight?" Big Red asked.

"I'm busy," she told him.

"So when are we gonna do us, River? I wanna take you somewhere nice."

"Red, we about business. I'm gonna be real, you know I ain't feelin' you like that. We cool peoples, and I want it to remain that way."

Red was a bit hurt. He'd heard the speech before, but the truth was, he craved River's undivided attention. She was beautiful, and he got jealous sometimes when he'd use River as bait and see her flirting with different men every night, even though he knew it was false and it was what they'd planned. He knew it was business and she was only doing her job, and she was the best at doing what she did. Red knew if River left, he wouldn't be able to find anyone as good as her.

"Ayyite, luv . . . go do you, you know what I'm sayin'?" Big Red said, trying to keep his gangsta composure and not show that River was getting to his heart.

River left without saying another word. And Big Red remained standing in the doorway, watching River's walk, watching her backside glide down his porch, her legs shimmering in the sunlight, and her long soft black hair falling off her shoulders. Big Red knew that one day, he would be with her. She resisted now, but he knew one day she would climb into his bed, especially when he started getting that money.

5

It was early morning, and the Dunkin' Donuts on Rockaway Boulevard was bustling with morning traffic. Employees on their way to work were purchasing a quick cup of coffee, tea, doughnuts, and bagels before their commute to work, quickly paying and leaving. Only those not in a rush and able to linger and watch the morning traffic pour in and out sat at the eight tables discussing nothing in particular.

One of these customers who loitered in the shop every morning around seven or eight was Pumpkin, a black male in his late sixties who'd been retired for about ten years now. He used to be a truck driver. He worked for many years and was able to save money and retire comfortably, living off his pension for the rest of his life.

He had salt-and-pepper hair and wore thick-framed glasses, looking a bit fatigued, since he'd smoked four packs of Newports every day since he was twenty-five. His face looked like crumpled paper. Pumpkin had lived a hard life, and had many stories to tell. He'd been through it all, Vietnam, the civil rights movement, racial profiling on the job, and even did time on Riker's Island for drugs and attempted murder.

Pumpkin was no stranger to the streets and the neighborhood. He was born in the South but came to live in Jamaica, Queens, when he turned twenty-two. He had two kids, a daughter and a younger son. He hadn't seen or heard from his daughter in over ten years, and his son was doing a five-year sentence in Upstate New York for drug possession.

Choosing not to wither away at home, Pumpkin woke every morning around six in fine comfort, walked down to the Dunkin' Donuts a few blocks from his home and ordered himself a cup of tea and two Boston cream doughnuts. His routine was predictable. Every morning you'd find Pumpkin, Leroy, Sherry, and John-John lounging around in Dunkin' Donuts, chatting and observing customers that poured in and out.

Eric walked into the shop around nine that morning, and saw his uncle Pumpkin seated at his usual spot near the window. If his uncle Pumpkin wasn't in Dunkin' Donuts with his three comrades, then he would probably be home, lying on the couch, watching an old Western movie.

"There he is, my favorite nephew," Pumpkin called out.

"Hey, Uncle Pumpkin," Eric greeted, pulling up a chair to the table. He greeted Sherry, Leroy, and John-John.

"Hey," all three greeted back in unison.

"What brings you around here, Eric?" Pumpkin asked, knowing his nephew didn't come around often.

Eric's father and Pumpkin were brothers. Pumpkin was the oldest of six siblings, all born in Durham, North Carolina. Eric's father had been a gun for hire back in the '70s and early '80s. He had even done work for the mob and had earned their respect. But in '85, Eric's father, who went by the street name Yung Black, was gunned down abruptly in front of his Hollis home one evening. Eric was eight when his father was killed, and his mother, who witnessed her husband's murder, became unstable and was admitted into psychiatric treatment in a Long Island institution a few months later.

Eric went to live with other relatives, aunts and uncles who looked after him. During the years of staying with his aunt Fran, he and his cousin Russell, a.k.a. Yung Slim, became really close, more like brothers than cousins. Eric never had any brothers or sisters, so to him Russell and his sister, Francine, became like siblings instead of cousins.

When they became teenagers, Russell took to the streets, hustling, fighting, and earning a credible street name for himself. Eric tagged along with his cousin, and they did practically everything together—drugs, pimping, fighting, stealing—everything, except for murder.

Russell took it that extra mile when he started carrying a concealed loaded pistol and started shooting homeboys in the foot or hand who owed him money or fucked with him. Eric wasn't down for the gunplay, he felt that murder and guns brought the cops harder down on you. Stealing and selling drugs was one thing, but when you start killing people, it was a different thing.

But Russell was always hardheaded, and was going to do what he wanted to do, nobody could tell him different. He was a bully, and he knew that niggahs in the hood feared him. He got off on the fear he caused, and put it into the streets, selling drugs, making money, and soon becoming a kingpin. And he was bringing his favorite cousin, Eric, along for the ride.

But in '97, Russell caught a murder charge because of a certain snitch. He was found guilty and sentenced to a ten-year bid upstate. So after that, Eric just did him, got himself a job and gradually left the streets alone. He feared prison, and didn't want to do time like his cousin. When Russell got sent upstate, they were both twenty years old. Eric missed his cousin, but he knew it was probably for the best, because Russell was on the road to destruction, and if he hadn't gotten locked up, he would probably be dead already.

Eric kept in contact with Russell once in a while, but when Russell had gotten transferred to different penitentiaries more than once, they lost contact, and Eric never bothered to locate his cousin. He let it be.

Eric sat across from his uncle, and asked, "Yo, Unc, is it true that Russell got paroled? He coming home?"

Pumpkin looked annoyed. "Where did you hear this?"

"From a reliable source," Eric said.

"You need to leave your cousin alone, Eric. That boy is the devil," Pumpkin said.

"How you gonna say that, Uncle Pumpkin? Russell is family, just like you and me."

"Well, sometimes family ain't no good for you. . . . Family get your soul taken away."

"Russell, he cool people. He's my cousin," Eric protested.

"Listen here, boy, you need to leave Russell alone when he gets out. I know that boy ain't changed in seven years. He ain't got one rehabilitated bone in his body. Prison ain't done him no good. It probably made him worse."

"But he's getting out soon," Eric said, looking content that his cousin was finally being released from Clinton Correctional Facility in Dannemora, New York.

"Eric, you doin' good for yourself. I know you don't want to hit them streets hard again. You already got shot one time. Fuckin' around with Russell when he gets out, you gonna damn near lose your life."

"Unc, how you know Russell ain't changed? You ain't heard or visit the man since he went in, much less written him some kind of letter. You just let him be up in prison and have him rot to death," Eric proclaimed.

"Listen, youngun', I've been in these streets harder and much longer than you've been pissing correct. I know a man like Russell will always be Russell. He's like your father, and just like your father, there was never no talkin' right in him. He was always hardheaded, just like your cousin. If your father would have listened to me, then he'd still be alive today," Pumpkin stated.

"Uncle Pumpkin, let's not speak about my father," Eric said, being sensitive about his father's death and how he was killed.

"Excuse me," Sherry interrupted, "but I'm gonna let y'all fellows be." She slowly rose from her chair. "Pumpkin, I'll talk to you tomorrow." Sherry slowly made her way to the exit.

"Okay, Sherry," Pumpkin hollered back.

Pumpkin knew that his nephew was being pigheaded about the topic. He knew Eric and Russell were family, like brothers, and Eric wasn't going to leave Russell alone when he got out. His nephew was becoming hardheaded like his father, and Pumpkin loved his nephew like a son. Eric was one of his favorites. He knew Eric was in the streets, but not heavy like his pappy, Yung Black, and Russell. The way Pumpkin saw it, Eric was just a small-time hustler, doing him with the strippers, and selling marijuana on the side. He was doing good for himself, keeping a low profile, and riding around in his Scion XB.

Pumpkin didn't want to see Eric end up like his father or his cousin. He had already lost one son to the system, doing a nickel upstate, and lost his daughter to the streets; he didn't know if she was dead or alive. But to Pumpkin, among the many nephews and nieces he had, Eric was his favorite. Eric was the one he saw occasionally, and Eric was a smart kid. Pumpkin knew how rough and deadly the streets could become, and he knew that Eric wasn't really built for the streets, for the game like that. Yeah, he looked the part, and had a little thug in him, but push come to shove, Eric wasn't his father and he wasn't his cousin—he was more calm and nonchalant.

Pumpkin warned his nephew again about keeping a low profile when Russell got out and not getting involved with him. But Eric waved off his warning and said good-bye to his uncle. The way Eric saw it, Russell was family, and you never turned your back on family because family was all you had sometimes.

6

It had been two weeks since River hooked up with Hubert Miller, a small hood who was making good money hustling nickel and dime bags, even pounds of the shit to his clientele in Long Island, Manhattan, and Queens. Hubert pushed a BMW 3 series. Hubert was a baller, a playa. He flashed money and jewelry like it was going out of style, and was a constant show-off. When he first saw River noticing him in the crowded bar up on Merrick Boulevard, he had to come over and say hello. River was looking stunning that night. Her sinuous long black hair was falling gracefully down to her back. She sported a minimicro denim skirt. Her long legs were gleaming in a pair of stilettos. Her cleavage was mashed together in a tight buttoned-down top that made any man—straight, gay, or bi—turn their heads and gaze at the eye-catching brown beauty all alone in a bar crowded with mostly men.

Hubert was flattered, in fact enthralled, when he caught the attention of this raving beauty giving him the eye across the room. Hubert wasn't the most handsome man in the place, but he was well dressed, and had enough money to pass around. He lounged by the teeming bar with his man, Kenneth. It took him ten minutes after catching her attention to go over and say hello. He offered to buy her a drink, and River smiled and played along.

Two weeks later, River had Hubert's nose wide open. He tricked on River every day, buying her expensive gifts, taking her out to classy restaurants and treating River as though she was wifey. And he still hadn't fucked her. River teased him constantly, giving him back rubs, jerking him off in the car, and allowing Hubert to catch a glimpse of her breathtaking naked brown-skinned figure.

Hubert thought that tonight was his lucky night. He had River over at his place in Cambria Heights and he thought tonight he was gonna finally fuck her, getting at the pussy he'd yearned for for the past two weeks.

Hubert was feeling River so much that he wanted to give her a baby, get her pregnant and leave his mark in her. He wanted her to himself, feeling River was too fine to share with any other man. He was falling in love, and when River stepped out of the bathroom clad in a red stretch-lace slip, with the scalloped edges and a derriere-skimming length, his dick jumped an extra inch. She wore transparent stilettos and her skin glistened with baby oil from head to toe.

"Shit, baby . . . you look good," Hubert complimented her, licking his lips as he gazed lustfully at River's gorgeous figure.

He grabbed his crotch and looked like a pervert in heat. Hubert was bug-eyed, sprawled across his soft king-sized mattress with silk green sheets, naked as the day he was born.

He wasn't much to look at, Hubert didn't have much of a body. It was rather shapeless and hairy, and didn't excite River to any extent. She slowly made her way over to Hubert, with his eyes dancing across her body.

"Yeah, come here . . . come to papa, sweetie. Come and sit on my lap and make a wish. Daddy needs some loving," Hubert sleazily said.

River kept her smile and made her way onto the bed. Hubert wasted no time grabbing ahold of her soft, warm, womanly figure, groping her from head to toe.

"Oooooooh, your body is so soft, River. Damn, I could touch and hold you forever," Hubert proclaimed.

He passionately squeezed her breasts, cupped her round succulent ass, and slowly wet her skin with his tongue against her neck. River looked away from Hubert and rolled her eyes. She had to put up with this corny, no-macking, no-class, wanna-be-pimp, hairy-ass fool.

Hubert's eyes were so wide open by beauty and pussy that he didn't know any better. He was blinded and didn't see the signs that she was playing him, using him. He'd never had a woman as bad as River, and one twirl of her hair around her index finger, batting of the eyes at him, smiling, and her soft touch against his skin, he was dumbfounded and open like Macy's after Christmas. Hubert was in his early twenties, and felt he had the gift of gab, but it was his money that attracted the women.

Hubert was so ready and blinded by the pussy he thought River was about to bless him with that he never noticed when River slipped his house key off his key ring and concealed it from his sight. She had fast fingers.

Earlier, she watched when Hubert opened his front door to the house, being all hugged up on him and frisky. She saw what key he used, and when they were downstairs in the living room, drinking and being flirtatious with each other, River quickly slipped off the key that Hubert laid on the glass coffee table, and hid it when Hubert went into the kitchen for a brief moment. She knew it was risky, but this was money. If caught, she knew all she had to do was give Hubert some phony excuse, show him some skin, and he'd forget all about it. She knew the power of pussy, and River used that to her advantage.

When they got upstairs in the bedroom, she told Hubert she wanted to go change in the bathroom, and come out with a surprise for him. Before she did anything else, she opened the bathroom window, where Big Red and Twinkie were waiting underneath, and she dropped the house key in Big Red's hand. Big Red smiled, and said to Twinkie, "It's on!"

Big Red and Twinkie had been casing Hubert's place for the past week, they knew all the exits and how many windows he had.

They both easily made their way through the front door, being wary of neighbors and anything else. But since it was after midnight, the neighborhood looked quiet and tranquil. Big Red and Twinkie slowly and quietly crept through Hubert's front door. After they were inside, their guns and masks came out.

River tried stalling Hubert. He was naked in front of her, and his dick was no bigger than five inches.

"Come on, River, I know you want it, look at this . . . I'm ready for you baby—give me some."

"I like foreplay first, baby," River softly stated, with her fingers dancing across his chest.

"Foreplay? I get it, no licky, no sticky, right?" Hubert asked, eager to drop down in between her legs and eat her out to please her any way possible. "I'm a man. I'm not ashamed to eat pussy."

River tittered and pulled his face back up as he tried to eat her out. "No, not that. I want you to talk to me, seduce me, make me feel like a woman," she proclaimed.

"Make you feel like a woman? But I'm trying . . . I mean . . ." It was obvious that Hubert was confused. "What you want from me, baby?"

"You know what I want . . ." River stated.

"Yeah. Tell me, I'll do it," Hubert eagerly replied.

River's eyes looked past Hubert and fixed on two males entering the bedroom quietly behind Hubert, dressed in all black and both gripping 9-mm pistols.

"Niggah, where that money at!" Big Red shouted, startling Hubert, who quickly spun around wide-eyed, his jaw dropping as he fearfully stared at the two masked gunmen entering his bedroom.

Hubert tried to run, but Twinkie smacked him with the gat across his back, dropping Hubert's naked frame to the floor. Hubert screamed out in pain.

"Yo, what y'all want? Don't shoot . . . please don't shoot!" Hubert whimpered, extending his arms and hands in a poor defense to protect himself in case they did shoot.

River, playing along, quickly covered herself with the bedsheets and looked frightened along with Hubert. She didn't budge but panted strongly and played her role in the robbery to a T.

"Baby, be cool," Hubert said to River. "I got this. Please don't touch her," Hubert said in a pathetic attempt to defend River. "I'll give y'all whatever y'all want, but just let us be."

"Niggah, where the money at?" Big Red asked, his voice was deep and strong and definitely intimidated Hubert.

Big Red menacingly pointed his gun at Hubert's head, and threatened to blow his brains out.

"I got about twenty thousand in a safe in the next room. . . . It's yours, ayyite . . . take it."

Twenty thousand definitely put a smile on Big Red's face, along with Twinkie. River, even though she wanted to smile, had to keep her composure.

"Get up, niggah!" Twinkie shouted, yanking Hubert up from the floor by his arm. "C'mon."

"You too, bitch!" Big Red shouted.

Assed out and feeling like a bitch, Hubert reluctantly led the masked gunmen to his hidden safe in the second bedroom.

Inside the plain eggshell-colored bedroom, Hubert led them to a hidden safe, pushing a piece of furniture back. He pulled back the carpet from the wall, and revealed his hidden compartment. Hubert then looked up at his captors. He glanced at Big Red gripping River strongly by her arm. She still had the bedsheet wrapped around her. He felt fear and anger. This was his night to be with River and these two goons fucked it all up for him.

"Niggah, you stupid . . . open the muthafucka!" Big Red shouted.

"Ayyite, man . . . let me think of the combination," Hubert replied.

"Niggah, you got three minutes," Twinkie threatened, pressing the 9-mm against his temple.

Under the pressure, Hubert began spinning the correct numbers to his safe, and shortly after, opened it, revealing the contents.

Eyes quickly lit up with excitement and greed. "Yeah, that's what I'm talkin' about. That money," Big Red proclaimed.

He and Twinkie peered into the safe, seeing the stacks of hundred-dollar bills piled up on each other. Twinkie pointed his gun at Hubert, keeping a keen eye on him while Big Red began emptying the safe into a black garbage bag he pulled from his back pocket.

"Don't fuckin' try anything." Twinkie sternly warned.

Within a minute, the safe was completely empty, and Hubert felt like crying. They had jacked him for twenty G's. After they had everything, Big Red looked over at River, stepped up to her and boldly gripped her in his arms and forced his tongue into her mouth while Hubert helplessly watched.

"Niggah, get the fuck off me—you don't know me!" River spat, looking disgusted.

"Yo, c'mon . . . chill, that's my girl. . . . Y'all already got my money," Hubert whimpered.

"Shut the fuck up!" Red shot back, aiming his gun between Hubert's eyes. "She too fly for you anyway, niggah."

Red looked over at River, and then said, "Fuck that, she coming wit' us."

"What?" River argued.

"Yeah, this cornball niggah don't deserve you. Get dressed, bitch," Red ordered.

"Fuck you!" River spat.

"What? Say it again," Red said, pointing the gun at River. River stared at Red, uttering not a single word. "Thought so, bitch. Now get dressed. We rollin' out."

"C'mon, man, that's my girl. Why y'all takin' her—" Before Hubert could say anything else, Twinkie hit him upside the head with his gun, knocking him out cold on the floor.

"Bitching ass, niggah!"

River quickly got dressed and followed Twinkie and Red outside to their rusty Pontiac parked around the corner. She had no remorse for Hubert. He was a cornball, a wannabe—and the way he'd bitched back there, River had to smile. Hubert was so dumb that he probably didn't have a clue she'd set him up.

Before Twinkie could pull out in the Pontiac, River quickly smacked Big Red across his head, yelling, "What the fuck was that back there?"

"Whaaaatt?" Red exclaimed.

"That kiss . . . callin' me a bitch . . ."

"I had to make it look real, right? The niggah fell for it," Red said, smiling and gloating that he actually got to shove his tongue down River's mouth and get that close to her.

"Well, next time, it's hands off. Fuck I look like to you, some cheap ho?"

"Ayyite, my bad, ma."

Twinkie smiled, throwing the Pontiac in drive and pulling away from the block. Between the three of them, they had twenty grand to split, and that was over six grand apiece.

7

"I can't wait to tear that pussy up," Bamboo exclaimed, gazing at Starr and closing the room door.

He grabbed Starr by her thick hips and stared into her hypnotic dark eyes with hunger. He was tall, towering over Starr by six inches, and he was horny.

He had paid fifty dollars for four hours at the Executive, a sleazy, cheap motel on the Conduit, and was willing to give Starr another hundred just to fuck her.

"Umm, you a big boy, right?" Starr said, grabbing his crotch and feeling him up. She definitely felt the bulge.

Bamboo was a corner thug, always out drinking in bars and clubs, hollering at every big-butt woman who passed his way, starting fights with strangers, and paying for pussy constantly.

"Your pussy tight, right?" he asked, moving his hand in between her legs and resting it against her damp pussy. He then pushed his index finger into Starr, causing her to jolt a little. She had on a short miniskirt, no panties, as usual, and her shirt was open, revealing her full-sized breasts.

"You like it? You like how tight my shit feels?" Starr said.

She began seducing him further by unbuckling his pants and reaching for his dick. She pulled out his dick and was awed by the size of it.

Bamboo smiled. "Yeah. You like that, right?" he said in a sleazy way.

"How big?" she asked as she stroked him gracefully, moving her hand slowly up and down his shaft.

"Ten inches," he boasted.

"Damn!"

"You ever had it that big?" he asked.

Starr shook her head. "No, to be honest."

"Well, you're in for a treat tonight."

Starr smiled and continued to jerk him off, hearing Bamboo moan as he felt her warm hands heat up his dick. But she stopped suddenly.

"Why you stop? I want that," Bamboo said, looking so desperate.

"You want it, then you gotta pay for it first," she proclaimed, stepping back from him.

Her eyes were fixed on his big dick. She thought, *Damn, I need to charge this niggah extra if he wanna put that shit in me.*

Bamboo pulled out a small knot of fifty-dollar bills from his pants pocket, and then dropped them to the floor. He stood in front of Starr, hanging like an anaconda.

"You said a hundred, right?" he asked.

"Bamboo, I'm sorry to say, but with that big dick, I gotta charge you an extra fifty," Starr stated.

"For what? You said a hundred," he snapped back.

"Niggah, do you see that thing? You can play jump rope wit' that dick," she quipped.

"Shit ain't fair, Starr. We agreed on a hundred."

"I know, but it's my pussy, and if I'm gonna be handling that, then you coming out your pockets, niggah."

Bamboo stood there with his pants lying around his ankles, contemplating if he should pay the extra fifty. Being horny didn't help him much.

"Fuck you, Starr. Here." He passed her three fifty-dollar bills.

"Nice doin' business wit' you," she said, placing the money in a secure location.

Starr started to get undressed. She got completely naked and motioned for Bamboo to come closer as she sat on the edge of the bed.

Bamboo moved toward her, eager like a child on Christmas Eve. He'd heard stories about Starr, niggahs claiming that she was the best when it came to giving blow jobs and fucking. He had to find out for himself.

Bamboo, clad in just a T-shirt, stood over Starr. His dick looked as if it weighed a ton. He was huge, and Starr knew that it was a challenge for her. But she was up for it.

She gripped his big dick in her hand and fondled him down to his balls. Afterward, she positioned her mouth near the tip of his dick, and taunted him by licking around the head and sucking on the tip.

Bamboo kept quiet as he waited and watched.

Starr looked at the dick for a quick moment, inspecting it, and then she swallowed him up completely. Bamboo was in shock watching ten inches disappear into her mouth.

"Yo, all that shit went down your throat?" he asked in amazement, peering down at Starr's bobbing head.

But Starr didn't respond. She was focused on her work.

"Where does it go?" Bamboo continued. No woman he'd ever fucked with had been able to deep-throat him like this.

Starr continued to deep-throat Bamboo for ten minutes, causing him to moan and pant, and feel as though his knees were about to buckle.

"Aaaaaahhh, shit! Damn! Yo . . . shit. Fuck, Starr! Ohmygod!" Bamboo carried on.

Starr continued to put him in bliss until he cried out, "Yo, Starr, chill . . . chill, you about to make me nut."

Starr pulled back, smiling up at him.

"Damn, girl . . ." He was lost for words.

"Told you," Starr said to him.

"Fuck that, lay on your back," he instructed as he held his dick in his hand.

"You got condoms?" she asked.

"Yeah."

"Magnums, I hope."

"Always."

Bamboo went over to his pants, which were on the floor, and pulled out a fresh box of Magnums. He quickly tore open the box and removed one. He ripped it open, quickly rolled it back onto his vast erection, and walked toward Starr.

"Listen, don't be tryin' to ram all that shit up in me, tryin' to have it come up my throat and out my mouth. I ain't that big of a woman," she stated.

"I got you, ma. I'm gonna try and be easy."

"Try?" Starr said, staring at him with some attitude.

Bamboo quickly pushed Starr on her back, having her spread her legs. He gazed at the pussy for a short moment, admiring how clean and well shaved Starr kept her goodies. He palmed his dick and slowly pushed a few inches into her, causing Starr to cry out loudly.

"Aaaaaahhh . . . aaaaaahhh . . . aaaaaahhh," she groaned, feeling as if a tree was in her stomach. "Ohmygod! Aaaaaahhh . . . ohmygod!"

Becoming excited by her constant moaning and panting, Bamboo pushed more into her, thrusting. Starr gripped his back, leaving scratches.

"Shit, niggah, you gotta big dick," Starr cried out, feeling her pussy opening wider the deeper he pushed himself into her.

Bamboo continued to thrust, pushing more and more of his swollen dick in her. Starr tightly gripped the bedsheets as her eyes rolled up in her head.

"You like it?" Bamboo asked, pressed against his knees in a vertical position, gripping her smooth brown thighs, and fucking Starr as if there would be no tomorrow for him. "Shit! Yo, you about to make me come, Starr."

"Aaaaaahhh . . . uuuummmm," she panted, tightening her love muscles around his erection and crying out.

"Shit, Starr! Fuck, you makin' me come!" Bamboo exclaimed, as he sweated and continued to thrust and thrust. "I'm coming!"

"That's right, niggah, come for me. You know my shit is good," Starr hollered, rotating her hips against his pelvis steadily, causing Bamboo to suddenly shudder, gripping her thighs tightly and screaming out, "Shit! Shit! Aaaaaahhhhhhhhhhh . . . Fuck! Fuck!" as he exploded inside of her. After that, he fell against her bare breasts, panting and wheezing.

Starr held him momentarily, whispering in his ear, "Told you my pussy was worth every penny. You need to tip my ass."

Bamboo remained silent, relishing the moment. But he was getting a little too comfortable. Starr thought that he was about to fall asleep on top of her.

"Okay, niggah, time is up. You gotta get up," Starr said, trying to push him off of her.

"Hold on, give me a few minutes," he said, not even trying to budge as he had her pinned underneath him.

Starr sighed. "Bamboo, get off me. Fuck, you starting to get heavy."

"Let me eat that pussy," he unexpectedly said in a whisper.

"Niggah, what? You gotta come extra for that," she said.

"C'mon, I'm giving you pleasure. I just wanna know how you taste," he said, picking himself up off her and giving Starr some breathing room between them.

"Fifty dollars and you can do whatever you want down there," she confirmed.

"Why is it always about money wit' you?" he barked.

"Niggah, you wanna taste it, fifty dollars," she said.

Bamboo sighed loudly, and retorted, "You know what, Starr, you ain't nuthin' but a money-hungry cunt! Next time I'm taking this shit for free." He swiftly grabbed between her legs tightly and felt her up with such force that Starr shrieked. His nails began to dig into her skin, and then he wrapped his hand around her neck suddenly, causing Starr to gasp.

"Don't fuckin' play wit' me, you bitch," he snapped, becoming a different person all of a sudden. Starr looked up at him in horror. "I'm being nice 'cause you young, and you cool. But you lucky I don't beat the shit out of you right now in this room and take my fuckin' money back."

Starr clutched his wrist, trying to loosen his grip around her neck, but he was strong and he became crazy. She kicked and squirmed frantically, but Bamboo just sat there, calm and collected as he tried to squeeze the life out of Starr.

"You want me to let go?" he asked, taunted her. "Huh?"

"Please . . . stop . . ." she managed to say, gasping.

"You got a hundred and fifty, huh? You wanna pay for your fuckin' life?"

Starr now regretted fucking him. Critter was a cheap and ugly bastard, but Bamboo was a lunatic, and just went off on someone unexpectedly. Starr didn't even see it coming. He just snapped.

Starr continued to fight for her life, never letting go of his wrist. She tried digging her nails into his skin, drawing blood, but Bamboo still didn't let go.

"I hate it when bitches be trying to play me . . . you know what I'm sayin'? I'm a nice guy, fo' real," he said, talking to her like they were friends.

"Please . . ." Starr begged for her life in a small whisper.

"What? What? You like me, Starr?"

Starr felt her young life fading from her. She couldn't even speak. She was losing the fight for her life.

"Bitch, you dying on me?" Bamboo asked in a cynical tone. "You can't die."

Suddenly he loosened his grip around her neck and Starr began to cough as she soothed her neck.

Bamboo got off the bed, and began talkin to Starr as if nothing had happened. "Damn, that pussy was so good, Starr . . . fo' real. I was just playing with you. I wasn't gonna kill you. We cool, right?"

Starr looked up at Bamboo with contempt, still massaging her sore neck. Starr had a small blade hidden in her skirt. She wanted to cut him.

Bamboo walked around the room naked, talking to himself, as he jerked off in front of Starr.

"I'm a king. I'm a king. I'm a king," he chanted.

This niggah is really crazy, she said to herself.

"Starr, I'm a king, right? You love me, right? I'm the best. I fucked you good. You my queen, right?" he asked, gripping his long big dick and pleasing himself as he walked toward Starr.

"Bamboo, get the fuck away from me," Starr said, moving herself off the bed and trying to reach for her knife.

"Bitch, don't diss me!" he shouted. "You know what? I want my fuckin' money back. You gonna give me my fuckin' money back."

"Niggah, you must be fuckin' crazy!" Starr said inching closer to her clothing and never taking her eyes off him.

"Bitch, don't diss me!" he yelled, and ran toward her.

Starr ran for her knife, but Bamboo was too quick. He darted across the bed and leaped on Starr, knocking her down on the floor.

Starr screamed and fought Bamboo. She kicked, punched, and bit him on his ear, causing Bamboo to cry out.

"You bit me you stupid bitch!" he shouted. He picked up Starr and hurled her across the room as if she was nothing.

Starr landed against the wall, in pain. But before she could look up, Bamboo was right on top of her again, grabbing her forcefully by her arms, and saying, "Get up, you stupid bitch!"

He picked Starr up and dragged her over to the bed, though she tried to fight, scratch, and free herself. Bamboo pushed her down on her back and jumped on top of her, straddling her and pinning her arms down with his knees.

"Bitch, I'm your fuckin' daddy!" he shouted, which was followed by a hard right hand slap across her face. "Starr, you hear me? I'm your daddy!"

"Fuck you!"

"Bitch, what?!" *Slap. Slap. Slap. Slap.* He struck her multiple times, drawing blood from her mouth.

"You got something to say?" he screamed.

Starr was crying, hurt, and she wanted to kill him. He had her arms pinned against the mattress, using the force of his body weight.

"I'm Bamboo, bitch. You better start respecting me," he stated. "I'm your daddy, bitch!"

"Fuck you!" she said.

This time instead of a slap he punched her with a closed fist against her jaw. He hit her so hard that Starr thought he knocked a tooth loose.

"I see that I'm gonna have to start teaching this bitch to have some respect for a man. Right, bitch? You a stupid bitch!" Bamboo began hitting Starr as though he was Mike Tyson in the ring.

Starr cried out loudly, trying to protect herself from the rain of blows that came down on her. But he was too strong and too crazy.

"C'mere, spread your fuckin' legs. Daddy got a surprise for you," he said, opening her legs and positioning himself between her thighs.

Starr just lay there motionless, her face battered and bloody, and her left eye swollen shut. She felt Bamboo in between her legs, but she couldn't do anything about it. Her body was weak and sore. Bamboo gripped his monstrous-sized dick, and without any compassion for her petite figure, he thrust himself so far into her that Starr felt him tear something inside.

She cried out in pain as Bamboo tried ramming all ten inches into her, hitting places in her that no man had ever hit before.

"Stop! Please!" Starr cried out. "It hurts—"

But her pleas fell on deaf ears. Bamboo pounded away into her, tearing away at her raw insides.

"Fuck you, bitch. I'm a king. I'm a king. I'm Bamboo. I'm Bamboo," he chanted, as he thrust and thrust, fucking Starr as if she was some lifeless rag doll underneath him.

"Fuck this!" he said, pulling out his erection, rolling Starr over on her stomach, and shoving his big black dick in her ass.

"Noooo . . . aaaaaahhh," she cried out. Even though she was familiar with ass fucking, the way Bamboo went about it was very fast and rough, with no lubrication at all, and it was even worse for her because of his size.

The situation reminded Starr painfully of when she'd lost her virginity at the age of twelve—just lying there having no control over her body, and having a man have his way with her. She'd thought she had control now, four years later, but Bamboo proved her wrong. He was worse than the man her mother had brought into her bedroom while she was sleeping.

Starr wanted to pass out, the pain in her ass was so unbearable. She tried to fight, but Bamboo beat the shit out of her.

"Turn over on your back again," he said, switching her to another position, and shoving his dick into her pussy again. "I'm coming again!" he shouted.

He thrust and he thrust until he came in Starr again, this time without any protection. Starr was sprawled out on the mattress, crying. She couldn't move, and she could barely see.

Bamboo beat her again, until he saw that she'd finally had enough. He got dressed, took his clothes and her shit, and left the room, leaving Starr unconscious.

8

River walked into her apartment ten minutes after midnight, ten thousand dollars richer. She, Big Red, and Twinkie had just caught another hustler slipping for some pussy. And surprisingly, it only took the young twenty-three-year-old drug dealer three days to trust River.

The first night they met, he took her to his apartment in Hollis and cooked a full meal for her. He was trying to show off his cooking skills, hoping that she'd give him some pussy. But all he got was a thank-you, a hug, and a hard-on.

River walked into her dark apartment, only to hear loud moans and grunts coming from her roommate's room, which meant that Tah-Tah's boyfriend, Kay, had come by for a booty call.

River sighed, hearing the two go at it. She walked into the kitchen to fix herself a quick snack before she went to bed. She was tired and wanted to sleep for hours.

She started to make herself a sandwich when she heard, "I know you heard us in there."

She turned around and saw Tah-Tah walking into the kitchen naked.

"I really wasn't payin' attention," River returned.

Tah-Tah had a lovely shape, with a phat booty and small waist-line. She had hypnotic green eyes and long sinuous hair; she looked like a candidate for Ms. America. But she was ghetto.

"You know Kay came by 'cuz he was missin' a sista', you know what I'm sayin'? I had to break him off wit' some pussy, 'cuz look what he just bought me," Tah-Tah said, holding up her wrist and showing off a diamond-encrusted bracelet.

"Nice," River said, glancing at it.

"I know. See the things a man can get you when you fuckin' him right?" Tah-Tah proclaimed, staring at her bracelet. "I got that nig-gah in my bedroom right now, knock the fuck out. My pussy gets me all kinds of things. I got niggahs down at the club begging to get wit' this. Shit, River, you need to come dance at Day Dreamz. I'm tellin' you, wit' your looks and that body, you gonna come off good. You can easily make a thousand a night if your game is tight. You coming up in here after midnight doin' what out there, girl, dating these broke niggahs and workin' some low-end job?"

Tah-Tah was unaware of River's dangerous occupation. As far as she knew, River worked a dead-end job somewhere in Brooklyn and dated broke-ass niggahs. River knew that Tah-Tah ran her mouth too much, sometimes to the wrong people. And she couldn't risk in-formation getting back to the wrong type of people.

"River, you need a man wit' some money, you know what I'm sayin'? Shit, I'm gettin' it good from the club and Kay. I ain't tryin' to be some broke bitch. I look too fuckin' good for that. And you can, too. You ain't ugly, that's fo' sure. I know plenty of niggahs that wanna holla at you. And they gettin' money."

River quickly made her sandwich. She was tired of hearing Tah-Tah's mouth. She was tired of hearing her talk about what car that one was driving, and how much money this one was making, and how her pussy was making them come out of their pockets to buy her nice things. Every day Tah-Tah talked about the same shit, noth-ing new.

And sadly, Tah-Tah's attitude and the way she saw life reminded River of her own mother, and how selfish and conceited she was. Her mother was a ho, abusive, and a money-hungry bitch.

River had met Tah-Tah at a Brooklyn strip club a year ago, and at first the two hit it off really well and decided to share an apartment together and go halves on the rent. But a year later, her friendship with Tah-Tah grew tiresome.

Tah-Tah was too raw, she didn't give a fuck about standing butt-naked in the kitchen and bragging about sex, her pussy, and how men were constantly buying her things after she had finished fucking them.

"I got a niggah for you, River. And he drive a Benz," Tah-Tah said.

"I can get a man on my own, Tah-Tah," River replied.

"Please, them broke niggahs you be wit' . . . they ain't doin' shit for you. I'm tellin' you, get wit' this niggah, and you gonna be able to quit your job in a month. And if you start dancing again and come work down at the club, you gonna be paid."

"Tah-Tah, please, stay out my business. I'm good for now. I don't need your help. I know how to get a man. So stop tryin' to pimp me," River lightly scolded her.

"Excuse me, Ms. High and Mighty. I was only tryin' to help you out. I was helping you to get a niggah that's worth keeping, but if you wanna be stingy wit' the pussy and fuck wit' these broke-ass nig-gahs, then fuck it . . . be a broke bitch!"

River let out a loud sigh, grabbed her sandwich and drink, and quickly rushed by Tah-Tah. Tah-Tah smirked at her as she passed, and blurted out, "River, you need some dick. When was the last time you had some?"

River ignored her and went straight to her room, slamming the door shut.

Like my mother, that fuckin' woman is impossible, River said to herself. She placed her food and drink on the night table next to her bed and just sat there staring at the wall. Talking to Tah-Tah brought back unwanted memories of her mother and the ordeal that she went through when she was young.

River went into her drawer and pulled out a framed picture of her younger sister. It was the only picture she had of her sister, the only picture of family she had around.

She peered at the picture quietly. Her sister was ten in the photo, and smiling as if the world was a great place to live. River's heart began to sadden as she continued to gaze at the photo. She felt guilty. Her conscience was eating away at her. River left home when she was sixteen, leaving Starr, her baby sister, in the grips of a madwoman who was very abusive and disturbed.

River wondered if her sister was all right. She hadn't seen or spoken to her since she left home five years ago. She had gone back to their old apartment once to see about Starr and maybe get her away from their mother, but they had moved. She had lost contact with everybody.

River continued to peer at the picture, forgetting about her snack. She wasn't hungry anymore. River started to reminisce about her mother, remembering when the abuse had first started at home.

She had been ten at the time, and it had been a Saturday night. Her father had left home when she was seven and never returned. River was in the shower lathering herself up when the bathroom door opened and in came her mother with a male stranger.

River shrieked when the shower curtain was pulled back. She tried to cover herself, and shouted, "Mama, what are you doing?"

"Hush your mouth, girl," her mother chided, glaring at her daughter.

"Mama, who is that? Get him out of here!" River screamed.

"River, I gave birth to you, and this is my house. You don't tell me what to do in my own home. You fuckin' hear me?"

"Mama, I'm in the bathroom . . . please . . . tell him to leave," River continued, not caring about her mother's previous statement.

Sheryl turned to the man, and said, "Excuse us a minute, dear. We need to talk."

The stranger walked out of the bathroom without saying a word. Sheryl closed the bathroom door behind him, removed her belt from around her waist, and glared at her daughter. She said, "Bitch, do I need to teach you some fuckin' manners in my home? Huh?"

But before River could answer, her mother quickly approached her with the belt and came down hard across her back twice, as River turned to protect herself.

"Mama, stop! Stop!" River cried out, trying to protect herself from the painful blows.

Her mother continued to rain down blows on her with the belt, which stung against her wet bare skin. Sheryl beat her daughter in the tub like a madwoman, ignoring her daughter's cries, while her younger daughter was asleep in the next room.

River dropped to her knees in the tub, hurt, her skin bloody, as the water above still cascaded down on her with tears mixing in.

Her mother stood over her, looking down fiercely at her broken young daughter.

"Bitch, don't you ever fuckin' talk back to me. You heard what the fuck I said? I'm your fuckin' mother. You don't run things here. I fuckin' do! You better start remembering that, River. You fuckin' hear me?!"

River continued to cry.

"Bitch, do you fuckin' hear me?" Sheryl screamed.

River slowly nodded.

"Now get the fuck off you knees and do what I say."

River slowly stood up, tears continuing to trickle down her face. Her mother went back out into the hallway to get her company.

She came back into the bathroom with the man. River couldn't even look their way, but stared at the shower wall.

"Give me my money," River heard her mother say to him.

The man passed Sheryl a hundred dollars. She took the money, looked at her daughter, and said, "Now, River, all he wants to do is watch you bathe, nothing else. If he tries anything else, you scream for me. Okay?"

River just stood there, not complying.

"River, I said okay?" her mother shouted more sternly.

"Yes, Mother," a tearful, frightened young River replied.

"Okay," her mother said, leaving the bathroom.

The stranger sat down on the toilet seat, crossed his legs, and said, "Please, continue. I won't hurt you."

River couldn't even look at him. She was afraid to. Reluctantly, she squatted down slowly and picked up the soap. She then slowly touched herself with the soap, but flinched when she gently pressed the soap against her broken skin.

Specks of blood from the beating covered her skin, and it hurt so much when she touched her wounds.

But scared of receiving another whipping from her mother, she began to bathe again while the man watched from a very short distance.

It took her ten painful minutes to finish. The water made her skin sting. The pain for her was unbearable. But out of fear, she got through it. She was so uncomfortable. The man watched and didn't say one word.

"I've seen enough," he said suddenly. He got up and just left the bathroom without even looking back.

Shortly after her mother came back into the bathroom and told River to get out of the tub. She was done. River dried herself off and went straight to her bedroom. She cried all night as she nursed her wounds.

Before River lost her virginity at thirteen, her mother made men pay to watch her shower or bathe. She had men come into their home and give up cash just so they could watch a young girl touch herself. It was sickening. River cried after every incident her mother put her through. The beatings continued, sometimes so severe that River couldn't even get up afterward.

She would miss school for days, sometimes weeks. And when teachers or the staff got too nosey, Sheryl would take her family and move away, shacking up with men she knew, and paying her rent by giving them some pussy. And if they didn't want her, then she would pimp her daughters. But by offering sex she survived the streets, not living off welfare and not being homeless. Men loved Sheryl, and she thrived off using her body and looks.

River used to look at her mother and say to herself, *How can such a beautiful woman be so ugly inside and carry so many demons in her?* She could never understand it.

River would be asleep some nights, but would wake up to hear loud panting and moaning coming from her mother's bedroom. Sometimes there would be as many as four or five guys who'd come visit her mother for sex in one night.

River was thirteen when her mother forced her to lose her virginity to a man who was in his late fifties. He was willing to pay Sheryl one thousand dollars for one night with her daughter. He wanted to be the first to fuck River, because he'd never had a virgin before.

Of course her mother agreed to the transaction, and, scared to suffer her wrath, River reluctantly agreed to fuck him.

River remembered his body being shapeless and hairy. He was bald, average height, and had a short fat dick. River got out of her nightgown as the man was sprawled out butt-naked on her mattress. His body disgusted her. But she blocked out the appalling image and continued to get on with it.

Her mother stood off in the corner, quiet and watching her daughter go on.

"Go ahead, River, he don't have all night," Sheryl said from the dark corner.

At thirteen, River's body was developing quite nicely in the right areas, and her mother was aware of that. The man in the room, Mr. Charles, had been begging dearly for a night with her daughter. At first he offered Sheryl a hundred dollars, but she turned him down, saying, "She's only a virgin once. You need to come higher if you want to be the first to fuck my daughter."

A week later he came with the offer of five hundred, but she turned him down again. Two days later, he offered her a thousand dollars for one night. Sheryl smiled and agreed.

Mr. Charles used to watch River leave for school on the mornings she actually went. He used to stare out his window at River and watch her walk past his house with his pants around his ankles and his dick clutched in his hand, masturbating.

He had a family, but desired young teenage girls with a fever. After a few quick, hot, and passionate nights with Sheryl for a hundred dollars a fuck, he started telling Sheryl how lovely her daughter was. One thing led to another and now Mr. Charles was having his fantasy come true.

River walked up to Mr. Charles naked. She was stiff as she lay down on the bed next to him. She couldn't even look at him. Mr. Charles leaned in toward her and began nibbling at her ear. His breath was hot, and smelled like cigarettes.

River bit down on her bottom lip, trying to put her mind somewhere else as she felt Mr. Charles's hand move slowly up and in between her young thighs and settle against her private parts. She tried not to tremble, but his touch was creepy, and a few tears trickled down the side of her face.

He continued to grope and fondle River for a long time, touching every inch of her body, enjoying every minute he had with her. River just continued to lie there motionless, crying softly, and seeing her mother watching her in the corner of her room.

She then felt Mr. Charles grab her hand and move it over to his dumpy fat dick. He pressed her hand against his penis, and made

River masturbate him slowly. For a thousand dollars, he was going to take his sweet time with River, savoring every moment he had with her.

River continued to lie frozen with her hand outstretched, gripping Mr. Charles's erection and jerking him off gradually. She heard Mr. Charles moan with each stroke from her small soft hand.

Forty minutes had passed and now Mr. Charles was ready for the main event. He got up on his knees, pressing heavily down on the mattress, and slowly climbed on top of River, not caring that she was stiff and unemotional, with a blank look on her face throughout the whole ordeal.

He slowly parted her thighs, positioned himself between her legs, grabbed his dick, and carefully inserted his manhood into her innocence—taking away the one thing that she would never get back.

River cried out as she felt his erection opening her up. He pushed more into her, ignoring her loud, painful cries. Moaning with pleasure at feeling how tight she was, he muttered, "Damn, you definitely are a virgin."

"Ouch . . . ouch . . . ouch," she wept, as Mr. Charles thrust and thrust himself into her.

"Oh, God . . . shit. Oooh, River . . . I'm so happy that I'm your first," he proclaimed, as sweat poured from his forehead. "I'm coming."

River continued to weep, having felt nothing like this before. She wanted it to stop. Mr. Charles rocked back and forth on top of her, fondling her by licking and sucking on her undeveloped breasts, kissing the side of her face, and gripping her butt.

He tore into River with his short erection like crazy. The only thing he cared about was coming. He gripped the sheets as he shouted, "I'm coming!"

A few more thrusts and he came in River, shuddering with relief. He lingered on top of River for a short moment, panting and sweating.

"Damn. Best money I ever spent," he said before collapsing on his back next to River.

River still lay frozen next to Mr. Charles. She so badly wanted to run into the shower and wash the smell and funk of sex off her. She continued to cry as she peered up at the ceiling.

"How was I?" Mr. Charles asked, glancing at River.

River remained silent. She felt so disgusted and used.

"River, you're done. Get up," her mother said, looming from out of the shadows. "You can go. Let me talk to Mr. Charles alone."

River rose quickly, reached for her nightgown, and left the room. She ran for the bathroom to take a long and needed shower. She cried the whole time she bathed, and still cried until she fell asleep next to her young sister.

She wanted to kill Mr. Charles and her mother, but being thirteen, fear made her consider otherwise. But she wanted revenge on Mr. Charles for being a fat, nasty pervert.

After her second encounter with Mr. Charles, River decided to get back at him by writing a letter to his wife, describing in detail his affair with her mother and a certain young girl.

Your husband likes to fuck young thirteen year old girls. The letter started off and continued in more detail. She gave the times and dates of his affair, and depicted certain marks and characteristics she'd noticed about him during the sex.

Mr. Charles was shocked when his wife read the letter out loud to him, calling him a child molester and a cheating, asshole husband.

Soon after the letter, word in the streets got out that Mr. Charles was a child molester. River made sure to tell everyone she knew about his dirty little secret. An investigation was soon initiated by the police. River's letter caused so much havoc and mayhem in his home and on the block that his wife left him and they began questioning him and many young girls in the neighborhood, and came to find out that River wasn't the first young girl that Mr. Charles had had sex with.

But before the cops could question River and her mother, Sheryl took her daughters and moved away from the block. But life was still the same for River and her sister no matter where they moved.

In a rage, River threw her late-night snack and glass of juice against the bedroom wall, screaming like a madwoman.

"I fuckin' hate you!" she screamed at the top of her lungs. "Why? Why?"

She fell to her knees, tears trickling down her face.

The unpleasant memories of the abuse and sexual assaults were forever embedded in her mind, and she could never forget. Her mother had fucked her up. It haunted her every night, and when she thought about what her sister must have had to go through after she left, the guilt of abandonment ate her up.

"River, are you okay?" Tah-Tah asked, knocking at her door.

River didn't answer. She sat on the floor with her back against the bed, her arms wrapped around her knees that were pulled up to her chest, and she continued to cry.

"River, you okay?" Tah-Tah repeated.

"Go away!" River shouted.

"We heard a noise," Tah-Tah said.

"Leave me the fuck alone!" River screamed.

"Fine, bitch!" Tah-Tah went back into her bedroom.

River continued to cry as she picked the picture of her baby sister off the bed and stared at it for hours.

9

It was Saturday afternoon, and Eric, Raheem, Donald, Mel, and the groom, Rah, stood by the church altar, handsomely dressed in their elegant three-button tuxedos waiting for Rah's bride, Vivian, to stride down the church aisle to join the man in her life. The church on Merrick Boulevard was filled with family and guests dressed formally and seated patiently as the bridesmaids, who stood across from the groomsmen, peered at the entryway. Moments later, after everyone was situated, the bridal march began to play, and everyone quickly got to their feet, peering back at the entryway, and there stood Vivian, clad in her off-white flowing bridal gown, arm in arm with her salt-and-pepper-haired father.

She gracefully began walking down the aisle with her father right beside her, smiling, with her eyes fixed on her groom. This was the happiest day of her life. Vivian couldn't wait to say "I do" to her man, her Rahmel. She loved him.

Family and guests smiled, eyes glued to Vivian's beauty, her sheer veil falling over her face. She clutched a bouquet of flowers in her hands that were wonderfully arranged. Within minutes, she stood next to her groom, and waited for the reverend to begin the wedding ceremony.

Eric was happy that his cousin Russell was coming home soon. He leaked the word out to his boys, Donald, Mel, and Raheem, and they, too, were equally excited. Eric stared ahead at Rah and Vivian as they held hands and pronounced their wedding vows in front of the many men and women who had assembled in the church on a beautiful, sun-drenched Saturday afternoon. He smiled at Rah, happy for his man. He gazed at Vivian, and thought to himself, *Vivian's a beautiful bride, and Rah's a lucky man.*

Eric knew that a wedding day for him, like this, would most likely never come. He knew Rah would probably make a good husband. But he felt he himself had too much loving to share and it couldn't be with one woman. He was a playboy and he loved women too much to settle down with just one when he was only in his late twenties.

Several hours later, guests and family unwound, drank, partied, and had a good time at the reception hall in Belmont Park, located in Elmont, New York. The DJ puffed up the revelers by spinning off some hip-hop and R&B jams like Jay-Z, Chingy, Jagged Edge, Mary J., and Beyoncé.

Rah and Vivian chose the famous wedding song by Luther Vandross, "Here and Now" to be played for their wedding dance.

Eric stared at the many beautiful females who crowded the reception, and he had to smile. He knew he probably could take any one of these women home tonight. The majority of them were giving him the eye and flirting with him, implying that they were definitely interested in him. And many caught his eye, but he remained nonchalant and chilled with his niggahs.

"E, yo, Yung Slim comin' home fo' real?" Donald asked. He towered over Eric and the majority of the crowd, and looked dazzling in his tux.

"Yeah," Eric answered.

"Damn . . . the niggah did seven years," Donald said.

"I know."

"You ayyite, E?" Donald asked, seeing Eric looking aloof from him and the wedding party.

"Yeah, Donald, just thinkin' about some shit, that's all."

Eric thought about his uncle's word, and he remembered how Russell had been before his incarceration. He thought: *Was the hood, and he himself, ready for Russell to come home?* His cousin was a bully, and for the past seven years, he'd been doing fine without Russell around. Things had been quiet for him, and he was making good money doing what he did. He loved his cousin, and he missed Russell a lot. But it had been different.

Donald looked at Eric holding a glass of champagne in his hand. "Ayyite, E, you know where I'm gonna be at. Too many females in this place for us to be holding up the wall just lookin'. I'm gonna get my dance on, and hopefully take one of these lucky ladies back to my place tonight."

Eric smiled. "Do you, Donald. Do you, yo?"

"To the fullest," Donald said, and casually walked off.

Eric remained standing and observed the reception. He needed a smoke, so he walked outside and pulled out a Black & Mild from his inner pocket. When he reached the exit, he noticed Rah standing alone, peering up at the sky and clutching a cigarette between his fingers. Night was soon to descend and the Long Island night began resting, heavenly and tranquil, over the heads of happy wedding revelers.

"Ain't you supposed to be with your bride, Rah?" Eric said, interrupting Rah's quiet moment.

Huh . . . what, oh, what up, E. . . ." Rah returned, looking lost in his own thoughts.

"What, your wife got you stressed already?" Eric joked.

"Nah, I was just out here, chillin' . . . thinkin' to myself."

"So how does it feel to be a married man?"

"Feels ayyite so far."

"I know you can't wait for the honeymoon. Where you takin' her?"

"Barbados. We're leaving in two days. I'm gone for two weeks, E. Getting the fuck outta here," Rah proclaimed.

"I feel you, Rah. Shit, I need a lil' vacation myself. Hood gettin' hectic and shit. You know Russell's coming home, right?"

"Yeah. I heard," Rah replied, looking halfhearted about the news. "He did seven years, right?"

"Yeah. Finally."

Rah shook his head lightly. He and Yung Slim had never really gotten along when Yung Slim was home. They were like oil and water. Russell felt that Rahmel was too much of a pretty boy, a faggot, and he'd never understood how his cousin Eric could be best friends with him.

But unbeknownst to Eric, the silent beef between Russell and Rah went further than unpleasant glares and small unkind words toward each other. One reason why Russell was locked up was because of Rah. But Rah never said a word to Eric about what had gone down between him and Russell. He'd figured Russell would do hard time, like twenty-five years plus, so it was a shock to him to hear that he was coming home soon.

Rah stood next to Eric, keeping his composure, looking nonchalant about the news.

"Eric, how long you and me been friends?" Rah asked, out of the blue.

"Shit, since the sixth grade. Why you ask?"

"Yo, we brothers, right?"

"Niggah, we family."

"So whatever pops off, you got my back, right?" Rah asked.

"Niggah, what kind of question is that? You know we ride or die together, Rah. You, me, Mel, Raheem, Critter, Donald . . . yo, you in some kind of trouble?" Eric asked, becoming wary of Rah's tone.

"Nah," Rah stated. "You know a niggah just got married, so you know . . . I'm just a little paranoid."

"Yo, I got your back, but any problems between you and the missus, you're on your own. That's where I don't have your back. You know I don't mess wit' angry black women, shit. I rather fuck wit' the feds than a mad, belligerent black woman."

Rah chuckled. "I hear you, niggah."

Eric looked at Rah, and said, "Congratulations, Rah . . . you doin' your thang. You stepped up and married shorty, surprising me and shit."

"Thanks."

"Fo' real. I'm happy for you, Rah. Vivian, she ayyite."

"She's more than ayyite, she's a blessing," Rah corrected.

"Yeah, I feel ya. You stepped up, tho', niggah. You're finally leaving these hoes alone, huh?"

"E, I'm 'bout to be thirty in two years. I need to start doin' me. You know? I'm thinkin' about moving out the city, getting a house in V.A. somewhere."

"You wanna move?"

"I need to. Queens is gettin' old."

"Damn, Vivian got you soft already?"

"Nah, I've been thinkin' about this for the longest. I wanna start doing me, and open up a business somewhere in the South. I just wanna be gone."

"What about us?"

"Yo, y'all can always come down and visit. You know I always got a place for my peoples. But I need a change, E, and Vivian's a start. I'm tryin' to relinquish my old ways and become a good husband, and soon father," Rah suddenly announced.

"Father?"

"Yeah, Vivian's two months pregnant."

"Word. Congratulations, Rah," Eric said, giving him dap and a hug. "Damn, you about to be a daddy."

Rah smiled. "You're the first to know. And I want you to be my child's godfather."

"Godfather?"

"Yeah. I know you ain't got any children yet, and Mel, he got a handful. So I know you'd be a suitable godparent to my child. I want you part of the family, E," Rah happily proclaimed.

"Rah, thanks. That's my word, I won't let you down. Your seed, I'm gonna treat it like it was mines," Eric stated, then giving his boy a manly hug.

"There you are," Vivian, the beautiful bride, called out. "Baby, I was looking all over for you."

"I just needed some air."

"Hey, Vivian," Eric greeted.

"Hey, Eric." Vivian returned, giving Eric a hug. "You were trying to keep my husband away from me?" she joked.

"Nah, never that. We were just having a one-to-one talk."

"I hope y'all two weren't talking about me."

"Nah. If so, we both had nothing but good things to say about you," Eric stated joyfully.

"Uh-huh, y'all better."

"Oh, by the way, congratulations," Eric announced.

She looked at Rah, and asked, "You told him?"

"Yeah."

"So you cool with being the baby's godfather?"

"What . . . I'm ecstatic."

Vivian smiled.

"Well, I think we should get back inside, before the guests think we abandoned them," Rah said.

"Yo, Vivian . . ." Eric called out. "What's up wit' your girl, the maid of honor? She single or what?"

"Why, you tryin' to get at her?"

"Maybe. She's cute."

Vivian smiled. "Go holla at her and find out yourself."

"I might just do that," Eric said, smiling. He just wanted to fuck her.

Eric followed Vivian and Rah back into the reception area where he'd make his move toward Vivian's friend. Seeing a bunch of single, sexy, and cute ladies clustered together in one room made him horny, and Charlene, Vivian's maid of honor, caught his eye the most and he definitely wanted to get at that for the night.

Eric wasted no time trying to get at Charlene, Vivian's girl. With the Dom Perignon champagne flowing through his system, his mind was on sex for the remainder of the reception and night.

Eric started a friendly chat with Charlene, getting her to smile and laugh. Rah looked over at Eric and raised his glass toward him, giving his friend the heads-up, seeing Eric doing his thang.

Two hours later, they both were tearing garments off each other at Charlene's Canarsie apartment in Brooklyn. Charlene jumped in Eric's arms, straddling him, and ramming her warm tongue down his throat. Eric, still clad in his tux pants and unbuttoned shirt, dropped Charlene onto the bed and stood over her. He was excited. Charlene was sexy—long jet black hair, exotic bedroom eyes, flawless brown skin, and stunning legs. Eric's manhood had risen profoundly just by the sight of her seminudeness.

Charlene went for his pants, slowly unzipping them, reaching for his dick, and pulling it out. She smiled. "I see we're gonna have some fun tonight."

Eric returned the smile as Charlene gracefully leaned forward and pressed her precious thick warm lips against his dick and engulfed him like a highly paid porn star.

To Eric, this was what life was all about—making money, his niggahs being happy, having pussy at his beck and call, and just doing him. He was happy. Rah got married and his cousin was coming home. He couldn't wait. He wanted to throw Russell a big coming-home party, and have mad bitches and strippers in the place—give Russell the welcome-home party he deserved.

He stood over Charlene, watching her head bobbing back and forth sucking hard on his dick, and causing him to grunt and moan.

He'd had a good day today. He told Charlene to stop. He pushed her on her back against the bed, and removed the rest of his clothing, along with hers, and then he slowly climbed on top of her and pushed his erection into her, melting in between her warm thighs.

Eric enjoyed Charlene's company throughout the remainder of the night. He felt contented, lying in Charlene's slim arms, both of them naked in her bed after having good sex. At this point in his life, things were going smoothly, and he wasn't stressed about anything much. Ever since Eric had got laid off from his airport job two years ago, his life went in a different direction—for him, a better direction. He didn't have any kids, and he wasn't committed to anyone at this point in his life. He did whatever he chose to do and bounced from one warm bed to another. Women loved him, and he loved them right back.

10

Starr lay motionless and still unconscious in Jamaica Hospital with tubes running in and out of her. Her vital signs were stable, but her body was badly beaten and abused. The nurses and doctors made continual room checks on her, monitoring her signs and nursing her wounds.

"How is she?" a city detective asked, walking into the room and peering down at Starr.

"Still the same," the nurse, Ms. Henderson, responded, jotting down some information on her clipboard. "She suffered some vaginal tearing, swelling in her right eye, and a broken nose. Whoever beat her like this had to be a big dude."

The detective shook his head in disgust and wondered what monster could do something so horrible to a young woman.

"Any information about her?" Ms. Henderson asked.

"Nothing. She has no ID, no name. Far as I see it, she's a Jane Doe," the detective informed.

"Well, we got the hospital sex-abuse unit on their way soon to check her out," she said. "But my guess, I say she's about sixteen or seventeen, and maybe a runaway. They found her where again?"

"The Executive Motel over on the Conduit," the detective stated. "One of the housekeepers found her sprawled out naked on the bloody mattress and freaked out. My guess, she was soliciting for sex, met up with the wrong guy."

Ms. Henderson let out a painful sigh. She peered down at Starr and shook her head, feeling sorry for the young girl. She'd worked at Jamaica Hospital for over fifteen years and saw young girls like Starr in and out of hospitals repeatedly because of abuse, sexual mistreatment, and pregnancy.

Ms. Henderson was one of the caring nurses who truly looked after her patients, especially the young men and women that came in off the streets.

Ms. Henderson was in her early fifties, and was a strong, positive black woman who had migrated to New York from the South when she was in her early twenties. She was a slim, gray-haired woman who wore wire-rimmed glasses and still had a good shape for a woman her age. She always gave off good vibes and was a very attractive woman who got asked out by the doctors and the male staff all the time. She had not one wrinkle on her fair brown skin. Men were drawn to her despite her age, but she was a Christian woman and loved her work, especially when it came to dealing with children. All her kids were grown and had moved away from home, leaving her to work late hours at her job.

She gently took Starr's hand and began rubbing the back of it soothingly, quietly saying, "It's all right, chile . . . everything is going to be okay for you. You're home now. You're gonna be okay."

"If she comes through, you call me right away, okay?" the detective said, walking towards the exit.

"Yes. And, Detective . . ." Ms. Henderson called out, stopping him at the doorway. He turned around. "If you find anything else on her, please notify me soon as possible."

He nodded. "Not a problem," he said, and walked off to continue his investigation.

Ms. Henderson continued to nurse Starr as she lay in bed motionless.

"We gonna get whoever did this to you, dear. I promise you. But you gotta wake up first and tell us what happened," she said, still soothing Starr's limp hand.

Ms. Henderson continued to talk to Starr as though she was her own child.

11

"Yo, E...when Yung Slim gets out, tell him to put a niggah on. I need to make that money," Critter said.

"Critter, just shut up!" Eric snapped.

"Fo' real, E . . . I need to get that money; my pockets are light right now. Shit, you know I got kids to take care of."

"Already, my cousin getting out and you ready to put him back in that life of crime. You thinkin' he gonna go back to his old ways?"

"Shit, what else is he gonna do, get a job?"

Eric cut his eyes over at Critter.

"Yo, that niggah was born a hustler. Niggah from the streets, just like you and me, E. I ain't got many options for myself, so I gotta get out here and grind hard so I can live and feed my kids. Shit, you out here pimpin' these hoes and selling weed, you should understand. Shit is hard for a niggah," Critter stated. He took a quick sip from his beer and glanced around the room.

"Niggah, I ain't pimpin' no hoes, I just throw parties and get a nice cut from them."

"Yeah, whatever. You got these hoes on lock, you call these hoes up, and them bitches come like that. Like Rah's bachelors' party, you ain't pimpin' them. But you charging niggahs to used the rooms for VIPs."

"Critter, I just do me. These hoes know that if they come to one of my parties, they gonna make at least five hundred and better for the night. Niggahs that I invite, they spend money, unlike your cheap ass."

"You need to hook a niggah up wit' some free pussy once in a while. The bitches I be seeing you with, I would love to break my dick off in some of that pussy. Look at me, E. . . . I'm on hard times here," Critter said, backing his chair away from the table, and allowing Eric to have a closer look at him. He was dressed in an old faded blue Rocawear T-shirt, old jeans, and Timberlands that had seen better days.

Both men were up in After Hours, a well-known lounge bar up on Atlantic Avenue. 50 Cent's hit single, "In Da Club," blared throughout the lounge as men and women mingled and reveled the night away.

"Niggah, you just too cheap to buy anything new for yourself," Eric countered back.

"Ayyite, E, you go out and have four kids and see how fast your money is squander away. My baby-mamas be stressing me every fuckin' day."

"See, that's your problem, I ain't having four kids by multiple women. You a pussy-starved niggah. Learn how to leave the pussy alone. Behave yourself, Critter. You meet a new bitch, and a month later, she's claiming she's pregnant. Niggah, how many abortions did you pay for?"

"Niggah, that ain't funny. Them other three bitches I got pregnant, yo, they were on some funny shit. I'm sayin', that dumb bitch, Angie, that bitch gave me gonorrhea and shit, and she had a man."

Eric shook his head, smiling over at his friend. "I'm gonna put you in rehab. You a nymphomaniac, niggah."

"Yeah, well, they say birds of the same feather flock together. You the same, E. You a pussy-craved niggah too. Shit, you just more quiet wit' yours, that's all. I see a couple of bitches that I would like to get at right now up in here," Critter proclaimed, guzzling down the last of his beer and then slamming the bottle on the table.

"Look at you, on the hunt."

"Yeah, well, we only live once, right? I need another beer. You still paying, E?"

"Yeah, I got you."

"I be back, I need sumthin' stronger this time." Critter got up from his chair and walked toward the bar.

Eric just remained seated, thinking Critter was going to overdose on the p-u-s-s-y. Critter was right about him, though. He was the same, but he was more discreet in his ways. That was why he couldn't really hate and talk down to Critter, because they shared the same ways. Eric just had better taste in women, and he took care of business more often than Critter, who was constantly broke and asking for a buck.

Critter made his way over to the bar, gazing at every big-booty cutie he came across. It damn near took him ten minutes to get to the bar.

"Damn, ma . . . let me get that number, you a cutie wit' a booty," Critter hollered at a passing female in a microminiskirt. "Ummm, let me bite that butt."

He laughed his way to the bar. And then gave the lady bartender a huge smile. "Hey, ma, what's up?"

"What you need?" the brown-skinned, short-haired, silver-hoop-earrings-wearing bartender asked Critter, being familiar with his loose ways toward women.

"You're cute, ma, what's good wit' you?"

"I already got a man," she quickly responded.

"So. He treating you right? Because you know I can treat you better. Honey, I'll rub you down in baby oil every night, and give you that massage. Yo, you'll be begging me for more."

She sighed, shaking her head, looking a bit annoyed by his words.

"Listen, I'm here to work, not to be some cheap thrill. What you want?"

"Damn, excuse me, luv. Shit, your man ain't giving it to you right, because—"

The lady bartender was about to walk off and take care of the next available customer, when Critter muttered, "Ayyite, ayyite, I'm sorry, ma. I'll take a glass of Alizé and mix me that Incredible Hulk, that green shit, you know?"

Critter looked around, dying for some female company tonight. He was definitely on the prowl and he was determined not to go home empty-handed. There was too much pussy in the place for him to come up short.

The lady bartender quickly went to work on his drink, wanting him to leave her bar as soon as possible. Critter looked around in awe when this stunning, drop-dead gorgeous brown-skinned beauty came squeezing her way toward the bar and stood next to him, trying to signal for one of the two bartenders.

Critter leaned back and exclaimed, "Damn! Ma, what's really good wit' that?"

River shot him an irate look, sucked her teeth with attitude, and focused her attention back at the bar. Critter wasn't going to give up that easy, even though River was high quality and would never give him the time of day.

River stood out in the place, sexily clad in a cropped red leather jacket with black collar, and matching miniskirt. Her lustrous long legs were set off by a pair of three-inch heels, and her long black hair fell smoothly down her back.

"Ma, I got your drink for you. It's on me," Critter told her, knowing it was Eric's money he was spending. But he didn't care; the niggah was pussy-struck right now.

River looked at him, displeased with his appearance and his pathetic attempt to pick her up, and said, "Niggah, did I give birth to you?"

"Huh?" Critter muttered out.

"No. So don't call me ma. I'm not your mother, nor would I want to be. Please, leave me alone. Fuck off!"

She shot Critter down like a bad contract. Critter glared at her, picked up his drinks from the bar, and countered with a quick, "Fuck you, then, bitch. You ain't all that anyway."

River glared at him, shaking her head in disgust, and then peacefully began to order her drinks.

Critter made his way over to Eric, wishing he could have really cursed out the bitch more.

Eric looked up at Critter, noticing the bleak look on his friend's face, and asked, "Damn, niggah, what happened at the bar? You look like you done lost your best friend."

"Nah. Fuckin' bitch got rude and shit, so I had to curse the bitch out."

"Who?"

"That bitch in the red, standing by the bar." Critter pointed out.

Eric took a peek, and shouted, "Damn . . . her?"

"Yeah. She a stuck-up bitch wouldn't even give a niggah the time of day."

Eric had a huge smirk on his face, knowing Critter didn't stand a chance with shorty—not his type. She had all her hair and all her teeth in her mouth.

"Man, knowing you, you probably came at her wrong and shit."

"Niggah, my game is tight."

Eric laughed. "If you say so."

Eric looked over at River again. He couldn't take his eyes off her, she was just too stunning. He also noticed that he wasn't the only man in the place noticing River's beauty. A lot of them were looking and pondering, but they saw that she came in with Big Red and Twinkie, who had a table across the room and were looking like two major ballers since their last holdup.

River carried both drinks over to Big Red's table, trying to avoid being bumped into and approached by assholes willing to maul and lust over her beauty.

She placed Red's drink in front of him—Hennessy and Coke—and then sat across from him. Big Red sat gangsta lean in his chair, observing the place. He wore a brown denim suit with a navy blue button-down by Akademiks, and a thick white-gold chain with a bulky Jesus-face pendant draped around his neck and a diamond pinky ring wrapped around his finger. He looked like a baller—that extra six grand in his pocket did him lovely.

"Yo, who was that niggah that tried to get at you at the bar?" Red asked.

"Some clown niggah. Why?"

"I've seen his face before," Red said.

"You can't miss it, he's ugly enough."

Twinkie let out a slight chuckle.

Red's eyes looked past the dense crowd in the lounge and landed on Critter's and Eric's table. He noticed Eric studying him. He watched Eric pull out a wad of bills and pass Critter a fifty.

"He a playa," Big Red said.

"Who, that ugly muthafucka at the bar?" River said, looking back.

"Nah, not him, his boy he came with. I know the face. The niggah got a string of hoes on lock. He be throwing parties with strippers. I've been to a few. He definitely makes his ends," Red said.

"Word, Red?" Twinkie asked.

"Yeah. We can get at that. You down, River?" Red asked, with his attention and eyes back on her.

"How much you think we can get from him?" she asked.

"I say about fifty thousand or better," Red answered.

"That'll do," River replied with a contented grin.

"What, I'll be good for a minute with that kind of cash in hand," Twinkie said, gulping down the last of his drink.

"Well . . ." Red began, gazing at River.

"Well what?" River asked looking at Red confused.

"Get to work. Get up and strut your goods, River. Get the nig-gah's attention like you did his friend," Red said.

River sucked her teeth; it seemed that her job was never over. It was always about that money, which was good. But damn, they had just hit up Hubert for twenty large a few short days ago, and she wanted to chill. But Red's eyes saw green constantly, and he was always willing to risk her life by putting her at the front line of his scheme.

River took a couple of sips from her Long Island iced tea and then slowly stood up. Her long gleaming legs stretched to heaven in her red miniskirt and heels. And like before, she made her way over to the bar, but not before she and Eric made quick eye contact and he held her gaze for a short moment, causing him to smile.

"Yo, E, fuck that bitch!" Critter cursed. "She's bad news."

"Yeah, for you, maybe," Eric replied. "But she's just my type."

"Yeah, whatever, niggah. Pussy probably boring anyway," Crit-ter said.

"Yeah, well, I'm willing to find that out for myself," Eric stated, rising from his seat and starting to head toward River where she stood by the bar about to order herself another round of drinks.

Clad handsomely in a red-and-blue button-down with knit sleeves and denim jeans, new Timberlands, and an iced-out lengthy chain adorning his neck, Eric effortlessly made his way over to River.

River didn't even have to turn around; she felt his presence com-ing her way. She had played this game so many times that she imme-diately knew how it would turn out. *All men are the same, all they see and care about is pussy, pussy, and pussy,* she said to herself.

Eric was a few feet from her. He knew he had to make his move quick.

Everyone was thirsty and trying to get at River from all direc-tions. But she was shooting them all down, waiting for that certain one who she knew was on his way over.

"You gonna turn me down too, beautiful?" Eric asked, standing next to her and smiling.

River turned and looked at him with a deadpan look. "Maybe," she replied.

"How can I turn that maybe into a sure thing with you?" Eric asked. He was charming, making direct eye contact and being confident.

"You figure that out. You look like a smart guy," River said, playing hard to get.

"Really. Well, let me start by buying you a drink." Eric pulled out a wad of bills. "Bartender, I got her. Give her whatever she's drinking." Then Eric turned back to River and asked, "What are you drinking?"

"Long Island iced tea."

"Make that two."

Eric stared at River from head to toe, but he glanced discreetly, not wanting to make her feel as if he saw her as a piece of meat.

"So, can I have the pleasure of knowing your name?" Eric asked.

"I don't give out my name to strangers."

"You don't, huh. Well, my name is Eric, but you can call me E." He extended his hand for a polite handshake but River just stared at him. "I'm trying, here, beautiful. You making me work this hard for your name, damn, imagine how it's gonna be on our first date." He got River to smile and chuckle a bit. "Oh, I see a smile and a laugh, finally."

"And what makes you think there will be a first date?" River asked.

"Because so far I'm still here talking with you. You didn't shut me down yet like you did them other niggahs. And plus, we caught eyes for a moment while you were walking to the bar."

"I could have been looking at anyone," River lied.

"Nah. I don't believe that, beautiful. You were staring at me. So I figure you like what you saw."

"Are you always this cocky towards all the women you meet?"

"Do you always play so hard to get? I still didn't get your name, and you know mine already."

River smiled, thinking he was cute. "I'm River," she said.

"River; that's a lovely name."

"Thank you."

"So let me ask you somethin', River. That fat light-skinned niggah you came in with, he's your man?"

"Nah, they're both my cousins."

"Oh, word, so is it safe to say that you ain't got a man?"

"Yes, it's safe to say so."

Eric smiled.

"Why, you looking to fill the position?" River asked, teasing just a bit.

"Hey, anything can happen, right?"

River smiled. The bartender placed both drinks in front of them, and River quickly took a sip from hers while Eric watched.

Big Red sat back and watched River work her magic. He was proud of her for easily reeling the niggah in. He felt the cash was already in his hand.

"Twinkie, it's in the bag for us. We got us another score," Red proclaimed.

"She's good," Twinkie said.

"Too damn good."

Critter just sat at the table and watched Eric get reeled in by someone who'd completely shot him down earlier. He felt envious but quickly got over it when he noticed another big-booty female and he made his way toward her, desperate to take anything home tonight and get his dick wet in some pussy.

The night continued to flow smoothly for the two. Eric kept River's undivided attention as he made her smile and laugh, and paid for her drinks. They both had forgotten that they came with other company.

An hour passed, and Eric glanced over at his boy and saw that

Critter was engaged in conversation with a woman. He smiled at his friend and turned his attention back to River.

"So, when can I call you?" he asked.

"Anytime. My cell phone is always on."

"I'm definitely gonna give you a call tomorrow sometime," Eric said, placing her number in a secure location, his wallet.

"I definitely had fun talking to you," Eric stated, holding her gaze. All night he'd been in awe of her beauty.

River smiled, leaned forward and placed a gentle, innocent, warm kiss against his cheek. "You're a sweetie."

She strutted off while Eric gawked at her backside and legs, and mumbled, "Umm . . . damn!" He knew niggahs in the place hated him, but he felt like the man. Every other niggah had tried to get at that but were quickly rejected.

He glanced at the time and saw that it was twenty minutes past one. He was ready to go. He'd already got what he came for and he wanted to call it a night.

He walked up to Critter and his lady company and asked if he was ready to go. But Critter, horny and desperate for a piece of ass, told his friend to leave without him. He was catching a cab back to shorty's place—pronto. Shit, Eric didn't care; it saved him the extra miles. He gave Critter dap and walked out the door a happy man, having River in his thoughts.

As River rode in the back of Twinkie's old Pontiac, she pondered about Eric. *He's cute*, she thought. River couldn't deny that she was definitely attracted to him. But she knew not to let her feelings get involved with the job, because it made it difficult to execute the plan. Her heart belonged to no one. Many men tried to claim it, but to no avail.

"You worked that niggah lovely, River," Red said, sitting shotgun, and peering out the windshield. "You know what to do, you know what I'm sayin'? You had that niggah open at the bar for over an hour. He's definitely feelin' you, you know what I'm sayin'? So how long you think it will be before we can move on this niggah?"

"Don't know yet, he's different from the others," River mentioned.

"Different? What the fuck you mean, he's different?"

"I mean, he . . . I just got a different vibe from him."

"Please, he got a dick, right? He sees pussy, right? Yo, that nig-gah's high off your shit and wants a taste of it just like the next nig-gah, and the niggahs that came before him. You can crack this one, River."

River didn't comment. She just stared out the window and thought about the night. *He was nice,* she thought. But Red was right, she had to crack him, get that money, and bounce. It was about sur-vival, not love. Love could get her killed. River wanted to save enough money to leave town and do her own thing. After a year, she wanted out. She wanted to do one big score and leave New York for good. She had North Carolina in her thoughts. She had a grand-mother living out there who she hadn't seen since she was seven. But she remembered her father driving her and her younger sister down to Durham, North Carolina, for a week or two and she'd loved it down there. She loved it so much that she hated it when her father brought her back to the city.

River was set to leave for North Carolina and wanted to leave her dreadful past behind state lines.

12

Starr's eyes slowly began to open, fluttering from the small light above her bed. It had been two days since she arrived at Jamaica Hospital and she had no idea of her surroundings. She saw that she was hooked up to a machine, and began to panic. She started to hoist herself up from the bed, but felt a pain race through her body, causing her to let out an agonized grunt.

"Rest yourself, chile, there's no need for you to try and get out of bed so soon," Starr heard a voice say.

She slowly turned her head to the left and saw a nurse standing by her bed.

"Hello?" Ms. Henderson greeted her with a warm smile and a friendly attitude. "I'm glad to see you up."

Starr didn't say a word. She just lay still, wishing she was somewhere else. But the woman continued to talk. "I'm Ms. Henderson, the nurse that's taking care of you. You took a bad beating and was brought here two days ago. How are you feeling?"

Starr didn't answer. "You have a name?" Ms. Henderson asked politely.

There was still no answer from Starr.

"I guess you're shy," Ms. Henderson said.

Starr glared at Ms. Henderson, watching her fix the bedsheets, checking the IV that was in her arm, and tending to other items around her bed. "Are you thirsty or hungry?"

"I guess not," Ms. Henderson said after a long pause.

There was a moment of silence between the two ladies, but Ms. Henderson was trying to make Starr feel really comfortable around her.

"Okay, maybe it's the motherly character in me, but I've been worried about you since you came in. You were in pretty bad shape. You mind telling me what happened to you out there?"

Starr turned her head away from Ms. Henderson and began peering out the window.

"Okay, I guess that means no."

Starr tried to ignore the nurse who was prying too much into her business and, instead, gazed out the window.

"Okay, you may not want to talk to me, but I'm gonna talk to you," Ms. Henderson said, pulling a chair up to Starr's bedside and making herself comfortable. "I'm a nice person once you get to know me. I've been working here for over fifteen years, and I took care of many young girls like yourself, and over time they begin to love me like I was their mother. I have four children and six grandchildren, but I do look good for my age, right, hon?" she joked.

Starr just continued to lie motionless with her face turned away from the nurse. She didn't care. It was dusk outside and Starr wished nothing more than to be back out on the track grinding for her money. And Bamboo, she was going to kill that niggah if she ever saw him again.

"You know, you're a beautiful young girl that could be doing so much with your life, and I'm not trying to be in your business—"

"Then don't!" Starr scolded, still not looking at Ms. Henderson. She watched the glare of city lights from her bedside window and felt so angry at herself for being stupid and ending up in a hospital bed.

"I don't want to offend you. I just want to help you," Ms. Henderson continued.

Starr sighed, mouthing to herself, "This stupid bitch!"

"You know, having an attitude and keeping quiet is not going to help you much. Sooner or later there's going to be a lot more questions from a whole lot of people coming into this room, even the police. They found you naked in a motel room not too far from here, with no ID and no money. Now, the person or persons that are responsible for your attack, do you really want them to get away with it by being stubborn with the people who want to help you?"

Starr wanted to answer that sarcastically but kept her mouth shut.

Ms. Henderson sighed, but she was not giving up on her. She continued, "Now, I know you feel alone, but don't be. I'm Ms. Henderson, and I want to help you."

"Bitch, please," Starr sternly returned. "You don't even know me."

Surprisingly, Ms. Henderson smiled and retorted, "I see I finally got a full sentence out of you. But if you give me a chance, I want to get to know you. I want to help you, and I know it sounds crazy, but that's why I love being a nurse. Because I get to help people, it's something I'm really good at. Trust me. Do this wonderful and charming face look like it will lie to you?"

Starr turned around, facing the nurse with a blank stare, not saying a word, and then she turned the other way, showing her back to Ms. Henderson.

"I don't know your past or what you been through in life, but let it go and look forward to the future. You're one of the lucky ones, chile, because you was given a second chance in life. You're still alive, and be thankful for that. God still wants you here on earth with us. I've seen a lot of young ladies who come into this hospital the way you came in and they leave here on their way to the morgue. Well, I've talked enough this evening, and I know you need your rest. But it sure would have been nice to know the name of the lovely young woman that I had the pleasure of meeting this evening. Good night, chile," Ms. Henderson said, making her way toward the exit.

"My name is Starr," she blurted out.

Ms. Henderson stopped in the middle of the doorway, smiling. She didn't turn around to face Starr, but she said, "Starr, now that's a lovely name to hide from the world. Well, Starr, if you need me for anything else this evening, just push that small buzzer by the side of your bed, and I'll be at your bedside within a moment. Okay?"

"Okay." She nodded.

"Get your rest, Starr. Good night," Ms. Henderson said, leaving the room feeling blessed that the girl had finally opened up to her somewhat.

Starr lay back against the pillows staring up at the ceiling. A few tears began trickling down her cheeks, because no matter how hard she tried, she always felt vulnerable in life. She wanted to be her own woman, but certain circumstances would occur, making it impossible to stand strongly on her own. Now she felt like a victim, and she knew it would only be a matter of time before they found out about her age and her illegal profession. And then the city would start investigating her case, and take her away and put her into a group home, or worse, foster care. Starr wanted no part of being dragged through the system. She knew when the time came she would fight and let it be known that she wasn't going down so easily.

13

Eric couldn't wait to call River the very next day. He sat with his uncle Pumpkin in the Dunkin' Donuts, nursing a cold cup of tea. He remembered her smile, her flowing hair, and thought that there was something different about her that definitely caught his interest.

"Something on your mind, Eric?" Pumpkin asked, staring at his quiet nephew, who hadn't said much to him all morning.

"Nah, just thinkin' about sumthin, Uncle Pumpkin . . . nothing important," Eric replied.

"You sure?"

"Yeah."

"So how's things going with you?"

"I'm doin' me, Uncle Pumpkin, just tryin' to live in the world I was born in," Eric casually stated.

Pumpkin nodded, studying his nephew. Pumpkin picked up his third cup of coffee and slowly sipped a few mouthfuls. It was only him and his nephew, his other comrades had left an hour ago. Pumpkin enjoyed these one-on-one talks with his nephew, because they rarely came. Eric was always too busy to spend time with him. And Pumpkin always cherished the moments he had with him. To Pumpkin, Eric looked just like his father, but was more humble and respectful.

"Uncle Pumpkin, I gotta be real wit' you, I met this woman last night. Shorty is gorgeous. I'm talking the total package," he proclaimed.

Pumpkin smiled, hearing his nephew become excited over a certain woman. "You just met her yesterday?"

"Yeah, at some lounge in Brooklyn. But she's been on my mind all night, and this morning. You know me, Uncle Pumpkin, I never stress a woman. Pussy is pussy, but yo, shorty got me thinking about her. We talked for an hour, and I'm definitely feeling her," he admitted.

"So call her. You got her number, right?"

"Yeah, she blessed me wit' the digits. But I ain't trying to sweat her like that . . . you know . . . you feel me, Unc?"

"Boy, what I always tell you about that pride and ego, especially over something you love?"

"Yo, love."

"Listen, Eric, don't miss out on a good thing because you're too arrogant to give a beautiful woman a simple phone call. Y'all young boys today . . . I tell ya, in my generation, we get a number from a beautiful woman, and we called her that same night to tell her good night and made sure she arrived home safe. But y'all boys today, everything is always a game, a damn joke. You gonna wait around too long and then have the next man take what you could have had. Let me give you a little advice Eric, there is two things to aim at in life. First, get what you want, and after that, enjoy it. Only the wisest achieves the second."

Eric sighed, looking at his uncle.

"I feel you, Uncle Pumpkin."

"Boy, give that girl a call. You probably done lost out already, waiting this long. It's your life, enjoy it while you can."

Eric smiled, then stood up, gave his uncle a loving hug, and told him he would talk to him later. He walked outside and pulled out his cell phone. He retrieved River's number from out of his wallet and started dialing up her number.

After the third ring, she picked up, and he was delighted to hear her sweet voice again.

"River?"

"Speaking."

"Hey, beautiful, you remember me from last night? It's Eric."

"Yeah, I remember you. So what's up?"

"Chillin', thought about you and decided to give you a call," he mentioned.

"Ah, that's sweet."

"Yeah, you know, wanted to hear your voice, say good morning, and all that good stuff."

River smiled at his charm and manners. "Thank you. This is a first that a man has ever called me to tell me good morning. I'm grateful."

"Well, you deserve it, beautiful," Eric said. "I didn't wake you, though?"

"No. I was already up. 'Bout to jump in the shower soon," she said.

Eric smiled and became slightly aroused at the image. He wished he could join her in the shower.

"So, when can we link up? I really want to take you out." he said.

"I'm free all week."

"So what about tonight?"

"Tonight's good."

Eric smiled. "Ayyite. Tonight, say around eight. That's cool wit' you?"

"Yeah."

"So, where you stay at?"

"I live with family. I just moved here from Baltimore," River lied.

"Oh, word, so you from B-more?"

"I was born in Brooklyn, and moved out to B-more when I was eight, with my mother. I just recently moved back to New York a few months ago."

"Welcome back, luv. Shit, if you stayed out in B-more, then we would have never met."

"I know."

"River, listen, I gotta make this run, so let me know where I can scoop you up later on tonight."

"You got a pen?"

"Yeah."

River quickly gave Eric her address and Eric jotted it down on a piece of napkin he'd carried out from Dunkin' Donuts.

"Ayyite, I got it."

"I'm gonna see you tonight, right?"

"Of course, beautiful. You know I'm there."

River smiled. " 'Bye, Eric." She said it so seductively and sweetly that it caused Eric to smile significantly.

"Damn!" he muttered to himself, thinking about her, River was a straight dime and more.

Eric had to make a quick run out to Brooklyn, to meet with one of his faithful clientele who'd called him earlier for a sale. He carried around four pounds of weed, that Purple Haze and Strawberry Hydro, which was popping off big in Brooklyn.

Eric knew that carrying around such large quantities of drugs was risky. But he trusted no one but himself, and felt more comfortable doing the transaction alone.

Eric's Brooklyn client was Willy, who had been in business with Eric for over a year now. Willy dealt only with Eric, because he was honest and was the one man in the game that he trusted. And Willy loved it when Eric would invite him to one of his parties, where Willy got free pussy because of his good business ventures with Eric.

Eric believed that a true hustler had to have more than one thing going for him. He learned that from his uncle Pumpkin, his father, Yung Black, and his cousin Russell, a.k.a. Yung Slim. So he popped off with the strippers and parties first, and then escalated into the drug game—marijuana, mostly. He believed anything else was an omen and bad luck to him, so he left the crack, heroin, and other hard drugs to the kingpins and street dealers. He was profiting well from both businesses, and wasn't complaining. He treated people fairly and kept a low profile. To him, as long as he had a knot of money in his pocket, and his wardrobe and ride were correct, he was cool.

Eric drove into East New York early that afternoon and met up with Willy over by Atlantic Avenue. Willy was happy to see him and even happier to see product coming his way. Eric gripped the small blue duffel bag in his hand, and followed Willy into the dilapidated two-story brick building on Logan Avenue.

"What's good, niggah?" Willy greeted, giving his friend dap.

"Same ol', you got the money?" Eric asked.

"Yeah, you know I'm on point," Willy said, pulling out a bulky bankroll from his pocket and holding it up.

Eric smiled, placed the duffle bag on the floor, unzipped it, and revealed four pounds of Hydro and Haze.

"That's what I'm talking about," Willy uttered.

Eric glanced around, observing the area, while Willy crouched down near the bag and picked up his product. "You always got that good shit, E, fo' real." He looked up and tossed Eric two bankrolls of big bills, fifties and hundreds.

Eric smiled, his hands going through the bills. He sold the Purple Haze for $6,000 a pound and the Strawberry Hydro went for $3,000 a pound. And Willy bought it all from Eric—$12,000 cash up front and the rest Willy got on consignment, because Eric knew he was definitely good for it.

"It's always good doing business wit' you, Willy," Eric said.

"Yo, you keep bringing good-quality shit like this around, and you know a niggah is always gonna give you a call," Willy said, zipping up the bag and slinging it over his shoulder.

"No doubt. Yo, what's good wit' you next month?" Eric asked.

"Why you ask?"

"My cousin is coming home, and I'm throwing him this welcome-home party. I got the drinks. I got the ladies, and you know I got the strippers coming through. It's about to be on, son," Eric proclaimed.

"Word."

"Yeah, you know my cousin Russell? He go by Yung Slim, though."

Willy shook his head, "Nah, name doesn't ring bells. If it ain't Brooklyn, I don't know nuthin' about it."

"Well, anyway, I want you to come through and have a good time. You know I always got you," he stated.

"I might just do that," Willy said, leaning forward and giving Eric dap and a hug.

They both left the building as quickly as they came. Eric jumped into his Scion and went his way, and Willy jumped into his BMW and went his way.

Later that evening, before his date with River, Eric wanted to do some shopping, so he hit up Jamaica Avenue and the mall over on Sunrise Highway. He knew he had to look his best for tonight and spend money. He purchased a few things, including new boots—Timberlands, his preferred choice—and got a quick shape-up at his local barbershop.

River wanted to look stunning for her first date with Eric. He was money, she knew it, and she also knew that he was a man with class and probably respect for himself, unlike the yo-yos she'd dated and scammed, who were loudmouths, obnoxious, rude, and had no kind of class. Eric seemed to be in a class of his own. She was kind of intrigued by him and his style, and wanted to learn more about him. But she also knew that this was work for her, and the quicker she got it over with and got that money, the better.

Her scams getting men for their jewels and money never surpassed two weeks. They trusted her after the first week, and were willing to give her the keys to their homes and call her wifey and shit. One time, she had to fuck one of them because he was getting hip to her scheme, so she gave him some pussy and quieted him down until Big Red and Twinkie made it in and beat him down and got away with $3,500 cash money. It was the downside of the job that once in a while, she would have to hit a trick off—fuck him to keep him in the dark. But it was very rare; it'd go down like that, because River was good, the best, and she had the gift of gab.

River stared at herself in the full-length mirror that hung on her closet door and admired her chosen outfit for the night, a white leather miniskirt and matching leather halter top with open-toe heels. She loved showing off her legs, because she felt they were one of her greatest assets that got men open and so horny.

Around seven, Twinkie came to her place to pick her up and drop River off at the location where Eric was supposed to pick her up. Rule number one in her game: never bring niggahs, the bait, to her home. On the phone, she gave Eric a bogus address in Queens; she told him Rochdale, building 16, and she'd be waiting for him in the lobby. River was familiar with the place, because she had a cousin who lived near there. Twinkie picked her up and dropped her off in front of building 16, where she walked into the lobby and began to wait for her date to show. It was like butter, worked every time. But for every scam, she gave a different location—Queens, Brooklyn, Long Island, sometimes Staten Island, just to throw them off if they ever decided to come around and look for her, becoming suspicious.

She stood patiently in the lobby of building 16, clutching her purse and watching the traffic go by on the streets and the bustling movement of people in and out of the lobby. She glanced at the time and saw that it was 7:50. Twinkie was still parked nearby, observing River and waiting for her date to show up. He tuned in to stations on the radio, reclined his seat back, and chilled until River was picked up.

. . .

Eric was looking sharp, dressed in a blue Rocawear button-down and some denim jeans, with new white-on-white Air Force Ones decorating his feet. He made a right on Bedell Street, rhyming along with 50 Cent's "How to Rob," and bobbing his head to the beat. He was excited.

He pulled up to the building number she gave him, looking out for River, slowing down the ride and profiling with the ice around his wrists and fingers.

He came to a stop when he noticed River standing in the lobby. He honked his horn twice, catching her attention. She smiled, seeing Eric in his Scion, and strutted out of the lobby, turning heads. Eric quickly got out and walked over to the passenger side and, being the gentleman, opened the door for his date. He smiled as she approached.

"Damn, you look really nice," he complimented her, eyeing her lovely figure from head to toe.

"Thank you," River returned, smiling and hopping into the vehicle.

Eric was definitely wide-eyed at River's choice of outfit. The skirt and heels definitely did her body right. He felt a slight jump in his pants as he continued to stare. He blew air out of his mouth, got his head right, and trotted around to the driver's side. When he jumped in, he glanced at River's long refined legs crossed over each other, and tried not to stare too hard.

"You lookin' for something?" River softly asked, catching him looking at her wonderful structure.

"Me, nah . . . you know."

"That's ayyite, they happen to do that to most men. I'm used to it," she stated.

"You're beautiful. A man can't help but to look. It's just, you can definitely put a niggah in a trance," Eric proclaimed.

River smiled. "Well, the only man I hope to put in a trance tonight is you."

Eric smiled. "Oh, word. It's like that?"

"It could be."

Eric had to control his hormones. He didn't want to look like some desperate perverted fool who had never been with a woman before. He got his head right, looked ahead, and put the car in drive.

"So, where are we off to?" River asked.

"Somewhere nice."

"I trust you," she said.

Eric never noticed Twinkie in the blue Pontiac sitting and observing his every move. As the Scion slowly passed his Pontiac, Twinkie quickly jotted down the tag number on the plates, the color, and the model. He smiled, thinking to himself, *This is too easy*. He pulled out his cell and called Big Red.

"Yeah, Red, she's set. He picked her up a few minutes ago. I got his tags and the car. The niggah drives a Scion, that box shit."

"Ayyite, Twinkie, you did good. Come on home now," Big Red instructed. "Our girl got it from there."

Eric and River dined at the exquisite Artie's Steak and Seafood in City Island. Their conversation never stopped, and he kept her smiling and laughing. The vibes were definitely there, and the more Eric talked and got to know River, the more he stopped seeing her as a piece of pussy and noticed that she was a woman really worth spending time with.

"So, what do you do anyway?" River asked. "I see you bling-bling out, with the ice around your wrist and the pinky ring. Making that money, huh?"

"A lil' sumthin' . . . I do me. I'm a party promoter," Eric explained.

"Really? What kind of parties?"

Eric smiled. "On the real, strippers and shit. I ain't gonna lie to you."

"Oh, so you're a pimp?"

"Nah, not even, luv. I know niggahs be horny, you know. I call a few strippers, get a place to throw the party, call up a few niggahs, pass out a few invites, make sure shit is right, and just collect what I charge at the door and a lil' extra on the side if it's that kind of party," he proclaimed.

"Oh, so you ain't a pimp, but you charging niggahs to fuck at your parties, right?"

"Hey, we both gotta get paid, right? Shit ain't free in this world."

"Ain't that the truth. So, I'm curious, you ever sample the strippers at your party? Be honest."

Eric chuckled. "Ah, man . . . you wanna know everything, I see."

"No, not everything yet. I'm just curious, that's all. You're cute, and I know you can get plenty of women. And I know being around a bunch of butt-naked hoes every night gotta turn a fine brotha like you on."

"Sometimes, but I look at it as business, that's all. I'm about that paper. Pussy comes and goes."

"I see," River said, then took a sip from her Long Island Iced tea, placed the drink back down in front of her, and suddenly came with, "So, am I only a piece of pussy to you?"

"Damn, are you always this blunt, luv?"

"I like to come straightforward with men. I'm not the type of woman to beat around the bush with shit."

"I see. I like that. That's what's up."

"So if you just wanna fuck me, and think going on one date is gonna accomplish climbing in between my legs later on tonight, then you got the wrong girl. It doesn't work that way wit' me," River stated sternly, gazing at Eric as she held her drink.

The patrons behind them overheard her comment. The lady started laughing and the young gentleman had to glance over his shoulder to see the young woman.

"I don't even see it like that, River," Eric began to explain. "On the real, I find you really attractive—fuckin' gorgeous. And the truth, when I first met you, yeah, you gotta niggah open, luv. But after tonight, I really wanna get to know you better, and not just after one night."

"I like that, you're honest."

"Listen, I have nuthin' to hide. What you see is what you get. I'm not one of these frontin' niggahs out here that gotta tell lies to impress you, River. All I ask for in a woman is, I'm real wit' you, so I want you to be real wit' me. No games. And so far, you're straight up wit' me. Blunt, too, and I like that. I love a woman who can speak her mind."

River held his gaze, feeling guilty about the situation she was putting him in. For once, her conscience was eating away at her. All the other men before Eric were bullshit, all they wanted was to get into her pants, play games, and have a trophy like River under their arm. She never had a second thought about going through with the scam with the previous ones. But with this one, she warned Big Red that it was different. She saw it in his eyes when he held steady eye contact with her, spoke the truth, and looked like there was more to him than the eye could see.

The waiter soon came to their table clutching a platter filled with food. He placed both their orders in front of them, and asked if they would like anything else.

Eric waved him off.

They started on their meals and continued to talk. River liked that he chewed with his mouth closed, and wasn't spitting out food while he talked, unlike Hubert, who was a total disaster at the table—no manners at all.

"If you don't mind me asking . . ." Eric interrupted.

"Ask what?"

"Your last boyfriend, how long ago was that?"

River sighed. "Two years ago. But he was a jerk."

"He wasn't treating you right?"

"He cheated on me, got some other bitch pregnant, and stole five hundred dollars from me."

"Damn."

"Yeah. But I don't like talkin' about it."

"It's cool. So what part of Baltimore you from?"

River looked up, shocked that he asked but flattered that he still remembered she'd told him Baltimore. "You get points for that," River said, smiling flirtatiously at him.

"For what?"

"Remembering things about me, unlike some men. You tell 'em something about yourself, and five minutes later they asking you the same dumb question you already gave an answer to. I hate that, turns me off. Goes to show that they're out for one thing. . . ."

"Pussy," Eric blurted

She smiled.

"Shit, I see enough of it every day, it ain't nuthin' new to me."

River smiled. "So, what about you, when was your last girlfriend?"

Eric sighed. "Too long now," he admitted. "I'm talking about since my early twenties."

"No kids?"

"Nah. You?"

River shook her head. "None here."

"Why not?"

"Choose not to. I want kids when I get married. I'm not chasing after no baby-daddies for child support, milk, Pampers, and other tedious shit. I want a stable man in my life, so we can raise our children together," River proclaimed.

"I'm impressed."

"Y'all niggahs be trifling. Y'all wanna get all up in it, enjoy it while it's good. Then when she's pregnant, and 'bout to have that baby, y'all wanna forget about it, and move on to something better, after your dick and your baby done stretched my shit all out. Nah, not this bitch. You give me a baby, you stayin' with me."

Eric chuckled. "Me, I don't see it like that. I love kids. I always thought about a family," Eric started, taking a bite out of his steak. "But, my life is too crazy right now to have kids."

"You'll make a good father," River stated.

"Why you say that?"

" 'Cause of your eyes, they say a lot. The way you look at me, direct eye contact, confidence, and they show sincerity."

Eric smiled, and said, "Well, they say the eyes are the windows to your soul."

"You believe that?"

"Yeah. To some extent."

River shrugged her shoulders and continued with her meal.

"Hey, you still didn't answer my question." Eric said.

"What question?"

"What part of Baltimore you from?"

"Damn, you don't forget shit, do you?"

"You wanna know about me, and I definitely want to get to know more about you," he declared.

River smiled, feeling his warmth, honesty, and humor, and then answered, "Park Heights."

They continued their evening touring Manhattan and its night life. River enjoyed every moment of his company. This was the first time she'd actually enjoyed a date, and the thought of conning him was far from her mind. They held hands, talked, and really got to know each other well.

By three in the morning, Eric was on his way back to Queens to drop her off at home. When he pulled up in front of her building, she stared at him.

"Got you home in one piece. Tell your family that you was in good hands."

"I will."

She had never done it before, but her heart urged for it. She was quiet, gazing at him, and then she softly said, "Come here," leaning toward him and pressing her lips against his, devouring his warm lips. They kissed passionately for several moments until she broke away and regained her composure.

"That was nice," Eric said, breaking the silence in the car.

"I gotta go. Thanks for the evening," River said, and quickly jumped out of Eric's Scion.

"I'll walk you upstairs," he volunteered.

"No!" River shouted.

"Why not?"

"Because I don't want you seeing my apartment yet," she said. "I barely know you."

"Understandable."

He watched her long refined legs as she strutted out of his sight.

"I'll call you!" Eric shouted through the window as River quickly made her way into the building. "Damn!" he muttered, and drove off.

Watching him leave, and seeing that it was clear, she pulled out her cell phone and dialed Big Red's number. He picked up after the fifth ring.

"Yeah?"

"It's me, come get me," River instructed.

"Everything went smooth?"

"Yeah. Just come get me."

"Everything ayyite, that niggah ain't do nuthin' stupid, right?"

"No. The date went fine. Just come get me."

"Ayyite. Twinkie will be over there in twenty minutes," Red informed her.

River never replied, she just quickly hung up and tried to keep herself from shedding tears. He was definitely different from the others, and finally her conscience was getting to her about the scheme.

14

"Ha, I win again," Starr declared throwing in her hand of cards on the bed as she and Ms. Henderson played a game of pitty-pat.

"Chile, you got some luck in playing cards," Ms. Henderson said. "No one has ever beaten me in cards like that. I'm always the best."

"Well, I'm not everyone, and your reign is finally over," Starr said, smiling at Ms. Henderson.

"Well, if I had to lose, then I'm glad it was to you," Ms. Henderson said. "How are you feeling?"

"I'm better, Ms. Henderson."

She'd been in the hospital for a little over a week and as promised, Ms. Henderson was making her stay very comfortable for her. Starr began to open up to the nurse and even began to smile when Ms. Henderson would enter her hospital room.

When the hospital sex-abuse unit came in to see her and ask her questions, Ms. Henderson stood by Starr's side. When detectives from the 103rd and 113th Precincts came into her room to get information about her attack, Ms. Henderson was by her side. And when Ms. Henderson thought that Starr had had enough of the questions and interrogations she would remove everyone from her bedside, pushing them out into the hallway, exclaiming, "Okay, she needs her rest now, that's enough." Ms. Henderson was strict and didn't play when she felt that they were badgering her young patients too much. Their health came first, and only if they were up to it would she allow for an interview to continue.

Starr definitely took a liking to Ms. Henderson and even trusted her a little.

Ms. Henderson would always talk to Starr about her four grown kids and her lovely grandchildren, and show Starr pictures of her family. Starr would hold back her emotions, thinking about her own family and the horror and abuse her own mother put her through.

As they played cards in her room, Starr peered at Ms. Henderson and wondered if her mother had been as kind and as sweet as the nurse, would she have turned out differently.

Starr remained quiet for a long moment, her expression looked troubled, and she didn't want to continue on with the game. Ms. Henderson saw the sudden change in Starr and asked, "What's wrong, Starr?"

"Nuthin', Ms. Henderson," Starr replied.

"You sure you don't want to talk about it? I'm here, chile. Whatever you have to say, I promise you that it won't leave this room."

"Ms. Henderson, what's goin' to happen to me? I'm sixteen, and I know what happens to young girls that end up on the street. They gonna put me in a group home, right?" Starr asked, lookin' a bit worried.

"Chile, the city has to do what they feel is the best option for you. I know you're scared, but try and have some trust in this system."

"I've been on my own since I was fourteen. I know how to take care of myself. What can the city do that I haven't already done for myself?" Starr asked, looking frustrated. "I'm a woman, Ms. Henderson, and I do what I have to do to survive."

"Yes, you're a young woman, but you still have some growing up to do, chile. The street is not a safe place for a young woman to grow up. And selling your body for sex, Starr . . . your body is your temple, and you should treat your temple with respect and care. God didn't give you that body to abuse it with drugs, sex, and have some man beat on it."

"Ms. Henderson, please don't talk to me about God. Where was He when . . ." she began to say, thinking about the horrible moments at home before she left.

"All I'm sayin' is, just because I'm sixteen, that don't mean I'm naïve to what's happening in the world. I left home when I was fourteen, and I've done things that I'm not proud of. But it's survival, Ms. Henderson. You gotta know how to handle yourself, and I've been doin' that."

"A sixteen-year-old girl shouldn't be trying to survive in the streets by selling sex for money or drugs. She should be nurtured, taken care of. She should be in school getting an education, learning how to become a respectful, beautiful, and educated young woman in life. Starr, are you proud to be lying here in bed, almost losing your life? Chile, don't you want something better out of life? How long do you think selling your body and soul for money is going to last you? Those same streets you're trying to survive in will take everything away from you and spit you out like you was nothing. I've seen many women like you come in here, thinking they know it all, bad as they want to be, and the next day, they're back out there in them streets doing the same thing. And you know, when they do come back in here, they're on their way to the morgue. Starr, don't make the same mistakes for yourself. You have a choice," Ms. Henderson preached.

"That's good and all, but growing up in my household, all I ever learned was to have sex, and how to use sex to get what I want from these niggahs. My mother didn't care about me! My older sister left home when I was eleven. My father left when I was two, and my mother . . ." Starr began getting choked up, reminiscing about certain events in her life that she'd tried to forget about. "My mother wasn't the best. In fact, she was the worst. She made us do things. . . ."

Tears began trickling down her cheeks and she started to pour out her hurt and pain to Ms. Henderson that had been buried within her for so many years.

"It's okay, chile, take your time. . . . I'm not going anywhere. You can talk to me. Sometimes we need to talk about it, it can be the only cure for our pain and suffering," Ms. Henderson assured. She moved closer to Starr and embraced her. Starr nestled against her chest and began crying in her arms.

"I hate her! I fuckin' hate her!" Starr sobbed. "She made me lose my virginity when I was twelve. She made me do things that . . . that . . . it hurts, it fucks wit' me, Ms. Henderson. Why did God give me a mother like that? If He really cared for me, then why did me and my sister end up with such a horrible mother, huh? Why? Why did He make my father leave us?"

"You can't question Him, Starr. His motives are His motives. But you got to forgive and let go. If you don't, then the pain and hurt will continue to eat you up inside until it will drive you mad. Can you forgive you mother for what she's done to you?"

"Hell, no!" Starr shouted. "I can't ever forgive that bitch! She made my sister leave. She made my father leave, and she made me leave. I wish she was dead and burning in hell right now."

Ms. Henderson shook her head, and said, "You have a lot of anger and pain in your heart. You have to let that go, chile. The past is the past, Starr. I want you to look forward to a positive future for yourself. And having all that resentment inside your heart will only make things worse for yourself. You think that you were the only child that was scarred from a wicked upbringing. Many folks have been where you've been, and it's sad to say, but it's the world we live in today, with so much of the devil going around. But we can't feed into the wickedness, Starr. We can only forgive the ones that brought harm and pain on us, because we can't change what they've already done to us. The Lord is very forgiving, and we have to be the same way in our life. Pray to Him, Starr. Talk to Him. Release that bitterness and anger you have for your mother, and move on with yourself. Take that pain and hurt and make something positive of yourself, and when you have children of your own, you make sure you give them the love and care that you wanted when you were young."

"You think it's that easy for me, Ms. Henderson? You think I can forgive my mother for all the abuse and hurt she put my family through? You don't know what I had to endure since I was ten," Starr proclaimed, drying the tears from her face.

Starr began enlightening Ms. Henderson about her past and what she'd had to bear while growing up. And when Starr talked to Ms. Henderson, she left nothing out, depicting a detailed picture of her life, from why her father left to the reason she herself left a few years after her sister. Starr held nothing back, telling her nurse everything about her first experience in sucking dick, and having men come into her room late at night to have sex with her. She even told Ms. Henderson the one thing that pained her the most, when her own flesh-and-blood mother ate her out for a mere thousand dollars.

Starr was in tears after explaining to Ms. Henderson everything she had to put up with at home. Ms. Henderson was in tears, too, thinking *What kind of mother can do such horrible things to her daughters?*

"Now, can you forgive a woman like that, Ms. Henderson?" Starr asked, drying her tears again.

Ms. Henderson was speechless for a moment. She now understood Starr's pain, and the resentment. She took Starr by her hand gently, and said, "Let it go, baby. Please, I know it's hard to forget, but try and forgive. Lord help this chile," Ms. Henderson uttered, squeezing Starr's hand lightly. "Please release her from the pain and hurt she suffered for so many years from the hands of a woman who knew no better. Lord, have her come to You, and know You are her way. Please, Lord . . . please, have her put You in her heart, and have her come to You."

Starr was taken aback as she listened to Ms. Henderson pray for her. No one had ever prayed for her, and it felt weird to her at first. Ms. Henderson continued to squeeze her hand slightly as she got deep into prayer, and Starr got a little nervous.

"Ms. Henderson, please . . . please, I don't need for you to pray for me," she said.

"You need *someone* to pray for you," Ms. Henderson replied. "You need help, Starr."

Starr sighed. "Where was help years ago?"

"Help is here now for you. I'm here, chile . . . remember that. I'm here for you now, and it's never too late," Ms. Henderson assured her.

Starr lay back against her pillows and thought about her sister. She missed her older sister so much and had been thinking about her a lot recently.

"You think that I'll ever see her again, Ms. Henderson?" Starr asked.

"Who's that?"

"My sister, River. You think God will ever bring her back to me? I miss her so much. She was always there for me, until Mama forced her to leave."

"Have faith, chile. All you need to have is faith, and believe in Him, and everything will turn out all right for you," Ms. Henderson stated.

Starr stared out her window and pondered her sister's whereabouts. If only she could reunite with River again. It would be nice for her, and a big change in her life.

Starr continued to lie in bed and Ms. Henderson went on holding her hand and praying for her quietly. She felt the motherly warmth coming from Ms. Henderson. She felt protected and so cared for whenever she was around. Starr looked at Ms. Henderson, and asked, "Ms. Henderson, why couldn't God bless me with a mother like you? Why I couldn't be one of your children? I guess He must hate me, then."

"He doesn't hate you. He loves you. But you're blessed with me now, chile. Maybe not when you was young, but you have me in your life now. And it's never too late," Ms. Henderson proclaimed. "Keep believing, Starr. Please, never lose faith. Get some rest and I'll see you in the morning."

Ms. Henderson slowly got up and watched Starr gradually shut her eyes and fall asleep. As Ms. Henderson stood over her bedside watching Starr sleep, a few tears trickled down her face. She thought about the hurt this young child had gone through at such a young age. And out of all the children and young women she had cared for and nursed, something about Starr drew her more to her heart.

She gently touched the side of Starr's face, and prayed for her one more time. And then, before she left, she said, "In due time, everything will be okay for you, Starr. I just have to check on a few things and when the time is right, you will never have to worry about anyone hurting you again. I promise, baby."

Ms. Henderson then left the room and closed the door behind her.

15

"You still ain't fuck her yet!" Critter said to Eric.

"It ain't even about that, Critter. Why everything gotta be about pussy wit' you?" Eric retorted.

Critter laughed. "Because, niggah, it is. Yo, the bitch is playing you, E. It's going on three weeks now, and you ain't fuck the bitch yet. She's playin' you out, son. Did you at least see the pussy?"

"Niggah, you hopeless," Eric returned, removing himself from the bar stool and going outside to smoke one of his Black & Miles.

"Hopeless, niggah—you the one hopeless. That bitch got you whipped and shit . . . blind where your dumb eyes can't see, niggah. I'm telling you, E, sumthin' is funny about that bitch!" Critter shouted, watching his boy exit the bar on Merrick Boulevard.

Critter sighed. "Man, fuck that niggah. Yo, shorty, what's up wit' that drink? It's been like ten minutes already."

The lady bartender sucked her teeth, looking at Critter with annoyance.

Outside, Eric placed the Black & Miles between his lips and slowly lit it with the matches he got off the bar. He exhaled the light cloud of smoke from his lips and leaned against the building with one foot propped up on the brick wall. River loomed into his head, and the past three weeks. He'd spent time with River almost every day the past weeks. He thought about River so much that he'd forgotten about his cousin Russell coming home. One more week, he thought, until Russell was a free man.

He made arrangements for a grand welcome-home party for his cousin, and invited everybody he could think of, and booked over two dozen strippers to work the party that night. He spent money, both on River and the party for his cousin, and knew that it was all worth it.

Eric pulled out his cell phone, scrolled down the numbers, and stared at River's. He was tempted to call but he wanted to lay off a bit. She had him open, for real, and he didn't want to look weak, calling her up with really nothing to say. He wasn't worried about pussy. He knew that at any given time he could call up any hoes from his phone list and make arrangements. But he resisted doing so, even though not having sex in a month was driving him crazy.

Later for that, he said to himself, and placed his phone back on his hip. *I'm not gonna sweat her.*

He took another drag from the cigarette and stared out into the street, watching the traffic go by. Five minutes hadn't even passed when Eric's phone started vibrating against his hip. He quickly flipped it open and saw who was calling—River. He smiled.

"What's up, beautiful? I was just thinking about you," he told her.

"You were?"

"Yeah. You know you stay on my mind," he said.

"That's sweet. So what you doing tonight, baby?" River asked.

"I'm free for anything. Why? What's up?"

"I'm wanna be with you tonight."

"That can happen. What you wanna do?"

"I mean I really wanna be with you, baby," she said softly, hoping he got the hint.

Eric thought about it, and then said, "Ohhh, that's what's up. Yo, I'll come get you and we can get a room."

"A room! I thought you had your own place?"

"I do."

"So why not there? I wanna wake up next to you and make you breakfast. I can't do that in a hotel," she stated.

"Oh, word, you wanna cook for a niggah? I didn't even know you could throw down like that."

"Well, I can. I've been thinking about you all day. I really want to do something special for you since you've been so nice to me these past weeks."

Eric smiled. "That definitely sounds like a plan."

"So what time are we talking?" River asked.

"I'm at this bar with my boy right now, say around nine."

"That sounds fine with me. I just bought something nice and sexy to wear tonight, too," River teased.

"Word, what you putting on?"

"It's a surprise, baby, you'll see me in it real soon. And I guarantee you'll love what you see."

"River, you ain't gotta tell me twice. I'll pick you up around nine."

"Okay, baby."

Finally, Eric thought to himself, after three weeks of waiting for it, it was time tonight. He finished off his cigarette, and couldn't wait to go back inside and tell Critter that tonight was gonna be his night—his patience had finally paid off. But he really cared for River and had felt that in the past weeks. He had actually gotten closer to her than he ever had before with any other woman, and without sex being involved.

"Shit, River, three weeks is too fuckin' long to be stringing this niggah along. We gotta make our move on this muthafucka," Big Red said as he polished and checked for dust and debris in the empty 9-mm he took apart. He passed Twinkie an empty Glock, and then removed the .38 from the small wooden table.

The inside of Red's basement looked like a small arsenal for a gang. They had every kind of weapon lying around, from .22s and .38s to the big guns, like Uzis and Tec 9s.

"You slippin', River?" Twinkie asked. "By now you should know this niggah's entire game plan, from what he wears to bed to what he brushes his teeth with."

"Yo, we ain't got time to wait on this niggah. We hitting this niggah up tonight," Red chimed in. "Twinkie already got this niggah's address. He lives up on Hillside, over by Jamaica Estates. Your little boyfriend got himself a swanky apartment over there, no one goes in or out, but him."

"Y'all stalking him now?" River asked, looking annoyed.

"Yeah, I wanted to see what this niggah was about, since you claiming he's different from the others. And besides, we can't spend too much time on this clown, I already got our next vic lined up. He's open market after we hit up our boy Eric tonight."

River sighed. She looked over at Big Red, giving him a disapproving look. She wasn't ready for this hit—not yet, anyway. Eric had been really good to her the past three weeks. There had been dinners, gifts, talking, and actually communicating with him on a different level. River was even tempted to tell him about her horrible past with her mother. She actually felt that she could open up to Eric and talk to him about anything.

Twinkie looked over at River as he began strapping up. "Yo, River, what's up wit' you? You actin' suspect right now."

Big Red looked up at her too. "Yo, River, don't tell me you're falling for this niggah?" he asked, looking upset. "What the fuck is wrong wit' you? This is our money, River, don't be getting soft on our victims now. He a mark, just like the rest of them fools we done hit up before him. He bank, and we gotta hit this niggah up tonight. Now, you never seen the inside of his apartment, so we don't know what he got up in there. It's risky, River," Red stated, staring at River.

He walked up to her, grabbed her chin in his hand, and continued, "I need you tonight, River. You down for this? I don't want you fuckin' this shit up for us. I want your head completely in this. This niggah, he don't give a fuck about you. He just like the rest, all this niggah sees is a quick piece of pussy."

"You don't know him, Red," River said in his defense.

"Fuck you mean? Like you do? Ain't nuthin' important to know about him but where he keeps his safe. River, this niggah don't even trust you to bring you by his crib one time. We couldn't even get a good scope of the place. But this niggah is still getting got tonight," Red proclaimed grimly, picking up the Glock and sliding a loaded clip into it. "Let's get this shit over with!"

Big Red was jealous. Seeing River displaying feelings for one of their victims didn't go over well with him. He didn't want her developing a real relationship with Eric, it was supposed to be bogus, ending the next day. He wanted to run up to Eric's crib, rob him, and if he tried to play gangsta then Red was going to give him a beating he'd never forget, and if push come to shove, murder him.

Big Red's feeling for River ran deep. And it pained him to see her talk about Eric as if they really had something going. He glared at her as he strapped up and thought about doing the unthinkable.

It was getting late, a little past ten, and River sat quietly in the passenger seat of Eric's Scion, staring out the window. They'd just come from doing some late-night shopping at an all-night Pathmark, and now they were on their way to Eric's place, where River promised to cook him up a late romantic dinner.

"Why you so quiet, luv?" Eric asked, glancing at her.

"Just thinking to myself," she softly returned, not even looking at him.

"You okay?"

River nodded. "I'm good."

"You nervous?"

"About what?" River snapped.

"Damn, I'm just talking about tonight. I mean, this is the first time you ever seen my crib. Yo, you good?"

"I'm sorry, Eric. I got into a huge fight with my aunt at the apartment before you picked me up," River lied. "It was over some dumb shit."

"Well, don't let it get to you. Tonight is our night, and don't let family fuck it up for us," Eric stated.

"I'm sorry, baby. I won't bring it up again. I promise."

"Ayyite. Yo, you lucky, River," Eric said.

"Why?"

"Because I never bring people by my place. You're one of the few that I ever had come through since I moved in."

River smiled. "Serious?"

"Yeah. I don't trust people like that. I live alone, don't like company coming by, especially unannounced. I like my privacy. It's like the bat cave to me."

River blushed. "I feel so special."

"So far, you're on the right track," Eric said, glancing at her and giving her the warmest smile.

River felt like a fake. Here Eric was, broadcasting how much he was feeling her and wanting to be with her, and she was setting him up. Twinkie and Big Red were parked outside Eric's apartment, waiting for the right moment to move in. She didn't want anything bad to happen to Eric, she really did care for him, and if she knew a way to avoid tonight's action, then she would have gone that route. But it seemed inevitable.

The burgundy Scion continued down Springfield Boulevard, with Eric clueless as to what was about to go down.

"So, how we working this, Red?" Twinkie asked. "We gotta run up on this niggah, hit him from the front? His apartment only got one way in and one way out. We don't know the fuckin' layout of his crib."

"I know, Twinkie. I worked that out wit' River. She gonna stall the niggah by his door while we come up from the stairs and run up on him before he opens his door, push him and River into the apartment, and you know the rest," Red explained.

"You trust her, Red? She's been acting suspect wit' this niggah recently," Twinkie observed.

"She ain't gonna fuck this up, Twinkie. That bitch sees money just like the rest of us. She on point, I know."

"It's your call," Twinkie said, and then reclined back in his seat.

Big Red thought about River. They were both counting on her, and if she decided to have a change of heart on this hit, then Red feared he might have to pop her, too.

They sat parked across the street from Eric's apartment. They were professionals. Red had the hookup at the DMV, where he ran Eric's plates and got his address within minutes. He'd slipped the worker at the Motor Vehicle Registration a C-note and slid out of the building as quickly as he came.

Big Red had tucked in his waistband a loaded Glock, and the .38, just in case. Twinkie concealed a Glock, too, and a .45. They both waited patiently until River arrived with their target.

Half an hour later, the Scion pulled around the corner, turning onto Hillside and catching Big Red and Twinkie's undivided attention. Both men stared at the car as though it might disappear into thin air. They were hunkered down low in their seats, watching every move.

Eric parked across from them and then stepped out first, soon followed by River, who carried two bags of groceries in her hands. Being the gentleman, Eric removed both bags from her hands and proceeded toward the solid ten-story building with River in tow. When Eric and River disappeared into the lobby, Red and Twinkie quickly jumped out of the car and hastily made their way across the avenue. It had to be quick. Both men weren't worried about security in the building or a doorman being present—the building's security was just a few cameras and a buzzer, which Twinkie had the code for.

He had studied the place for a week, constantly watching folks come and go. He had it mapped out.

Twinkie made it in first, pushing the four-digit code, and he and Red quickly headed for the stairs, knowing that Eric was taking the elevator up to his fifth-floor apartment.

When the elevator reached the fifth floor, Eric stepped out first, holding the plastic bags. He walked down the brightly lit corridor, confident that his night was going well, and he didn't have any doubts or worries about bringing River to his apartment. He was happy to invite her, and definitely pleased to have her spend the night. His bed had been lonely since the day he moved in, and he got tired of having sex outside his place, and waking up with naked hoes in motels or their apartments or on the floor at the wild parties he threw. It was going to feel good to wake up in his own bed for once, with River lying next to him.

"Baby, hold the bags for a minute while I get my keys out," Eric said, passing the groceries over to River.

She easily complied. As Eric searched for his keys, River looked back over her shoulder and peered down the hall. Her eyes rested on the illuminated red Exit sign suspended over the stairs, knowing that any second Big Red and Twinkie would be emerging from the stairs with guns drawn. It was the way Red had planned it, since they saw no other way to come at Eric. It had to go down that way—forced entry into his apartment at gunpoint.

With his back turned, placing his key in the lock, Eric was oblivious to the setup. He trusted River.

River wanted to shriek when she saw Twinkie and Red looming up from the stairs, masks covering their faces, dressed mostly in black, with their guns out as they quickly came toward her.

The hall was quiet until the point when Big Red let out an intimidating threat. "Niggah, get the fuck in the apartment!"

Eric quickly spun around to see two men dressed in black, pointing guns at him. "Yo, what the fuck!" he shouted.

Not wanting to arouse attention and being wary of nosy tenants, Big Red quickly pushed Eric and River into the apartment, slamming the door shut behind him.

"Yo, y'all serious?" Eric shouted, as his eyes went from River, Twinkie, and finally landed on Big Red. He watched the burly man with a Glock pointed at him carefully. He stood about six feet two, and his voice was dense and menacing. Eric knew he was the leader of the scheme.

River remained quiet. Her heart fell to the pit of her stomach. Seeing the look on Eric's face made her want to cry and forget about the ordeal, but she knew it was too late for any change.

"Yo, where the money at?" Red demanded, the Glock pointed at Eric's head.

"What . . . ain't no money—fuck y'all here for?" Eric scolded, not being so easily intimidated by a gun in his face.

That pissed Big Red off. He quickly stepped up to Eric, grabbed him violently by his collar and brought the butt of the Glock across his face, dazing Eric and causing a gash over his eye.

"No! Red, please—leave him alone!" River cried out.

Red heard this and turned to look at River as he still had Eric clutched in his grip. Eric wanted to pass out from the powerful blow but he still stood, and prayed that they wouldn't kill him.

"What—yo, fuck this niggah!" Big Red shouted. He glared at River, angry that she'd called out his name in front of their victim and then expressed concern and care for the niggah. Envy and hate steeped in Big Red's heart again. The look in River's eyes said a lot, and that caused Red's rage.

Eric wasn't stupid. He glared at River, knowing he'd been betrayed. He knew she had to set him up, because River couldn't even look him straight in the eye.

"Niggah, I'm gonna ask you again!" Red said angrily, "Where the fuckin' money at?"

Eric, knowing that if he answered wrongly again it could cause him severe pain, and probably his life, focused his concern on Big Red, who seemed to be more belligerent than his partner. Twinkie just stood behind Big Red quietly with his gun pointed at Eric.

Eric touched the side of his face where Red had struck him. Blood was trickling down his skin. He glanced at his hand and saw the blood coating his fingertips.

"Niggah, you think we fuckin' playin' wit' you!" Red shouted, seeing that Eric was taking too long with his answer. He grabbed Eric violently again and punched him in the stomach, causing Eric to fold over and let out a gust of air.

"Eric, just tell him, please!" River pleaded.

Hunched over and holding his stomach, Eric looked up at his attacker, knowing he was in a no-win situation. He reluctantly obliged by saying, "The money is in my bedroom."

Red grabbed Eric forcefully and dragged him to the bedroom like a small child being reprimanded by his parents. Twinkie and River followed.

Once in the bedroom, Eric stood up. Big Red and the rest took quick notice of the bedroom setup, and had to admit, the man had taste: green leather imported furniture in the living room area, with a wide-screen TV, and rich plush green carpeting throughout the apartment. The bedroom area was decorated with a brass-and-iron bedstead, finished in cream, and matching mahogany nightstands on both sides, with a gold ceiling fan suspended above the bed.

River was definitely impressed. She wished she could have seen his bedroom under different circumstances, but it was what it was.

"Niggah, what the fuck you standing around for? Get that money!" Red shouted, pushing Eric around. "You definitely a baller, niggah. Got all this antique fancy imported shit set up in your crib. You living like a king, niggah, huh!"

Eric ignored him and walked to the center of the bedroom. For once, he wished he had taken his cousin Russell's advice and always carried a gun on him. But he was opposed to the idea. He didn't have beef on the streets, and he feared getting picked up by cops and catching a gun charge, and doing time for some petty bullshit.

Eric had a piece around, a loaded .38 he kept concealed under his bed. But it was impossible to retrieve in the predicament he was in with a gun pointed to the back of his head.

He walked to his hidden drawer safe, which was spring-loaded and solenoid-activated, constructed of ten-gauge steel that contained $35,000 in cash, jewelry, and some weed. It was hidden so well that you could walk into the room and be right next to it and you wouldn't realize it was there.

Eric went over by the lamp, flipped a switch, and his safe opened, revealing the precious contents inside. Big Red's eyes lit up as he went for the gold.

Twinkie kept his gun on Eric while Red began emptying out the safe, tossing everything into a black garbage bag. River stood motionless, trying to avoid eye contact with Eric. All Eric could do was watch while the two thugs robbed him of the $35,000 cash he'd made a month ago.

Within minutes the safe was completely empty and Big Red was a happy man. River was somber, feeling like she'd just betrayed her best friend.

"We good, baby!" Big Red shouted, throwing the bag over his shoulder.

Eric stood still, his anger seething. He was hurt, frustrated, and wanted nothing more than for the two thugs and the rat-bitch who'd set him up to leave his place immediately.

But Big Red had other plans, though. He hated Eric the most of all the victims they'd robbed. Eric had managed to have River go soft on him, and he knew that River actually liked Eric.

Big Red glared at Eric. The gun was still gripped in his right hand and the bag containing the money was slung over his shoulder.

"Yo, let's go," Twinkie called out, happy with what they'd come for.

"You like her, right?" Big Red asked, looking Eric in his eyes, searching for fear or some kind of raw emotion in Eric. "You wanted to fuck her, huh?"

River became confused and worried. "Can we go?" she demanded, fearing Red might do something to Eric out of jealousy and rage.

"This your boyfriend, right, River? He actually thought y'all were a couple. Damn, you stupid." Red chuckled. "Niggah, that's my bitch. She ain't got nuthin' to do wit' you. You got played, niggah!"

Eric stood there, not replying, not budging. He knew Red was in control. He had the gun. He had the manpower. Eric just glared back at Big Red, hoping to run into the fat, greasy bastard again one day. Even though Big Red's face was masked, Eric knew that if he came across this niggah again he would recognize him and it would be on.

"Twinkie—catch," Red said, tossing Twinkie the bag of money and jewelry. Twinkie seized the bag in his arms, and continued to look over at Big Red, wondering about his partner's next move.

"Fuck you lookin' at, niggah?" Big Red scolded. "Say sumthin' muthafucka. Go 'head, you gangsta, right? Talk, niggah!"

Eric remained quiet. Now he feared that he wouldn't make it out of the room alive. He saw the look in Red's eyes, and knew Big Red wouldn't hesitate to shoot him.

Unexpectedly, Big Red's large arm swung around, and struck Eric in the head with the gun, knocking him down on his knees. Eric cried out, holding his face, hunched over, and staring down at the floor. Red didn't even give him a chance to breathe or recover from the sudden blow as he began raining down on Eric blows from his fists and feet.

"Noooo . . . Red, stop it—please!" River shouted, running up to Red and grabbing hold of his arm. "No—please, don't do this!" River pleaded.

"River, you feelin' this niggah?" Red shouted. He pointed the Glock down at Eric's abused body, lying sprawled out across the bedroom floor. "Go ahead, tell me you feelin' this niggah!"

By the tone of his voice, River knew not to answer what her heart was telling her. She looked down at Eric, who looked as if he'd definitely had enough of the abuse, and then turned her eyes back to Red.

"Let him go—please! We got what we came for," River said, her eyes glossy, looking as if she wanted to cry. "Please, he's not worth it."

Eric moaned in pain, sprawled on his stomach. Twinkie wanted to leave quickly; he didn't want death on his hands. He gripped the bag of money as though his soul was in it and peered at Red, knowing not to interfere when Big Red became enraged like this.

"You disappoint me, River. I know you got better taste than this . . . liking this clown-ass niggah," Red said.

"I don't, Red."

"Say you love me, River," Big Red said.

River didn't hesitate. "I love you, Red." She would tell Red anything to keep him from putting a bullet in Eric's back.

"Yo, you know I love you, right, River? I'll do anything for you. Don't fuck this up for us. We gettin' money, River, I'm lookin' out for you, baby. This niggah here, he ain't worth your time. River, I know niggahs like him. They spit that game, and when they fuck you, then it's bye-bye, you don't hear from him again."

"I know, Red. I'm good, right. I never liked him. He was the plan, and we got that money, so let's be out and spend his money," River said, trying to sound convincing.

"C'mon, Red, she's right. We got that money. Let's go," Twinkie chimed in.

Big Red finally came to his senses, and fell back from Eric.

"Fuckin' clown-ass niggah!" he said before giving him one more swift kick in the ribs.

Eric lay still, almost passing out from the beating and the pain. His eyes were swollen shut and his breathing ragged.

He heard the culprits exiting his bedroom and felt a sense of relief that he was still alive.

River turned around and gave Eric one last look, wishing she could run over to help him. But Big Red pushed her out of the bedroom and warned her not to look back at him.

River held back her tears for Eric, knowing she had wronged him. Of all the many men had she set up and robbed in months, Eric was the one hit that she wished she could turn back from and prevent. She tried not to think about it. She climbed into the Pontiac and held back her tears, knowing not to let Red see her cry. For once she didn't give a fuck about the money. She'd actually found someone she liked and who held her interest.

When Twinkie pulled away, River glanced back at the building and wondered, *Would he try to kill her if they met again?*

16

THE PAST IS THE ONLY DEAD THING
THAT SMELLS SWEET

Man, I told you not to trust that bitch," Critter scolded, mocking Eric in his own apartment as he peered at the wide-screen television.

"Yo, Critter, I ain't in the mood right now," Eric replied, not bothering to look over at Critter, who was slouched down in the leather chair, holding a bottle of E&J in his hand. Critter was mad that his friend got set up by some pretty snake bitch. He wanted to go after the niggahs that jacked his boy, but Eric lay around, being nonchalant about the situation.

"So what you gonna do about it, niggah? They came at you, bashed your fuckin' face in, stole thirty grand from you, and you sitting around actin' like you a scared niggah. What you say, the niggah go by the name Red?"

Eric finally turned and looked over at Critter. "Yo, let me think on it," was Eric's only response.

"Think on what? You got the three-eighty under the bed; you should be lookin' for these niggahs. Niggah, you know I'm down," Critter said.

"Man, they probably long gone by now, Critter. Plus, they both wore masks," Eric stated.

"So find the bitch. You know her face."

Eric sighed, redirecting his attention back to the TV.

"I don't know about you, E," Critter said, then took another swig from the E&J. "Yo, your fuckin' cousin getting out next week."

"And?"

"You still throwin' him that party wit' the strippers? Shit, you ain't worrying about the niggahs that got you, so you need to be focus on sumthin," Critter said, rising from his chair and about to walk to the kitchen.

"Yeah, the shit still on, I ain't gonna let this beef stop me from throwin' a welcome-home party for Russell."

Critter smiled, thinking about all the strippers that were going to show up. He couldn't wait. Critter smirked down at Eric, and then smartly said, "Niggah, did you at least fuck the bitch before her chubby boyfriend played tennis wit' your face?"

"Fuck you, niggah."

Eric was trying to forget about the ordeal with River, and Critter was throwing the robbery in his face. Eric knew he should have been more careful, but beauty and pussy made him slip, and he promised himself never to make that same mistake again.

He couldn't get mad at Critter, though, for teasing him. While Eric lay beaten and bleeding on his bedroom floor, he managed to call Critter from his cell phone and Critter rushed over and took him to the hospital to get checked out. Eric suffered nothing serious, just some cuts requiring a few stitches across his bruised eyelid, and his wounded pride. He couldn't believe that he was set up so easily. He wondered if he'd ever come across River again, and if so what his reaction should be toward her. He admitted to himself that she did save his life; she kept Red from shooting him. But it was because of her that he had been robbed in the first place.

He told Critter that he didn't want a word of this getting out, es-

pecially to his cousin. He didn't want it to look as if he couldn't handle himself out on the streets. If anything, he would say to anyone
that asked about the bruised eye and stitches that he got into a dispute
over some money with a client and the man sucker-punched him
with a blunt object and ran off. Critter promised he wouldn't tell
anyone what had happened, and they both left it at that.

The remainder of the day, Critter and Eric lounged around the
apartment, drinking beer, smoking, and slowly passing the day away.

The private club on Hempstead Turnpike had been jumping off
since nine in the evening on a beautiful spring night. It was the spot
for Russell's coming-home party. The turnpike was lined with sump-
tuous foreign coupés, trucks, and SUVs that decorated the strip as
dozens of high-end cars with blaring audio systems were literally
stopping traffic. Hustlers, pimps, thugs, dons, and even wannabes
stood outside the Long Island club profiling with their high-priced
jewelry gleaming and knots of money clutched in their hands. The
ladies and hoochies—dressed scantily in miniskirts, weaves, and tight
jeans—were craving the ballers' attention and hordes of folks were
waiting to enter the place.

A few local cops were on hand, hoping their mere presence would
guarantee a peaceful night with no gunshots and no fights.

The owner wasn't expecting the turnout to be so large, but he had
over a dozen bouncers present and had notified the police department
just in case. He was a middle-aged white man who'd catered to urban
parties before and definitely knew that without the right security and
cops present, things can go bad really quickly. But he couldn't turn
down the money that Eric and his crew gave him to throw the party
at his club.

Rock-Rock, the owner, was dressed casually in khakis and a
T-shirt, wearing a pair of loafers. He approved of the strippers that
were going to be in his place, and allowed Eric to collect from the
door, though he still profited from the bar all night. It was a fair ex-

change, since Eric was charging the guys thirty dollars to get inside the place. If you purchased tickets in advance, then it was twenty-five.

It was Russell's night, and Eric went all out for his cousin's party. He had VIP set up for Russell and his boys, with their own personal servants and a handful of strippers to please Russell, knowing it had been a long time since Russell had had sex. And for after the party, Eric had earlier rented three suites at the Marriott, where they would continue the after party.

Around midnight, the place was almost jam-packed, and if you weren't inside, then you were definitely going to be locked out. Capacity was one thousand revelers, and the club was about to reach that in another forty minutes, with five-hundred-plus people still waiting outside to get in.

The 2000 S-type Jaguar twelve-passenger limo Eric rented pulled up to the club just a few minutes before midnight. Eric eyed the madness that the driver had to navigate through, the sea of cars and people that flooded the block. He had Critter, Donald, and his cousin—the big man himself, Russell—with him. The limo finally moved its way through the dense traffic, parked around in the back parking lot, and out stepped Eric and his peoples dressed like ballers.

Eric was nicely clad in a navy blue-and-white pinstriped leather suit by Shadez; he had a long white-gold chain adorning his neck and looked like a major figure as he strutted up to the club flanked by his cousin and his boys.

Donald was wearing denim Phat Farm shorts that came down to his knees and a plain white-T, wearing massive jewelry.

Critter, who looked decent for once, wore a gray-and-blue button-down by Sean John, baggy Polo jeans, and sported beige construction Timberlands. He wore white gold also.

Russell, the man of the night, walked beside his cousin sporting a full denim suit, with a navy blue button-down by Akademiks underneath. He also wore beige-and-white construction Timberlands fresh out of the box. A thick long chain hung from around his neck with a colossal diamond pendant of Jesus' face hanging low by his abs.

Russell was six feet two and well built—seven years in prison, and he was cut like an action figure. He held a strong presence, with his braids extending down to his back and his thick black beard trimmed. He was dark-skinned, with diamond earrings embedded in both ears, and he personified a real thug image. One look at the man and you knew he was not to be trifled with. He turned heads with his demeanor and definitely attracted women. One look into his dark onyx eyes and they showed something that intrigued most women and made his enemies wary of him.

Previous to their arrival at the club, Eric had hooked up with his cousin at Sherry's place, Russell's longtime girlfriend. Sherry rented a two-bedroom apartment on Farmers, where Russell fronted her some money to keep her bills in order. When the two finally met, Eric and Russell, coming face-to-face after seven years of separation, Eric embraced Russell and shouted, "Damn, I missed you, cuz. It's been a long time. It ain't been the same without you."

"I know. I'm glad to be home, yo," Russell returned. He rarely showed emotions, but this was family. Eric was jovial about his cousin being home, and so was Sherry. But Sherry wanted him home alone for a few hours, so she could stretch out on that dick she'd been missing for years. Sherry peered at Russell, and stated, "Baby, you look good."

Russell smiled, admiring Sherry's goods, and replied, "You know what time it is."

Russell looked over at his cousin, and he had to excuse himself. "E, you know, it's been a minute . . . I ain't had none of this in a long time," he said, hugging Sherry and grabbing her firm backside with his strong hands.

"Yeah, I know. Do you, Russ. I'll be back around tonight to scoop you up for the party," Eric told him.

"That's what's up."

Eric gave Russell another hug, once again saying to him how

good it was to have him back home. He then left the apartment, leaving Russell with Sherry to handle his business.

Russell wasted no time divesting Sherry of her clothing, peering at her superb figure, and then carrying her into the bedroom, where he was about to get ready for business. He was seven years backed up, and couldn't wait to release all of his pent-up sexual frustration. He had demons to let loose.

"Russell, it's good to have you back, word. You know it ain't been the same since you got locked up," Critter said, brownnosing a little. "You know the hood wasn't the same without you, son. Shit's been all fucked up. But you home now, niggah. You home to take care of business."

"Yeah, niggah . . . welcome home," Donald chimed in.

"All for you, my niggah," Eric said, raising his glass filled with champagne in the air over his cousin.

Russell looked around, feeling the love and the party. He greeted many guests upon his arrival to the VIP section. Some came to show him respect and tell him it was good to have him back, and some wanted to talk business and personally meet the legend themselves. Russell admired and stared at the two dozen strippers who walked around topless or scantily clad. It had been a long time since he'd seen a beautiful, half-naked woman besides Sherry. And he thirsted for more sexual attention from the ladies.

They all sat in the VIP area, observing the outsized crowd from above, sipping on Cristal, Dom Perignon, and Hpnotiq. 50 Cent's "In da Club" blared throughout the club as revelers below moved to the catchy beat and flow of music the DJ poured into the crowd, causing sweaty revelers to hit the bar repeatedly and dispense more money into the place.

In the VIP area, there were over thirty people mingling along with Eric, Russell, and the rest, some well known, and some lingering, trying to feel important and make their impression on Russell.

Everybody knew what he was about, and the majority feared him but craved his attention and respect, and would go to the limit for that.

Six exotic, voluptuous strippers pranced through the VIP area, flirting, mingling, and collecting huge tips all night. It felt like paradise to Critter, who looked around in awe and stuffed twenty-dollar bills down every G-string that passed by him.

"Everything good up here?" Rock-Rock asked, checking in.

"Rock-Rock, we good," Eric stated.

Rock-Rock was down-to-earth, and Eric liked him. He went up to Rock-Rock, and said, "Yo, Rock-Rock, let me introduce you to my cousin."

Rock-Rock didn't mind, he was dying to meet the man of the hour, the man he'd heard about from his security team, and the man who brought over fifteen hundred people to his club.

Rock-Rock walked beside Eric and approached Russell, who was engaged with Mindy and Mandy, the beautiful Hershey twins. Russell poured Cristal down their chests, and began sucking it off their nipples and in between their breasts.

"Yo, Russ," Eric called out.

Russell turned around, laughing, and looked over at his cousin, then rested his eyes on Rock-Rock. "What up, E?"

"Yo, let me introduce you two. Russ, this is Rock-Rock, the owner of the club. He looked out for us tonight," Eric informed him.

Russell examined Rock-Rock, doing a quick size-up of the white man, and then said, "Good lookin' out. I appreciate this."

"If y'all need anything, come to me," Rock-Rock recommended.

"Definitely," Russell said, and then turned his attention back to the topless twins, who were dying for his undivided attention.

"Well, that went good," Rock-Rock said.

Eric smiled. "He just came home. He did a seven-year bid."

"Understandable."

Rock-Rock then left the VIP section and went to see about his workers down in the club.

The DJ began to spin some extended Jamaican mixes, piercing the large club with Sean Paul's "Get Busy" and "Like Glue." Revelers got excited and were grinding their pelvises against their partners'. Some of the females stared up at the VIP section, hoping to catch Russell's attention. But Russell was too busy sucking champagne off a stripper's nipples to pay attention to the floor below.

As the night went on, more people started entering the VIP section; females tried sneaking in or bribing the bouncers at the foot of the stairs, in search of that next big baller to trick on them. And the fellows wanting in were wishing to see Russell, knowing that he was home now, and wanting to get put on to make some money out on the streets.

Lying low among the crowd and trying to be inconspicuous about their presence were two black agents who kept a keen eye on Russell and his crew upstairs. Being aware that he was home, they knew it would be a matter of time before he hit the streets again and returned to his life of crime. They both were dressed in velour sweatsuits, and Yankees caps. They knew seven years ago Russell had been a very major figure in the drug trade. He was only twenty years old then but was a rising kingpin.

But luckily for cops, with the right informants and Russell making a stupid mistake by committing murder, they were able to shut him down and put him away for a long sentence. Now it seemed as if the years had gone by too fast, because Agent Merchant and Agent Morris couldn't believe that he was out again. They felt Russell should have done life. He was ruthless and he'd terrorized the neighborhood for too long, as his family did before him.

Making their way through the thick crowd in the VIP section in search of the man of the night were Barnes and Bishop, two well-known street thugs. They'd been tried in court twice, but were never convicted of the four murders they allegedly committed.

Barnes was a solid six feet three, brawny, and always wore a menacing look on his face. He was in his early thirties and had thick black eyebrows and smooth brown skin, with a baldy. He loved wearing leather coats and jackets, even in the summertime, because he was able to conceal any kind of weapons in his coats.

Bishop was six feet one, slimmer than Barnes but just as deadly. One look into his dark eyes and you knew he was a crazy sonovabitch. He had a pierced tongue, nose, and both eyebrows, and had taken the life of his father when he was fifteen. He caught his father stealing from him, a dope package out of his bedroom. Late one night, Bishop spotted his pop walking up Rockaway Avenue, so he quickly ran up behind him and shot him twice in the back of the head. Bishop didn't care, his father didn't raise him anyway, and he was a junkie on top of that. Bishop saw himself as doing his father a favor by putting him out of his misery.

They both spotted Russell, whom they knew as Yung Slim, fondling some redbone stripper as she sat on his lap. They walked up to him, wanting to catch him off guard.

Bishop crept up behind him and quickly slid his arm around Russell's neck, squeezing him in a little choke hold, and said, "You slippin', niggah. I know prison ain't made you soft."

Bishop then let go, and Russell quickly turned around and looked up at his boy, Bishop, and then Barnes came into view.

"My niggahs, what's up, what's up, what's up!" Russell exclaimed, jumping from his chair, and giving Barnes and Bishop dap and embracing them in a manly hug.

"Good to see you again, niggah," Barnes stated.

"Oh, shit. It's been a long time," Russell exclaimed.

"Too long, niggah. So, what's good, Russ?" Bishop asked.

"Back home, baby. You know what's good," Russell said.

"So you ready to get back to work and hit these blocks again?" Barnes asked with an impassive look.

"Barnes, you know what's up. I'm home, baby. I'm here to take back what was taken from me a long time ago."

"That's what I'm talkin' about, niggah," Bishop chimed in. "I'm glad to see the state didn't make you go soft."

"Never that, yo . . . fo' real. We gonna be on point again, my nig-gahs. I got a lot of deadweight to deal with first, and then it's on," Russell proclaimed, then took a sip from his glass.

"Ayyite, Yung Slim, we out. Do you, niggah. Enjoy the night. I'm gonna get at you wit' some info later on," Barnes stated.

"Y'all niggahs leaving already? Stay . . . you got pussy roaming free all over this muthafucka, enjoy y'all selves."

"Nah, we got other business to attend to," Bishop proclaimed. "We just came to check you, and see what's up. Welcome home, Yung Slim," Bishop said, and gave him dap again.

"Same here, niggah . . . see you around," Barnes said, and then they both left the way they came, intimidating the revelers as they lightly pushed their way through the dense crowd.

From a few feet away, Eric noticed Barnes and Bishop leaving the room while he was talking to a young female. He knew they both came to see Russell, and he knew that both men were dangerous, and only came to drag Russell back into the game. He'd never had any beef with them. In fact, since Russell's incarceration, Eric remem-bered seeing the duo only a handful of times. After Russell got locked up, they just left the hood. And now, coincidently, they were both back. Eric gazed over at his cousin, watching Russell down a bottle of Cristal, and rub his hands across a stripper's breasts.

The night was still young, and the only thing that was on Eric's mind was pussy. He had three suites waiting for him and his company at the Marriott, and he planned on bringing as many strippers and hoes as he could along for the ride in the limo, and continuing their party back at the Marriott.

The party continued at the Marriott in downtown Brooklyn. The limo ride was nothing but an early orgy, where Critter got a blow job from two hoes who got naked during the ride. They both were clearly drunk. They kissed and fondled each other, and molested Critter, who sat back with his jeans around his ankles and his huge erection ready for action. Eric, Russell, and the rest sat, drinking and getting drunk as the petite, light-skinned ho engulfed Critter's dick down to his balls, never coming up for air.

Critter had the largest smile on his face as he looked over at his friends and gripped a handful of the woman's hair, forcing her farther down on his big dick. He groaned and she choked, gagging on dick and spit.

"Critter, you still a wild boy," Russell proclaimed, smiling and then downing his drink. "This niggah still ain't fuckin' change."

"Yo, Russ, I live life fuckin' these hoes and doing me, niggah," Critter replied.

Shorty finally came off the dick and wiped her mouth, smiling, and allowed her friend to go down on the dick next.

This was Critter's moment. His homey, Yung Slim, was home, a beautiful bitch had his dick in her mouth, and he was tipsy and on his way back to the hotel to fuck two, three, or all seven of the hoes they'd brought with them to the hotel.

Critter wasted no time shoving his big black dick into the light-skinned shorty who'd deep-throated him in the limo earlier. He ran up in her raw-dawg, without protection or anything, and had her panting and scratching at his back as she lay naked on her back with her legs spread like eagle's wings, Critter's big dick opening her up like the Grand Canyon.

"You gonna be my next baby-mama, right, bitch!" Critter shouted, thrusting his dick into her.

"Yes . . . yes . . . Fuck me! Fuck me. . . . Oooh. Shit . . . yes . . . fuck me! Damn, you gotta big dick," she cried out.

Donald was also engaged in an orgy, having himself a ménage à trois in the adjacent room. He had two butt-naked hoes with him, and heard the loud cries from the young hoochie Critter was banging in the other room, and he wanted to drown out their sounds of ecstasy and see who could make the hoes cry out louder.

Russell and Eric, they put the sex and hoes on pause for a moment, and went to have drinks down at the hotel bar. The pussy wasn't going anywhere, and Russell wanted to have a talk with his cousin alone.

"Damn, cuz, that's like your tenth drink tonight," Eric remarked, seeing Russell throwing back champagne as if it was water.

"A niggah didn't get to drink like this in seven years, E. The three most missed things in prison while I was locked down was pussy, liquor, and money. . . ." He was a bit tipsy but still remained focus.

"Yo, I saw you talkin' to Bishop and Barnes at the club earlier," Eric said. "What those two wanted?"

"They happy to see a niggah home, E. You know, came to say what's up," Russell stated tersely.

"I haven't seen them around lately. Thought they both were dead or locked up by now."

"Nah, them niggahs are soldiers, E . . . they handle their business correct."

Eric looked at his cousin for a long moment before saying, "You know they watching you, Russell."

"Who?" Russell slurred.

"The feds, cops . . . your enemies. Everybody and their mama know you back home now, so they watching."

"Fuck 'em, E. . . . you think I'm stressin' muthafuckas. Yo, the king is back. And he's back for good now."

"Yo Russ . . . slow your roll, don't get caught up in the game so quickly. Things changed since you were locked down. A lot of people stepped up, doing their thang now. They see you out, they gonna take you as a threat, and wanna put you back down."

"Fuck 'em, damn right I'm a threat, E. I've been out of action for too fuckin' long. I got a lot of things to take care of," Russell proclaimed, gazing angrily at his cousin. "I'm better now, fuckin' wiser. I got Bishop and Barnes by my side again, we gonna take back what belongs to us in the first place. Who da fuck these niggahs out here you telling me to back down from?"

"Russ, I'm just sayin', I want you home for good now. I don't wanna lose you again. We family, niggah. I don't wanna see the state take you away again . . . this time for good," Eric stated. His voice became softer and his eyes rested on Russell.

Russell peered at his cousin, his gaze became gentler, and his tone became calmer. "E, I'm not goin' anywhere, you feel me? A niggah out now and a niggah home for good and there ain't no changing that. You feel me, niggah? I fucked up before, you know what I'm sayin', but believe me . . . I'm gonna make it right. I'm back, baby, and you know me, I'm about this money, getting it by any means necessary. And like before, back in the day, I want you right by my side, holding shit down; you know what I'm sayin'? We're kings, niggah. We share the same blood, our family been running shit in these streets since forever. Your father, our cousins, uncles, we were built for this game here. Don't let shit deter you from making that money. Whoever's out there now, thinking they holding down the throne, cuz, believe me when I say this, they about to get put down." Russell stated.

Eric looked at his cousin, and he knew he meant everything he said. It was like the saying, There's a new sheriff in town. But this sheriff wore the black hat instead of the white. Eric feared that with Russell being home, bloodshed was about to come because Eric knew—the players who were running the game now, whether selling drugs or pimping, they weren't going to back down from Russell one bit. It was going to be an all-out war.

Eric knew the key players around the way, and he was cool with them. He kept a low profile and operated his marijuana business with no problems. He wanted Russell to lie low and keep a low profile for himself. But his uncle Pumpkin always told him that his father, Yung Black, and Russell, they were the same—greedy, hardheaded and crazy. Both were smart men, and were highly respected in the hood, but didn't know how to back down and keep a cool head about most things. Yung Black and Russell, they did business with their gun in one hand and the pen and money in the other.

"Yo, I've been meaning to ask you, E," Russell blurted out.

"What?"

"Who tapped your eye up like that? You got beef, niggah? What's up wit' that?" Russell wanted to know.

"Nah, just a little dispute with a fuckin' crackhead who caught me off guard with an object. Nothing serious." Eric lied.

"You sure, niggah? 'Cause if you got problems out there, we need to handle that shit now. We need to let niggahs know not to fuck wit' family. You feel me?"

"Yeah, I feel you, Russell. But everything good," Eric assured.

"Ayyite, niggah," Russell said. "Yo, I don't know about you, but I know Critter a horny fuck, and I'm 'bout to run up in one of those suites for some pussy before Critter sticks his nasty dick in all them bitches. Niggah might fuck around and give one of them hoes an STD."

Eric laughed. "Ayyite. I'll be up there shortly."

Russell gave his cousin dap, and then strutted drunkenly back to the elevators. Eric sat at the bar and ordered another drink. He thought about River, and then angrily had a flashback of the setup. He figured that she and her associates were probably long gone and out of town by now. He wanted to see River again, for mixed reasons, the majority of them not good. Part of him thought about bashing her face in, but then thinking of her smile and her charm made him think against it. He hated to admit it but River had a strong effect on him, and he had to give her credit, she had him open and so blinded that she'd made him slip up in the game. He hadn't even got to see the pussy yet, and he was already open like a fat man's pants.

"Fuck this," Eric muttered to himself. He came to reason with himself, thinking he had over half a dozen naked freaky bitches roaming around on the tenth floor in three suites, and he was sitting in the bar worrying about one bitch who did him wrong. Coming to his senses, he removed himself from the bar stool and joined his cousin and the rest for a night of craziness.

17

Starr was dressed and finally ready to leave the hospital accompanied by two social workers from the Child Advocate Center who were joined by a uniformed officer. Ms. Henderson assured her that everything would be fine, but in Starr's mind she wanted no part of the system, or living in a group home. She wanted to be on her own, and cursed herself for not being eighteen soon enough.

"Starr, everything's going to be okay," Ms. Henderson assured her, helping her with her clothing. "I know Mrs. Barkley personally, and she's a very good woman."

Starr kept quiet and frowned at Mrs. Barkley, showing her disapproval of the situation that she was being forced into. Mrs. Barkley went over to Starr, and said, "Ms. Henderson tells me that you beat her in cards. That's impressive because she never loses. Maybe one day you and I can play a few hands."

Starr remained quiet, smirking at Mrs. Barkley. *Does this bitch think I'm ten?* Starr thought. But Mrs. Barkley still kept her warm smile and reassuring attitude. Starr hated what she was dressed in, baggy worn jeans, old dirty white sneakers, a T-shirt that was clearly too big for her, and her hair in a long ponytail. They had her looking like some poor sixteen-year-old misfit from the block. For once,

Starr looked her age, but like a dirty sixteen-year-old girl without a pot to piss in. She was used to being scantily clad in the best name-brand clothing, having money to burn, and having grown men lusting after her and guessing her to be in her early twenties. She knew that after she left the hospital and got thrown into a group home, her life would change dramatically, and she wasn't about to let that happen. If they had her dressed like this, her skin itching from the cheap fabric they put her in, then she definitely wasn't looking forward to the Brooklyn group home that they had her assigned to.

Ms. Henderson looked at Starr with glossy eyes, trying not to become too emotional, as she sometimes did with her young patients before they checked out. She went up to Starr and gave her a deep, loving hug, and said, "This is not the end for you, chile. It's only the beginning. You have a second chance to get your life right. Please do. And in time, I'll come for you. You have my number, and please don't hesitate to call me if you need anything."

"Thank you," Starr replied, not wanting to let go of the one woman who ever cared and loved her in such a short time.

"Remember, I'm always here for you, Starr. So give me a call, and I promise we'll hang out someday," Ms. Henderson said.

"I'd like that," Starr replied, smiling.

"It's time to go," the male worker said, glancing at his watch.

Starr collected the few items that she'd acquired since her stay and followed both social workers out of the room. Ms. Henderson lingered back in the room peering at Starr with tearstained eyes, getting emotional over Starr's departure. Starr quickly glanced back, and mouthed "Good-bye," to a friend and a woman who'd been more of a mother to her than her own biological parent.

Down in the lobby, Starr had other motives. She peeped at the ugly brown van parked outside the hospital entrance and knew it was there waiting for her. Her heart pounded rapidly as she took in her surroundings.

Mrs. Barkley was engaged in a conversation with the cop while her male friend played her close, as if he knew what was up.

"So, where is this place?" Starr asked, trying to feel him out.

"Someplace where they won't hurt you," the man replied, being short.

"Well, can I use the bathroom before we go anywhere?" Starr asked.

"You should have thought of that before we came downstairs," the man replied angrily. "We're on a schedule. We have two more kids to pick up."

"Well, you want me to go in the van?"

He let out an irate sigh, and heard Mrs. Barkley say, "William, just let her go. She's not going anywhere."

"Fine," he muttered, and escorted Starr to the nearest bathroom. "You got five minutes. Make it quick."

Starr went into the bathroom and thought about her quick escape. She was determined not to get into that van with anyone. She went into the stall and tied her sneakers really tight. And then she went to the sink and filled her hands with lots of liquid soap. It was a desperate attempt, because the man in the suit looked really fast, but the cop and the woman she knew didn't have a chance in hell of catching up with her when she ran. The cop was overweight, and Mrs. Barkley looked as though she hadn't seen a gym in ages. But her colleague looked fitter than either of them, and he was the one who worried Starr.

After spending a moment in the bathroom contemplating her plan, she told herself that it was now or never.

"Hey, young lady, hurry up in there, we ain't got all day!" he shouted, banging on the bathroom door.

Starr emerged from the bathroom with both her hands in tight fists. She tried to keep her composure and started back to the lobby looking nonchalant.

"Is everything okay?" Mrs. Barkley asked.

"Yeah, I'm fine," Starr replied.

"Good, let's keep it moving," the man said.

They all walked outside the hospital toward the van. Starr's heart started to race. She knew doing this was going to definitely disappoint Ms. Henderson about starting up a new life for herself. But Starr didn't care. She had to do what she had to do.

When it looked as if everyone was distracted by something outside, Starr quickly made her move.

"Excuse me," she called out to her male escort.

"What?" he said, turning to face her, and that's when Starr leaped up and smeared the liquid soap in his eyes, causing him to scream out, "Aaaaaahhh, that little bitch put soap in my eyes!"

In one rapid motion, Starr took off running. The cop gave chase as Starr bolted across the busy Van Wyck Expressway, almost getting hit by a car. She ran toward the overpass down Jamaica Avenue. She glanced back and saw the cop was right behind her. She'd underestimated his speed, because he was gaining quickly on her.

She sprinted down five blocks, never letting up her speed, and when she glanced back at the cop, he was more distant from her. He was fast, but Starr had much more stamina, and ran as though her life was in jeopardy.

After the eighth block she finally slowed down until she stopped, assuming it was now safe for her. She was out of breath, and leaned against a steel gate for rest. She glanced around, making sure she didn't see any unwanted company coming her way.

She only had one place to go, and that was the apartment she was previously staying at in the Forty projects before her beating. It was a risk getting there, but she was willing to take it.

She went into a nearby McDonald's and cleaned herself up in the bathroom, washing the sweat off her face. She stared at herself in the mirror and sighed, looking at a hot mess of herself. Some of her bruises still showed, but they weren't that bad. *I need to get out of these clothes*, she said to herself. She remained in the bathroom for fifteen minutes and then cautiously exited, watching her back carefully.

She only had three dollars in her pocket and was so hungry. She went to a nearby pay phone on Sutphin and called the apartment where all her belongings were; at least she hoped they were still there.

The phone rang a few times before a male picked up. "Yo, who this?"

"Rome, it's Starr—"

"Bitch, where the fuck you at?" he cursed. "You don't know how to bring your fuckin' ass home. It's been almost two weeks, Starr. I got niggahs calling for a date wit' you every fuckin' day and night. I'm missin' out on lots of money, Starr."

"Rome, I was in the hospital," she said.

"What the fuck you doin' in the hospital?" Rome shouted.

"I got jumped by Bamboo," she explained.

"I'm gonna fuck that niggah up when I see him. You okay, Starr?"

"Yeah, but I need help. They were tryin' to put me in a group home, but I ran away, and now they're after me," she quickly explained.

"Where are you now?"

"I'm at a pay phone on Sutphin, near Jamaica Avenue," she mentioned, then glanced around for any cops or that ugly brown van.

"Ayyite, you stay there, I'm comin' now," Rome said.

"Rome, meet me in the McDonald's on Sutphin. I can't stay out on the streets lookin' like this."

"Don't go anywhere, Starr. You hear me?"

"Just hurry up," Starr said, and hung up.

She quickly went back into the McDonald's and ordered herself a cheeseburger and some small fries and took a seat at one of the tables.

Half an hour later, Starr saw Rome walking into the McDonald's looking around for her. He went up to where she was seated, clad in dark jeans, a black T-shirt with a picture of Biggie on the front, and

Timberlands. He was decked out in lavish jewelry and swathed with tattoos on his upper torso. He sported a low-cut Caesar, and a small scar ran down his cheek.

"C'mon, get up and let's go," he told Starr, grabbing her by her arm and not caring who was watching.

"Damn, Rome, you ain't gotta be manhandling me like that," Starr shot back.

"Yo, you heard what the fuck I said," he said loudly, catching the attention of a few bystanders. "C'mon, get your fuckin' shit and let's go."

He noticed a family of four watching his every move. He glared at them, and shouted, "What the fuck y'all lookin' at? Eat your fuckin' food and mind y'all business!"

They quickly turned their heads, intimidated by Rome's thuggish behavior. Starr got up and followed him out the door. Parked outside was a black Escalade sitting on twenty-inch chrome rims. One of Rome's henchmen was sitting in the driver's seat. He shoved Starr into the backseat, jumped in on the passenger side, and the truck drove off moments before the brown van turned the corner.

Starr was happy to be back at the apartment, even though Rome was acting hostile toward her. But she was used to his abusive ways.

"Bitch, how did you let Bamboo put you in the hospital? I told you about those motel dates," he barked.

"Baby, I'm sorry, but he—"

"You know Bamboo crazy!" Rome shouted, cutting her off. "You know what, go in the bathroom and wash your dirty ass, you stink, bitch!" he said, pushing Starr toward the bathroom. "You're makin' me some money tonight."

Starr did as told, moving toward the bathroom, slowly undressing. She gave both her wife-n-laws, Juicy and Sin, nods as she passed them slouched down on the couch.

Inside the bathroom Starr turned on the shower and finished undressing. She put up with Rome's mistreatment because she had nowhere else to go when she walked the streets. He gave her shelter when she was out on the cold streets starving, trying to survive. Rome put Starr up in his apartment, and she agreed to work for him on the streets, making him rich, while he supported and took care of her.

As the shower ran, Starr pulled out Ms. Henderson's number from her jeans pocket. She stared at it and felt sad that she had run away from the two social workers. But she refused to be placed in a group home.

Ms. Henderson was the only person who ever took time out to be with her and really talked to her, and prayed for her. Already Starr was missing her a little bit. She tried to block from her mind what Ms. Henderson had said to her about becoming a respectful and educated young woman, and tried to focus on making money for Rome tonight.

Starr slightly crumpled the phone number in her grip, tempted to throw it in the trash, but she decided to hold on to it. She placed the paper back in her jeans pocket and jumped into the shower. It had been a rough two weeks for her, and she needed to make up for lost time—money needed to be made. She dismissed Ms. Henderson from her mind and said to herself, *I'm never getting caught out there like that again. She doesn't understand me, and never will.*

She was determined not to get caught up in a situation with Bamboo or the CAC ever again. In fact, she wanted to get revenge on Bamboo. She wanted to kill him. Starr knew that in due time, her sweet revenge would come.

She quickly washed and dried off, and wrapped herself in a large towel. She wanted to relax for a few hours. But when she stepped out of the bathroom, she saw Rome standing in the living room with one of her male clients.

"Bitch, you might as well not get dressed, you got business to take care of," Rome said. "He's been wanting to see you for a week now."

Starr sighed, securing the towel around her tightly. "C'mon," she muttered, heading for one of the back bedrooms.

The man gave Rome a few twenty-dollar bills and followed Starr to her room. Starr closed the door behind him and then walked up to him. He took a seat on her bed, looking as though he was raring to go for some ass.

Starr stood over him, untied the towel from around her, and dropped it around her ankles. She stood naked in front of him, fresh from the shower. He reached his hand up to her breasts and fondled her gently, his dick getting hard as he pinched her nipples softly.

Starr got down on her knees, unbuckled his pants, and pulled out his dick. He was average, and she felt relieved that she didn't have to put in too much work handling a big dick. She rolled back a condom on his dick and then engulfed him slowly, causing her trick to let out a slight moan as her head bobbed up and down.

Starr's two-week vacation was over. Her first day out of the hospital and it was back to business, being in her bedroom sucking dick. But even though she'd been in the hospital, for her it felt good to just chill out and talk to Ms. Henderson and not think about the track that often.

But this was her reality, and this was how she got paid. And she felt that there was nothing more for her, especially an education. She had street smarts, and the hood showed her how to get paid. And being young, she thought that all she needed to get by on was her looks and her sexual skills.

But then Starr asked herself, if this was all it was about for her, then why did she keep Ms. Henderson's number?

18

River sat alone at a booth, sipping on a strawberry daiquiri and thinking about her life. She was sitting in a Harlem lounge collecting her thoughts. No one knew her in Harlem and she figured it was safe for her uptown. A small jazz band serenaded the crowd in the dim atmosphere, as everyone felt at ease nursing their drinks and letting the night carry them away.

River thought about Eric and hoped that he was okay. She decided to stay out of Queens for a few days despite Big Red's disapproval. Things were getting too hot for her in Queens.

With the money and jewels they had gotten from robbing Eric, it totaled $15,000 apiece for them. Big Red had pawned over $10,000 worth of jewelry, and mixed the proceeds in with the loot.

River decided to take her share and leave the hood for a while. She rented a lavish room at the Sheraton in downtown Brooklyn. It cost her two hundred a night. But for her, it was worth it.

She lingered in her booth looking like money herself. She was clad in a beige glazed leather wrap miniskirt, a sheer boat-neck sweater with side ties at the hip, and stilettos. Her flawless beauty attracted unwanted attention from the many men who occupied the lounge. Around her neck she sported a diamond, seed pearl, sapphire, platinum, and pink gold necklace, and wrapped around her right index finger was a diamond-encrusted platinum ring.

She glanced around the lounge and noticed a man in a gray suit raising his glass of wine at her, trying to catch her attention. But River ignored him and focused her attention on the band. She wished she hadn't come alone, being prey to a roomful of men. River knew it would only be a matter of time before someone came up to her.

Her pager went off in her purse, and she dug into it and looked at the number. It was Big Red paging her. She sighed, tossed the pager back in her purse, and said quietly, "Not tonight."

Moments later, a tall, well-groomed man clad in a three-piece black suit appeared at River's table. He was decked out in diamonds and jewelry, and gazed at River with a smile.

Without her permission he took a seat across from her in the booth, and said, "You look familiar. I know you from somewhere."

"I don't think so," River shortly replied, clearly implying that she wanted to be alone.

"Nah, I do know you, but I just can't place where," he continued.

Something about his presence made her nervous. She didn't want to make a scene, so she continued to sit casually in the booth, acting as if they were old friends.

By his demeanor, River knew he was a thug disguised by a suit. His eyes were black, and even though he was handsome, she knew his attitude was very ugly.

"Why you here alone?" he asked.

"Can you please leave?" she said.

"Nah, not until I place your face. There's something about you that got me trippin' right now. I don't know why." He sat there and studied her. "What's your name?"

River sighed. She knew sooner or later that the situation was going to turn ugly. She slowly reached into her purse for her blade.

"You must know my boy, then," the man said, looking across the room.

River turned to see who he was looking at, and suddenly fear spread across her face. The man who sat with her noticed this and said with a smirk, "Yeah, you know him, right? I see it in your face, and it can't be for anything good."

"No, I don't know him," River replied.

"Bitch, don't lie to me," he barked.

"Excuse me, but I have to go," she said, slowly moving out of the booth.

"Nah, fuck that, you ain't goin' anywhere," he said, quickly grabbing her by the forearm with force, spilling her drink.

"Please—" River uttered, sounding helpless.

The man held on to her tightly as he nodded over to his friend Hubert. River saw Hubert get out of his chair and start to come her way flanked by two other goons. Panic struck her suddenly, and she knew that she had to make her move, even if it meant causing a scene. With her one free hand, she reached for her blade, and when the man wasn't looking, instantly she came down on his right hand with the blade, pinning his hand to the table.

"Aaaaaahhh! Aaaaaahhh, this bitch stabbed me!" he screamed, trying to free his blood-soaked hand.

River bolted from the table and made her way for the door. Hubert and both his goons gave chase as patrons looked on in awe. Everything stopped for that moment.

River quickly ran outside, racing in her stilettos down the block. She glanced back and saw Hubert and his men running quickly for her. She dashed across four lanes of traffic and oncoming cars, making a minivan stop short to keep from hitting her.

She scurried down a busy street, trying to hail a cab. She saw one parked and quickly made her way to it. But before she could open the back door, one of Hubert's goons grabbed her, twisted her around, and gave her a backhand smack across her face. River dropped to the concrete, peering up at her attacker.

"Bitch, where the fuck you going?" he shouted, revealing a .357 in his waistband.

The cab driver got frightened and pulled away without even trying to help. Hubert was there shortly. He glared at River, and said, "You remember me, bitch?"

"No!" River replied sarcastically, with a little bit of blood trickling from her lips.

Smack. Hubert struck her, and River fell back against a parked car.

"You set me up," he said.

"You got the wrong bitch," River replied.

"You must think I'm stupid, right?" Hubert exclaimed, glaring at her. "Bitch, you're about to breathe your last breath on this earth. But not before me and my niggahs finish raping your ass. Gene, get the fuckin' car and go see if Dino is all right—stupid muthafucka!"

Hubert forcefully grabbed River by her arm, but suddenly fell back when he heard the far-too-familiar sounds of *whoop-whoop*. Police sirens blared at a short distance.

"Shit!" he mumbled.

A squad car pulled up to them, and two white officers stepped out. River quickly wiped the blood from her mouth.

"Is there a problem here?" the tall blond officer asked, glaring at all three men.

"Officer, my ex-boyfriend was trying to attack me," River exclaimed. "We were having a fight."

"Are you okay?" he asked.

River nodded. "I just want to go home."

Both cops looked at Hubert and his men. "The three of y'all were trying to jump on this one lady?"

"Nah, it ain't even like that, Officer. Nothing but a misunderstanding between me and my woman, that's all," Hubert calmly informed him.

The man concealing the .357 was hoping that it didn't get ugly and they wouldn't try to search him, because he was already on parole.

"Officer, I don't want to press any charges," River continued. "I'm tired and I just want to take a cab home. Me and him are so through, right, Hubert?"

"Yeah, we're through, you're like dead to me right now," Hubert dryly returned.

"You need a cab?" the tall officer asked.

"Yes. Please."

While his partner maintained order with Hubert and his men, the blond officer helped River hail a cab. Hubert stood back and helplessly watched River jump into a cab and ride off. He glared at the cab, and bit down on his bottom lip wishing tonight had turned out differently for River—like seeing her lying dead in a ditch somewhere.

"Okay, tonight's your lucky tonight. She's gone, so turn around and go back where y'all came from," the shorter officer instructed. "I don't want to see the three of you around here anytime tonight."

Hubert sighed and walked away reluctantly with his two goons right behind him.

In the backseat of the cab, River sighed with much relief. She came so close to losing her life tonight that it took her a minute to tell the cabbie her destination. She thanked God for the officers' perfect timing.

"Please take me to the Sheraton, downtown Brooklyn," she told the cabbie.

Her heart pounded rapidly as she stared out the back window. She'd known it would be only a matter of time before she ran into a victim that she had helped set up, but tonight had caught her off guard. She quietly shed tears in the cab as she thought about her options. It was becoming too risky. Robbing tricks on the track was one thing, but going after full-blooded hustlers was another. And River was too wise not to know that everything comes to an end sooner or later. She definitely wanted out after tonight. Her life came first.

19

The burgundy Escalade pulled up to the parked four-door sedan at a pier in Far Rockaway. It was three in the morning, and quiet. Yung Slim sat in the passenger seat while Critter was driving. Yung Slim lit a cigarette and sat in the truck for a while, peering out at the beach.

"Why you deal wit' these muthafuckas, Yung Slim?" Critter asked, glaring at the sedan.

"Cuz, I rather side with them than be against them. Everybody comes in useful, remember that, Critter. Besides, I need some information from our friend," Yung Slim said, then stepped out of the truck.

Detective Monroe stepped out of his car and Yung Slim followed him toward the boardwalk. Critter sat back and watched his boy disappear onto the dark boardwalk with a cop he didn't like or trust.

"I can't believe they let your monkey ass out in seven," Detective Monroe said. "Whose dick did you have to suck to get paroled?"

"Fuck you, too!" Yung Slim chided. "I can't believe your crooked ass is still a cop. I thought the DA had a case against you."

"I've been a cop for too many years to let some snitch rat mutha-fucka get the drop on me," Monroe said. He pulled out a cigarette. "You got a light?"

Yung Slim passed him his lighter and the two continued to walk down the boardwalk. Monroe took a long drag from his cancer stick and exhaled, peering up at the stars.

"What you need from me?" Monroe asked.

"Some information."

"So I take it that a nine-to-five for you is out of the question? You ain't even out one week yet."

"There's five grand for you."

"Five grand for what kind of info?" Monroe asked, taking an-other drag from his cancer stick.

"I need an address or location of a certain individual," Yung Slim said.

"I need a name first."

"His name is Rahmel, but he goes by Rah," Yung Slim said.

"Rahmel. Ain't that your cousin's homeboy? What you want wit' him?"

"I just need to talk. I heard he got married some time ago, but he never came back to the States. I know he's running," Yung Slim in-formed him.

"I see what I can do. But I want half up front."

Before Monroe could say anything else, Yung Slim pulled out a knot of hundreds and passed it to Monroe. "You ain't changed a bit. There's twenty-five hundred in that knot. Get it done."

Monroe gave Yung Slim an unsmiling stare. "So we're back in business?"

"It never ended," Yung Slim said.

"So no hard feelings?" Monroe asked, remembering what went down seven years ago.

"Even though your bitch ass hanged me out to dry for that mur-der beef, nah, there ain't no hard feelings. It's always business, right?"

"Yung Slim, you have to understand, shit was hot back then. You were on the rise too fast and making a name for yourself. You made enemies everywhere, even in my precinct. A lot of men wanted to see you dead, so be happy you got jailed for those seven years and get to see the streets today. I did you a favor, you remember that. If I had got involved with your case then it would have made it difficult for the both of us, and the DA would have fucked us both."

"Muthafucka, I'm the one that got fucked! But it's all good, I'm home now, Monroe, and shit gonna change."

"Yeah, well, remember you're still on parole. You violate that, and there ain't shit I can do for you."

"Let me worry about my PO. I'm better now. These streets, I'm gonna own 'em again, and you either gonna ride wit' me or die coming against me," Yung Slim proclaimed.

Monroe took one last pull from his cigarette and tossed it onto the beach. "I see your mind is made up."

"It's good doin' business with you again, Detective Monroe. Get that info for me. I'll definitely see you around," Yung Slim said, back stepping away from him.

Monroe shook his head, knowing that they'd just paroled a monster back on the streets. He'd been a cop for twenty years and seen them come and go, and knew that Yung Slim was not the one to let out. The detective was in his midforties, a black man of average height, with a short haircut, trimmed beard, who dressed hip-hop style—Timberlands, baggy jeans, jerseys, leather coat, and so on. He knew that he was in Yung Slim's pocket for a long time, because the man had too much dirt on him. But the extra money was good coming in, and with him retiring next year, it would mix in very well with his pension. But Monroe knew that he had to watch his back with Yung Slim. They might be in bed together but he didn't trust him. And if push came to shove, then Monroe would take it that extra step and put a bullet in the back of his head if Yung Slim ever tried to turn against him or rat him out.

. . .

The following night, Yung Slim, Critter, and Donald sat in the same parked burgundy Escalade, observing the track on Rockaway Boulevard. They watched two young ladies in short denim skirts and stilettos strut up Rockaway Boulevard waving down cars and trying to get a quick date.

"Slim, there's definitely money out here," Critter proclaimed. "Hoes be up and down here on a regular basis now."

"I see," Yung Slim uttered.

"Some of them rent out rooms at the Executive around the corner, make it safer to turn tricks," Donald chimed.

"Who's workin' this area?" Slim asked.

"Some young pimp named Reality," Donald informed him. "But his man Rome is the one we gotta watch out for. He got about eight hoes working out here, on South Road, and Brooklyn. He's back and forth from Atlantic City constantly."

"Matter of fact, them two hoes that just passed, them his hoes," Critter said.

"But some nights, cops make it hard out here for the ladies to work. They may constantly patrol the area, or do sting operations, scaring the tricks off," Donald stated. "If we come in, we gotta come in smart."

"I'll take care of that," Yung Slim said, peering out the passenger window.

Yung Slim sat in the passenger seat and continued to observe the two young ladies in the miniskirts. He definitely liked what he saw and wanted in on the action. Critter was in his ear about this pimping business, continually telling him how much money there was to be made by selling pussy. Critter even informed Slim about Eric and his underground business with the parties and the strippers, and told him how much his cousin was profiting.

"Yeah, Slim, he be doin' his thang," Critter would say to Yung Slim when they were alone.

"Cuz done stepped up a bit, huh?" Yung Slim would reply. "That's what's up."

Yung Slim gazed out the truck, watching a white Lexus pull up to one of the girls. The ho with the long black hair walked up to the car, peered inside, and said a few words to the driver. Moments later she got in and the Lexus pulled off.

"Yeah, we in on this," Yung Slim said. "I'm gonna bring Barnes and Bishop in."

Critter turned and looked at Yung Slim with an uncertain stare. "You sure? Those two niggahs are crazy. I ain't tryin' to doubt you or nuthin, Slim, but they make the block hot wit' the murder game."

"Nah, I'm gonna tell them to be cool wit' the gunplay unless it's necessary. But with their presence on the track, niggahs gonna know I mean business."

"What about Rome and Reality, they ain't gonna like it too much you moving in on their turf," Donald mentioned.

"Donald, I ain't worrying about these niggahs. I'm home now, if they wanna bring it, then let 'em come. But starting tonight, I'm running this track, and if niggahs wanna sell pussy out here, then there's a percentage that's gotta be paid to the family. Y'all niggahs hear me? Any niggah or bitch grinding out here or on South Road, they pay us sixty percent of their profits, and if they don't, then we fuck them up till they understand we mean business. Get the word out."

"Ayyite," Critter said.

Yung Slim glared at Donald and Critter, and shouted, "Yo, what y'all niggahs waiting for? I said get the fuckin' word out!"

"Oh, you mean now?" Critter replied, giving Yung Slim a perplexed look.

"You see that bitch across the street—you think she knows about the new rules in effect yet?" he barked.

Knowing what he meant, Critter and Donald stepped out of the truck and made their way across the street to the young streetwalker.

She stood on the corner of Rockaway Boulevard and 137th Avenue in three-inch clear stilettos, a denim miniskirt and a tight T-shirt that accentuated her big tits.

She noticed two men coming her way, and got nervous. Not wanting to take any chances, she made her way down 137th Avenue into the back streets.

"Yo, shorty, c'mere. . . . We just wanna talk to you," Critter called out, moving faster as he watched her move quickly down the block.

She got extremely nervous and started to run in her stilettos. Critter gave chase; he was faster than Donald, and caught up with her in the middle of the block and threw her against a parked car in the shadows.

"Bitch, why the fuck you makin' me chase you?" he yelled, having a tight grip around her T-shirt.

"Please . . . get off me. . . ." she pleaded with her soft babyish voice.

"Why the fuck you running for? I ain't tryin' to hurt you," Critter said, pushing her against the car.

Donald came up to them; he wasn't a runner and was glad that he had Critter with him. He looked at the frightened young girl, and asked, "How old are you, ma?"

"Seventeen," she answered.

"Who you work for?" Critter asked.

"Reality," she quickly answered.

"How much you made tonight?" Critter asked, searching her for any money stashed away on her. He grabbed her breasts and then moved his hand up her thighs, pushing up her short skirt and felt in between her smooth, soft legs. He even took it a step further and placed his hand on her pussy, feeling that she didn't have on any panties. He got excited, feeling his dick getting hard as he molested her by pushing two fingers inside of her. She began to squirm, feeling the raw entry, and tried to move his hand from within her. But Critter was adamant, and said, "I'm checking to see if you ain't lying to me."

He searched her, and she came up clean.

"Bitch, where you keep your money?" Donald asked.

"Dynasty holds everything for me," she said.

"That's that bitch that got in the Lexus?" Critter asked.

She nodded.

"Ayyite, listen up. As of tonight, if you workin' this track, you and your girls choke up sixty percent—you hear?" Critter proclaimed.

"But Reality—"

"Fuck Reality!" Critter shouted. "You on this track selling pussy, you pay my boss sixty percent. Bitch, you fuckin' hear me! If not, then don't ever bring your ass on this track again."

Critter lifted up his shirt and revealed a .45 tucked in his waistband. She nodded.

"Good. But we gotta come up wit' sumthin. Your girl Dynasty, where does she like to get dropped off at?" Critter asked. "Because we gonna need that loot tonight from y'all."

At first, she was reluctant to reveal the information, but because of the looks on her two captors' faces she uttered, "Over by the Executive."

"Good girl," Critter said, taking control of the situation while Donald mostly stood by and watched.

Ten minutes later, Critter sat in the Escalade with Yung Slim and Donald waiting for Dynasty to be dropped off. All three men observed the white Lexus pull up in front of them at the Executive Motel and watched Dynasty step out, pulling down her skirt. She walked toward the motel entrance and glanced around for a moment. She was beautiful, with fair brown skin, long sensuous black hair, and a body that would make any man's dick get hard just by sight alone.

"I want my money," Yung Slim said to Critter. "Make these bitches and niggahs out on this track understand we mean business."

Hearing that, Critter stepped out of the truck and walked up to Dynasty. He stood by her near the entrance, and said, "What up, ma, how you doin' tonight?"

Dynasty gave him an unpleasant look, and said, "If you want a date, it's a hundred and fifty."

"Nah, I'm not here for that," he replied.

She sighed, and asked, "Then what are you here for? You a pimp?"

"We need to talk business," he stated.

"Get the fuck away from me!" she barked.

With that, Critter quickly grabbed Dynasty by her arm and began pulling her toward the Escalade. She began fighting, shouting, "Niggah, is you crazy? Get the fuck off me! Get the fuck off me! I'm gonna get my pimp to fuck your ass up!"

The back door to the Escalade opened and out stepped Donald. He grabbed Dynasty as if she was paper and tossed her into the backseat and quickly shut the door behind him.

"Y'all niggahs know who y'all fuckin' wit'?!" Dynasty screamed. "I'm Rome's bottom bitch, and he gonna get Reality to fuckin' murder y'all niggahs for disrespecting me like this."

Critter pushed his .45 into her face and told her to shut the fuck up. With that, Dynasty got quiet suddenly.

"Bitch, we know who you work for," Yung Slim began to say. "That's why you're here."

"Empty your purse, bitch," Critter demanded.

Reluctantly Dynasty poured out the contents of her purse on the backseat. Donald quickly picked up the roll of twenties and tens and went through it. "Fifteen hundred," he said, counting the cash again.

"Look, from now on, you sell pussy on this track, you give up sixty percent to my crew," Yung Slim instructed.

"I don't work for you," she scolded.

Slap! Dynasty caught a hard right-hand slap from Donald in the backseat. Dynasty held the side of her face in shock. "Bitch, now you do," Critter said.

Donald peeled off nine hundred from Dynasty's wad of bills and tossed her the remaining six hundred. "Here, you lucky you get that much," Donald said, passing Yung Slim the cash.

"You spread the word to your girls, ayyite, Dynasty? You let them know I'm in town now, and I'm running things on this track. You're a cute girl, so I don't wanna fuck up your face by you being stubborn," Yung Slim said, gazing at Dynasty with ice-cold eyes. "You take me serious, right, bitch?"

Dynasty nodded.

"I'm nobody to fuckin' play with. And if y'all want a job, come ask for me. I'll hook y'all up. Fuck that niggah Rome and his bitch Reality. If they want a job too, give them this number," he said, passing her a small piece of paper with two cell phone numbers written on it.

Dynasty took the paper and placed it in her purse. Something about Yung Slim's demeanor made her extremely afraid. She knew that with him around, things were going to pop off really ugly. When she spoke Rome's name, he didn't flinch or cringe like most men would have done. He looked unemotional.

"Ayyite, get the fuck out my truck," Yung Slim said. "I'm done talkin'. You pass the word around and give your bitch-ass pimp my number and tell him to holla."

Donald pushed Dynasty out the door, almost causing her face to hit the pavement. She stared at the Escalade as it hastily drove down the North Conduit. She didn't take her eyes off the truck until it disappeared into the night. She then went into her purse, pulled out her cell phone, and dialed Reality's number.

The phone rang twice before Reality picked up.

"Dynasty, you better give me a good reason why you're callin' my phone and not out makin' my money," Reality chided.

"Reality, we got a problem. I need to talk to Rome," she said.

"He's in A.C."

"Well, you better call him. . . . I just got robbed," she proclaimed.

20

Eric sat in the crib, watching TV and having some solitude. He'd been distanced from everyone the past few days—not so much as a phone call or anything. He'd been hearing about Russell on the streets setting up meetings, paying off certain cops, and now he heard that Russell had moved in on Rome's territory down on Rockaway Boulevard, even demanding 60 percent from the key players on the block. Eric knew that the bottom was going to fall out quickly, and he knew that in a matter of time, all hell might break loose. His cousin had been home a little over a week and was already causing chaos in the hood.

But when he found out about Critter and Donald running up on one of Rome's ladies and smacking her up on the streets, he was mad at Russell. Critter and Donald were his homeboys and he knew that Russell was getting them into a world of trouble. But the one thing that lingered in his mind was River. It had been three weeks since the incident, and he hated to admit it, but he was falling in love with her.

As he lounged in his chair, he heard a loud knock at the door. He sighed, not wanting any company, but was cautious, carrying his .380 to the door just in case.

"Who is it?" Eric shouted.

"Niggah, open the fuckin' door! I ain't some bitch tryin' to rob your ass," Critter shouted, mocking Eric.

"Niggah, fuck you," Eric replied, turning the locks.

Critter stepped into the apartment dressed like a young fresh hoodlum off the block. He was clad in baggy Sean John jeans, a throwback Lakers jersey, a fitted baseball cap, and sporting jewelry like a rap star.

Eric stared at Critter's new image and shook his head. "My cousin got you lookin' fresh now, huh," Eric stated.

"Niggah, I'm finally gettin' this money now, like how you used to do. At least your cousin putting me on, niggah."

"Man, you don't even know what you're gettin' yourself into, Critter. That world that my cousin lives in will put you in the ground so fast," Eric proclaimed.

"I'm gettin' paid now, that's what matters, E—this money," Critter countered, reaching into his pocket and pulling out a wad of cash. "You need to be down, E . . . fo' real. Yung Slim was asking about you today. He wants you present at this meeting in two hours."

"I ain't going," Eric stated, walking back to his chair.

"Yo, he wants you there," Critter said, following Eric into the living room. "Niggah, I know you ain't still trippin' over that bitch. Yo, we see her again, then it's bang-bang, lights out for that scandalous ho." Critter lifted his jersey revealing a .45.

"Critter, chill, she's probably long gone by now," Eric said. "And she's not even on my mind," he lied.

"That bitch better not be, son."

Eric sat in his chair and stared at the TV.

"Yo, E . . . what's up wit' you? Why you acting so fuckin' distant? We boys, niggah. Ever since Yung Slim got out, you've been actin' unfamiliar. I know you ain't hating on your cousin."

"Nah, it ain't even that," Eric replied.

Critter stared at Eric, studying his expression and his movement. "Niggah, why you playin' yourself? You is stressing that bitch, niggah!"

"I told you I wasn't," Eric snapped back.

"Yo, E, we knew each other since the fourth grade. I know you like a book, niggah. Right now you actin' like that time Lisa broke your heart in the tenth grade, moping in the chair, not even watching shit on TV. You didn't want to do shit when she dumped you, now you actin' the same way. Yo, this fuckin' bitch set you up and you still caring for this slut bitch. Yo, niggah, get your ass up and get dressed, we goin' to see your fuckin' cousin at this meeting," Critter shouted.

"Yo, I said I ain't going, fuck him and his meeting," Eric retorted.

"You really want me to tell your cousin that?" Critter asked. "You want me to give him the true reason why you ain't checking him?"

Eric stared at Critter. "Fuck you, Critter," was all he could say. He got out of his chair halfheartedly and made his way to the bedroom to get dressed.

Outside, Critter hit the alarm button to a four-door black Acura.

"This you?" Eric asked.

"Nah, not yet, but give me time," Critter replied. "I borrowed it."

About twenty-five thugs and key player from the streets met up in the basement of a local strip club on Hillside Avenue. The owner and Yung Slim went way back and he allowed Yung Slim to set up a discreet meeting there with his crew. Yung Slim paid the owner off with a few hundred dollars and the owner didn't have a problem renting out his spot for a few hours.

Everyone stood around the barren unfurnished basement waiting for something to start. They all knew Yung Slim was home and word had quickly got out about how Yung Slim was moving in on Rome's business—how he smacked up his hoes, robbed them, and demanded 60 percent from rival crews. It was definitely a brazen move for someone who'd been out of action for a long time.

The majority of the men were eager to get down with Yung Slim, while some were skeptical about going to war with Rome. Before

Yung Slim came home, Rome had things on lock, and he had definitely proved himself over the years by going head-to-head with the most ruthless men in the game and living to tell about it.

Yung Slim walked into the room cocky and assured. He wore a white wifebeater and his upper body was swathed with tattoos. A bulky chain hung from around his neck as he stared into the crowd with an intense look. He was flanked by Bishop and Barnes.

"Yo, y'all muthafuckas shut the fuck up!" he screamed, catching everyone's attention.

The room suddenly became quiet, and everyone's attention was focused on Yung Slim. He continued with, "Y'all know why y'all here?"

Some shrugged, some were too intimidated to answer, and some just wanted to be down.

Yung Slim answered for them. "To get this money, that's why y'all are here. Everybody in this room wanna get paid, right?" he shouted.

"Yeah!" the small crowd of men shouted in unison.

"I'm sure every one of y'all niggahs heard about my move on Rome's turf and slapping up his bitches the other night. That's how we fuckin' operate. We don't ask, we don't compromise. Niggahs in my crew regulate on any muthafuckas that's against us. We fuckin' take. That's how you put fear into your rivals' hearts. I know some of y'all know who I am by name and recognition, but for y'all new jacks that's tryin' to get down, you staring at the niggah in charge and that's about to start up a fuckin' empire in this muthafuckin' city," Yung Slim proclaimed.

"I'm Yung Slim," he continued. "I'm that niggah that's home now, and gonna put that paper in all y'all niggahs' pocket. And to get this money right, all that competition out there is gonna stop, so me and my crew will be the only ones eating out this bitch. You either gon' ride with us or die coming against us. Y'all niggahs understand?"

"Yeah!" the crowd shouted.

"Yo, we selling pussy, cocaine, heroin, and whatever product that's gonna bring this family money, we pushing and selling. And as for muscle, you see these two niggahs right here?" Yung Slim pointed out Bishop and Barnes. "Yo, any niggah that they had beef with ain't living to tell about it. These are my two enforcers. Any one of y'all niggahs cross me or this crew, and I'm gonna set the dogs loose on you. So as of right now, I'm giving y'all niggahs in this room a choice. If you down with makin' paper like 50 Cent and living that baller's life, stay. But if you ain't got the heart for this shit here, I'm warning niggahs to leave now, because once you in, you in, and there ain't no halfhearted shit done with anything in my crew. I don't care if you peddling drugs to putting the murder game down. You do your job right and sufficient, 'cause if not, you gonna deal wit' the consequences. And believe me, you don't wanna piss me or my enforcers off.

"So right now, who's ever down, stay the fuck in the room, and if you ain't . . . there ain't no hard feeling, just get the fuck out!"

The room was suddenly quiet as everyone glanced at each other to see who would stay and who would leave. Three men walked out, leaving ample soldiers behind to start a fierce crew.

"That's what I'm talkin' about. . . . Fuck them other niggahs that walked out, let 'em starve on the streets while we gettin' this paper," Yung Slim shouted out.

Yung Slim started to get more detailed about his operation. He wanted to call his empire Queens Notorious. Niggahs were definitely feeling the name.

"As of today, QN niggahs ride or die for theirs. We're strictly about paper, and putting fear in rivals' hearts. Our motto, you either ride wit' us or die coming against us," Yung Slim proclaimed.

He got cheers from the men.

"Business is gonna be good. We gonna set up shop over on Rockaway Boulevard and the Conduit, South Road, One Hundred and Fiftieth Street, Sutphin Boulevard, Guy R. Brewer, Baisley, and even in these cheesey motels in the hood. And if y'all niggahs got any problems wit' anyone, you get at Barnes or Bishop for muscle or fire-power," he stated.

"Critter is gonna be my eyes and ears on the streets," Yung Slim said, looking around for Critter. "Yo, where the fuck is Critter?"

"He ain't here," a voice shouted out.

Yung Slim bit down on his bottom lip, upset about Critter and his cousin's absence. "I said I wanted everyone present. Fuck it, I deal wit' them later."

Moments later, Critter walked in with Eric following right behind him.

"Yo, Slim, sorry about being late, but—" Critter tried to apologize.

"Shut the fuck up, Critter! I'll talk to you later," Yung Slim chided.

Critter remained silent and stayed in the background with Eric. He listened to Yung Slim speak to the crowd. Eric couldn't believe the turnout Yung Slim had—eager young men who were ready to get rich quick by any means necessary. Eric knew what waited ahead for the streets of Queens, New York.

Half an hour later, the meeting was over. Eric and Critter still lingered, hearing Yung Slim say to the crowd, "I'm glad y'all niggahs showed up. Tomorrow will be a new and richer day for all of us. Y'all ugly muthafuckas go upstairs and enjoyed that pussy, and tip them bitches and stop being cheap muthafuckas. But I want my lieutenants to stick around."

As the majority of men headed upstairs to the strip club, eager to drown themselves in the sea of women that waited, Donald, Critter, Barnes, Bishop, and Eric stayed in the basement with Yung Slim.

Yung Slim looked into the faces of all his lieutenants, and said, "Y'all niggahs standing in this room with me right now are my back-bone to my organization. I need y'all. I need for y'all to hold it down in them streets when it gets rough. We family, and family don't snitch, rat, or turn on each other. Y'all hear? Family ride or die for each other. Together we can take over this whole fuckin' borough, even this fuckin' city. We got the soldiers, we got the manpower, the firepower, and most of all, we all got heart."

Yung Slim gazed at Eric and noticed that he looked aloof from the rest. But he was going to address that later.

"We build this together as a family or we don't build this shit at all," Yung Slim stated. "We blood in, we blood out. Anything goes down, no matter how big or small, we handle that with a sense of urgency. Any niggahs come against us, we lay 'em the fuck down. Us in this fuckin' room right now, we keep this shit tight, this is all we got right here—each other. I want y'all to swear to give your life to this shit."

Everyone nodded, agreeing to Yung Slim's terms. Yung Slim spoke for a few more minutes and allowed his lieutenants to go upstairs.

"Not you, Eric, let me holla at you for a minute," he said.

Eric stayed, and wondered why his cousin wanted to speak to him alone. As they heard the door shut upstairs, Yung Slim walked up to Eric, and said, "You and me could run this city with an iron fist."

"I got my own thing going, Russell," Eric stated.

"I know, Critter informed me. That's why I want you down. You've been doin' this pimping shit before I got home."

"I wasn't pimpin' them, Russell. The ladies I used for my parties know that it's a business understanding. We're cool like that."

"Well, it's time for you to step up your game, cuz, that's why I want you running things for me on the track. You know how to work things, you a money niggah. Niggah, you a Beaumont, gettin' rich is in your blood. Your father was the notorious Yung Black, you need to carry on his legacy and help me run this shit. Also, I want you to stop that side hustling."

"What side hustles?" Eric replied.

"You selling weed, right, to some connect out in Brooklyn?"

Russell brought up. "Nah, niggahs in my organization don't do any outside business with anyone unless I approve of it."

"You serious?"

"Like a heart attack, niggah. You fuck around and get locked up, cops or the feds might try to roll on you to get to me. I don't know your Brooklyn connection, so end that shit," Russell proclaimed.

"I'm your bitch now?" Eric sternly replied.

"What? Niggah, you family," Russell returned.

"You're forcing me into your organization. You want me to become like my father. You ain't home but two weeks and already you trying to tell me what to do. Like when we were kids, always gotta have control of everything," Eric stated.

"E, I ain't trying to control you, I'm just trying to advise you and look out for you," Russell countered.

"Look out for me?" Eric tittered. "Russell, you've been gone for seven years, and I've been handling myself pretty good since you been gone. I haven't had any problems or beef wit' niggahs or police so far. I know how to handle myself."

"Then how you let a bitch infiltrate your business?" Russell stated.

"What?"

"Niggah, you think I'm stupid. You give me some bullshit story about how some buyer of yours sucker-punched you while your back was turned. You expect me to believe that one man fucked your face up like that?" Russell said. "I know it was a crew that ran up on you, E, and they had a bitch set you up."

"I told this niggah Critter—"

"Critter's a soldier," Russell stated proudly. "He wants us to come back on them niggahs that came at you. We need to, E—that move they pulled on you makes us look weak. We need to make an example out of your attackers."

"Russell, it's my beef, let me handle it."

"Then handle it, niggah. You family, you represent me and this crew out there. If one niggah got a problem, then we all got a problem," Russell proclaimed. "You got names, right?"

"I got one name."

"What about the bitch?"

"Nah, I don't even think she gave me her real name," Eric said.

"Then what the bitch look like?"

"Russell, we done here?" Eric asked, looking irate.

"Fuck it, then, niggah, we talk about this later. But you gotta understand, E, I'm tryin' to harden you up. You my blood, and if you show weakness in these streets, niggahs will definitely come at you. And I can't have my cousin lookin' weak," Russell stated.

"I survived this long," he returned.

"Surprisingly," Russell snapped back.

"Whatever," Eric muttered as he made his way to the stairs.

"E . . . niggah, I ain't done talkin'," Russell called out, watching Eric leave.

"Well, I am," Eric returned, ignoring Russell.

Russell was angry, but let the disrespect slide because Eric was his cousin. But if it had been any other fool who had turned their back on him while he was still talking, they would have gotten shot down immediately.

Eric quickly strutted through the crowd of men and scantily clad strippers in the club, making his way to the exit. Critter noticed his boy moving hastily through the crowd, as he had a young well-endowed woman on his lap with his finger embedded in her pussy.

"Excuse me, ma," Critter said, pushing her off his lap and following Eric outside.

"Yo, E, what's up?" Critter called out.

"Fuck off, Critter!" Eric cursed, still walking toward his car.

"Niggah, what the fuck is your problem?" Critter shouted.

Eric turned around, and shouted, "You really want to know what my fuckin' problem is? You, Donald, and all y'all low-level mutha-fuckas that put my cousin on that pedestal thinking he's a god. He home two weeks and y'all kissing his ass like his bitches!"

"Yo, you sound like you hating right now, son," Critter said.

"It ain't hate!"

"Yeah, whatever," Critter snapped back. "Yung Slim is doin' a good thing right now, E. He's lookin' out for me and his peoples." Critter reached into his pocket and pulled out a wad of hundreds.

"You see this," he continued. "It's never been like this for me be-fore. I got money. I got respect. And I got that love, especially from the ladies. And no offense to you, but he's doin' more for me that you ever did."

"I never had your back, Critter?" Eric asked.

"Yeah, you did. But you wasn't putting this much money in my pocket."

"And you can't keep your fuckin' mouth shut," Eric shouted. "You had to tell him!"

"Yeah, niggah . . . Yung Slim ain't stupid. He knew you got jacked. He came to me and told me to be real wit' him. I can't lie to Slim, we like brothers, E."

"Brothers?" Eric questioned.

"E, you down wit' us, right? C'mon, in this game, the more of us, the stronger we are. You're smart, and you're my friend. You see that up in there," Critter said, pointing to the strip club. "That's what life is about, having fun wit' your peoples and running things, and gettin' paid to do it. You remember how we always had each other's back when we were kids. Any niggah stepped to us, no matter how many or how big they were, we went at them to-gether . . . you, me, Donald, Rah, and Mel. We weren't scare of no-body, and niggahs knew it, too. You fuck wit' one of us, and you fuckin' wit' all of us. And the majority of niggahs hesitated to step to us, because they knew how strong our bond was. It's the same way now, E. I'm in this game wit' your cousin, but if I got you by my side, I know I'm in good hands, because I trust you. You got my back, E?"

Eric stared at Critter. He was quiet for a moment.

"I got your back, Critter," Eric said, giving Critter dap and embracing him.

"Thanks," Critter blurted. "I'm sorry I told your cousin about your beef."

"Nah, don't sweat it. It's water under the bridge now," Eric proclaimed.

"This is us, Eric, we were meant to live like this. You see me, having money in my pockets, and running wit' your cousin is my only way to earn the respect I deserve on these streets. I ain't no Denzel, and the only way these bitches and niggahs feel me is if I'm a cold-blooded hustler. You feel me? I'm not a nine-to-five office muthafucka. I'm too ugly for that," Critter joked.

Eric let out a slight chuckle. "Yeah, you're right."

"I know what I'm gettin' into, E. C'mon, I've been on these streets since I was ten. You know Mom never give a fuck about me; she was too busy riding that white horse. You and Slim, y'all like family to me. Y'all the only family I have. Without you and him, I probably wouldn't be here today," Critter proclaimed. "Brothers, yo?"

"Brothers," Eric returned.

"Yo, we could survive in this game if we stay strong, E. . . . I got your back, and I know you got mines," Critter whispered in Eric's ear, as they held each other in a quick embrace.

"One, my niggah," Eric said, meaning he was out.

"One, E—be safe out there."

Eric walked back to his car with a different attitude. Even though he was against Critter and Donald working for his cousin, he knew that he had to be there for them, they both were still his boys. And the only way to watch their backs was to do what they did. Critter had had his back so many times that it almost felt as if he was his guardian angel. And despite Russell's warning about earning outside money with the Brooklyn connection, Eric took that lightly, saying to himself, *Who is he to tell me what to do and what not to do?* Business was business, and he knew that he was going to continue doing business either with his cousin or with Willy.

Yung Slim walked into his parole office early Wednesday afternoon looking fresh and clean. He strutted into the Jamaica Avenue office in a pair of black Dickies, beige Timberlands, a white-collared shirt, with a few pieces of jewelry, including an eighteen-karat white-gold pinky ring encrusted with diamonds.

He sat in the waiting area alone, and was cocky, while waiting to hear his name called. Critter sat in the truck parked on Archer Avenue trying to hit on every cutie who passed by.

"Russell Beaumont," he heard a woman call his name.

He quickly got up and smiled. *Oh, shit,* he thought, as he followed the red-bone cutie in the black skirt, heels, blouse, with wavy light brown hair. As he followed her to her office, she never looked back.

Inside, Russell took a seat at her desk while she closed the door behind him and then positioned herself behind her desk.

"Mr. Beaumont," his PO said, not even giving him eye contact as she shuffled some papers on her desk.

"Damn, you're in law enforcement now," Russell said, smiling and staring at her.

"Yes, and as your PO I must inform you about the stipulations of your parole," she said, trying to be stern with him.

"You can't even look at me, Meeka," Russell said. "You look good, though, damn . . . really fuckin' good." He stared at her with dark eyes, and just wanted to rip her blouse off. "You miss me, Meeka?"

"Please, Mr. Beaumont, I'm your PO, and you will treat me with respect or I'll have you in violation and you can continue your three years back upstate," she warned.

"You really wanna do that, Meeka?"

"My name is Karen, Mr. Beaumont," she sternly stated.

"Yo, stop callin' me Mr. Beaumont. How many years we go back, Meeka? How long have you been a PO?" he asked.

"Four years."

"Damn, a lot of shit done changed since I've been gone. You were in college when I got locked up," Russell said. "And now look at you, damn! You do look good, Meeka . . . really good. Don't sit behind that desk and front, forgetting how we used to get down. You still got my name tattooed above your breast?"

"Mr. Beaumont—"

"Meeka, c'mon, you know the deal. It's ironic that you're my PO. Do your supervisors know that we used to fuck our brains out?" he brazenly asked.

Karen was quiet. She stared at Russell, trying to do her job adequately without letting old feelings get in the way. They had a past together, and when she saw that he was being released and was assigned to her, she knew she should have informed her supervisors that she knew the parolee, or to be more exact, that she was in love with him. But something inside of her stirred and she wanted to see him again.

"You wanted to see me again, admit it, Meeka. You saw my name, you could have pushed me off to another officer, but you still got feelings for me," Russell proclaimed.

"You're still a cocky sonuvabitch, Russell," she spat.

He chuckled.

"Listen, just because we used to fuck, you're still a felon, and ex-con, and you're on three years' probation with this office. You violate anything by failing a piss test, arrests, or doing the same shit you did that got you locked up, and I'm going to violate your ass and have you finish your time in a maximum prison," Karen stated.

"So, how long have you been married?" Russell asked, peering at the diamond ring on her fourth finger, and looking unaffected by threats of being sent back to prison.

"Did you hear what I just said?" she barked.

"Yeah, I heard you, but you really think I take that shit serious?" he countered, looking smug.

Karen let out a faint smile, shaking her head in disbelief. "You were always impossible."

"And that's why you loved me."

"And you loved that bitch Sherry more than me," she angrily said.

"C'mon, Meeka, Sherry was pregnant at the time," Russell informed her.

"And so was I," she uttered.

Russell was shocked. "By me?"

She nodded.

"And what happened to the baby?"

"I had it. But I didn't want to take care of it, so I gave him up for adoption," she stated, looking upset.

"Damn!" Russell muttered. "I'm sorry."

"You should be, muthafucka; I should violate your ass right now for how you hurt me so much. I loved you," she announced. "And all you ever cared about was yourself and the streets."

"Meeka, I'm a gangster . . . this is what I do. I was born into this shit here," he said. "Yo, when I was locked up, why you never wrote me and let me know what was goin' on wit' you?"

"Because I wanted to forget about you. I wanted to hate you," she admitted. "And here you are, and I told myself that I can handle you. I'm more mature, wiser. I'm over you. And I plan on treating you like all my other parolees. So are you looking for some kind of employment?" She stared at him, noticing the gleaming diamond ring on his pinky finger, his clothes, and the diamond earrings embedded in both his ears. She knew he was hustling again.

"You're not over me, Meeka," Russell said, gazing at her. "The way we left it, it wasn't right."

"It was fucked up."

"I know, but I'm home now, so why can't we continue where we left off?" he asked.

Karen sighed. "You must be crazy. I'm married now, and I'm your fuckin' parole officer."

"I know, but you know I don't give a fuck. Who's your husband anyway?"

"I'm not telling you about him," she snapped.

"Is he treating you right?"

"Russell, please respect me and my position—okay?"

"Ayyite," he said dryly.

"Are you lookin' for employment at this time?" she asked, trying to focus on work.

"What you think, Meeka?"

"I assume no. I need your place of residence, a number where I can reach you, and you need to take a urine test before you leave this office," she instructed. "And also, your curfew is at nine o'clock every night."

"Curfew! Let's be fo' real here, Meeka, you know I ain't doin' no fuckin' curfew," Russell said, slouching in his chair.

"Why do you have to make this so difficult for me, Russell?"

He smiled, looked at her, and boldly returned with, "Because I can. Meeka, you know what I'm about."

"Believe me, I know, and I'm trying to forget."

"Meeka, are you happy wit' your life now?"

"What?"

"I know you, don't forget that. We fucked wit' each other for years, and I know what you're about. You like the finer things in life. And now you're a parole officer, doin' your thang, I suppose. But before I got locked up, you had dreams of going to school to become an actor, and you wanted to own your own business. What happened?"

"Life, and this pays the bills," she said.

"You need your bills paid, Meeka, you know I got you. I know you're not happy doin' this. I can look out for you," Russell said.

"I get involved with you and lose my career and my freedom, no thanks."

"You call this having a career?" Russell went into his pocket and pulled out a roll of hundreds. He tossed it on Meeka's desk.

"Russell, are you stupid?" she barked, staring at him angrily and then looking down at the money.

"Take it, it's yours."

"You must be crazy. I can't take that."

"Why not? Who's watching? They got cameras on you?" he asked.

"No."

"So, there's fifteen hundred in that roll for you. My gift to you. I won't tell a soul what I saw in this room today," he said. "I owe it to you."

Karen was tempted. She had many bills past due, and the payment on her Benz was behind by two months. Russell read her like a book. She loved having the finer things in life and her paycheck some weeks just wasn't cutting it for her.

"Meeka, you can trust me. That money is nothing for me. All I ask from you is cut me some slack when I'm in here and on the streets. I know you can be a bitch about things. I'll pay you fifteen hundred a week, and all you gotta do is look the other way wit' me," he suggested.

Karen looked at him and then glanced down at the cash. She was tempted. She contemplated it for a moment. Then she sighed and picked up the cash off her desk and flipped through the hundreds quickly. She was extremely nervous when she placed the money in her desk, hoping it wasn't a setup.

"That's my girl," Russell muttered.

"I can't believe you," she replied, staring at Russell. *How can he make it so easy?* she thought.

"We cool?" Russell asked.

"Yeah, we cool."

"So, now that we got an understanding . . . what about us?" Russell continued.

"What about us?"

"I miss you, Meeka," he proclaimed. "I thought about you every day in prison, wondering why you didn't write me, or come see me."

"I already gave you my reason," she responded.

"I know, but that ain't good enough for me. Listen, I'm a changed man now. I'm better and wiser. I'm taking back what belongs to me. I can use your help; I'll definitely pay you extra plus the fifteen hundred every week. And honestly, Meeka, lookin' at you right now is turning me the fuck on." He moved forward, placing his elbows on her desk, gazing into her light brown eyes, and continued with, "You remember how we used to get down. I used to fuck the shit out of you every night. Remember how I used to eat that pussy out on your mother's sofa when we were young? You remember how crazy we used to get?"

Karen reluctantly let out a smile, remembering her past with Russell.

"You used to love fuckin' me; I was the only niggah that could make you come. Your husband makes you come like how I used to? I used to love the way you would grab and hold me tight when you were about to explode. Word! We can make it happen again, Meeka. I want you again so fuckin' much."

"Russell, stop. . . . We're done here," she said, rising from her chair.

"You sure?" he asked, staring up at her with a proud look.

"Yes."

Russell slowly stood up. "Ayyite," he muttered. "What about that piss test?"

"Please, just leave," she instructed.

Russell made his way out of the office, looking content with himself. When he left, Karen plopped down in her chair, letting out an agonizing sigh. "God, please help me," she whispered to herself.

Outside, Russell made his way to the Escalade where Critter was waiting for him. He jumped into the passenger seat.

"Everything okay, Slim?" Critter asked.

"I got that bitch in my pocket," he proudly stated.

"You the man, Slim . . . fo' real," Critter said, starting up the truck and driving off.

21

Something in River made her extremely nervous as she traveled in the cab on her way back to Queens. She was quiet, noticing the cab driver peering at her from his rearview mirror. He smiled when she noticed him watching, and then focused his eyes back on the road.

She kept out of the loop for a week, ignoring phone calls and forgetting about business with Big Red. She had twenty missed calls from him and over a dozen threatening messages from Red demanding that she call him immediately. The last call he made to her, he threatened her life.

That run-in with Hubert and his goons had River shook up for a few days. She knew that she had to watch her back.

The cab continued to drive east on the Belt Parkway on a calm and warm Friday night. River's cell phone went off. She removed the phone from her hip and looked at the caller ID. It was Tah-Tah calling. River was stunned, because Tah-Tah never called River unless it was an emergency.

"Hello," River answered.

"River, where the fuck are you?" Tah-Tah shouted. "I tried calling you before but I got no answer."

"What happened?" River asked nervously.

"You got niggahs lookin' for you and shit," Tah-Tah said.

"What?"

"About four niggahs came up in the crib asking about you. They were lookin' serious. They went through your room and shit, tossed shit around like they were lookin' for somethin'. They threatened to kill me if I didn't tell 'em where you were," Tah-Tah said, her voice panicky.

"You okay, Tah-Tah?" River asked, concerned that her beef came to her home.

"Yeah. I called Kay, he's here wit' me now. We need to talk," Tah-Tah stated. "You in some kind of trouble?"

"I can't talk right now," River said. "How long ago was this?"

"They came by yesterday."

"What they look like?" River asked.

"One was light-skinned and fat," Tah-Tah informed her.

"Fuck!"

"River, please tell me you're coming home soon."

"I'm on my way home now," she said.

"How soon will you be here?" Tah-Tah asked.

"I'm on the Belt right now," River said, not giving away too much information.

"You alone?"

River didn't answer. She was wondering why Tah-Tah was asking her if she was alone.

"Tah-Tah, where's Kay at right now? I wanna ask him sumthin."

"He went to the store," Tah-Tah said.

Something bothered River deeply. Kay never went to the store, he always sent Tah-Tah if they needed something. They would fuck like crazy, and he would rarely come out of her bedroom.

River knew Tah-Tah had to be setting her up. She thought Big Red and Twinkie had to be at her crib right now, waiting for her to show up. She'd dissed Red by not calling him back, and she knew how he got. *But what if it's not Big Red, what if niggahs found out my location?* she pondered.

The thought of running into a trap scared her, because she was on her way home, and if Tah-Tah hadn't called, who knows what might have happened.

"Tah-Tah, I'll be there in fifteen minutes," she lied.

"Okay. Please hurry. I'll tell Kay you wanted to talk to him."

River hung up. She needed a change of plans. "Shit! Shit! Shit!" she shouted.

"Everything okay?" the driver asked.

Going home was not an option for her anymore. She thought of someplace else to go, but nothing specific came to mind for her at first.

"Excuse me, I have a change of location," she told the driver.

"You're not going to Hillside Avenue?" the driver asked, glancing at her through his rearview mirror again.

"No."

River thought of one place to go, but it was risky for her—she might end up getting her head blown off. But it was her only hope. She just prayed that he was a very forgiving person.

River looked at the driver and told him the new location.

River walked up to the ten-story building on Hillside, extremely nervous. She had no other options for herself. She didn't have any type of weapon on her, the one knife she did carry she'd left stuck in a man's hand.

She walked behind a woman toward the lobby, and when the lady got buzzed in, River walked into the building with her. She got on the elevator and pressed the button for the fifth floor. As the elevator ascended, her hands felt clammy, her heart rate increased, and she was fidgeting with her cell phone.

She slowly stepped out on the fifth floor and made her way toward his apartment. Her beauty and attire made her look as if she was working for an escort service. She strode down the hallway clad in a belted Lurex herringbone skirt, stilettos, a white sleeveless mock turtleneck, and her long wavy hair falling onto her shoulders.

She stood in front of the apartment door, hesitant. *What if he's not home?* she thought. She glanced down the hallway, and took a deep breath. She rang the bell twice and waited.

Eric heard the doorbell and wondered who was at his door so late on a Friday night. He wasn't expecting company, and except for Critter, he rarely got visitors at his home.

He gripped his .380 in his right hand and made his way to the door. He looked through the peephole and thought he was seeing things. He saw River at his door and got nervous. He wasn't making the same mistake twice.

He cocked the gun, securing a round in the chamber, and shouted, "Who is it?"

River hesitated for a moment, and then answered, "We need to talk."

Suddenly the door flew open and Eric yanked River into his apartment by her arm and shoved the gun in her face. "Bitch, why you come back here? I should blow your fuckin' head off right now," he shouted, but his bark was worse than his bite.

"Please, please . . . let me explain," River pleaded, looking sad as she gazed into Eric's eyes.

"Start talking."

"I'm not here to set you up. Eric, believe me. I wanted to see you again," she proclaimed.

His grip around the .380 tightened as he glared at River, her back pushed against the wall. "Where's your crew?"

"I don't fuck wit' them anymore. I had to leave. Look, if you think I'm lying, then shoot me. But I'm here on my own account."

Eric wanted to believe her, but fool me once, shame on you, fool me twice, shame on me. He still had the gun near her face. *She looks good*, he thought. But pussy got him robbed in the first place.

"Can we at least talk without the gun in your hand?" River gently asked of him. "Look . . ." She began to remove the expensive necklace that was around her neck. She unclasped it and dropped it to the floor. Then she took off her rings, bracelet, and took out the cash that she had left over after her spending and tried to force it on Eric.

"There's five grand in that envelope. It's yours. I just wanna talk, that's all. No surprises. I came alone," she said.

Eric was still skeptical.

"Answer me this one question," he said with the gun still aimed at her.

"What?"

"Was it real? Was the attraction you had for me and the bond we created, was it ever real?"

"Yes," she honestly answered, never taking her eyes off him. "It was. You think I would risk coming back here to see you again after what happened if it wasn't? I can honestly tell you from my heart that I miss you."

With that, Eric lowered the gun from her, and held it down by his side. River looked depressed. He saw a few tears trickle down her face as she told him, "Eric, my life is so fucked up right now that I felt you were the only person I could turn to. I'm sorry for everything that happened. If I could take it back, I would."

His passion for her, and his kind heart, soon won out over the anger and resentment he'd felt for River. Instead of wanting to beat her and curse her out, he wanted to embrace her.

It seemed too easy.

"I'm alone, and I have no one else," she cried out.

"You in trouble?" he asked.

She nodded.

"Are people after you?"

She nodded again, with tears still trickling down her face.

I'm gonna hate myself for this, he thought, moving closer to River and taking her in his arms. When it came to women, he was weak, especially the ones for whom he truly cared. Some might say that he was a sucker for love. He nestled River against his chest as she cried.

"I got you. Don't worry," Eric said, trying to comfort her.

River faintly smile and turned her tearstained face up to his caring eyes. "Thank you."

She held his gaze for a moment in silence. He cupped her chin tenderly and moved his lips toward hers, and gently kissed her. Her lips were soft and inviting. River didn't resist but poured herself onto him, feeling his grip around her tightening. He embraced her with passion and fire. The gun fell from Eric's hand and they tore at each other's clothing.

He pulled her shirt over her head, exposing her lacy purple bra, and River pulled his T-shirt over his head, seeing his upper-body six-pack physique. She was definitely impressed. They kissed passionately again as River straddled Eric and covered his neck with her kisses.

Eric carried River off to his bedroom where he laid her down on her back on his plush king-size bed. River quickly unfastened her skirt, and Eric removed his jeans and boxers. He was so hungry for her that his long erection was clearly visible.

River smiled and sexually positioned herself for him as she moved back near the headrest and spread her legs. Eric was in awe of her womanly figure. She was perfect from head to toe—shaved pubic hair, hour-glass figure, with a pedicure and her gleaming long legs looking like they belong to a Playboy pinup.

He climbed on top of her, positioning himself between her inviting thighs, and slowly pushed his dick into her. River gasped, "Aaaaaahhh," as she felt him slowly penetrate her with a deep hard thrust.

It had been months since River had sex. With Eric it was real for her, the attraction was there, and it showed between her thighs.

Her sweet juices flowed against his dick as he pounded away into her. She gripped him tight, rooting her manicured nails into his back.

Eric gripped her thighs and continuously pushed himself into her. He'd been longing for her since the day they met, and had never thought that he would get a chance to be with her sexually.

Neither cared about using a condom, he wanted to feel her raw. He clasped her outstretched hands, pinning her against the mattress, and ground deep into River's soft thighs as if it would be his last time.

"I'm coming," he announced, pushing himself into her harder and deeper.

River moaned, feeling his dick hardening more inside of her, feeling his manhood about to explode. They both were sweaty and didn't want the sex to end. River owed him this, but she also wanted it for herself, to make sure it was real. She knew after tonight, there was no turning back from him. She had never felt so strongly for a man, and it scared her somewhat, because she risked her life coming back to him not knowing what his reaction would be.

Eric began fucking River rapidly. River let out a passionate cry as tears trickled down her face, loving every moment of being in the missionary position.

He grunted, squeezing her thigh and her hand simultaneously as he quivered between her legs, exploding into her. He continued to pant while their juices mixed into each other. He loved the touch of her soft smooth skin against his, and lingered on top of her, kissing her, touching her, fondling her plump breasts.

"Shit!" he muttered contentedly, rolling off her and lying on his back, peering up at the ceiling.

"Was it good?" River asked, nestling against him for comfort.

"Fuck, yeah," he answered, breathless.

River smiled.

"On the real, I'm glad you came back. You did save my life," he mentioned, stroking her soft black hair with her face pressed against his chest.

"They're gonna come for you . . . for us," River told him.

"Who?"

"Big Red and Twinkie. He gets jealous, and he has a very violent temper," River said, peering at Eric. "He loves me."

"You love him?" Eric asked, fearing she might say yes.

"No, I never loved him; it was just business with us. But he thinks I owe him sumthin. He wants so much more from me. He hates the fact that I'm really attracted to you. And if he finds out that I'm with you, he'll kill you and me."

"I ain't worried about that fat fuck. Let him come," Eric stated.

"But you don't know him, Eric—he's crazy."

"Listen, you're safe wit' me. I know people, and if he comes, then he's gonna regret ever fuckin' wit' me. I still owe that niggah from the last time. But I want you to stay wit' me. Where's your stuff?"

"At my apartment. But I can't return there. I have dangerous men waiting for me. I think my roommate tried to set me up," River explained.

"Then first thing tomorrow morning, we go shopping, get you some new clothes and shoes," Eric said.

"Thank you. I knew you were so different since that night we met at the bar."

"Yo, I like you, and from now on, you gotta be real wit' me, River. Ayyite? I don't want anymore surprises poppin' up."

"I have nothing to hide from you anymore," she confessed.

"First off, is your name really River?"

"Yes. But I'm not really from Baltimore, I was born and raised in Brooklyn." With that, River continued to confess everything to Eric, even confiding in him about the violent and sexual abuse she'd end-lessly endured from her mother when she was young. They shared

stories, and Eric let River know what he was about. He spoke briefly
of his cousin Yung Slim, who was now released on parole.

They talked for hours until she fell asleep in his arms, nestled
against his chest. As River slept, Eric was feeling somewhat uneasy.
He slowly slid himself from underneath her precious comfort, not
wanting to wake her, and went into the living room to retrieve his
.380. He stalked back into the bedroom naked and hid the gun under
his pillow for that just-in-case incident. He stared at River sleeping
on his bed. She looked like an angel, lying naked against his satin
sheets as if she had falling from heaven itself. He wondered if he
could trust her again. Was she worth the risk? But he thought about
the superb night they'd just had together, and he felt so connected to
her that he forgave her. He wanted River, despite the risk.

"Please let this be real," he whispered to himself, gazing at River.
He then got back into bed with her and softly held her in his arms
again, never disturbing her from sleep. He nestled against her womanly figure and knew that loving her wasn't going to come easy.

22

"Aaaaaahhh, yeah ... fuck me! Fuck me! Fuck me!" Starr chanted, as she rapidly moved her thick young hips back and forth with eight inches of hard dick deep in her pussy.

She pushed against his broad chest as he gripped her hips and thrust all he had into her. Starr rode him as if she was trying to win a race. Her trick got excited, lifting his back off the mattress, grabbing at her hips tightly, sweating, and feeling himself about to come as Starr tightened her love muscles around his dick, being so wet. But Starr pushed him down on his back and pinned him with her hands against his chest, her legs straddled around him like Vise-Grips.

"Stay down," she instructed, never missing a beat as she rode that dick.

"Damn, Starr . . . I'm coming. You makin' me come. You got that good pussy. Oooh, you got that pussy. Oooh, you got that good pussy," he hymned.

Starr rocked back and forth, feeling him about to explode soon. Suddenly the bedroom door opened and Reality walked in, loudly saying to Starr, "Yo, hurry up and make that niggah come. He got four minutes, because Rome wants all of y'all out here in five minutes."

He walked back out of the bedroom leaving Starr to finish her business.

"C'mon, niggah, come for me," Starr said, putting more pressure on him by clinching her ass cheeks against him. "You wanna come in me. My pussy's good, right? I'm the best. I'm worth every penny right?"

"Oooh, shit! Hells, yeah. Aaaaaahhh . . . you feel so fuckin' good," he cried out. "I'm coming!"

Soon afterward he trembled underneath Starr, letting free millions of babies into the condom as he grabbed at her hips, panting and grunting.

"Damn!" he whimpered.

Starr let him savor the moment for a few seconds as she remained on top of him, feeling his dick becoming flaccid inside of her. She then climbed off him, reached for a nearby towel, and wiped in between her legs.

She watched him get up, reach for his jeans, and start to get dressed. He was cute, and had a big dick, and she got hers off right before he got his nut. It was rare that a trick made her come.

Starr put on her panties and jeans and threw on a T-shirt, trying to look somewhat decent for the meeting with Rome. She heard about what happened with Dynasty and Cherry. She overheard the conversation Reality had with one of his men about someone moving in on their turf and demanding 60 percent from all of Rome's workers—it was extortion. Both men were furious, and Dynasty got reprimanded with a few bruises on her face by Reality for being so stupid.

"I'm gonna see you later, Starr," her client said, giving her a kiss on her cheek and leaving the room, knowing to mind his own business.

"Okay, baby. You gonna see me next week?"

"Of course, you know my wife can't fuck like you," he proclaimed, smiling.

Moments later, Reality walked into the room shouting at Starr to hurry the fuck up. Starr quickly hurried behind Reality into the living room, where the others ladies were present.

Reality was a menacing-looking man who stood six feet two inches and was as solid as a rock, with long braids and biceps like a heavyweight boxer. He was fierce and spoke with a deep raspy voice that intimidated the ladies and many men.

"Y'all bitches shut the fuck up!" he shouted throughout the room.

Knowing not to make him repeat himself, the room got quiet, and Rome suddenly appeared in the room. He was shirtless, and a thick platinum chain hung around his neck. Both men stood in the center of the room and looked as though they were not to be fucked with.

Starr kept her distance, being seated between Chyna and Tara, two hoes that were down for anything, even murder if tempted. Starr gazed at Dynasty, who stood behind Rome. Her eye was swollen and her face bruised. She looked a hot mess.

"Yo, first off, don't end up like this stupid bitch here, giving away my money to some niggah like he takes care of her," Rome proclaimed, pointing to Dynasty, who stood still and quiet behind Rome. She looked embarrassed, her eyes glued to the floor.

Rome violently grabbed Dynasty by her hair and yanked her forward as though she was some kind of mule. As he held Dynasty strongly with his fist gripped around her hair, he glared at his hoes, and continued with, "Any one of y'all bitches give away sixty percent of my money, or anything else that belongs to me, and I'll kill you."

Everyone in the room knew he meant business.

"And second, I'm giving each of y'all bitches Nextel phones. If you got a problem while out on the track, or you see something that ain't right, you get on the horn and hit up Reality. He's gonna be around tonight, making sure everything goes smooth," Rome exclaimed.

"Y'all bitches need not to worry about this bitch-ass niggah named Yung Slim! If y'all lose out on makin' my muthafuckin' money again tonight, there will be hell to pay. Y'all bitches hear me?" he shouted.

"Yes, Daddy," they all shouted in unison.

"I got soldiers for that niggah who got at Dynasty. I'm the fuckin' king, right, Dynasty?" Rome scolded, still gripping Dynasty tightly by her hair with her head lowered to him.

"Yes, Daddy," Dynasty meekly replied.

"You're my bottom bitch, and I expect you to act like it tonight. You fuckin' hear me?!"

"Yes, Daddy. I won't fuck up again," she responded.

Reality stayed in the background and smiled, watching his boy Rome humiliating Dynasty in front of her peers.

"You know what, Dynasty, get on your fuckin' knees and kiss your daddy," Rome ordered.

He pushed Dynasty down on the floor and unzipped his jeans. Dynasty moved toward him on her knees, reached into his pants and pulled out his monstrous dick. Rome was well-endowed, eleven inches and better. Dynasty gripped his huge dick in her fist and began stroking him gently.

"I said kiss it, not play wit', you dumb bitch," Rome scolded.

Dynasty leaned forward and took him into her mouth, sucking him like a lollipop. Rome grabbed the back of her head and pushed more of his big dick down her throat, causing her to choke on it. Dynasty gagged, but Rome showed no mercy.

"You know how to deep-throat, bitch, teach these hoes how to please a man," Rome said.

Dynasty was able to shove nine inches down her throat, trying to handle the dick like a porn star. As Dynasty sucked Rome off, he continued to lecture his hoes. "As I was sayin' . . ." He let out a slight moan. "There you go, Dynasty, make your daddy proud. Y'all bitches better come fuckin' correct tonight with all my fuckin' money. You got problems, you don't hesitate to get on that fuckin' horn and hit up Reality. He's gonna take care of your problems."

Rome let out a satisfied moan as Dynasty took in all of him and licked his nuts. She wanted to make her daddy happy and have him forgive her for being so stupid, so she went all out.

Dynasty sucked Rome's dick as if they were alone, despite the seven hoes that watched her. Rome grabbed a handful of her hair and gazed at everyone in the room. Dynasty's head rapidly bobbed back and forth, stroking and sucking Rome simultaneously.

"Reality," Rome said, turning to face his right-hand man. "Any problems tonight, you know how to take care of it."

Reality nodded, knowing what Rome meant.

Rome then looked down at Dynasty, and said, "Don't fuck up again tonight."

Dynasty pulled his dick from her mouth, with it still gripped in her fist, and replied, "Daddy, I got you. I'm gonna make you proud of me tonight."

"Y'all bitches get dressed," Rome instructed.

Dynasty started to get off her knees until she heard Rome shout, "Bitch, did I tell you to stop suckin' my dick? Fuckin' finish what you started."

Dynasty obeyed orders and shoved his huge erection in her mouth, trying to make her man come. Rome moaned, loving how his bottom bitch sucked his dick. It was one reason why she was his bottom bitch; her head game was a 100 percent on point. Dynasty continued to suck Rome off until he burst into her mouth, making her swallow his kids. Afterward he looked down at Dynasty, and said, "Now you can get up and get dressed."

It was ten after midnight and the track on Rockaway Boulevard was busy with prostitutes from Rome's camp. He had five workers over by Rockaway Boulevard and the Conduit, and another three of his ladies were working South Road, and 150th Street.

Starr strutted down Rockaway Boulevard in a white drop-waist skirt, her long legs gleaming with baby oil in a pair of clear stilettos, and a tight pink T-shirt that accentuated her breasts and slim waistline. Starr was one of Rome's best bitches. He recruited her when she was only fifteen, which was a year ago. Starr was alone, dining in a Burger King on Jamaica Avenue, when Rome approached her with his thuggish attitude and good looks. He spotted Starr as potential when he first walked into the fast-food restaurant. Rome paid for her meal, talked to her for an hour, and took her back to his truck, where he fucked her and gave her two hundred dollars. He promised to take care of Starr if she took care of him, and from there on, she was in his pocket.

Starr waved down a few passing cars driving down 136th Avenue but to no avail. They honked their horns, looked on in amazement, and kept it moving.

Reality patrolled the track in a black Escalade, rolling on twenty-inch rims. He had Butter and Jay in the truck with him. Under Reality's seat was a loaded .50-caliber Desert Eagle, and in the backseat Butter gripped an Uzi and Jay carried a .45. They were armed and ready for anything. They watched all the girls like hawks and kept an eye out for anything unusual.

Starr stalked across Rockaway Boulevard, hoping to do better on 137th Avenue near the Howard Johnson. Her money had been slow in the past hour, but she knew things usually picked up around one in the morning—the later the better. She carried her Nextel in her hand and was very wary as she made her money, making sure that what happened to Dynasty didn't happen to her. As she stood on the corner of Rockaway Boulevard and 137th Avenue, a green Cherokee pulled up beside her and rolled down his window.

Starr peered into the jeep and saw a Hispanic male gazing back at her.

"How much?" he shouted out.

Starr cautiously made her way toward the jeep and answered, "It's fifty for a blow job, and a hundred and fifty for a fuck."

"Damn, that's a little steep for some pussy," the Hispanic man replied.

"Baby, I'm worth it. I'm the best out here," she boasted about herself.

But the driver still looked reluctant. To give him more encouragement, Starr lifted her skirt and revealed to him that she didn't have on any panties. The man gazed at her shaved pussy, and his hormones went raging.

"This could be yours right now. I know you ain't scared of pussy, baby. You look like you got a big dick," she said, slightly playing with her skirt with the man watching.

"Fuck it, get in," he said, unlocking his doors.

Starr quickly jumped in, and when she got in on the passenger side, she quickly chirped Reality, saying, "Reality, I got a date; I'm getting into a green Cherokee jeep."

Reality chirped her back, saying, "Ayyite, Starr, you know the rules, that niggah got twenty minutes."

"I know."

The jeep drove off down the block to find a secure and inconspicuous location where Starr could earn her money.

As Starr drove off with her date, Reality noticed a burgundy Escalade driving toward them. Reality remembered Dynasty saying that they pushed her into a burgundy Escalade. His senses heightened, and he reached under the seat for his gat.

Donald pushed the truck down Rockaway Boulevard, looking out for hoes to tax. He had Tank with him, and they both were ready to run up on some hoes and give them a hard time.

"Look at that, these bitches are out here tonight, and they thinkin' we a joke," Donald said, looking very unhappy. "They think it's a game. We gonna show these hoes we mean business."

Donald looked around for his first victim, and he quickly spotted her sauntering down 154th Street, coming toward 137th Avenue. She had just stepped out of a car and was making her way back to Rockaway.

Donald slowly moved the car down 154th Street and pulled up close to her. The young lady got nervous, knowing she was in trouble, and she started to run in her spike heels. But Tank quickly got out and pushed her against a brick wall.

"Bitch, where you goin'? Don't fuckin' run from us!" he yelled. "What we tell you about being out here and gettin' this money? This is Yung Slim's territory. Anything being sold out here, from drugs to pussy, he gets a percentage of."

The young lady stared at Tank in horror. He was slim, dressed in baggy jeans and a T-shirt, and brandished a 9-mm pistol in front of her.

"You either get the fuck off this track now, or you pay the fuck up!" Tank yelled.

"Please, I need this—my daddy said—"

Slap! Slap! Slap! Tank smacked her multiple times in her face with an open hand. "I don't give a fuck who your daddy is—you know what's up!"

Donald stayed seated in the driver's seat, observing Tank go wild on shorty, and smiled. Tank was one of the young recruits who got on the team and was eager to make this money and earn a name for himself. And he definitely had heart.

Both men were unaware of the black Escalade that turned off of 134th Avenue and slowly moved down 154th Street with its headlights off. Reality cocked back his Desert Eagle and was now positioned in the passenger seat while Jay drove.

Reality saw Luscious getting smacked near the corner, and was upset.

"Drive by real slow," he told Jay.

Jay moved the truck down the block at a turtle's pace. Reality couldn't just do a drive-by because of Luscious being in the way.

Tank gripped Luscious by her neck and continued his abusive onslaught, enjoying his work. He was going hard for his reputation by beating up helpless women.

Donald continued to watch, but something suddenly caught his attention. He turned to look and noticed a black Escalade was pulled up beside his, and before he could react, two shots were fired into his head, pushing his wig back. The .50 caliber left two crater-sized holes in his head.

Tank quickly spun around, only to see Butter coming at him with his .45 trained at his head. Butter quickly fired. *Blam! Blam! Blam! Blam! Blam! Blam! Blam!*

Tank dropped suddenly, hit by all seven shots that came at him.

Luscious screamed in horror as blood splattered on her. Butter quickly yanked the screaming woman off the ground by her arm and shoved her into the truck.

"Yo, chirp all the hoes and tell 'em to get off the fuckin' track ASAP. Tell 'em to meet up at the rendezvous," Reality instructed Butter and Jay, knowing that they just made the track hot for police activity.

Starr sucked her date's dick with passion and skill while he reclined in his seat, moaning and grunting. The loud slurping sounds she made while deep-throating his dick were music to his ears.

"Ah, yeah . . . damn . . . that feels good. Ooh, so good!" he cried out.

He fingered her pussy with her legs spread for him as Starr simultaneously sucked on the tip of his dick and jerked his shaft, playing with his balls.

Suddenly from a short distance, they both heard numerous shots ring out. They were parked in the nearby parking lot on 140th Avenue.

"Yo, was that gunshots?" Starr inquired, stopping her actions.

"They shooting?" her Hispanic date said, raising his seat up.

Moments later, Starr received a loud chirp over her Nextel, hearing Jay shout, "Starr, get off the track now! You know where to meet up at."

"Oh, shit!" Starr blurted out, becoming nervous.

"Yo, what happened?" her date asked, becoming nervous himself.

"I need to go," she told him, pulling down her skirt.

He started the ignition and quickly drove out of the parking lot. He dropped Starr off in front of the Executive. She apologized to him for the trouble and walked toward the entrance.

When the jeep pulled away, she got on the horn and chirped Reality. "Yeah, I'm in front of the motel."

"Somebody will be around shortly to come get you. You stay there," Reality instructed.

Moments later, a dark Yukon quickly came to a complete stop in front of the Executive. Starr went to the truck and quickly jumped in and was greeted by three other ladies in the backseat.

Within ten minutes, Reality cleared the track of all activity and hauled business off to a different location—Newark.

An hour later, the block was inundated with police activity. Flashing police lights and the loud sirens blaring awakened many neighbors to the crime scene.

They found Donald slumped over the steering wheel with two large holes in his head, and Tank sprawled out on the concrete riddled with bullets.

Detective Monroe pulled up to the scene, not really knowing what to expect. He'd got a call over the radio indicating two dead, and decided to check it out.

He walked up to the bodies and instantly knew what crew both men belonged to. "Shit!" he muttered. He examined Donald and shook his head in disbelief. His brains were leaking all over the dashboard, and his body was contorted. The next victim didn't look so good either; he was riddled with shots, with brain matter all over the sidewalk.

Detectives began asking around for eyewitnesses, but no one had seen a thing. Cops knew that the area was frequented by prostitutes, but it didn't surprise them that they couldn't find one girl in sight for questioning.

Monroe got on his cell phone and quickly made a few calls. He had some indication of what went on. It wasn't a coincidence that a few weeks after Yung Slim got out, bodies started dropping. But he was shocked that the two dead belonged to Yung Slim's camp; he'd thought it would be the other way around. Detective Monroe knew about Rome and his violent hold over some areas in south Jamaica, and what he feared was starting to come through. A war over drugs, pussy, and territory was brewing between two notorious men.

23

Eric lay nestled against River in the comfortable confines of his king-sized bed on a sunny warm afternoon. She'd been secretly staying at his apartment for a few days, and he loved every minute of her company. As promised, he took her shopping and splurged on $3,000 or more of clothes, shoes, getting her hair done, and a night out with her in the city.

He had completely forgotten about business with his cousin, Critter, or even Willie, his Brooklyn connection. River had him in complete bliss since she'd arrived at his apartment unannounced.

"I can lay in your arms forever," River said.

"Ditto," he replied, squeezing her tightly.

On the nightstand, Eric heard his cell phone going off repeatedly, but he ignored it.

"You're not going to answer it?" River asked.

"Nah, niggahs can do without me for a few days," Eric returned, gazing into River's hypnotic dark bedroom eyes. The phone rang a few more times, but Eric just tuned it out, and had River straddle him in the bed. She climbed on top of him and began riding his dick slowly, causing him to moan.

"Ooh, I love this so much," he cried out, gripping her hips.

Out of the blue, Eric's apartment phone began to ring, and that shocked him, because nobody ever called his home line. If they wanted to reach him, they knew it was through his cell phone only.

Eric stopped midthrust and stared at the phone.

"What's wrong?" River asked.

"My phone," he said, looking troubled.

"What about the phone?"

"That phone doesn't ring, unless—" He stopped when he heard the answering machine pick up.

"E, where the fuck you at?" he heard Critter shout through the answering machine. "I've been calling your phone all fuckin' morning. They got Donald last night, shot him twice in the head. Pick up, niggah. Shit is fucked up right now."

Eric couldn't believe what he just heard. He had no immediate reaction. He just looked emotionless. River still was on top of him, but all sexual activity stopped for them as soon as he heard the message. She didn't know what to say or do. She knew it had to be a close friend of his.

"Baby," she called out, trying to snap him out of his sudden trance.

"Just get off me," Eric said calmly.

River didn't say a word but got up and positioned herself near the end of the bed, staring at Eric.

"Muthafucka!" Eric shouted, knocking over the lamp on the nightstand and jumping out of bed. He walked around naked, angry and upset. He picked up his cell phone and dialed Critter's number.

Critter picked up after the second ring.

"Yo, where the fuck was you?" Critter shouted.

"None of your business. What the fuck happened?"

"Rome's men murdered Donald and that new niggah Tank last night. They got gunned down on One hundred and thirty-seventh Ave, it's a fuckin' mess," Critter informed.

"Where's my cousin?" Eric asked.

"I don't know. He called me, said he wanted everyone to meet up at the club this evening, and that's it," Critter said. "You know it's on, right?"

Eric was quiet over the phone.

"E, you still there? E . . ."

"Yeah, let me call you back," he said, and clicked off.

Donald was a childhood friend, and what he feared came true. Donald and Tank were the first victims in a war that was brewing. Eric didn't want to admit it, but he was scared. Everything was happening too fast for him. First there was the stickup with Big Red, then his cousin coming home and trying to reclaim the streets again. Then River had come back into his life, and having such strong feelings for her, he couldn't let her go. And now his boy Donald was dead.

"Eric, you okay?" River asked, being concerned.

"No, I'm not," he replied, trying to hold back his emotions. He stared out his bedroom window, trying to hide his teary eyes from River. He didn't want her to see him in this state.

River, knowing he was upset, slowly walked up to him as he gazed out his bedroom window, gently placed her arms around his waist and embraced him.

"It's goin' to get ugly, River . . . really fuckin' ugly," Eric proclaimed, his attention still focused out the window.

"I know, but it's been ugly for me," she replied. She began massaging his chest, trying to comfort him.

"I just wanna escape and go somewhere where nobody knows me and start over. I just wanna be happy, and this game I'm in, I fear I might not come out of it alive, like my father," Eric said.

"Baby, please don't talk like that," River countered.

"Why not? It's the truth. Donald's dead, and how many murders will come after him? You don't know me, River. You don't know what my family is about. I grew up around this shit all my life, from my father, uncles, and my cousins," Eric stated. "My father was Yung Black, you ever heard of him?" he asked.

"No," River answered.

"He was one of the most feared gangsters in this city back in the eighties. He used to work for the Gambino crime family as a gun for hire, and ran around with a notorious crew known for murders and extortion. I remember when I was six, he put the first gun in my hand and told me what I held in my hand gave you respect and power on the streets. My father took shit from no one, and had so many men's blood on his hands that I used to think it was normal to do what he did.

"When I was seven, I remember cops with guns kicking in our front door and shouting, looking for my father. He was upstairs in the bedroom wit' my mother when they raided the crib. I just stood there, watching them drag my father down the stairs. He was fighting back, and they jumped on him, cuffed him, and took him away from us for a month. He eventually got out on bail, and was still doin' the same old shit, like nothing affected his dangerous lifestyle. I used to think he was untouchable, until I was eight. My father and mother were having this huge argument, I think it was over money. Somebody owed him for a hit he did, but they shitted on him. He was out the door ready to do what he did best, murder. But my mother tried to stop him, I guess she felt something wasn't right. I remember it was a gloomy night when he walked out the door with his gun, and my mother was chasing and pulling after him. But he wouldn't listen, he was intent on handling his business. They argued outside, and then that's when I heard the shots, about ten shots rang out. I quickly ran to the door and saw my father sprawled out on the sidewalk in a puddle of his own blood, and my mother clutching his body in her arms, crying out hysterically. He was dead on the spot. It was a hit, and till this day, his death is still unsolved. But my father made many enemies, and he died the way he lived.

"But seeing that, it didn't stop for me with his death. A few months later, my mother went crazy and she got admitted into an institution. But she got worse over the years, and never came home. So

I moved in with my aunt Fran, and became close wit' my cousin Russell. Yo, we did everything together, so that people thought we were brothers. We ran the streets like it was our playground.

"I remember the night I got shot fuckin' wit' Russell. I was eighteen at the time. We had beef wit' these Brooklyn niggahs who wanted to muscle their way onto the block we had set up shop on. Yo, we ran up on them and fucked them up, I mean we came at them wit' bats, chains, and everything, and embarrassed them on the block, so that some of them had to be carried away by their homeboys. We wasn't playing. But we underestimated them, thinkin' they were pussy. They came back on us that same night, guns blazing and everything. We were at this social club, hanging out and drinking, and this car came from around the corner and niggahs stepped out. Yo, they must have fired at least twenty rounds into the crowd. I got hit in my shoulder, but my man Links caught it bad. He got hit four times, and died right next to me."

River squeezed him gently, listening to him tell his story and open up his heart to her. Just like her, he had a painful past, and she figured that was the reason she felt so connected to him.

"That's why when I met you and we bonded, I knew I could be happy wit' you. I never been in love," he proclaimed. "I just wanna die happy, and knowing that I didn't miss out on something good. I wanna love you."

"Eric, I'm so fo' real wit' this, and I promise, I'm not going anywhere," River said. "We both share the same troublesome past, and you make me happy. That's why I risked coming back here."

Eric heard what she said, and the thought of dying scared him.

"Do you believe that everything in your life happens for a reason?" River asked him.

"Excuse me?"

"I mean, do you think that the steps we take, the pain we go through, the trials and tribulations we endure, all lead us to some important part of our life or maybe someone?" she continued. "Growing up, when I used to visit my grandmother in the South, she used to tell me and my sister that the day we're born, God already has a plan for us. We just have to listen to Him closely, and everything will fall in place. I believe that I'm here for a reason. I believe our destiny was to find each other, Eric, and help each other. I've done many bad things in my life, and I'm not proud of what I've done . . . but I'm ready to change and leave this behind. I'm ready to make something right out of my life.

"I have a younger sister that I haven't seen in five years. I left home when she was eleven, and I would do anything to see her again."

"What's her name?" Eric asked.

River thought about her sister with a smile, and then answered, "Starr."

"Starr . . . why does that name sound so familiar to me?" Eric said, trying to recall where he'd heard that name before. "She's still in New York?"

"I don't know. I don't have a number or address. I don't even know if she still alive," River said, her voice saddened by the thought of not knowing anything recent about her sister.

"But if we get the chance to escape the world we were born into, I want to find her, Eric. I want to know if she's okay. I need to know."

Eric looked her in the eyes and saw this compassionate, innocent woman, and his heart melted. The vibes he got from River were real. He said to her, "When I was living wit' my aunt, the one thing she instilled into me and her own kids was having faith and learning forgiveness, because you may never know when you may ask for forgiveness from someone else someday. She used to tell us that those are the two ingredients for a healthy soul. She had so much faith in us. She always believed that her kids and myself would achieve so much in life. She believed that we would overcome the stigma of our family created by my father and uncles in the streets. No matter what happened wit' us on the streets, she kept her faith in us until the day she died. She was a strong woman. The only one who would have made her proud is her daughter. She's living in New Jersey, got married, and is enrolled in law school to become a criminal attorney. It's ironic wit' my family's history that she chose that profession. But my cousin, he holds too many grudges, and I see that in him every day. He thinks the world owes him something because he did seven years. It's odd that my aunt, the sweet and caring woman she was, gave birth to him.

"C'mon, we gotta go," he exclaimed, reaching for his clothing.

"Go where. I can't stay here?" River asked.

"No. It's too dangerous. You said yourself that Red will come after you. He'll come back here sooner or later. And I don't want to chance it by leaving you here by yourself," Eric stated, quickly getting dressed.

"But where are you taking me?"

"Someplace where nobody will look for you," he informed her.

Parked outside Eric's building on Hillside Avenue was a black Nissan Maxima, and the occupants of the car were Big Red and Twinkie. They both sat patiently scoping out the lobby, watching who went in and who came out. Big Red was furious about River's sudden disappearance. It was slowing up his money and his affection for River grew into hatred and rage when he thought about the possibility of her dissin' him by coming back to see Eric.

Big Red, Twinkie, and two other thuggish-looking men paid a visit to River's place, being disappointed that she hadn't been home in days. Tah-Tah quickly gave up River's business, but she had no idea where River was. Big Red didn't believe her, and had both his men manhandle her to get some truth from her. Tah-Tah had relentlessly called River's phone until she finally picked up, and tried to convince River to come home to a trap. But River was too smart for that. Tah-Tah was selfish and put her life first before anyone else's. It was easier to have River killed than endanger herself any further. But her plan backfired when River never showed up. And being furious, all four men raped and beat Tah-Tah in her bedroom, cut her up afterward, slit her throat, and left her bound to her bed, naked and saturated in her own blood, where she still lay—dead.

"I fuckin' knew we shouldn't trust that bitch," Twinkie exclaimed. "You think she chillin wit' homeboy?"

Big Red was seething with jealousy and hatred. "Yo, if she is, we gonna handle this bitch and that niggah like we did her fuckin' friend. I fuckin' swear I'm gonna rape and torture that bitch," Red exclaimed. "I shoulda murdered this niggah when I had the chance. How the fuck I let this stupid bitch talk me out of puttin' a bullet in his head!"

Both men were armed with automatic weapons, and two Glock 17s and a .45 rested under the car seats.

"Handle your business, niggah," Twinkie encouraged.

"Believe me, I will."

Moments later, River walked out of the lobby with Eric looking as happy as ever. Twinkie tapped Red, pointing out the two, and cursed, "Sheisty bitch!"

Big Red's face was twisted with anger and disgust as he gazed at River from a short distance.

"You wanna kill 'em both now?" Twinkie asked, retrieving his gat from under the seat.

"Nah, not now," Red answered. He wanted to murder them both where they stood, but it was too risky with so many people around. And he wanted to take his time with River, make her feel pain and have her suffer as he slowly plunged his knife into her, wanting to cut out her heart.

"Follow them," Big Red said.

Twinkie started up the car and followed the Scion at an unnoticeable distant.

Eric stopped his Scion in front of his uncle Pumpkin's house, believing that River would be safe with his uncle at his home. He was unaware of the Maxima that followed him the whole trip.

He rang his uncle's doorbell, and a minute later, Pumpkin answered. He looked out at his nephew with curiosity.

"Eric, everything okay?" he asked.

"No, Uncle Pumpkin, I need a favor from you," Eric said.

Pumpkin gazed at River, admiring her beauty, and knew that the young woman Eric brought to his home had to be dear to his heart.

"Uncle Pumpkin, this is River, the woman I told you about. She needs a place to stay," he informed his uncle.

"She's in danger?" Pumpkin asked.

"Some dangerous men may be after her and me as well. They know about my location, so she can't stay there by herself. Nobody knows about you, I figure she be all right here," Eric mentioned.

Pumpkin looked at his nephew and then at River. He couldn't tell them no, so he said, "Okay, but you owe me."

"I know," Eric uttered, pushing River into the house.

They both walked into the living room, and Pumpkin quickly closed the door behind them, securing the front entrance with four thick double bolts.

River glanced around his home and wasn't impressed. *A simple place for a simple old man,* she thought. Wooden floors, no style or decoration, old furniture positioned sparsely throughout the room, and the room was clustered with bits and pieces. In fact, his home kind of reminded her of *Sanford and Son*. But she didn't mind because she felt safe there.

"Excuse me, young lady, while I talk to my nephew privately," Pumpkin said, pulling Eric away from River.

They went into the kitchen and Pumpkin asked, "How much trouble are you in?"

"My friend Donald was killed last night," Eric mentioned.

"I'm sorry to hear that. How are you holding up?"

"Could be a lot better," Eric replied.

"So what are you about to do?"

"Unc, there's a lot happening, and I ain't got time to explain," Eric said, looking hurried.

"It's Russell, isn't it?" Pumpkin inquired. "That boy ain't even been home a month now, and already one of your best friends is killed."

"Uncle Pumpkin, I ain't got time for this," Eric said, walking back into the living room.

Eric looked at River, and said, "You'll be okay here. My uncle knows how to hold it down if there's any trouble."

River was content with what he said. She pulled him toward her, and kissed him passionately. "Be safe, baby."

"I will."

Eric then pulled out his .380 and put it in River's hand. "Take this just in case."

River was reluctant to take the gun, but Eric insisted. "You ever shot a gun before?" he asked.

River replied no.

"It's simple, you raise it, point, aim, and squeeze," he quickly instructed.

"I know the basics," she replied.

"And what you gonna use just in case them fools come at you?" his uncle asked. "Since you leaving my house unarmed."

"Don't worry about me, Uncle Pumpkin. You know I can handle myself," he countered.

"Boy, I've heard a lot of men said that before they were murdered," Pumpkin said. He went into his cabinet and pulled out a .357

and handed it to Eric. "You take care of yourself. I don't want to hear about you on the news."

Eric nodded, concealed the gun in his waistband, and headed for the door. River watched him exit, and said a small prayer for both of them. She knew things were definitely going to get ugly.

Outside, Big Red and Twinkie watched Eric leave the house without River.

"What you wanna do, Red?" Twinkie asked. "He left her alone, so now's our chance to get at the bitch."

"Nah, too risky," Red said. "We don't know how many people up in there, and what they holding up in that crib. It's a blind move."

"So I say we murder this niggah right now," Twinkie suggested.

"Something else is goin' on . . . I feel it," Big Red said, looking transfixed on something.

They both watched Eric get into his Scion and drive off.

"We not gonna follow this faggot?" Twinkie asked.

"Nah, we gonna hold off for a minute. The one thing we're good at is being patient. Our time will come, when we'll catch 'em both slippin', and believe me, when we do, it ain't gonna be pretty. We know where he's stashing her, so the bitch ain't goin' nowhere," Red said.

Twinkie nodded.

"So we just gonna sit here?" Twinkie asked.

"Fo' a minute, see what kind of activity pops off, and watch and see who else comes out that crib. I don't wanna take any chances," Red said.

"Just say the word, and I'm down."

Big Red stared at Twinkie. He was proud of his right-hand man.

24

"Ain't no niggahs gettin' money out here, fo' real," Critter exclaimed, furious about Donald's demise. "It's on! It's muthafuckin' on!"

He brandished a loaded .45 around the room while he spoke to his peers in the basement of Dreams, the local strip club on Hillside Avenue.

"Word, son! I'm ready to do this," another cohort shouted, his face twisted with anger.

The room was packed with twenty bloodthirsty thugs, ready to revenge the death of one of their lieutenants. Guns were displayed everywhere, from shotguns and Uzis to the typical street handguns, .45s and a few 9-mm pistols.

News of Donald's death spread quickly throughout the hood, and there was going to be hell to pay. The strip club Dreams had a bunch of trigger-happy thugs ready to shoot up the whole hood.

Yung Slim walked into the room with Barnes and Bishop. His face was tightened with sadness and hostility. He was dressed in black army fatigues. He stared into the crowd, and announced, "Yo, I'm puttin' up ten grand for any niggah that bodies that faggot niggah, Reality. And another fifteen for that faggot niggah, Rome."

Everyone in the room nodded at Yung Slim's offer. Every man wanted the cash for themselves.

"He wants a war, we gonna bring it to him," Yung Slim said. "Yo, y'all see any one of his hoes out on the track, y'all know what to do. Niggahs ain't gettin' no money out there while I'm home. And anything that's connected to that faggot niggah, Rome . . . lay 'em the fuck out."

"We got you, Yung Slim," a voice shouted out.

"Ayyite, y'all niggahs get the fuck out, and lock shit down out there," Yung Slim exclaimed.

As everyone was leaving the basement, Eric was making his way in. Yung Slim glared at him, and shouted, "Niggah, you always fuckin' late!"

"Yo, what the fuck happened?" Eric shouted back.

"Where you been?" Critter asked.

"Critter, stop tryin' to interrogate me, I ain't in the mood right now," Eric chided back.

"Donald's dead," Critter replied. "You should have been here earlier."

Eric looked at Yung Slim with contempt in his eyes. Yung Slim gazed back, and sternly said, "What? You blaming his death on me now? E, this is the game, you ain't new to this. Shit happens. Donald knew what he was gettin' into. He went out like a man. But I guarantee you this, muthafuckas are gonna pay lovely wit' their lives."

"An eye for an eye, right, Russell," Eric returned. "Aunt Fran would be so proud of you," he added sarcastically.

"Niggah, don't fuckin' bring my moms into this. This is how the game is, we win some, and we lose some. This is what our family is about, what we been about since you and I was born. You need to be more like your father, niggah—ready to murder niggahs. Don't be actin' like some scared bitch!" Yung Slim barked. "I need to know if you're in my corner, E. Are you down for this payback on niggahs that got at Donald?"

Eric looked over at Critter, who was quiet in the background.

"You strapped?" Yung Slim asked.

Eric nodded.

"I got niggahs rollin' out tonight to put the word out, that they fucked wit' the wrong niggahs in my camp. So don't come up in here tryin' to preach to me like you my moms; that bitch is dead and in the ground. She never understood what our family was about," Yung Slim said.

"You rollin' too, Critter?" Eric asked, staring at his friend.

"Niggah, that was my man . . . I ain't gonna let him go out like that," Critter returned.

"E, look at you, what got into you? You lookin' unfamiliar right now. We're like brothers . . . nah, fuck that, we *are* brothers, and you been actin' distant from your family fo' a minute now. You lookin' weak, out here pushin' that bullshit box shit, Scion, thinkin' you making yourself some real money by peddling some weed and throwing parties. What's really good wit' that?" Yung Slim asked.

"I'm just comfortable, Russell, trying to be happy. You always wanted the world at your feet, tryin' to be God," Eric replied.

"That's where it belongs," Yung Slim countered back. "We come from history, niggah, you need to understand that."

"I understand that this life put my father in the ground, made my mother go crazy, like a half dozen of our cousins are locked up or on the run, and now one of my best friends is dead," Eric returned.

"So what you sayin', E, you bitching out on us? Am I hearing you right?" Critter asked. "I thought you had my back. We need you now when it's more important—this is critical for us."

"I don't wanna lose you, Critter," Eric said. "You know I got your back, but this war y'all gettin' into, it's gonna bring down so much heat on us. How many more men will fall for you to rise to the top, huh, Russell?"

Yung Slim stepped up to Eric. "Niggah, I'm done talkin'. E, don't dare turn your back on us, or I swear to my mother's grave, I'll treat you like any other niggah out on them streets, if you walk out on us."

Eric didn't feel threatened, he held down his cousin's hardened gaze and returned with, "I'm not turning my back on y'all, just watching my back more carefully."

There was a brief silence.

"I'll get back with you. I got things to take care of," Eric said, leaving the room.

Critter, Yung Slim, Barnes, and Bishop all watched Eric leave the room in silence. When he was gone, Yung Slim said to Critter, "I know my cousin. That niggah's hiding something from us."

Critter nodded, agreeing. "What you want me to do?"

"Keep an eye on that niggah, see what he's about," Yung Slim instructed.

"Got you."

"I wanna know what my cousin is hiding," Yung Slim added.

When Critter left, Barnes walked up to Yung Slim and asked, "All due respect, but do you trust your cousin? He's lookin' kinda weak in my eyes, and you don't wanna make that same mistake you did seven years ago. We don't need any more weak links in this crew, or having niggahs snitching."

Yung Slim looked at Barnes without saying a word. He knew where he was coming from and knew Barnes was only watching his back.

"Let me worry about my cousin, you just handle your business in the streets," he said to Barnes.

Barnes nodded and backed off.

But that's how it starts, having one man in your ear about a soldier or your man being disloyal to the crew, and then the mistrust begins.

The following night, three young thugs in a black Acura Legend circled the blocks around South Road and 150th Street. They were armed and looking for anything remotely connected to Reality or Rome. They were looking for payback and ready to start up some trouble before the night ended.

"Yo, pass that shit," Sean said, reaching for the blunt from the backseat.

"Niggah, calm the fuck down," Omar exclaimed, seated in the passenger seat, taking a long pull from the L.

The driver of the car kept a keen eye out as he cruised slowly from block to block with a loaded .380 resting in between his legs. He wasn't taking any chances and made sure his gun was within his reach.

"Row, ain't no bitches out here tonight, we just wasting our time out here," Sean said, finally taking his pull from the blunt. "They know we comin' for them, so they hiding," he added, exhaling a cloud of smoke.

"Nah, something's out here, we just ain't looking hard enough in the right areas," Row replied, making a right on South Road.

"Shit, a niggah need some pussy right about now," Omar said, slouching down in his seat as he stared out the window.

"Yo, I heard that niggah Rome been marking all his bitches by forcing them to get his name tattooed on their bodies," Sean stated.

Row chuckled, and replied, "There's only one way to find out."

They drove past the 40 projects and kept looking for something, but so far their night was coming up empty. They searched the South Road area for an hour, and got tired of searching.

"Yo, I'm 'bout to say fuck this, ain't shit out here," Omar exclaimed. "It's damn near two in the fuckin' morning."

"I feel you, O," Sean replied.

As they drove down South Road, heading toward Sutphin Boulevard, Sean spotted something, and hollered for Row to slow the car down.

"What you see, niggah?" Row asked.

"Back up, niggah!" Sean shouted.

Row backed the car up, and Sean peered down 155th Street. He saw something in the shadows that appeared to be a woman striding down the block.

"Yo, I think I saw some ho down that way," he said.

"Oh, word," Omar said.

Row slowly turned down the block and moved at a snail's pace. Sean was right, as they gazed at a redbone cutie from the back sauntering down 155th Street in a short denim skirt and black stilettos.

"You think she's one of Rome's hoes?" Sean asked.

"Only one way to find out," Row replied, moving the car closer to her.

The young lady was out looking for work, but the track was slow since the murders on Rockaway Boulevard. But she didn't care. She had two kids to feed, and a debt to pay off. She knew everything was hot, and she was willing to take her chances out on the streets just to feed her kids.

She glanced over her shoulder and saw a black Acura rolling up on her really slow. She got nervous, but tried to play it cool as she continued to walk down 155th Street. She carried her Nextel in her purse, and knew she needed to chirp Reality, who was unaware that she was working the track tonight against his orders. After the murders, Reality had told all the girls not to work anywhere in Queens, but Royal still took her chances.

When she got to the corner of 107th Avenue, that's when the Acura took action and hastily drove up to her. Three men stepped out, brandishing guns. Royal tried to run, but she had on three-inch stilettos and they were wearing Nikes and Timbs, so she knew it was impossible to escape from them.

"Bitch, what's up?" Omar shouted, running up to Royal and grabbing her by her thin arms.

"Please, I'm just tryin' to make some money to feed my kids, I don't want any trouble," she pleaded.

"Oh, you got kids. Can I be your baby-daddy too?" Sean joked, feeling up her breast.

"Who you out here for?" Row asked.

"I'm workin' for myself," Royal replied.

Row said, "Bitch, you lying to us?"

"No."

"You sure? You ain't workin' for that bitch-ass niggah Reality?" Row asked, glaring at her.

"Who?" she responded, playing stupid.

"Yo, see if she got the tattoo," Omar suggested.

All three men stared hungrily at Royal, admiring her tight petite body in the denim skirt, and snug black shirt. Row pointed his gun at her and then sternly pulled at her skirt, shouting, "Bitch, take this shit off!"

Royal tried to resist, but Omar and Sean quickly grabbed her, trying to strip off her clothing. She fought though, scratching and biting at her attackers.

"Bitch, you think we playing!" Row shouted, cocking back his .380. "I will murder you out here tonight. Take everything the fuck off right now!"

Royal stared down the barrel of the gun, frightened. She knew he was serious. "Please, why are y'all doin' this? I have two kids."

"Bitch, we ain't got time for your sad excuses. If you wanna see your kids again, you better start takin' that shit off," Row demanded.

Royal began to shed a few tears as she started unfastening her skirt. She removed it, and then pulled her shirt over her head, her tits coming into view. She stood sobbing in a red thong.

"Bitch, I said everything," Row exclaimed.

Crying, and shaking, Royal slowly pulled down her thong and removed it too. She stood stark naked in high heels, her arms covering her breasts.

"Yo, this bitch is makin' my dick hard," Omar expressed, grabbing his crotch.

Royal had a nice body, she was flawless from head to toe.

"Yo, check if she got that tattoo," Sean said.

Omar walked up to Royal and observed every inch of her body. He finally found Rome's name tattooed across the back of her shoulder. It was in script and read *Daddy Rome*. Omar and the rest laughed, seeing it was true that Rome marked all of his girls.

"Yo, Row, let me fuck this bitch," Omar said, glancing around the area and then looking at Royal as if she was a piece of meat.

"Nah, put that bitch in the trunk. She may know something," Row instructed.

Upset that he couldn't get himself some quick pussy, Omar roughly grabbed Royal by her arm. She tried to resist, shouting, "No! Please, no! No! I have two kids that need me!"

"Bitch, you think we give a fuck about your kids! Get your ass in that trunk," Sean snapped.

But Royal was reluctant.

Row walked up to her and punched her in the jaw, almost breaking it. Royal lay unconscious in Omar's arms as he stuffed her into the trunk. The three men then quickly got back in the Acura and drove off, unaware that they were all being watched.

A half hour later, all three men met up with Critter at his home. Row called his cell phone, requesting that he meet them outside. Ten minutes later, Critter stalked outside in his robe and slippers.

"Fuck y'all niggahs want?" he barked. "I got this bitch I'm 'bout to lace tonight, and y'all better not be calling me out here for some bullshit."

"We thought you might want to see this," Row explained, placing his key in the lock and unlocking the trunk.

The trunk popped opened, and Critter stared down at a naked, gagged, and tearful Royal in stilettos lying in the trunk.

"Who the fuck is this?" Critter asked.

"We picked her up off the track; she's one of Rome's hoes. Thought she might be useful to us," Omar explained.

"Useful?"

Row shrugged. "Hey, maybe the bitch knows something about where to find Rome and Reality."

Critter sighed.

"You wanna keep her?" Sean chimed in.

"Fuck it, take her down in the basement, and keep her quiet. I got a bitch upstairs. I don't need her making noise and fuckin' my night up," Critter told them.

"I'm sayin' . . . can we at least fuck her first?" Omar said, being a horny bastard.

"Niggah, just take the bitch in the basement, and come by tomorrow night and we can handle her then. See what she knows," Critter said.

Omar and Sean removed Royal from the trunk, and Omar tossed her over his shoulder and carried her down into the basement.

"Yo, when is the funeral?" Row asked.

"Thursday night," Critter answered.

"I'll be there."

Critter nodded.

With that Critter went back into his crib and Omar came walking back out after leaving Royal bound and gagged in Critter's dusty basement. But he was definitely coming back tomorrow night to get himself some pussy before anyone else had their way with her. She was too cute, and he wanted her badly.

It was game time now.

25

"You keep doin' what you doin', Starr, and you gonna be my right-hand bitch," Rome proclaimed, gazing at Starr's naked body.

He was lounging in his La-Z-Boy chair watching Starr rub her body down with baby oil from head to toe. His dick got hard just at the sight alone.

Starr smiled and continued to smear herself with the oil. She was definitely attracted to Rome, but she knew he only saw her as his working bitch. And she liked hustling for Rome, he protected her and promised to take care of her.

"You're young, beautiful, and that body is tight. You never come up short wit' my money and you fuckin' listen. I like that," Rome stated.

"You know I gotta do you right, Daddy," Starr replied, smiling at her pimp.

"Word, you wanna do me right," Rome said, displaying a lustful smile.

Starr smiled back, rubbing the oil in between her thighs.

"I gotta surprise for you," Rome stated.

"You do, Daddy?"

"Yeah, you definitely gonna like this," he said.

He began unbuckling his jeans, and pulled out his huge dick, and began stroking himself lightly.

"Ooh, I like that surprise," Starr said, staring at his big dick.

"Nah, this ain't it. I'll show you later after I fuck you first," Rome said. "Come jump on this dick and make your daddy proud."

He didn't have to repeat himself. Starr walked up to him still naked, glistening with oil, and straddled him in the chair. He slowly pushed the tip of his dick into her, and she gasped loudly, clutching Rome tightly as he opened her up with his thick and long erection.

"Show Daddy you can handle it," Rome said, thrusting about eight inches into her, with three extra inches left to spare.

Starr bit down on her bottom lip, clawing at his back as she rocked back and forth on his lap, tightening her love muscles around his huge shaft.

Rome devoured her plump breast in his mouth, sucking and licking on her nipple as he grabbed her ass firmly and repeatedly thrust himself into her, causing Starr to scream out.

"Aaaaaahhh, Daddy . . . Aaaaaahhh . . . you got a big dick, baby," Starr cried out.

Rome fucked her the way she wanted to be fucked—long, hard, and deep. There was a knock on Rome's bedroom door.

"What?" Rome shouted, still deep in Starr.

Reality walked in, and said, "We ready."

"Then wait, muthafucka!" Rome shouted.

"Ayyite," Reality replied, and walked out.

"I'm coming, baby!" Rome uttered, clutching Starr's butt tightly.

"I'm coming too, Daddy," Starr said.

Rome grunted, discharging himself into Starr. He shuddered and gripped her hips tightly. Starr came a short moment afterward, clutching her pimp tightly and quivering along with him.

Rome panted, and then said, "Ayyite, get the fuck off me, Starr."

Starr jumped off his dick, satisfied that she got her nut, and started to get dressed. Rome began to make himself decent again, and then told Starr to hurry up, he wanted to show her the surprise he had waiting for her.

A half hour later, Starr followed Rome into another apartment he had in the same building. This apartment was off limits—she and the other girls were strictly kept out of it. Only Rome, Reality, and a handful of his soldiers came in and out.

Rome knocked on the door, and Reality opened up. Starr followed behind Rome, feeling uneasy. The room was empty, no carpets, pictures, rugs, or furniture. It was strictly bare, looking vacant. Starr stopped in the center of the living room. But Rome nodded to Starr, gesturing that she should keep following.

They headed to one of the back bedrooms, and Starr heard some kind of activity behind the door. Before they walked in, Rome looked at Starr, and said, "You take care of me and I'll take care of you. Here's my surprise for you."

He then opened up the bedroom door, and Starr was shocked by what she saw—they had Bamboo tied to a chair, and he was naked. They had worked him over terrible before she arrived. He was bleeding from his head, with his eyes swollen and his lip busted.

"This the muthafucka that attacked you, right?" Rome asked.

Starr nodded.

Rome walked up to Bamboo, and shouted, "You put one of my girls in the hospital, you fuckin' bitch! You dare harm my product. You know who I am?"

"Fuck you!" Bamboo cursed. "I'm Bamboo, niggah. I'm gangsta. Fuck y'all!"

Rome viciously struck him a few times in the face, causing Bamboo to spit blood from his mouth.

"Shut the fuck up!" Rome shouted, glaring at him.

Starr just stayed in the background and watched. She didn't want to get involved despite his being the one who'd put her in the hospital.

"Yo, pass me those Vise-Grips," Rome said, reaching for them.

Reality passed Rome the tool and Rome immediately went to work on Bamboo. He clamped the Vise-Grips around Bamboo's nipple and twisted, breaking flesh.

"Aaaaaaaaaaaaaaaahh—fuck y'all!" Bamboo continued to curse.

"What, niggah, fuck us! Fuck us! No, fuck you!" Rome screamed, twisting the tool again, ripping the nipple off. Rome then went for his other nipple, twisting the Vise-Grips against his skin, causing a piercing scream throughout the room.

Starr reluctantly looked on, becoming squeamish.

"You see this bitch right here, she belongs to me, and you put her out of work for a few weeks, so you gotta pay, muthafucka!" Rome shouted.

Rome then had his men hold Bamboo down, as he pulled out his tongue with the Vise-Grips. "You like this? You die slow tonight, niggah. Reality, cut this niggah's tongue out."

Reality walked up to Bamboo with a huge blade in his hand, and didn't hesitate to slice off Bamboo's tongue as though it was butter. Reality then held the tongue in his hand as if it was nothing.

Vast amounts of blood poured from Bamboo's mouth. He gagged on his own blood, twitching and squirming around in the chair.

"Ohmygod!" Starr cried out, turning her head from the gruesome sight.

"Starr, he made you suffer, now you make him suffer," Rome said, picking up a metal baseball bat and passing it over to Starr. "Do your thang."

Starr looked on in awe, thinking, *Is he serious?*

She reluctantly gripped the baseball bat and walked over to Bamboo, who was coated in his own blood, and spitting up. She glanced at his tongue near his feet, and felt the urge to throw up.

She couldn't will herself to do it. Rome looked at her and said, "Give me the fuckin' bat and let me show you how it's done." He grabbed the bat from her hands, raised it, and violently came across Bamboo's head, nearly snapping his neck back. Bamboo's face was contorted. He shook as if he was having a seizure. Rome raised the bat again, and hit him across the head again, again, again, again, again, and again.

Starr was wide-eyed, her stomach beginning to turn. There was blood everywhere, puddles of it on the floor. Rome stood over Bamboo's lifeless body panting, looking like a butcher covered with blood. He passed Reality the baseball bat.

"Next time, you don't hesitate to kill a man before he kills you," Rome said to Starr.

Starr tried to keep her composure. She'd never seen a man tortured before, and she knew this crew was ruthless. Everyone in the room looked calm and collected. But Starr wanted to run out of there.

Rome walked up to Starr, and said, "That's for you, baby. Any niggah touch you, and that's how they get dealt wit'."

Rome looked as though he just finished doing housework. He kissed Starr on her forehead despite having just beaten a man to a pulp with a baseball bat.

"Yo, get rid of that faggot. Cut him up and dispose of that niggah. I want his body out of here by tonight," Rome ordered.

Starr followed Rome out of the apartment and back to his other apartment down the hall. She was terrified. She remained quiet the entire time.

Reality was a few steps behind them when his cell phone rang. He picked up and watched Rome and Starr walk into the apartment.

Inside, Rome began stripping away his clothing and washed his face off in the kitchen sink. Starr just stood in the living room and watched him. Moments later, Rome walked up to Starr shirtless and asked, "You okay wit' this? You ain't gonna bitch up about what you saw back there?"

"No," she said.

"The same thing can happen to a woman if she crosses us," Rome sternly explained. "You understand that, right?"

"I understand," she replied meekly.

Reality walked into the apartment looking troubled. Rome saw that, and asked, "What's up?"

"We gonna have problems wit' this niggah Yung Slim," Reality told him.

"What the fuck you mean?"

"They kidnapped Royal," he informed Rome.

"What?" Rome snapped. "Take care of this shit, Reality. Find my bitch, and murder this niggah."

Reality nodded. "You know I am."

Starr looked at both men and her heart began to beat rapidly. She became scared. This was the first time she had doubts about Rome since she'd left the hospital. She thought about Ms. Henderson and the love she gave her when she was so messed up.

She thought about the advice Ms. Henderson gave her, and deep inside, she did miss her. After witnessing Bamboo being murdered in a horrendous way, she knew it was time to get out. But she knew Rome was a gorilla pimp, and no ho got out unless he said she could leave, and that was very rare. He was very possessive and controlling and made all his hoes get his name tattooed somewhere on their body. She got hers on the small of her back.

"Starr, you and the girls get ready to hit the track in two hours," Rome instructed. "Cash is driving y'all out to Hunts Point tonight."

Starr nodded, reluctant to turn tricks after what she just saw. Before Rome left with Reality he looked at Starr, and coolly asked, "You're not gonna bitch up on me, right? I need you tonight. I want you to continue makin' the money you've been makin' me since you been wit' this crew."

"Yes, Daddy," she softly replied.

"Ayyite, now is not the time to begin fuckin' up! You never made me angry, and don't start now," he continued as he held her chin in his grip, gazing into her eyes.

"I'm okay, Daddy," Starr replied, keeping her composure around Rome.

"Ayyite, that's my girl. Any problems tonight, Cash is goin' to be around. You chirp that niggah on your Nextel," Rome instructed before he walked out of the room with Reality.

Starr sighed, and then reluctantly began getting ready to hit the track that night.

26

Yung Slim and Bishop pulled up to the parked sedan where Detective Monroe sat waiting, smoking a Newport.

"I don't like waiting," Monroe barked.

"You got something for me?" Yung Slim asked, disregarding his remark.

"Your boy got picked up for a DWI last week," Detective Monroe informed him.

"Who?"

"Rahmel. I got his information. He came back into town two weeks ago, him and his new bride."

"That's good," Yung Slim replied.

"He got himself a cozy Long Island home in Brentwood," Monroe said, passing him the address.

When Yung Slim had the address in his hand, he then passed him the rest of the money owed to the detective. Detective Monroe quickly went through the bills, making sure it was all there.

"You don't trust me?" Yung Slim joked.

"I don't trust anyone," he replied.

Satisfied that it was all there, Detective Monroe laid the cash down on the passenger seat, and then said, "Listen, I know it's your business, but what do you want with this man? He's not in the game."

"You're right, it is my business, and not yours to go snooping around on," Yung Slim replied. He tossed an extra two grand into the car, and said, "That's a little extra to forget about this meeting we had. You hear or see something in the future, you forget about this information I required from you."

Detective Monroe nodded.

"I'm sorry about your boy Donald. When is the funeral?"

"Thursday. Any leads from the precinct?" Yung Slim asked, but not really caring.

"We're on it. But it's not my case. My hands are clean from the bloodshed," Monroe said. "Y'all two want to kill each other, it's fine by me. You keep me away from this beef, Yung Slim."

"I could care less about your old ass," Yung Slim said.

The less said, the better, Detective Monroe told himself. He planned on retiring next year and didn't want to get caught up in the war with two arrogant assholes who wanted to cancel each other out. He wanted to keep a low profile till his retirement, and knew that wouldn't happen if he constantly got involved with Yung Slim. He would slip him some information from the NYPD database and that was about it. But as far as getting his hands dirty in murder, drugs, and other illegal activities, he wanted to be through with that. Monroe had lasted this long by being smart and not being too greedy. He knew Yung Slim's era was going to come to an end soon, and he refused to get dragged into it anymore. He had a family, and wanted to be around to see his kids grow.

Detective Monroe drove off, aware that the streets were going to get a whole lot uglier. He wished that they would have waited an extra year to parole Yung Slim, because by then he would have been retired and moved out of state.

. . .

As Eric made his way to the funeral, his cell phone rang in the passenger seat. He looked at the caller ID and saw that it was Willie calling. He knew it was about that time for him to re-up. But he'd been so busy that he had forgotten about his Brooklyn client. And that cash would definitely come in handy for him.

"What up?" Eric answered.

"Same o, same o, E," Willie replied. "I need them thangs from you again."

"How many thangs we talkin' about?"

"I got a large order this time," Willie said.

"How large we talkin' about?"

"About eight. You can do that for me?" he asked.

"I might. I gotta call my peoples," Eric stated.

"And one more thang, I'm stepping my game up, tryin' to hit a home run. I need a lil' extra points on the scoreboard," Willie mentioned.

Eric was surprised. He knew what Willie was talking about. He wanted that yayo.

"Yo, you know I don't pitch at that speed," Eric said.

"I know, but I'm doin' a few practice runs. My coach is beggin' for it. Might go MVP this year," Willie informed him.

Eric sighed. He knew it was more money in his pocket, but the deal was risky. He didn't see the warning signs, because since business had started with Willie, he only ordered four pounds of weed, nothing more and nothing less. And it had been that way for a year now.

"Can you make that happen?"

"I'm gonna see what I can do for you. I'll call you," Eric told him, and hung up.

Crowe's Funeral Home on Sutphin Boulevard was packed with friends and family on late Thursday evening. Everyone came out to give their condolences to Donald's family. It was a closed-casket viewing because of the shots he received at such close range.

Eric walked in dressed in a pair of black pants and a button-down shirt. He came alone to pay his respects to his childhood friend. He greeted the family and said he was sorry about what happened. Donald's mother, Brenda, a southern woman in her late sixties, hugged Eric close, and cried out, "They took my baby from me, Eric . . . they took him from us. Why they killed my baby? Why?"

"I don't know, Mrs. Jones. He didn't deserve this," Eric said.

"I know he wasn't an angel, but my baby was trying," she cried out, still gripping Eric. "He was trying to get his life right."

A relative next to Mrs. Jones pulled her off Eric, embracing Donald's mother in her own arms. Eric stood there for a moment, gazing at the grief-stricken mother, and tried to compose himself. He then turned around and peered at the closed casket his boy was lying in.

He took a deep breath and made his way over to the viewing. There was a large picture of Donald encircled by dozens of flowers arranged formally by the casket. Eric stood over the casket, lowered his head, and said a small prayer to himself. A few tears started trickling down his face as he thought about his longtime friend.

It could be any one of us lying here tonight, he thought. He couldn't take standing over the casket too much longer, so grief-stricken in his heart and soul, and he made an exit from the room. He met up with Mel and Raheem out in the foyer. And to his surprise, he noticed Rahmel walking into the building with his wife, Vivian. Rah noticed Eric and gave him a slight nod and smile.

Eric walked up to Rah and hugged him.

"I just recently heard," Rah whispered in his ear. "They know who did it?"

"Nah," Eric lied. "How long you been back in town?"

"Two weeks now," Rah said.

Eric looked over at Vivian, and she was so beautiful dressed in a black skirt and white blouse with her hair in a French twist.

"Hey, Vivian," Eric said, giving her a hug and kiss on the cheek.

"Hey, Eric, I'm so sorry about your friend," she sadly said, embracing him tightly. "You okay?"

"I'll be fine," he replied.

"If you need us for anything, don't hesitate to call," she suggested.

"Thanks."

"Baby, can you give us a minute alone?" Rah asked of her.

"Sure. I got to use the ladies' room, anyway." She walked off to the bathroom.

"I can't go in there. I just can't do it to myself." Rah said. "I know it's a closed casket, but the last memory I want of Donald is when he was at my wedding having himself a good time."

"I understand," Eric said.

"Shit is goin' to hell, E. Everything's changing," Rah continued.

Mel and Raheem joined Eric and Rah, and soon afterward, Critter walked into the funeral home alone. It was a small reunion, minus Yung Slim, and unfortunately, Donald.

As they all talked, Eric noticed that Rah was aloof from everyone else. He looked troubled about something. Eric gazed at his friend, and asked, "Rah, you okay?"

"E, we need to talk," Rah said.

"No doubt," Eric replied. "Yo, fellows, we'll be back."

Rah and Eric walked outside the funeral home and continued up the block. Eric wanted to know what was troubling his friend so much. They stopped at the corner and Rah proclaimed to Eric, "E, I'm a saved man."

"What?"

"Vivian, she changed me so much, and I love that woman. Because of her, I'm not wit' that rowdy shit anymore. I made my peace wit' God, and I need to make my peace wit' you tonight," Rah said.

"What you talkin' about?" Eric questioned, looking at Rah with bewilderment.

"I ain't gonna lie to you, I got beef wit' your cousin. I was the one that helped to get him locked up," Rah stated.

"What?" Eric replied, trying to understand where he was coming from.

"A few years ago, I was stressed for some cash, so I got down wit' this dude named Loco . . . some Spanish niggah from Brownsville. We did a few stickups here and there out in Brooklyn. One night, Loco's cousin put us onto one of Yung Slim's stash houses he had out in Brooklyn, told us there had to be about fifty thousand or better in the place. So I was down. I wanted payback. You don't know this, but remember Tammy I used to fuck wit'?"

"Yeah, you were lovin' that girl," Eric said.

"She was cheating on me wit' your cousin, and she ended up gettin' pregnant by that niggah," Rah proclaimed.

Eric was shocked. "You serious?"

"Russell used to throw that shit up in my face every chance he got. He always thought I was pussy. But I let it be, 'cuz that was family to you, and I respect you. So I kept my mouth shut about it and ate that pain. The bitch had his kid, a son, and he doesn't even take care of it. All due respect, but I hate your cousin, E . . . he a grimy niggah. So Loco and I ran up in his spot, and robbed that niggah. It was risky, but we pulled it off, and came off wit' fifty G's. We laid low for weeks, because we knew the status Russell had, and I thought he would use you to get to me, but he never did. A month after the hit, Loco came up dead, shot four times in his head. I knew Russell had a hand in that. I got scared, and went to the police. I told them everything I knew, and they set up a sting for him, with me as their pawn. They knew Russell wanted me dead. The cops started using inside informants to get the word out to Russell about my location, 'cuz they knew he was going to come after me for my life and his money.

"An inside informant in Russell's crew gave him bogus information about my location, and Russell believed him. He told Russell that I was hiding out in an apartment on Atlantic Avenue, and I was alone and scared. But the police was staking the place out twenty-four/seven. Only something went wrong, and the informant ended up dead, shot twice in his head. But he was wired when he was murdered, and cops ran up on Russell and arrested him. I gave my testimony to the police and grand jury and left town soon afterwards. I thought that they had enough evidence on Russell to give him life. But he still outsmarted the judicial system and got only ten years. And now the niggahs is out early on parole. You believe that shit?

"E, I didn't mean to keep this from you, but I was scared to tell you. We've been boys since forever, and somehow I felt that I betrayed our friendship by keeping so much from you."

"Fuck, Rah!" Eric exclaimed.

"You needed to know this. This shit been eating me up since it happened," Rah stated.

"Does Vivian know this?"

"Yeah. I told her everything. She was the one that encouraged me to confess to you. And she got me believing in God now. After my wedding, I wasn't planning on coming back to New York. I was goin' to take my bride and start a new life far from here. But her family's here, and they're very close, and they love me to death. So I got this home out in Brentwood, Long Island, and took my chances coming back. I know if Russell finds out I'm back, he'll come after me."

"What you need from me?" Eric asked.

"I want you to come through, so we can really talk. E, this lifestyle, it ain't us anymore. I don't want my soul condemned by my past. I'm a changed man now, and I want you by my side. We're like brothers, E . . . fo' real. And I know if I can change, you can, too. Have Donald's death open your eyes. The streets done took so much from you already . . . your father, your mother. I don't want it to take your life and soul too," he said.

"I feel where you're coming from, Rah. We gonna link up and we gonna talk. I won't let my cousin come after you," Eric said.

Rah smiled. "I ain't worry about him anymore. I'm wit' a higher power now. I just had to get that off my chest. I've been holding that secret from you fo' so long. But try and come by tonight," Rah told him. "And plus, I want you to see the new crib I bought for my wife."

"I'm glad to see you're happy," Eric said.

Then Eric thought about his cousin, and asked Rah, "Who else knows you came back into town?"

"Nobody, I've been keeping a low profile. But I had to pay my respects to the family tonight," he explained.

"Keep it like that."

"I ain't stupid. I know I still got that beef wit' Russell. I've been hearing about him through the grapevine. I know he's family to you, E . . . but you need to stay away from him," Rah proclaimed.

"It's funny, my uncle told me the same thing," Eric mentioned.

"Listen to that man, E, he knows what he's talking about."

Vivian came down the block in search of her husband and smiled when she saw him and Eric having a private talk.

"Why do I always find the two of y'all outside? Y'all trying to hide from me?" Vivian joked.

"No, baby, why would we do a thing like that? You know we both love you," Rah commented back jokingly. "We were just having a one-on-one talk. I asked E to come visit us tonight so we can get more in-depth with what we were talking about earlier."

Vivian knew what her husband meant, and smiled.

"I hope you can come by to see our new home," Vivian said. "I would love to have you over."

"I will definitely make it. I promise," Eric said, gazing at Vivian.

"It will mean so much to us," she replied.

"I'll be at your place around midnight. I just wanna make sure everything is okay here with the family," he explained.

Vivian smiled and gave Eric a deep hug. "Thank you for being a good friend to my husband. He needs your support in his life right now," she whispered in his ear.

"He's a brother to me," Eric replied.

Eric then gave Rah a hug and dap, and said to him, "Whatever happens, Rah, I got your back. Don't worry about the beef wit' my cousin. You're family to me too, just like him. Nothing will come between us."

Hearing that definitely put a smile on Rah's face, and made it concrete that Eric was a true friend. Eric then watched Rah and Vivian walk off hand in hand to their car in silence. He wanted what Rahmel had, a loving and caring woman by his side. And that made him think of River.

He'd been by his uncle's place every day for the past week to see how she was adjusting, and to his surprise the two of them were getting along just fine. River didn't mind hiding out in his uncle's home. Eric took care of her, and warned her to watch her back when she left the house and not to wander off too far. She still carried around his .380, and only left if there was a reason to, and only in the daytime. She was wise to the streets and knew Big Red and Twinkie were going to be looking for her. But she was unaware that they'd been stalking her every move and waiting for the right time to strike.

Rah and Vivian walked into their Brentwood home only to be greeted by a half dozen thugs loitering in their living room.

"What the fuck!" Rah shouted in shock. He wanted to run for the gun he had stashed in the bedroom but he was outnumbered and outgunned. He was a saved man, but he wasn't stupid. He still had some street in him.

Vivian shrieked as the men all pulled out guns and warned them to shut the fuck up.

"How was the funeral?" Yung Slim asked, slouched down in their chair, staring up at them.

"Look, leave my wife out of this, she has nothing to do wit' us. This is between you and me," Rah pleaded.

"Niggah, she married your bitch ass, so till death to y'all apart," Yung Slim said.

That statement enraged Rah, and he went charging at Yung Slim only to be beat down by a few thugs with their guns. He dropped to the floor, bleeding as they kicked and stomped him out.

"*Noooooooooooo!!!*" Vivian screamed, trying to run to her husband's aid, but being restrained by two men who gripped her tightly.

Rah moaned, clutching his side as he peered up at Russell. "Why are you doin' this?"

"Niggah, you put this on yourself," Yung Slim shouted. "You steal from me, snitch on me, tried to set me up, and you think it was goin' to be all good? What, you thought I would get life? I always come back to get mines, niggah."

"Please let him go . . . please don't hurt him. I know you must have a soul," Vivian exclaimed with tears streaming down her face.

Yung Slim looked at Vivian, and replied, "You gotta pretty bitch here. Maybe I'll put this bitch on the track and have her turn tricks to pay back the fifty grand you stole from me."

"Fuck you! I'll kill you," Rah shouted. He tried to rise to his feet but was violently knocked back down.

"Yo, Rah, her pussy good? Maybe I should have a few of my boys take her to the bedroom and find out," Yung Slim tormented him.

"No! Leave her alone. Please, I beg of you—just let her be. She has nothing to do with us," he said, gasping in pain.

"Niggah, I wanna see you suffer, that will turn me the fuck on," Yung Slim said. "What would make you suffer, Rah? . . . Seeing your bitch get fucked right in front of you, huh?"

"Russell, I beg of you, please let her go."

"It's good to see you beg and cry over this bitch. She's definitely fine, though. But you think I give a fuck about her, or you? Matter of fact, yo, y'all take that bitch to the bedroom and handle y'all business. I wanna see this niggah endure the pain of watching his wife gettin' raped," Yung Slim instructed.

"*Nooooooooooo!*" Rah screamed out, as he watched three thugs carry Vivian away into one of the back bedrooms. She tried to fight and resist, but to no avail.

Rah watched them disappear with his wife into their main bedroom. He was sobbing uncontrollably, thinking about the abuse that was happening with his wife while he painfully heard her screams from the bedroom.

Yung Slim walked up to Rah, crouched down beside him, and said, "I always hated you, niggah. My cousin befriended your bitch ass, and I don't know why. But tonight, you get yours. I always come out on top; you should know this by now, Rah. I fucked that stupid bitch of yours, Tammy, and she loved every minute of this dick, and now I got your wife."

"I hope you burn in hell for eternity," Rah spat, glaring at Yung Slim with bloodshot eyes.

"Well, before I burn in hell, it's gonna be heaven for me to watch you endure living hell on earth right now," Yung Slim countered back. "Yo, drag this muthafucka to the bedroom and have him watch the show."

Two thugs carried Rah to his bedroom, and when the door opened, Rah saw his wife sprawled out on her back, legs spread, her clothes ripped off her, pinned in the missionary position and crying out as one thug ground in between her legs while his friends held her down.

"God! No! No! *Nooooooooooo!*" Rah yelled, teary-eyed and trying to free himself. But he was helpless as he watched them rape his wife.

"Yeah, niggah, watch and see how we do," Yung Slim continued to torment him. "That ain't your pussy anymore, niggah. I own that now."

The young thug fucked Vivian raw, thrusting his dick into her, panting and fondling her breasts. "I'm coming," he shouted, and then didn't give a fuck about pulling out but came in Vivian.

"I got next," the next thug called out, unzipping his pants quickly, and positioned himself between her naked thighs and pushed his dick into her. He grunted and began moving rapidly in between her thighs. He came within minutes, and then the next man jumped on her.

"How could you?" Rah cried out.

Rah helplessly watched man after man have their way with his wife as he sobbed like a two-year-old. Vivian stopped screaming and reluctantly gave in to the men. She stared at her husband, still subdued on the floor, tears trickling down her face, and she said, "God is still with us, baby. They took my body but they will never have my soul. Everything is going to be okay."

After the last man was done, Yung Slim stepped up, pulling down his jeans. Before he went any further, he looked down at Rah, and said, "Let me show you how it's done. Let me show you how you fuck your bitch." He gripped his dick and pushed himself into Vivian. But she was quiet as he thrust himself into her.

Vivian peered at the ceiling and began reciting the Lord's Prayer. "Our Father Which art in heaven, hallowed be Thy name. Thy kingdom come, Thy will be done on earth as it is in heaven. Give us this day our daily bread and forgive us our trespasses, as we forgive them that trespass against us. And lead us not into temptation, but deliver us from evil—"

"Bitch, shut the fuck up!" Yung Slim screamed, covering her mouth and muffling her prayer as he grunted and came in her.

Vivian just lay there still, her body frozen against the bed. She stared at her weeping husband and whispered to him, "I love you."

Yung Slim buckled his pants, gripped a loaded .45 in his hand, and put the gun to her temple. He glanced at Rah and said, "You really care for this bitch."

"Russell, please don't. If you have a soul, a conscience, just let her go. You already humiliated me. You took everything. Please, don't! She's pregnant," he begged of him.

Vivian looked up at Yung Slim and said, "May God have mercy on your soul."

Russell displayed a smirk, and replied, "I don't give a fuck about her or your unborn, religious bitch!"

Boom! He blew her brains out while her husband watched.

"Vivian!!!" Rah screamed, trying to break from his captive's grip. His face was filled with anguish. The bedroom sheets were saturated with her blood and brain matter.

"Aaaaaahhh, no! No! No! You're a monster! Vivian! Vivian!" Rah cried out.

Everyone stood around nonchalantly and watched Rahmel pour his heart out. Yung Slim stepped up to Rah, pointed the gun down at his head, and uttered, "Pathetic. Go out like a man, niggah. Crying over your bitch."

Boom! Boom! Boom!

Yung Slim fired three shots into his head. He felt vengeful. He then turned to his soldiers, and ordered, "Yo, burn this bitch down."

Eric slowly made his way down the block, coming to a stop at flashing police lights and fire trucks that flooded the quiet Long Island street. The block was shut down, with dozens of firefighters trying to put out the heavy fire that engulfed an entire house. Neighbors came out in swarms, clad in their robes and slippers, witnessing the scene.

Eric suddenly got this funny feeling in his gut as he stepped out of his ride and slowly came closer to the blaze. He stood next to a neighbor, and asked, "What happened?"

"They don't know, I woke up and the entire house was on fire," a slim Caucasian male informed Eric. "Sad, they just bought that house not too long ago."

"They?" Eric inquired.

"Yeah, a couple. I heard that they just got married," he continued to explained.

"Black?"

The man nodded.

Eric stood frozen, fearing the worse. "Where are they?"

"It's funny, I haven't seen them. They're probably out of town."

"Ohmygod!" Eric muttered to himself. His eyes started to dart around the street in search of Rahmel and Vivian but they were nowhere in sight.

Eric got on his cell phone to call Rah, but he instantly got his voice mail. He continued to call Rah's phone repeatedly but all his calls went straight to voice mail. Eric began to fear the worst. He had just spoken to Rah a few short hours ago.

An hour passed, and the fire was finally put out. The house was completely destroyed, but the news got grimmer when firefighters informed their crew that two bodies were found in the main bedroom burned beyond recognition.

The news quickly spread throughout the neighborhood, and when Eric heard, he knew who the bodies belonged to. His face saddened, and he banged his fist hard down on the hood of his ride. His eyes were filled with tears.

"Fuck!" he cursed.

"Ohmygod," a neighbor cried out on hearing the news. She stood next to Eric and looked horrified.

Eric knew who was responsible for the horrendous act of violence against his friend. He wondered how his cousin found out about Rah's location so soon.

Now it was two close friends that he had to bury. He got back in his ride, did a quick U-turn, and made his way back to Queens. He broke down weeping a few times on the highway, but regained his composure and quickly tried to make it to his uncle's house in one piece.

27

Starr sat at the foot of the bed, giving herself a pedicure. It had been days since Bamboo's murder, and Starr tried to forget about the horrible events she had witnessed. But seeing Bamboo tortured was messing with her head, and she began having nightmares about it. She witnessed firsthand how deadly and cruel this world she was living in can get. Bamboo's ghastly death, the brutal rape and assault on her, and the murders were starting to open her eyes to what Ms. Henderson was trying to preach to her earlier.

The apartment was quiet, and it gave her time to think. Rome was in the kitchen discussing business over his cell phone, and the only girl in the apartment was Dynasty, satisfying a trick in the adjacent bedroom.

Starr heard Dynasty's moans coming from her room as she fucked a customer. She thought deeply about Ms. Henderson. She still had her number and was tempted to give her a call. She needed someone to talk to, and Ms. Henderson was the right woman she could run to.

Moments later, Dynasty walked into the bedroom naked while Starr continued to paint her toenails.

"Hey, girl," Dynasty greeted her, walking over to the closet and donning a red robe.

"Hey," Starr said, still focusing on her nails.

Dynasty looked exhausted. She stared at Starr and complained, "Rome had me out on the track all night, so I could make back his money. Now he got me fuckin' niggahs twenty-four/seven. I ain't got no sleep in two days."

Dynasty was only twenty-six but looked to be in her early thirties. She'd been in the game a long time, and it was starting to show in her appearance.

Starr looked up at Dynasty and noticed that her bruises were healing up really well. She was starting to look like the old Dynasty again.

Starr respected Dynasty and her position. She was Rome's bottom bitch, and she knew the game like the back of her hand.

"Starr, how old is you?" Dynasty asked.

"Sixteen."

"Damn, you're still a young thang," Dynasty replied. "I've been in this game for over ten years. I've been wit' Rome for six years now. You like what you do, Starr?"

"I'm gettin' paid, the money's good," she replied.

Dynasty chuckled. "I used to think it was always about the money when I first started. I would fuck ten niggahs in one night and make my daddy a thousand and more every night I was out grinding on the track. I was good at fuckin' and suckin' these niggahs like I was they bitch. Sex was my profession. I was the baddest bitch on the track and every pimp wanted my ass, and every trick used to request a date wit' me."

"But you're still beautiful, Dynasty," Starr told her.

"I'm not anymore on the inside. Look at me, Starr, I'm twenty-six. Do I look twenty-six to you?"

Starr studied her features and, honestly, when Starr first met Dynasty, she thought she was in her early thirties.

Starr shrugged.

"This game will add ten years to your life. I feel used, baby girl. I have nothing left, and these pimps, they will pimp you till your shit is dried up and you have nothing else to give. No man doesn't want a used-up ho. I'm scared, Starr, because when my time is up, what's next for me? Retirement? A pension? I have nothing to look forward to. I had three miscarriages, and I can't have anymore kids. I was pregnant with Rome's child once, and he made me get rid of it. Now my insides are so fucked up, and this lifestyle has prevented me to give birth to a child of my own. . . . You want kids, Starr?"

"Yeah."

"Well, my advice to you is get yours and bounce. Don't end up like me; you still have a chance, baby girl."

"Why are you telling me this?" Starr asked.

"*Because I see a lot of you in me. I was like you* when I was young. I was Rome's favorite bitch. I was his boo. I used to bring in so much money for my daddy that I became his bottom bitch. And I see how Rome looks at you, you're becoming his favorite. And soon he's gonna replace me wit' you, because you're bringin' in what I used to bring in for him. My clientele is diminishing and my money is becoming less and less every night. And when you don't bring in his quota every night, this is what happens to you," Dynasty said, pointing to her eye, the one that was healing.

Starr gazed at Dynasty. She was quiet, listening to her like an attentive young child.

"These streets are no joke, Starr. It ain't the same anymore. Niggahs wanna kill each other over some pussy, and the tricks are always trying to get over on you. They always wanna pay you less for more. They don't know how to treat a bitch anymore. Too many young niggahs tryin' to be pimps, and don't even know the first thing about pimpin'. I've been selling pussy since I was twelve, and I've seen many young girls come and go. Some end up locked up for their pimps, and some end up being murdered in this game, either by a trick or their pimps. My best friend, Sherrill, was murdered by her pimp ten years ago. He thought that she would leave him to go work for another pimp, and he stabbed my girl forty times.

"You heard about Royal?" Dynasty continued.

"I haven't seen her around," Starr said.

"They kidnapped that bitch."

Starr's eyes widened. "Who?"

"Reality told her not to go out, but she needed to make that money to feed her kids. Now niggahs got at her, forced her into the trunk of a car and drove off."

"Ohmygod," Starr exclaimed, shocked.

"It's gettin' dangerous out there, Starr. I see so much more in you than this. And I understand, I was in your same situation when I was young. You ran away from home to escape the abuse, the beatings, and you were constantly being mistreated. But let me pull your coat to something. Did you actually escape the abuse by coming here? It's the same thing, and even worse. My father couldn't stay off of me every night. I got pregnant by him and had a miscarriage two months later. I was only eleven at the time. Like you, I ran away from home and stayed over at an older guy's house, and he used me for sex. I got turned on by it, and been selling my pussy in the streets since I was twelve. I never had a boyfriend. I don't even know what it's like to fall in love wit' a man. All I know is having him climb on top of me to do his business and paying me for my services. I don't even come anymore, and my pussy, I gotta rub lubrication on it, that's how I get wet for these tricks. Don't any man want a woman who can't get aroused or wet for him. I'm so used up, Starr, that this game is all I got left. I have nothing else goin' on for me."

As Dynasty talked to Starr, her tone was gloomy, even hurt. For her it was too late, and she felt there was nothing more for her. So she tried to advise and help Starr, make sure she didn't end up making the same mistakes she had when she was young.

"Yo, Dynasty—bitch, come here!" she heard Rome shout.

Dynasty stood up and quickly went to see what her daddy wanted. Starr continued to sit at the edge of the bed, thinking about what Dynasty had told her. Starr didn't want to end up like her.

Starr abruptly heard Rome yelling at Dynasty from the kitchen, and then Dynasty let out a loud shriek. She went over to the door and looked over at Rome choking Dynasty, with her robe on the floor. Dynasty was in tears as she gazed at Rome with fear in her eyes. Starr wondered what was Rome's beef with her now. It seemed as if Dynasty had had to walk on eggshells around Rome the past few weeks.

Rome glared at Starr, and shouted, "Bitch, mind your fuckin' business. Get your ass back in that bedroom before you make me upset, too!"

Starr obeyed his orders and quickly went back into the bedroom and shut the door behind her. She continued to hear Dynasty's terrifying cries as Rome beat her.

Reality walked into the apartment with another man and stumbled on Rome reprimanding one of his bitches. Reality watched Rome assault Dynasty for a few seconds, and then said, "Rome, we need to talk."

Rome stopped, looked at Reality, and asked, "About what?"

"They found Royal," he said.

"What?"

"They found her naked and dead in Baisley Park last night," Reality informed him.

Rome's tight grip around Dynasty loosened, shocked by the sudden news of one of his best girls murdered. He wasn't sad, he was furious. They murdered Royal, who was always coming to him with her money correct. Royal had been with Rome's camp for eighteen months and that was his product that they took away from him.

"Get the fuck out my face, Dynasty!" Rome said loudly, clearly upset.

Dynasty moved from his sight quickly with tears in her eyes. But they weren't tears of pain that Rome inflicted on her earlier, they were about hearing that her friend Royal was murdered.

"Yo, Reality, soldier up. I'm 'bout to be on some extermination shit wit' this niggah Yung Slim," Rome barked.

Dynasty ran crying into the bedroom where Starr sat, her bottom lip trickling blood, her right eye slightly bruised, and naked again.

"Dynasty, you okay?" Starr asked.

Dynasty looked at Starr and proclaimed the depressing news that Reality had relayed to Rome. "They found Royal, she's dead," Dynasty cried out.

Starr cupped her hand over her mouth, shocked by what she just heard. "Royal?"

"Yeah. They found her naked in Baisley Park last night," she informed Starr.

"Ohmygod," Starr cried out.

A short while later, Reality walked into the bedroom and instructed the two girls to get dressed. Even though they had suffered a loss in the crew, money still needed to be made. Both girls felt reluctant to turn tricks after hearing about their girl Royal being murdered. But the men didn't care. Now that they were short one girl, that just meant all the other hoes had to step their game up even more to cover Royal's share.

At that moment Starr knew she needed to get out of the game.

28

Eric quickly pulled up to his uncle's house and dashed up the steps. He was very upset about Rahmel's death. He knew his cousin had set up the hit. He wanted revenge, but felt conflicted. Rahmel was his boy from way back, though. He banged on the door, and Uncle Pumpkin answered with an irate look on his face.

"Boy, you crazy, knockin' on my door like you the police or something," his uncle barked.

"Where is she?" Eric asked, hurrying by him and into the house.

"She's upstairs in one of the bedrooms," his uncle said.

Eric ran upstairs to see River. She was lying in bed, watching TV in some sweats and a T-shirt.

"Baby, pack your shit, I'm gettin' you out of here," Eric said.

River looked surprised, and asked, "Why?"

"I can't explain to you, but something terrible just went down, and you need to bounce while I handle things."

"Eric, calm down. I can't leave yet. I still have business here in Queens," she explained.

"It's too dangerous here for you, for everyone. You still have that three-eighty, right?" he replied.

River nodded.

"Good, keep that wit' you at all times," he told her.

"Eric, you're scaring me. What you about to do?" River nervously asked.

Eric stared at River, knowing it wasn't wise to tell her the truth. The sudden death of both his friends, back to back, put him in a zone, and Eric honestly didn't know what he was capable of doing.

"Become more like my father, if I need to, to survive out here," he finally admitted.

"So you gonna become a murderer like you father?" Pumpkin asked, coming up the stairs.

"Uncle Pumpkin, they just murdered Rahmel and his wife. He's dead!" Eric cried out.

"Damn!" Pumpkin said, his face sad.

"Russell is trippin', he's on some other shit right now, there ain't no talkin' sense to him, Uncle Pumpkin. And he's at war wit' Rome," Eric said.

"Baby, I'm with you," River said. "But before I leave, I need to find my baby sister. I know she's still alive and close. I can feel her in my heart."

Eric sighed.

"You're not built for this game, Eric. You're not like your father, or your cousins. You have a heart. You're smart. You still have a chance to do right with your life. I'm sorry about your friends, but there's nothing you can do for them now. You can't go up against Russell or Rome," Pumpkin explained.

"I just can't take this shit anymore, Uncle Pumpkin. Ever since Russell got out, it's been hell."

"That boy will always be the devil," Pumpkin proclaimed. "But don't go crazy on me, boy. Keep a level head. You gotta start thinkin' straight."

"I know, Uncle Pumpkin."

"How much money you got on you right now?"

"About thirty grand. But I can get more by tomorrow night. I got a deal set up," Eric informed him.

"This is what you continue to do, keep a low profile, act like you don't know about anything. Do not go out and get revenge for both of your friends' murders. You have a beautiful woman by your side, boy. We gotten a chance to talk while you were out running your errands, and y'all do look good together. She's got a good head on her shoulder. She told me everything."

"Everything?" Eric inquired.

"Everything about how y'all met. She's real, Eric. And there aren't too many women out there that will come clean like she did. It's a bold and risky move, but she's real," Pumpkin said. "Now you make your deal, and be careful about it. You got so many snakes in the grass that you can't trust anybody. And when you do, you leave town with her, and don't come back. Sooner or later, everything's gonna work itself out, and when it does, you don't need to be around for that, Eric. Take River and run. Start a new life together."

River stood in the background listening. She liked his uncle, he was so cool, street smart, and down-to-earth.

"I told your father the same thing once, when everything started boiling over. But he wouldn't listen to me. I told him to take you and his wife and leave town, but he was arrogant and wouldn't listen to me. Your father never ran from anything or anyone," Pumpkin informed him. "That's what got him killed that day."

Eric stood, listening to his uncle speak about his father. The day he saw his father murdered was still fresh in his mind—the blood and the screams.

Pumpkin continued, "Eric, I don't ever want to see you go out like your father. And you're not a killer. You can start a new and better generation for this family. We have this black cloud over our names about being gangsters and killers. You can change that by taking your woman and raising a family far from this. Look at your cousin Francine, follow in her footsteps."

Eric understood where his uncle was coming from. And he wanted a change too. He'd wanted out a long time ago.

"I understand you, Uncle Pumpkin," Eric replied.

Suddenly his cell phone went off, it was his Brooklyn connection. He talked for a few minutes, hung up, and then said to River and his uncle, "I gotta go handle this deal. I promise you, Uncle Pumpkin, it's my last. I'm out. I'm done wit' the game."

Pumpkin smiled and gave his nephew a hug. "Thank you for listening. You have a chance."

River went up to him and embraced him passionately. She gave him a deep kiss, and said, "Remember when I told you I have faith. I know this is meant to be, for us to have a better life. We were both meant to meet, even though it was under such critical circumstances. But I believe God brought us together for a reason. And I know He will not take you away from me so soon."

"I'm coming back," Eric promised her.

They hugged and kissed one last time, and River followed him to the door.

"You still strap?" his uncle asked.

Eric nodded.

"Only use it if you're in a life-or-death situation," Pumpkin said.

Eric nodded.

He walked outside, but he was unaware of the eyes that were glued to him. Twinkie sat alone parked a few cars down, staking out the house. Meanwhile, Critter was parked across the street in a tinted Honda Accord, trying to observe his friend's movements. He wanted to know what Eric was hiding and he soon found out when he saw River standing in the doorway, giving Eric a hug and kiss good-bye.

"Damn, E . . . bitches always made you weak. And you thought I was the one that was always trippin' over some pussy," Critter proclaimed to himself.

Critter had gone over to Eric's apartment a few times, but he was never home. So being Eric's best friend, he knew where Eric would be resting his head, knowing he was safe, and that was at his uncle's place.

Critter and Twinkie both watched Eric get into his Scion and drive off. Twinkie got on his phone and called up Red to inform him what had happened.

Critter got on his phone and called up Yung Slim. He hated to give him the news about his cousin, but he'd made a vow to Yung Slim and the crew never to keep secrets from anyone.

Yung Slim sat at the edge of the bed peering at the wall, being deep in his thoughts, with a cigarette in his hand. He had his cousin on his mind. He was naked in room 425 at the Holiday Inn. The pussy was still the same, even better. They spent the night together, rekindling their affair.

Yung Slim turned around and looked down at the naked parole officer Karen as she still slept. They'd been fucking a few weeks after he got out, and Yung Slim loved her because she took it in the ass, swallowed his kids and everything. Too bad she was now his parole officer. If it hadn't been for his wifey, Sherry, Yung Slim would have married Karen.

But Karen/Meeka was already married, and, he found out, to a fellow parole officer. He smirked, knowing her husband put the ring on her finger but her heart and pussy still belonged to him.

As he sat smoking a cigarette and peering at the wall, he heard his cell phone go off on the table. He got up and checked the call. It was Critter.

"What up?"

"Slim, I don't know what to say to you . . . but your cousin is resting his head over at your uncle's crib," Critter informed him.

"And?"

"And he got that bitch that had him set up stayin' over there, too," he went on.

"My fuckin' cousin is a joke sometimes," Slim exclaimed.

"But yo, I think he's being watched," Critter added.

"Why?"

"I peeped this Maxima parked in front of his crib fo' a minute. I don't know if it's her peoples or five-0.

"Ayyite, I'm 'bout to come out there. I need to have a one-on-one talk wit' my uncle anyway," Yung Slim said.

"You want me to stay parked?"

"Yeah."

Yung Slim hung up and walked back over to the bed. Karen was just beginning to wake. She peered up at Yung Slim and smiled.

"What time is it?" she asked in a drowsy voice.

"Time to get that naked ass up and do a niggah right," Yung Slim joked.

Karen smiled up at him, reminiscing about last night. He had a big dick and knew how to make her come all over the place.

"You know if the job ever found out I was fuckin' you, it would be over for me," she said.

"That's ayyite, 'cuz you know I would take care of you."

He rubbed her legs as he stared at her.

"Listen, baby . . . I need a favor from you again," he said.

"A favor like what?" she asked, rising up.

"Information about a few individuals that need to be taken care of," he mentioned.

"I'm listening."

"There's five grand for you, if you can do this for me," he continued.

Karen looked hesitant at first, but returned Yung Slim's gaze, and said, "Murder?"

"You don't need to know all that. All you need to know is I'm payin' you healthy for the information you attain for me."

"You got names?"

"Rome and Reality."

Karen nodded. "I got you."

"That's my bitch," Yung Slim said as he climbed on top of her.

Karen positioned herself on her back again, opening her legs, and allowed him to enter as she let out a moan, feeling his hard dick opening her up. She was still in love with him, and even though she worked in law enforcement and was married to another parole officer, that street was still inside of her. She loved the thrill and excitement Yung Slim aroused in her. She'd hidden her feelings for thugs and the streets behind a badge for so long, and it took Yung Slim to bring the hood out of her again.

Eric went to meet Snowman, his drug connection, at his Long Island establishment. It was a local bar in Hempstead that was frequented by thugs and gangsters. Eric only came once a month to link up with Snowman for his drugs, but besides that, it wasn't worth coming to the place for any reason. He always got bad vibes when he showed up.

Eric walked around to the back of the establishment near an alley and was greeted by Sneak, a soldier blocking the entrance to the back door.

"Yo, I'm here to see Snowman," Eric told him.

Sneak, who was tall and stocky, sported a tight wifebeater and a visible .45 tucked in his waistband. He glared at Eric for a moment and then got on the horn and called the visit in downstairs.

"Let him in," a voice came through from the horn.

"Ayyite," Sneak replied. He then looked at Eric and said, "Niggah, you know the routine, throw them arms up."

"Yo, Sneak, why we always gotta go through this?" Eric said.

"Because, niggah, I don't trust y'all Jamaica, Queens, niggahs," Sneak quickly replied.

Eric sighed and spread his arms to get searched. "I ain't never packin' when I come here. You know that, niggah."

"So what. Better safe than sorry," Sneak said as he patted Eric down, checking for weapons.

When he was satisfied, Sneak let Eric past. Eric gave Sneak an unpleasant glance and walked in.

"Fuck you too, niggah!" Sneak mumbled under his breath.

Eric slowly walked down the dimly lit stairs into the basement. They creaked with every step he took. He was always uneasy when he came to see Snowman. He was aware of his notorious reputation and knew one false move with the Snowman and they'd find pieces of him in ten different zip codes. He and his family had been in business with Snowman for years, and it had been good so far.

Snowman was a stocky black male who sported a thick grizzled beard, bald head, and had very menacing features. He was like Suge Knight, always had a lit cigar in his hand. He mostly sported expensive suits, or sweatsuits, he was rarely seen in jeans or T-shirts. He was in his early fifties and had been in the game for a long time—so long, that he was a major drug distributor in the northeastern seaboard. Eighty-five percent of the drugs on the streets probably came through from the Snowman.

Eric walked into his basement office after passing about seven armed guards and some loose women who were playing a game of pool and flirting with the men.

"Mr. Beaumont," Snowman called out, seeing Eric walking into his office. "Keeping the family business going as usual."

Eric nodded.

Snowman was clad in a three-piece gray pinstripe suit, had a cigar clutched in his hand, a gray derby on his head, and sported $15,000 worth of diamonds and jewelry on his wrists, fingers, ears, and even in his mouth. He had a brown-skinned bitch in a tight miniskirt seated on a corner couch, playing around with her nails.

"How you doin', Snowman?" Eric greeted.

"Every day I'm alive and out of jail is a good day for me, baby," Snowman replied. "What brings you back around here? A re-up, I assume."

Eric nodded.

"You bring me good business, Eric. I always liked you and your family. You come from good peoples. You lucky I knew your father, that muthafucka was a born gangsta. You definitely come from good genes. And your cousin, I'm hearing about him on the streets already. That boy ain't been out less than two months now and he's already making a name for himself again. Now I see more of your father in him than I do in you. You sure y'all wasn't switched at birth?" Snowman joked.

Eric let out a slight chuckle.

Snowman's presence was solid and very intimidating. The way he would look at people made them feel that they had screwed up sometimes, even though they could be as innocent as a mouse.

"What you need from me this time, Eric? The same as usual?"

"Nah, I got kind of a larger order this time," Eric proclaimed. He walked up to Snowman, pulled out an envelope filled with cash, and tossed it on his desk. "That's the ten grand I owe you from before. It's all there."

Snowman picked up the cash and went through it real quick. He then nodded at Eric.

"How large?" he asked.

"Ten pounds of that Purple Haze, and four keys," Eric said.

"That's not your speed, Eric. Why the change?" Snowman asked.

"Clientele," Eric explained.

Snowman stared at Eric for a moment, feeling him out. Snowman was contemplating making the sale.

"C'mere," Snowman called out, indicating for Eric to come closer with his two fingers.

Eric moved in closer toward his desk, and Snowman leaned in more toward Eric with the palm of his hands rooted flatly against his desk.

Snowman looked at Eric and then asked, "This clientele, it's the same, or did you suddenly switch up on me?"

"The same guy I've been dealin' wit' for the past year," Eric admitted.

"And all of a sudden, this man stepped up his game for more products. You ever asked yourself why?" Snowman said.

"Honestly, no," Eric admitted.

"You trust this deal?"

Eric hesitated before answering. "Yeah."

Snowman got quiet, thinking about something. He then peered at Eric, and advised, "When a man switch up on you so sudden, you gotta ask yourself why. What's his motive . . . his routine? Has he been gone for a long time or not? Ask yourself these questions. I don't trust that shit, Eric. You be careful. I've been a free man for a long time, and I plan to die a free man."

"I understand," Eric said.

Suddenly Snowman's expression changed dramatically. He glared at Eric, and warned, "If you do this deal, and if it don't come out right, you keep my fuckin' name out your mouth. You fuckin' hear me?"

Eric nodded.

"I'm gonna give you what you need, only because I know your family and who your father was. But niggah, if you fuckin' cross me, I swear to my kids, the only things that will find your body is the rats and maggots as they nibble away at you one day at a time."

"I understand, Snowman," Eric returned.

Snowman then looked at his young lady friend on the couch, and instructed her, "Peaches, bring Moe into my office."

Peaches nodded, got off the couch, and walked out of the office, pulling down her skirt as she exited.

Snowman took a seat in his expensive leather chair and peered up at Eric. "Our deal is the same as before—points and everything. You and your cousin are the only men I give product to on consignment, because y'all always come correct with my money."

A short moment later, Peaches entered the room with Moe right behind her. Moe was tall and stocky like Sneak, with long dreads reaching down to his back.

"Moe, you know what's up. Supply our friend here with ten pounds of PH and four keys," Snowman instructed.

Moe nodded and walked out of the office.

"Eric, you know the routine," Snowman said. "You'll pick your stuff up in a half."

Eric nodded.

"I hope you know what you're doing, I always liked you more than your cousin. You're smart. Your cousin brings too much attention to himself," Snowman said before Eric left the office.

Eric quickly left the building and got into his Scion and drove about ten miles. He parked at the assigned destination where he always picked up his product.

He waited for about fifteen minutes near an empty park, until he noticed headlights approaching behind him. Snowman never supplied any drugs in his building, or did any transactions. Customers had to link up somewhere far away and that's where the transaction took place.

Two men were in the car, but only one got out. Eric stayed seated and watched from his rearview mirror. The passenger of the car walked around to the trunk of their car and removed a small duffle bag. Eric unlatched the back of his Scion as the man approached his ride. The man dropped the bag in the back, tapped on the window, indicating delivery of the product, walked back to his car, and then they drove off.

Eric drove away right after, satisfied with the transaction.

29

Two black Denalis drove slowly down the block and stopped where Critter was parked watching the home for the longest time.

The driver's-side window rolled down and Yung Slim leaned over the driver, and asked, "They still parked?"

"Yeah, I think there's two in the car. A stout light-skinned niggah," Critter told him.

Yung Slim nodded.

"You think they police?" Critter asked.

"Listen, this is what I want y'all to do. Tell Tango and Rob to roll around the block, and tell them to stay parked at the end of the block. And on my orders, open fire on them muthafuckas. But only on my orders," Yung Slim instructed.

"Ayyite," the driver said.

Yung Slim, Critter, and an unknown soldier approached the house.

Big Red and Twinkie gazed at the two black trucks that drove down the block and wondered what was up. Too much activity was going on around the house they were watching and targeting.

Twinkie looked at Red, and asked, "You want me to call it in?"

"Nah, not yet. We might have something here," Big Red said.

Twinkie shrugged and continued to watch three men walk to the house.

Pumpkin heard a loud knock at his door and wondered who it could be. River was in the living room, and her heart jumped, thinking something was about to go wrong.

Pumpkin glanced outside through the blinds and was shocked when he saw his nephew Russell and Critter standing outside his door.

He turned to River, and said, "Go hide upstairs. I'll take care of this."

He watched River dash upstairs and then slowly opened his front door to his nephew. Russell flashed a quick smile at his uncle, and said, "It's been a long time, Uncle Pumpkin."

His uncle stared at him.

"I don't get a hug or sumthin?" Russell exclaimed.

Pumpkin let out a faint smile and gave his nephew a hug, and reluctantly invited him and his friends in.

"Nice place, Uncle Pumpkin. A bit cluttered, but you always made do, ain't that right?" Russell said.

"What finally brings you around to see me?" Pumpkin asked.

"I was in the neighborhood and decided to stop by. You don't miss me?"

"You've been out for almost two months now, Russell. So what you been up too?" Pumpkin asked, walking near the kitchen.

"Don't act like you don't know what I'm about, Unc . . . what our family always been about. Money," Russell proclaimed, as he followed his uncle to the kitchen.

Critter and the other man took a seat near the door, listening to the two talk.

"And Critter, you come into my home and don't have the manners to say hi. Shit, I remember when my wife used to change your diapers every morning," Pumpkin said.

"How you doin', Mr. Pumpkin?" Critter greeted him.

Pumpkin let out a slight cough as he messed around in the kitchen.

"You're gettin' sick and old on me, Uncle Pumpkin?" Russell asked.

"I'm gettin' better every day," he countered.

Russell smiled.

Pumpkin stared at his nephew clad in diamond jewelry, Timberlands, baggy jeans, and a throwback jersey. "You look good, Russell."

"Like you, every day I'm gettin' better."

"Better comes with becoming wiser," Pumpkin said.

"Learning more about black folks every day."

"So honestly, what brings you around here to come see an old man all of a sudden?" Pumpkin asked.

"You're family, Uncle Pumpkin, right?" Russell said.

"Yeah."

"And family doesn't keep secrets from one another. Family supposed to be tight, and always have each other backs. Why you never came to see me while I was locked down?"

"I've seen enough prison in my times, Russell. And coming to visit you would be no different," Pumpkin replied.

"No letters, nothing. . . . You and the rest of the family left me in there to rot, thinking I would never come home again," Russell said.

"If you came for an apology, then you won't get it from me," Pumpkin told his nephew.

"I'm not lookin' for an apology. I'm lookin' for the truth," Russell returned.

"Truth?" Pumpkin laughed.

"You ashamed of me, Uncle Pumpkin?"

"You should be asking yourself that question when you look in a mirror every day. You got the game twisted, Russell. Look at you—" Pumpkin started.

"Yeah, look at me, Uncle Pumpkin!" Russell shouted. "I'm continuing on with our generation, something that you and your brothers helped build. Now I'm the new! The strong! I'm the man in the streets, and I'm gettin' what's owed to me, even if it means spilling blood."

"You're a fool, that's what you are, Russell. This ain't about power. You wouldn't know the first thing about power. My brothers and I, we had power in the streets. We knew how to control things, and we were well respected. We took care of our own, and they took care of us," Pumpkin proclaimed.

"You're a washed-up old fool who got scared of the game and became a fuckin' truck driver," Russell countered. "You weren't nuthin' like your brothers. They went out shooting, they went out wit' dignity. You, what you have to show . . . Nuthin'."

"I'm alive and I'm free. I'm the richest out of all of them," Pumpkin said.

Russell snickered. "Free! You call this free? Your wrinkled old ass ain't free. You stay dusting away in this junk of a place you call home every day, this ain't free. This is living scared. You're running away from what you used to be. You can't hang like Uncle Omar and Uncle Mike. You're the biggest pussy out of all your brothers."

"Niggah, don't you come in my home disrespecting me and this family's name, because you don't know the first thing about being a gangsta or respect. You think running around here making noise for yourself is supposed to make you tough. You're a bitch niggah inside. It ain't always about the gun. You know, Russell, when I look at you, I see this scared, powerless little boy like when you were young, five years old, and you were afraid of your own shadow. I remember a scared eight-year-old boy running home to mama trying to escape bullies, hiding behind his uncles. Your mother would be spinning in her grave if she saw how her own flesh-and-blood son came out. You're running this family's name into the ground with the continuous drugs and bloodshed you advocate on the streets. I woke up from that a long time ago, and it's too bad you can't do the same. You're still that insecure and powerless little—"

"That's enough, old man!" Russell shouted as he pulled out a Glock and pointed it at Pumpkin's head. "You're family to me, but you keep disrespecting me and I won't hesitate to blow your brains out on that kitchen floor. Now, enough of the games and our little family reunion. Where's the bitch?"

"I'm alone," Pumpkin replied.

"Uncle Pumpkin, don't play wit' me. I know that bitch that robbed Eric is up in here. We just wanna talk to her."

"And your version of talk is having a gun pointed at my head," Pumpkin commented.

"Fuck it! Yo, Link, you and Critter search this dump and find that bitch," he instructed.

Link and Critter started searching from room to room while Russell remained in the kitchen.

"You will never learn, will you, boy? Your cousin is happy. It's not your fuckin' business! He already forgave her, so why can't you?" Pumpkin asked.

"Because that bitch and her crew disrespected him and me. I gotta be the one to uphold this family's notorious reputation, even if means killing that bitch,'cuz you and my bitch cousin aren't man enough to do it. And you know me, Uncle Pumpkin; I'm crazy enough to do it, too. I ain't that scared little boy anymore, running behind you and Yung Black."

Pumpkin stared tensely at his nephew as he slowly moved himself near the kitchen drawer, trying to retrieve a hidden loaded single-action .22 caliber.

"It's a new day for me, Uncle Pumpkin," Russell exclaimed.

Critter ran upstairs moving aimlessly from bedroom to bedroom searching for River with a .380 gripped in his hand. He turned over furniture and kicked down doors, but his heart was saddened by his actions, because this was Uncle Pumpkin's crib, and his family had practically raised him when he was young. But he was on a mission. Yung Slim was on the rise, and he wanted to be his right hand.

"Yo, I can't find this bitch, Slim!" Critter shouted.

"Keep lookin' . . . that bitch is hiding in here somewhere," Yung Slim shouted back.

"C'mon, Uncle Pumpkin, just tell us where the bitch is at and we can make this easy," Slim said.

But Pumpkin remained quiet as he slowly gripped his weapon discreetly.

Critter went into the last possible room she could be in, and as he walked in—*Whack!* He got hit upside his head with a broomstick. Critter screamed out as he fell back, squeezing two shots off in the air.

River ran past him and darted down the stairs, but ran into Link, who smacked her across her face, dropping her to the ground.

"What the fuck?" Yung Slim exclaimed as he turned his head.

"You'll never learn, Russell," Pumpkin shouted as he sprang into action and pointed his gun at Russell.

Russell turned around, shocked. "Uncle Pumpkin, you fuckin' crazy or what?! You don't even know this bitch!"

"Let her go, Russell!" Pumpkin shouted.

River struggled to get free from Link's tight grip. Critter came down the stairs clutching his face, visibly upset over the sudden attack on him. He stared at River, and said, "You a feisty fuckin' bitch!"

Smack! Critter hit River like she was a man.

"Fuck you!" River spat back.

Suddenly everyone's eyes were focused on the showdown between Yung Slim and his uncle.

"Uncle Pumpkin, I didn't come here to hurt you . . . but are you ready to give your life for this bitch? She had Eric set up and beat, and right now, she got two men parked outside your front door, and she's setting you up, too," Yung Slim proclaimed.

"Is not for you to judge, Russell. It's his life and that's his woman. And I promised to protect her," Pumpkin replied, slowly moving toward his nephew with the gun gripped in his hand. "He wants to change, and you won't allow it."

"Niggah, is you fuckin' serious? Yo, take that bitch outside and put her in the fuckin' truck," Yung Slim instructed. "Uncle Pumpkin, I'm gonna show you power. Critter, make the call."

"Russell, I said no!" Pumpkin shouted.

Big Red and Twinkie were still parked outside waiting to see what was transpiring.

Twinkie looked at Red, and said, "You know we gotta kill this bitch. She can link us to too many things. And I ain't goin' down for a bitch, Red."

Big Red nodded. "I already got everything planned out. We about to retire from this game after we pull off one more big score."

Suddenly both men heard distant shots coming from the house.

"Ah, shit, they shooting!" Twinkie shouted.

"Call it in!" Red shouted, leaping from his unmarked car.

As Red stepped out of the car with his Glock gripped in his hand he noticed from his peripheral vision a figure coming quickly toward them. But before he could turn, multiple rounds were fired into the car striking Twinkie in his chest as he was about to exit the vehicle.

"Twinkie!" Red screamed, taking cover as he shot back.

Boom! Boom! Boom! Boom! Boom! Red hit the man point-blank five times.

"Twinkie—Twinkie, answer me!" Red cried out. He got on the horn and exclaimed, "Officer down! I repeat, officer down at One Hundred Forty-Seventh Street and One Hundred Twentieth Avenue!"

Red then turned and noticed two men leaving the building, carrying River as a hostage. He ran over, and shouted, "Freeze, NYPD!"

"What the fuck!" Critter shouted.

River was shocked, staring at Red's face. "You're a cop?"

"I said put the guns down, now!"

"Fuck you!" Link shouted, and opened fired, but he missed and was quickly mowed down by Red's Glock.

Yung Slim came out and he and a few other soldiers opened fire at Red. Red quickly took cover, hoping backup would arrive soon.

"Get in the truck!" Yung Slim shouted.

He grabbed River by her hair and dragged her to the truck as he continued shooting at Officer Gibson, a.k.a. Big Red. Critter quickly got in the driver's seat and pulled away hastily.

"Shit! Shit! Shit!" Red cried out as he peered over at his partner of five years who was slumped out of the car with his gun still gripped in his hand. "Damn, Twinkie."

"Who the fuck are you! You police, too, bitch?" Slim shouted, pointing the gun at River.

"No!" River cried out.

"Shit! Yo, Slim, we just killed a cop, they gonna be all over us," Critter exclaimed nervously.

"Fuck that cop! I'm gonna take care of this," Yung Slim snapped, pulling out his cell phone.

"Snowman," Yung Slim greeted.

"Yung Slim, it's always good doin' business with both Beaumonts in one day," Snowman proclaimed.

"What you mean by that, Snowman?" Yung Slim asked.

"Your cousin just left here a few hours ago with some purchase. I assume you're well aware about our business dealings for the past year now," Snowman said.

"Fuckin' snake. I told that niggah no outside business," Yung Slim barked.

Snowman chuckled at Slim's remark. "A small family feud between the two cousins, I assume."

"Nuthin' that I can't take care of. But some shit just went down between me and some cops. It's really bad. You owe me, Snowman. I need this taken care of," Slim said.

"You're too hot, Slim. I'm hearing about you through all my peoples on the streets. You're at war with Rome. Why couldn't you let the boy be?"

"Snowman, you and my family go way back. I need this taken care of. You gonna leave me out to dry? After the tons of money I've made for you over the years, even while I was locked down. I ran that prison for you, don't forget that. I'm a commodity to you, Snowman. You need me as much as I need you."

"Young blood, I don't need anyone. I've been in this game long before your daddy even thought about fuckin' your mama," Snowman replied. "But I owe you, and I never forget about friends. Come to the warehouse tonight."

"I'll be there."

After Yung Slim hung up, he turned to River, and said, "You and my cousin are some snake-ass muthafuckas . . . y'all probably do deserve each other."

"Where we headed to, Slim?" Critter asked, pushing the Denali to sixty down the Conduit.

"To see the Snowman," he replied.

Hearing that name made Critter extremely nervous.

As Yung Slim beefed with River, his phone went off again. It was Karen this time.

"Hey, baby," she greeted him.

"You got that info for me, boo?" Yung Slim asked.

"You know I got you. I got Reality's info. His real name is Bobby Johnson, and his family resides in Queens. He was paroled four years ago. Rome has a younger brother in Brooklyn, a crack dealer who goes by the name Sleepy," Karen informed him.

"Damn, you're good, baby. That's why I love you. Didn't I tell you I was gonna look out for you? I got what I owe you plus a little extra."

Karen smiled and continued to feed Yung Slim information she had obtained discreetly from the files and computers at her workplace.

An hour later, the block was flooded with marked and unmarked cars, even Emergency Service Unit vehicles blocked off the street. Uniformed officers canvassed the area, as detectives and Crime Scene Unit personnel looked for witnesses and tested for forensic evidence at the crime scene. And above their heads, a police helicopter surveyed the entire neighborhood with its blinding blue spotlight in search of a black Denali truck. They had a dead cop on their hands, and that meant all the toys came out in searching for the suspects responsible.

Red kept his composure as he gave scant details to the police captain about what had transpired. He told the captain that he and Officer Steward got a lead from an informant about drugs and guns being moved out of the house that they were staking out. He explained that they got a lead on a deal happening, and were watching everything go down until something bad happened and he informed his superiors that two suspects came out shooting. But he neglected to give his fellow officers a vivid description of the suspects who fled the scene in a black Denali. His excuse was that it happened too quickly for him to give accurate information. He was nervous about River. She now knew his true identity as a New York City cop, and he feared she might snitch on him if captured.

Red was an extremely dirty cop. He'd been on the force for seven years, and had hidden behind his badge and gun the majority of his career, robbing drug dealers and scheming to get money.

Three men were dead, including Officer Steward, the suspect who fired four rounds into the cop's chest, and the owner of the house, Ronny Pumpkin Beaumont.

The captain looked at Officer Gibson and the other officers, and exclaimed, "I want a full investigation into this case. I want to know why one of my officers is dead tonight. And why no one knows a fuckin' thing! I want every fuckin' rock turned over. I want every snitch, informant, or any niggah with an arrest record or priors picked up and questioned before dawn. I want this case closed and the men responsible processed on Riker's Island before I lay on top of my wife."

Everyone nodded and quickly got to work.

Red was furious. His partner and right-hand man was dead.

Eric pushed his Scion down the Conduit on his way to Brooklyn to meet up with his connection for a sale. Willie agreed to meet him at the same location on Logan Avenue, right off Atlantic Avenue.

Eric was unaware of what had occurred with Russell and his uncle a few hours before. His mind was focused on River's safety and trying to leave town in one piece after he made this deal with Willie.

He thought about Donald and Rahmel but stopped himself from getting too emotional. Donald had understood that he was in the game and that shit happens. But Rahmel was a civilian, and he had gotten his life right with God and his wife. Eric was furious that his death was so tragic and appalling.

"Fuck it, I'm gonna do this and I'm out," he told himself. "Fuck this family!"

As he drove, he thought of what River said to him about her younger sister, and ironically he suddenly remembered where he'd heard the name Starr before.

"Oh, shit!" he muttered, remembering that Starr was a sixteen-year-old girl that Critter had in his apartment a few months back.

He instantly knew he had to get at Critter to find out more information about Starr. He wanted to reunite River with her younger sister. And he thought to himself, it had to be fate for them to link up and for him to forgive her. The events that encircled them were too ironic.

He pulled up to the buildings on Logan Avenue and already noticed Willie's car parked in front. Eric stepped out, removed the duffle bag from the backseat, and headed toward the entrance. Before he went inside, he canvassed the area around him, looking for anything unfamiliar. Snowman's words about walking into a setup made him nervous. When he felt everything was okay, he proceeded into the building.

Willie was alone, as usual, waiting for Eric's arrival. He smiled and greeted Eric with a dap and hug.

"You never let me down, E. You got my stuff?" Willie asked.

"Let's make this quick," Eric said, passing Willie the duffle bag. "I got everything you asked for."

Willie smiled. He took the duffle bag and surveyed its contents quickly. "Eight pounds and four keys, it's always good doin' business wit' you, buddy," Willie said as he passed Eric the cash in return. "You're my number-one guy, E," Willie added.

Something in Willie's tone of voice made Eric nervous. Eric held Willie's gaze and knew something with this deal wasn't right.

Then suddenly there was a loud shattering sound and the doors to the room came crashing in and Eric heard the frightful sound of someone shouting, "Get down on the ground now! DEA! Get down! Get down! DEA!"

A dozen agents raided the place with their guns gripped tightly in their hands. Eric's heart dropped, and panic showed on his face. He had nowhere to run as he gawked at the agents charging on him with their guns trained at him.

Willie looked at Eric with a sad expression, and said, "I'm sorry, E . . . they had me in a tight squeeze."

Eric was then forced to the ground and handcuffed. He knew his life was over. He bowed his head and felt he'd failed his uncle, River, and himself. He'd managed to escape prison all his life, but now, being caught with the amount of drugs he had on him, Eric knew it would carry a sentence of up to twenty-five years in prison.

He went off with the agents peacefully.

A few hours later, Eric sat in a bare room, handcuffed to the chair and waiting patiently to be interrogated. He held back his tears and tried to keep his composure. He thought about a few lawyers he could call. He needed a really good lawyer. He couldn't believe Willie had snitched him out. They'd been in business with each other for a little over a year, and just like that, it was over.

Two DEA agents entered the room, and surprisingly, two FBI agents followed in right behind them with their IDs showing.

Ohmygod, Eric thought to himself.

One agent came over and uncuffed him from the chair. Eric massaged his wrist as he peered at the agent.

"I'm DEA Agent Merchant, and this is Agent Morris. To be blunt, you're fucked, Eric," Agent Merchant stated. He was a tall black man with dark hair who was clad in a flight jacket.

Eric stared at the two FBI agents across from him who had their IDs clipped to their dark suits and wore polished wing-tip shoes.

"The four keys alone are enough to put you in jail for life," Agent Morris stated. He was tall, too, with a bald head and a thick goatee.

"What y'all want from me?" Eric asked. "I know it's something, because we both know I wouldn't be wasting my time sitting in this room with four agents."

"You're a smart man, I assume," Agent Morris remarked. "We can help you."

"Listen, I'm not the one to dance around, but as you can see, the feds are involved in this too," Agent Merchant said. "Now, this can work out two ways for you. You can become very useful to us and tell us what we need to know, or you can sit there, be an asshole, and go to jail for a very long time. You have a choice."

"Why are the feds involved?" Eric asked.

"Listen, we ask the questions for now, not you," Agent Merchant sternly replied.

"Eric, it's not you we're after, you're just the poor sap in the middle of it all. We want your cousin Russell. Now, since he's been home, all hell done broke loose. Seven years ago, your cousin should have done life in prison, but unfortunately that didn't happen for us, and he's now a free man again, and trying to regain what he once lost," Agent Morris informed Eric. "We know he linked back up with his old crew, and we know about the war with a rival named Rome. These are dangerous men on the streets, and with your cooperation, you can help get them off the streets and in jail where they belong."

"This is my cousin we're talking about," Eric replied. "My family has never snitched on anyone."

"Are you ready to do heavy time for your family, huh, Eric?" Agent Merchant asked.

Eric remained silent, staring at Agent Merchant.

"Your family has a notorious history," Agent Morris chimed in. "Your father was Yung Black, and your uncle was once part of the Gorilla Black family. Damn! From generation to generation, it continues. You can put a stop to it. We're giving you a chance here, all you got to do is work with us and you can have your life back."

"Work with us and we promise you full immunity," Agent Merchant assured.

Eric let out a slight chuckle, shaking his head in disbelief. He was definitely set up. "Y'all are a piece of work. I was set up. Y'all have been watching me the entire time. Let me guess, you knew I was in business with Willie. Y'all bust him, get him to talk and have him fabricate some phony deal with me, and I fall for it, knowing it wasn't Willie's style to fuck wit' the keys. But I'm stupid enough to get caught up in it. I should have seen it coming. I'm your only link to my cousin, and this is the only way to have me snitch out on him . . . by having this heavy charge over my head. I feel pressure by the number of years I'm facing and suddenly take the easy way out," Eric said.

"See, I told you he was a smart man," Agent Morris stated.

Agent Merchant walked over to Eric, leaned in near him with his hands against the table, and said, "I really hope you're a smart man, because there's no other way out for you."

Eric sighed, looking pressured. No one in his family had ever snitched or taken the easy way out, and he was reluctant to do so.

But the agents kept pressuring him and pressuring him, scaring him with large sentences and life.

They got desperate, because they wanted Yung Slim with a hard-on, and even promised to put Eric in the witness protection program.

Agent Morris looked at Eric, and said, "Look, I know this man is your cousin, but he's not worth going to prison for. I look in your eyes Eric, and I see a nice guy . . . too nice of a guy to go to prison for a very long time. And I assume you know what they do with nice guys like you in prison, Eric."

"Tell us about your uncle," Agent Merchant said.

"What?"

"You really care for him, right?" Agent Merchant continued.

"Where we goin' wit' this?" Eric asked.

Agent Merchant nodded over to Morris and Morris dropped two glossy photos on the table in front of Eric. "I just received those from the NYPD a few hours ago. You know him?"

Eric stared in shock at the two photos of his dead uncle.

"He was shot twice in his chest not too long ago," Agent Morris informed him. "I had a friend in the department quickly develop them so you can see the truth about your family. Your cousin is responsible for that, Eric . . . and this is family to him, so you see how he does family."

"Yo, that's fucked up," Eric cried out, saddened by his uncle's murder. He then thought about River and feared for her safety.

"Was he alone?" Eric then asked.

"We have one witness who says they saw a group of young men carrying a woman out the door," Agent Morris mentioned.

Eric knew it had to be River.

"Work with us, Eric, that's all you have to do. . . . Work with us and we can make everything okay for you," Agent Merchant assured him.

Eric stared at the photos of his uncle once again and said to himself, *Enough is enough . . . this shit has got to stop. Fuck family*.

Eric nodded toward the DEA agents, giving them his full cooperation. They both smiled. But he wasn't in the clear yet. The feds stepped up, and they dropped another picture in front of Eric, and asked, "Do you know this man?"

Panic and fear engulfed Eric quickly as he stared at a picture of the Snowman.

"We've been investigating him for several years now and, unfortunately, we haven't been able to get a man in close enough to bring him down," one of the federal agents informed Eric. He was slim, curly-haired, and clean-shaven, with green eyes. "He goes by the name Snowman, and he's a major cocaine and heroin distributor in the northeastern seaboard. Does he supply you your drugs?"

Eric was hesitant to answer the question. He peered over at Agent Merchant, who simply shrugged, and said, "They want everything. You deal with us and you deal with them."

Eric felt himself getting pushed into a tight squeeze, and he remembered Snowman's dreadful words to him, "You get caught, keep my fuckin' name out your mouth."

Eric felt his heart pounding rapidly. He knew snitching out the Snowman wasn't just death alone, it was dismemberment and torture, and Eric knew not to take the Snowman's threat lightly.

"We need viable information on him and an inside man," the federal agent continued.

Eric contemplated the offer. River was heavy on his mind, and he loved her. He needed to get to her and her sister, and he knew that couldn't happen if he was locked away in a jail cell. For love, it was worth the risk. He agreed to work with the feds and the DEA, and became a snitch.

After signing papers and becoming an informant for the law enforcement, Eric was allowed to leave after spending several grueling, long hours in a downtown precinct. His nerves were shaky, but he felt he'd done what he had to do. He had a plan, though.

As Eric walked away from the building, and got a few blocks away a black Ford Taurus came to a sudden halt in front of him and out stepped Big Red/Officer Gibson. He sternly grabbed Eric by his shirt; twisting his arm and slamming him facedown on the hot hood of the Taurus.

"Where you goin', muthafucka?" Red shouted, pressing Eric's face against the hood.

"Aaaaaahhh, what the fuck y'all want from me?" Eric shouted.

"Your cousin a fuckin' cop killer!" Red exclaimed.

"I ain't got shit to do wit that—fuck you and my cousin," Eric harshly countered.

"What, niggah!"

"Fuck you!"

"I should have put a bullet in your ass a long time ago," Red shouted.

Suddenly his voice seemed familiar to Eric. He didn't have on the mask this time, and was without his partner. But Eric knew it was him.

"You're a cop?" Eric questioned. "Oh, shit!"

"Where is she?" Red asked.

"I don't fuckin' know. What do you want wit' her anyway?"

Red spun Eric around facing him. "I want that bitch."

"Fuck you!" Eric chided. "She's better off without your trifling ass. I hope she rats your crooked ass out, you fuckin' pig. You steal from me and think you can get away wit' it."

Red slammed Eric against the car again violently, and said, "Listen here, niggah, I'm the law, you fuckin' hear me? I take what I want. And you or that bitch ain't gonna stop me from gettin' mines."

"Yeah, whatever, niggah . . . I find River—and believe me, I will—I'm bringing your crooked ass down, and have the DA bring a case against you to the grand jury. You don't deserve that badge. You're a criminal, just like us."

"Fuck you! I find her, and your little girlfriend is dead and then you're fuckin' next! Don't fuck wit' me, niggah, I'm a cop, but you already know what I'm about!" Red exclaimed.

Red loosened his grip around Eric and stepped back. Eric smirked at the officer. He knew that Officer Gibson couldn't do any harm to him near the precinct building. And he also knew Red was looking for River, because she knew everything about him—she had too much dirt on his underground lifestyle, and her loose lips could sink his ship and put Red in jail for a very long time.

"See you around, Officer," Eric mocked as he slowly stepped away.

"Yeah, I'll definitely see you around!" Red remarked, shaking his head, knowing what had transpired with Eric and the feds in the building. "You'll get yours—fuckin' snitch!"

30

Who's the bitch?" Snowman asked Yung Slim as he approached with River.

"Collateral," Yung Slim replied.

"She's cute," Snowman stated.

Critter was not too far behind.

"I need you to clean this up for me," Yung Slim said.

"It's already done," Snowman replied.

Two men walked up to the parked Denali and got in, driving away in the truck. They had to burn it and get rid of any evidence and fingerprints.

"I talked to a few friends of mines down at One Police Plaza, so far the police don't have anything on you," Snowman informed them. "From now on, you need to keep a low profile, and stay the fuck away from Rome and his bitches." Snowman then drew on a cigar as he stared at Yung Slim.

Yung Slim laughed, and replied, "My hands are clean, Snowman." He threw up his arms in a joking manner. "I just might take the dogs for a walk, that's all, and maybe do a little spring cleaning—right, Critter?"

"Right, Slim," Critter responded, knowing what Yung Slim meant by that.

Everything was set. Yung Slim had made the call right after he'd spoken to Karen.

"Bitch, why you so late bringing me this muthafuckin' money? You know I gotta check in with Reality soon," Cash chided, scolding one of Rome's hoes about bringing in her earnings an hour late.

"I'm sorry, Cash, but this one trick was taking forever to come." Pepper replied. She was glued to the passenger seat and only spoke when she was spoken to.

"Bitch, you know the fuckin' rules, each trick only gets twenty minutes wit' you. If they don't come, you fuckin' leave, unless they're paying you extra to stay. Pepper, don't let this shit happen again," Cash threatened as he glared at her.

Pepper nodded meekly.

Cash was a ride-or-die soldier and had been in Rome's camp since the beginning. He sat parked in his burgundy Benz and counted money on the corner of 150th Street and 107th Avenue.

Pepper remained seated in her short denim skirt and was quiet as a mouse while Cash counted her share for the night. Rome let out a few girls to work the track, thinking it was safe for them to work and get that money. Rome had Cash and N.O. working security on the tracks and so far the night was going smoothly for everyone.

As Cash counted money, Pepper noticed a man coming toward them, but she really paid him no mind. He was dressed like one of the crack locals in the area. He was clad in tattered pants, dirty sneakers, and wore a long stained and ragged brown trench coat in the spring weather.

Pepper thought he was out of his mind and turned her attention elsewhere. Cash glanced up and saw the man, but ignored him, too. He thought that he was just a harmless crackhead.

As they sat in the Benz, the stranger approached the car. He discreetly reached into his coat and walked up to the driver's side.

"Yo, you got a light?" the stranger asked.

"Get the fuck away from my car, you dirty crackhead!" Cash screamed. "Fuck off!"

"Fuck you!" the man shouted back. He suddenly reached into his dirty trench coat and pulled out a double-barrel shotgun.

Cash was wide-eyed.

Boom! Bishop blew Cash's head clean off at close range, leaving a bloody mess all over the windshield, dashboard, seats, and even Pepper.

"*Aaaaaaaaaaaaahhhhh!*" Pepper screamed frantically, covered in Cash's blood with half his head in her lap.

Bishop stared at her with ice-cold eyes, raised his shotgun again and fired—*boom!* He air-conditioned her by putting a basketball-size hole in her chest.

Barnes pulled around the corner in a blue Chevy truck and Bishop got in on the passenger side and they quickly took off.

N.O. was blocks away when he heard the echo of the loud shotgun blast that killed his friend Cash, and Pepper.

Sleepy, who was Rome's younger brother, was chilling and smoking in a small Jamaican restaurant on Ralph Avenue with a few of his friends.

Sleepy was a notorious hustler in Brooklyn and fed off his older brother's reputation. He wasn't feared like his older brother, but he did have a reputation. He was accompanied by two of his friends in the place that night, and they joked and waited for their orders.

"Sleepy, what up wit' that bitch you met the other night, you gonna pass her on to me?" a friend of his joked.

"Fucked that bitch," Sleepy replied. "She ain't tryin' to fuck. Bitch pussy probably stank anyway." Clad in a throwback Chicago

Bulls jersey and Nike sneakers, he was sporting cornrows and wore platinum around his neck and wrist.

"Niggah, your game falling off. Let me find out, Sleepy," his other man said. He was leaning back in the chair, and noticed two thuggish-looking men entering the joint. He tapped Sleepy and gestured at the two. "Check it out."

Bishop and Barnes walked into the restaurant and focused their full attention on Sleepy, their eyes never leaving his. Both men had on black denim jackets and jeans, looking casual.

"What up? Your name Sleepy, right?" Barnes asked.

"Niggah, do I fuckin' know you?" Sleepy responded harshly, glaring at Barnes and Bishop and feeling secure around his boys.

"I know your brother . . . we go way back," Barnes said.

"Word," Sleepy uttered nonchalantly.

"Yeah, I need you to give him a message for me," Bishop continued.

"And what's that?" Sleepy asked.

"Fuck you and him!" Barnes shouted, and then quickly pulled out a .45 and opened fired. *Bam! Bam! Bam! Bam!*

"Oh, shit!" Sleepy's man shouted as he reached for his gat, but abruptly caught a shot to his head by Bishop's hand cannon.

Panic spread throughout the restaurant as bystanders ran out screaming or took cover behind chairs and tables. Sleepy's other friend ran out the door after the first couple of shots.

Just the way they came in, Barnes and Bishop casually walked out and got into their truck and drove off.

Reality hurried his baby-mom into the car, cursing at her for being a stupid bitch. Even though he was a killer, he cared about his family, and hustling in the streets paid his bills and bought him and his son's mother a duplex condo near the Conduit.

"Bobby, why you being so stupid?" his baby-mother, Nicole, shouted. "You trippin' right now!"

"Nicole, shut the fuck up!" he cursed.

Reality had a strong feeling that something was about to go down. He always listened to his gut instincts, and something told him to get his son's mother and their child out of her mother's home and get them out of town, or somewhere safe. He survived on the streets by being smart. He was unaware of Cash's and Sleepy's murder.

"Bobby, what about T.J.? It's four o'clock in the morning. I know you ain't tryin' to wake our son up this fuckin' early in the morning," Nicole barked.

Reality sighed as he opened the trunk to his Lexus and retrieved his 9-mm Beretta and checked the clip. It was fully loaded. He concealed the gun in his waistband and closed the trunk. But something caught his immediate attention. A car was slowly creeping down his block in the dark.

He removed his gun, cocked it back and continued to watch the car creep. He gripped the Beretta and waited, thinking it was his nerves getting to him.

His cell phone suddenly went off. Reality answered the call with his eyes still glued on the car.

"Who this?" Reality asked.

"Reality, we got hit hard tonight. They got Cash, Pepper, and Sleepy, Rome's little brother," N.O. informed Reality. He sounded frantic.

"What?" Reality exclaimed.

"It was a hit. We got set up," N.O. stated.

"Fuck!" Reality shouted. His eyes stayed glued to the black BMW creeping his way. He knew it was a hit. Suddenly tires screeched and guns came out the front and back windows.

"Nicole, get down!" Reality shouted.

*Tat!-Tat!-Tat!-Tat!-Tat!-Tat!-Tat!-Tat!-*Tat!-Tat!-Tat!-Tat!-Tat!-Tat!-Tat! Glass shattered as dozens of rounds penetrated Reality's Lexus.

"*Aaaaaahhh!* Bobby! Bobby!" Nicole screamed, ducking and trying to get out of the car.

Reality took action, firing shot after shot at the BMW. But the occupants of the car were bold, and the car stopped and two men stepped out, gripping guns and firing rapidly as they started to approach Reality even closer.

An all-out shootout transpired on the street. Reality tried not to panic as his car took on heavy gunfire.

"Nicole! Nicole!" he shouted. He started to fear the worst.

Boom! Boom! Boom! Boom! Boom! Boom!

Reality could hear the shots coming closer. He quickly stood up and returned fire, almost emptying his clip. He knew he was doomed.

"Die like a man, muthafucka!" Jerry shouted. He was part of Barnes's deadly crew.

"Fuck you!" Reality shouted back.

Suddenly Reality heard the sounds of distant police sirens coming toward them. He would never have thought that hearing a siren would be music to his ears.

Jerry glanced at his partner and they both ran back to the car and sped off. Reality stood up, knowing that they had left, and went to see about Nicole. She was sprawled out in the front seat.

"Baby, get up!" Reality shouted, pulling Nicole out of the car. "C'mon, baby . . . don't do this to me . . . get up."

She had been shot twice; one bullet hit her in the shoulder and the other bullet struck her in the abdomen. Reality had to think quickly. He hid his gun in a stash box in the Lexus, and signaled for the police to help.

Two squad cars were rapidly on the scene, and two officers rushed out of their cars with their guns out, and shouted to Reality, "Get on the ground now!"

"My girl is shot!" Reality shouted back.

"Get on the ground!" the officer loudly and firmly repeated himself with his gun trained on Reality's head.

Reality reluctantly complied. He got down on his knees and locked his fingers behind his head, but he continued to shout, "My girl is shot. Y'all need to fuckin' help her!"

Two officers went to check on Nicole while one kept his gun aimed at Reality.

One cop got on the horn, and said, "Dispatch, we need a bus at South Conduit, and . . ."

For Starr the nightmares were continual, almost every other day. Bamboo's murder still lingered in her mind, and her mother's violent abuse still haunted her.

Starr remembered being thirteen and hearing her mom in the bathroom getting high. She slowly walked to the bathroom, noticing the door ajar, and saw her mother getting high while sitting on the toilet.

Her mother was naked, her eyes were drowsy, and that's when Starr saw the needle stuck in her arm. That's when Starr knew her mother had finally graduated to using heroin.

Sheryl looked over at her daughter standing in the hallway, and she slurred, "Starr, baby . . . c'mere."

Starr reluctantly walked into the bathroom, seeing that it was a mess.

"Starr, you know Mommy loves you, right?" Sheryl exclaimed, peering at her daughter as she moved her hand through her hair.

"This makes the pain go away. Your father was a bitch-ass niggah who couldn't handle himself or this family," Sheryl mumbled.

Starr's face tightened when her mother spoke disrespectfully about her father. She knew the true reason why her father had left, though she kept her mouth shut. But every day, she missed him dearly. And every day Starr wished her father would come back and rescue her from hell on earth. But it never happened.

"So what, I fucked a few niggahs? He couldn't handle it, my pussy was too much for him. Your father wasn't much of a man, if you know what I mean," Sheryl continued.

"But he took care of us," Starr replied suddenly.

"He couldn't take care of shit! He left. He doesn't give a fuck about you and your sister. . . . They both abandoned us. We gotta help take care of each other, baby. Pussy is our business. Men love us. And they love you," Sheryl proclaimed as she opened her legs and began touching herself.

Starr gazed at her mother in fright. Her mother was unpredictable at times. She could be so calm and cool one moment, and then become a raging, out-of-control, abusive bitch the next.

"Selling my pussy and gettin' high is what gets me by every day, baby. . . . I'm just teaching you about life. Shit ain't fair for us, Starr. . . . Life is hell, so we gotta find ways to make it to heaven without dying," she stated. "And this is one way."

Sheryl pulled the needle out of her arm, and then said, "You down?"

Starr was shocked and appalled. She slammed the bathroom door and ran back to her bedroom.

Starr was abruptly awakened by a loud crash coming from the living room. She was jolted out of sleep, sweating and wide-eyed.

"I'm gonna murder that niggah where I find him!" she heard Rome scream from the other room. "I'm gonna fuck his ass up! I'm gonna kill that muthafucka! He don't know who he fuckin' wit!!"

Starr heard more crashing sounds like something breaking, maybe glass. Starr got out of bed and started to go and find out what all the commotion was about.

Dynasty and another girl ran into the bedroom, looking as if they were taking cover.

"Dynasty, what's up, girl? What's goin' on out there?" Starr asked.

"Someone murdered Rome's brother, Sleepy, the other night," Dynasty informed Starr with tears trickling down her face. "And they killed Cash and Pepper."

"Ohmygod!" Starr whispered, cupping her mouth.

"Rome is fuckin' furious," Dynasty said.

All three girls remained in the bedroom until Rome calmed down or left the apartment. They knew better than to get in his way and risk his wrath. He might end up killing one of them in his frenzy.

Eric drove aimlessly in his car, collecting his thoughts. He was in a bind, and he tried to think of the best way to come out of his situation alive. He'd become an informant for the feds and the DEA, and agreed to testify against his cousin in court. That didn't bother him, but knowing that Russell had kidnapped River, killed his uncle, and that both his friends were dead was messing with his head. *This game is spiraling out of control,* Eric told himself.

Eric knew that he had done a lot of wrong in his life, and he told himself that he would start making things right for himself and River if he got a second chance.

He got on his cell phone and called up Russell. They needed to talk. Russell picked up after the third ring, knowing it was Eric. "Where you been, cuz?" Russell asked.

"Is she okay?" Eric asked, not beating around the bush.

Russell let out a slight chuckle. "She's good. I ain't touch her, not yet, anyway. You disappoint me, Eric. I thought you were stronger than this. You gonna let pussy come in between us?"

"What the fuck is wrong wit' you, Russell? You had to shoot Uncle Pumpkin? He was our fuckin' uncle!" Eric barked.

"Niggah, you know better—not over the phones. But you're a snake muthafucka, E!" Russell chided.

"Fuck you talkin' about?"

"I told you, no deals outside of the family. And what do you do?

Continue dealing with that Brooklyn niggah. You think I wouldn't fuckin' find out. I told you, no fuckin' secrets. And you had the nerve to hide this bitch at our uncle's crib, after she set you up."

"You don't control me, Russell. This is my life and you need to stay the fuck out of it!"

"Niggah, I always had your back, and you betray me for this bitch," Russell shouted.

"I never betrayed you! You always talk about family, but you don't know the first thing about family. All you do is kill, control, and hold grudges for every muthafucka that does you wrong. You killed Rah!"

"Eric, what I told you? Not over the phone."

"We need to talk," Eric stated.

"I'm listening."

"I want River back."

Russell laughed. "Niggah, you'll get this bitch back in pieces."

"Russell, please—don't hurt her! I'll pay you for her."

"Niggah, is you serious?! You're ready to pay for this bitch after what she done did to you?" Russell questioned.

"I love her," Eric said.

"Love? Eric, is her pussy that good? Is her pussy worth losing your life over?"

"You will never understand the meaning of forgiveness and you will never know love, Russell. I got eighty thousand in cash in a small duffel bag. The money's yours, in exchange for River."

"You were always the fool in the family, Eric. You disgrace me and your father," Russell stated. "Fuck it, ayyite . . . we can do business, no problem. You wanna pay for the bitch, then it's all good. You come correct, though, Eric, or I swear, I'll take my time killing this bitch and then I'm gonna do you."

"We cool. I got the money, just let me know where to meet."

"You remember where Uncle Black and his crew used to hang out at?" Russell asked.

"Yeah, that old warehouse in Five Towns," Eric said.

"I'm there. Come alone."

"I'll be there around midnight," Eric said.

"You better come alone, E. And don't fuckin' cross me. We family and all, but I won't hesitate to kill you."

Eric hung up.

Eric stopped at a local chicken spot on Liberty Avenue when he spotted Hershey from a distance. He knew Hershey had the information he was searching for. Hershey was a girl who had been into everything from drug trafficking to prostitution. She even did a few of Eric's parties and blessed Rah with some ass at his bachelor party.

Hershey was standing outside the chicken spot talking to a male friend when she noticed Eric rushing out of his car coming toward her.

"Eric, what's goin' on? It's been a minute," Hershey said, greeting him with a smile, looking enticing in some tight jeans and a fitted basketball jersey.

"Hershey, we need to talk," Eric said.

"You got another party for me to do?"

"Nah, I need to talk to you in private," Eric stated, glancing at her male friend.

"Ayyite, no problem. . . . Mike, I'll be right back," Hershey said, and strutted off with Eric to his car.

Hershey got in and Eric drove off.

"So, Eric, what's good? What you need from me?"

"Do you know a girl from around here named Starr? I know she works the tracks on occasions. If I can recall she's about five-five and beautiful, with long black hair, beautiful brown eyes, and she's about sixteen."

"Starr . . . Starr . . . oh, I know who you're talkin' about. She works for Rome. The little bitch got some attitude on her," Hershey stated. "What do you want wit' her?"

"You know where I can find her?"

"Rome has a few apartments in the Forty projects, moves girls in and out of there all the time," Hershey informed him.

"I know. It's been a while since we talked. I need to get wit' him," Eric said.

"You sure?"

"Yes."

"Ayyite, I'll see what I can do for you," Hershey said, pulling out her cell phone and making a call.

An hour later, Eric nervously walked past three armed men on his way to see Rome in his fourth-floor apartment. Rome and Eric were very familiar with each other, since they both were in the business of profiting from the sex trade. They had done business with each other a few years ago, but for Eric business with Rome had gotten too risky, so he backed off and they'd gradually gone their separate ways.

Eric came to the apartment door where two soldiers stood guard outside. They both were expecting Eric to show, but were totally against his arrival. Eric's cousin had Sleepy killed, and they resented Eric just walking up on them and not being able to do anything about it.

"Niggah, put your arms up," one man said sternly, about to frisk Eric for any weapons. He glared at Eric as he patted him down.

"I'm clean," Eric stated.

"I don't give a fuck! You lucky Rome won't let me put a bullet in your fuckin' head," he countered.

Eric ignored his threat and allowed him to continue with the search. After Eric came up clean, the soldier opened the door to the apartment, allowing Eric entry.

Eric slowly walked in, not knowing what to expect. Rome was at war with his cousin, and it could be a setup for Eric. But he took the risk and continued without any weapons. It was a large three-bedroom apartment, but Rome had renovated it a few years ago, knocking down the walls to the adjacent apartment and combining both rooms.

A few soldiers stood guard in the room when Eric walked in. They all glared at him, and they were all strapped. Some ladies stayed in the background, staring at Eric as the enemy. Word got out that Eric was Yung Slim's cousin, and the tension in the room could be sliced by a butter knife. They were just waiting for Rome to give the word so they could tear him apart.

"Where's Rome?" Eric asked, being short and simple with his words.

"Niggah, shut the fuck up and wait! You don't say shit!" a man loudly stated as he motioned to Eric with a pistol in his hand.

Eric returned his hard gaze, not backing down or looking weak. Then Eric's eyes danced around the room looking for a girl who resembled Starr. He'd met her once for a moment, and knew if he saw her again, he would recognize her.

Rome entered the room, shirtless, in a pair of baggy jeans and Timberlands, gripping a black-and-silver 9-mm in his hand. He glared at Eric as he approached, and then shouted, "Niggah, tell my why I shouldn't blow your fuckin' head off in this apartment right now!" Rome raised the gun to Eric's head, inches from his skull.

"Because right now we need each other," Eric replied.

"Fuck you talkin' about, niggah? Because of your cousin, my little brother is dead," Rome said.

"On my father's grave, I swear to you, Rome, I had nuthin' to do wit' that."

"Explain yourself for coming here to see me, then." Rome said.

"I got something you want, and you have something that I want," Eric stated.

"Like what?" Rome then lowered the gun from Eric's head and was now listening.

"I'll give you the location of my cousin right now. Fuck him! We ain't family anymore. As of tonight, I have nuthin' to do wit' him," Eric said.

"And?"

"For the information I give to you . . . I'm lookin' for one of your girls."

"What?" Rome said.

"Her name is Starr," Eric told him.

"Fuck you want wit' Starr?" Rome questioned, giving Eric a perplexed gaze.

"It's personal between me and her," Eric said.

"So you ready to give up family for some pussy?" Rome asked.

"It's much more than that. . . . I can't get into details."

"Niggah, you must be buggin', Starr is one of my best earners. What makes you think I'm supposed to pass her over to you for information? How I know I can trust you?"

Starr was deep in the background when she heard her name being mentioned. Wide-eyed, she tried to get a peek at the man who was asking for her. When she saw him, his face suddenly began to register in her memory as she tried to place where she'd seen him before.

"Yung Slim killed my uncle in his own home, and he kidnapped my girl," Eric informed him.

"That niggah is goin' crazy," Rome said.

"I'm not lying to you, Rome. I know where he is hiding, and he's waiting for my arrival around midnight. You can have him—I'm giving him to you on a stick."

Rome stared at Eric. "We used to do good business together, E. I always respected your family, but your cousin got a fuckin' problem. The niggah just came home and wanna tax me and my hoes like he the muthafuckin' government. How do I know this ain't a setup, you telling me this, but walking me into a trap?"

"It's not. I swear to you, on my soul, my family, my father. . . . I don't want nuthin' to do with that niggah anymore. To me he's better off dead than alive," Eric loudly proclaimed. "I came here alone, on the strength of us being cool wit' each other at one point. All I want in return is Starr."

"How that bitch get so important in all of this?" Rome asked.

Starr moved her way to Rome's side as she stared at Eric with resentment.

"I'm not leaving. I don't know him," Starr said.

"Bitch, shut the fuck up!" Rome scolded. "You have no fuckin' say in this."

Eric stared at Starr. She was beautiful and so young.

Rome was quiet, contemplating the proposal. His brother's death was in his thoughts, and nothing would satisfy his thirst for revenge more than torturing and killing Yung Slim himself. Rome knew Eric was good people but had bad blood in his family.

"I have twenty thousand cash in a brown bag in my Scion downstairs. That's all the cash I have left, Rome. It's yours, for Starr," Eric stated as he tossed Rome the keys.

Rome looked at his man, tossed him the keys, and said, "Yo, go get that."

Rome then looked at Starr, who stood clad in tight Daisy Duke shorts, a tank top, and black-and-white Nikes. Twenty thousand in cash and a chance to get his revenge for his brother's death: Rome knew he couldn't pass up the opportunity.

"You must be crazy like your cousin to give up that much cash for a bitch." Rome said.

"We have a deal?" Eric asked.

Rome hesitated to give his answer right away. He looked at Eric and then diverted his eyes back to Starr, and knew she was hard to give up. But she was sixteen, and he knew young girls could become a headache sometimes, especially if they got locked up.

"Fuck it, we have a deal," Rome said.

Starr looked at Rome in shock. "But Daddy—"

"Bitch, shut the fuck up!" Rome shouted. "You belong to him now."

Starr looked at Eric with contempt. She tried to register his face, knowing she had seen him previously. Moments later, Rome's man came through the door gripping the brown bag Eric had told them about.

"Bingo," he shouted, passing Rome the bag.

Rome nodded. He quickly opened the bag and his hands went through the bills.

"Starr, even at the end, you still pay off big for me," Rome said, smiling.

Eric then went on to inform Rome and his men about Yung Slim's location. He laid out the blueprint of his father's old warehouse. He even informed Rome who Yung Slim had probably hired for the information needed to carry out the hits.

"A woman named Karen, who became a parole officer," Eric told him. He had never liked Karen; he always thought she was a money-hungry two-faced bitch.

After their meeting, Reality came bursting into the apartment, gunning straight for Eric. Word got out to Reality that Yung Slim's cousin was meeting with Rome, and Reality wanted to blow his head off. His son's mother, Nicole, was in critical condition at Jamaica Hospital, and doctors didn't know if she would survive another night.

"Muthafucka, I'm gonna murder this niggah where he stand!" Reality cried out, aiming his gun at Eric.

A few soldiers moved out of his way, hoping he would shoot first and ask questions later. Eric stared at Reality wide-eyed as panic overwhelmed him.

"You come at me and my girl!" Reality continued to shout. It was the first time anyone had ever seen Reality in tears, and his men were shocked.

"Reality, chill, niggah!" Rome shouted, trying to calm his boy.

"Nah, fuck that, Rome!" Reality shouted, viciously grabbing Eric by his neck and pressing the gun to his head. "Why you bring this niggah here, and have him still breathing?"

"Because this is business!" Rome explained.

"Reality, I had nuthin' to do wit' what happened to you, believe me," Eric told him, trying to save his ass.

"Shut the fuck up! I'm gonna murder this niggah Rome."

"Reality, he just gave up his cousin's location. You can have your revenge . . . but E . . . let him be," Rome instructed. "He had nuthin' to do wit' it."

"And you believe this niggah, Rome?"

"Me and him go way back. Let him be, Reality. We got the information and the bitch that set us up," Rome stated. "Remember your old parole officer?"

Reality continued to glare at Eric but lowered the gun and backed off. "Yeah."

"That bitch is in Yung Slim's pocket. How you think that niggah got the information needed to hit us so hard?" Rome said.

Reality was furious. He wanted to see blood spilled, even if it meant losing his own life.

"Yo, we cool?" Eric asked.

Rome nodded. Eric then looked at Reality, and said, "I'm sorry, but that blood is not on my hands. I'm out the game."

Eric then glanced at Starr, who looked reluctant to leave, and called out, "Starr, come on."

Starr turned around and stared at Rome. "I'm not leaving," she exclaimed.

Rome became furious. He raised his gun at her, and said, "You either leave wit' him or in a fuckin' body bag. Your fuckin' choice."

Of course she chose the first option.

"Eric, I swear, if you're lying to me . . . I'll find you, and believe me, when I do . . . a bullet in your head is gonna feel like heaven when I'm finish wit' you," Rome warned.

Eric took Starr by her hand and went out the door.

When they left, Rome stared at Reality and his soldiers, and said, "Y'all niggahs get ready, we gonna finish this war tonight."

. . .

Eric quickly moved down the stairs with Starr cursing and raving at him.

"Niggah, you don't fuckin' own me! Who the fuck you think you are?!" Starr shouted as Eric pulled her by her arm down the stairs.

"Listen, stop being a bitch for a moment and let me explain," Eric said.

Starr stared at Eric and finally recognized where she had seen him before. "Ohmygod. I do know you. You're Critter's friend. Why are you doin' this?"

"I'm here to help, not hurt you," he explained. Before they left the building, Eric said, "I know your sister, River."

Starr was shocked and wide-eyed. She couldn't believe what just came out of his mouth. She had never spoken about River to anyone except to Ms. Henderson, so she knew Eric had to be telling the truth somehow. She stopped being so reluctant and willingly followed him to his car.

Starr wanted to ask Eric a thousand and one questions, but Eric said he would explain it to her in due time. He was in a rush.

Yung Slim stared at River, who was bound to a chair, gagged, and helpless.

"You got my cousin trippin', bitch. . . . Your pussy gotta be made out of platinum or gold," Yung Slim said. "Because of you, I might have to murder him tonight. But not before he watches me kill you."

River was in tears. It was hopeless to try and struggle to get free. The ropes that burned into her skin were tight and knotted well. She figured this was her end.

Yung Slim had a dozen soldiers at his side, including Bishop and Barnes, his most lethal enforcers. He was ready for anything. Snowman was helping him out with the slain officer, taking care of things at his end. And Yung Slim was cleaning up his mess, starting with River and a few others.

"Slim, why you keeping this bitch alive?" Barnes asked.

"She's a commodity right now. If my cousin is willing to pay eighty grand to get the bitch back, then hey . . . I'm about business. He's gonna get her back, but she won't be alive for that long," Slim proclaimed.

Critter overheard them talking and his conscience was eating away at him. He regretted making the phone call to Slim, informing him about everything. Now Uncle Pumpkin was dead and a New York City cop was murdered, and Critter knew that there would be a massive manhunt for the shooters responsible. And he'd recently heard on the news about Rahmel's death. He was starting to believe what Eric was saying to him, that maybe this game was becoming too much for him to handle. The money was good, but the extra stuff that came along with getting paid, like the murders, were burdening him. Critter was stressed, and he knew it would only be a matter of time before his past caught up to him.

As Yung Slim talked to Barnes, his cell phone went off. He wasn't familiar with the number, but picked up anyway.

"You have something that I want," a voice said to him.

"What?"

"You murdered my partner, but I'm willing to let that be, in exchange for the girl you're holding hostage," Big Red informed him.

"What's wit' this bitch, why is she so important to everyone?!" Yung Slim shouted through the phone. "Fuck you, pig! How the fuck did you get this number anyway?!"

"Listen, we can do this real easy and on some gentleman shit, or I swear to you, I'll have the entire NYPD task force down your throat by tomorrow morning," Big Red threatened. "Now, I'm willing to make a deal wit' you. . . . I have some valuable information that I know you will want to hear."

"And what's that?"

"About two snitches in your crew," Red told him. "So, do we have a deal? You give me her, and I'll give you their names."

Yung Slim thought about it. "How do I know you're not lying?"

"Can you risk having snitches in your crew?"

Yung Slim knew he was right. He couldn't risk going back to jail, and whoever it was, he knew he had to take care of that immediately.

"We have a deal," Yung Slim announced.

After a meeting place was agreed on, Yung Slim hung up and proclaimed to his people, "Change of plans. I want her alive."

32

Eric met up with DEA agents not too far from the meeting site with his cousin. They passed him eighty thousand dollars in cash in a brown duffle bag, and wired him up.

"They're gonna search me once I'm there," Eric said.

But one of the agents explained to Eric that the wire was wired inside his belt and could not be seen. Eric was nervous, but allowed them to continue.

Starr was baffled. Eric explained to her how he met her sister, and she was so relieved that River was still alive and nearby. But when she also got the news of her being kidnapped, her joy was short-lived. She'd never prayed so long and so hard in her life. She would do anything to see her sister alive again, and she was willing to give her own life to save River's.

One of the agents passed Eric the cash, thinking the money was for Eric to purchase several kilos of cocaine, but Eric went in there with the intention of buying River back from Russell. He misinformed the agents about the deal.

"Okay, once you're in there, we'll be listening to everything from a small distance. You get your cousin to talk about the murders, and have him make the transaction very quickly. Time is vital," Agent Morris informed him.

Eric nodded.

"You're doing the right thing," Agent Merchant stated.

It was still hard for Eric to set up and snitch on his cousin, despite all the grimy things he had done. But he was in love with River and knew this was the only way to get her back and maybe still have a decent life with her.

Eric slowly walked to his ride, placed the money on the passenger seat, and got in. He stayed still in the driver's seat for several moments, getting his head right and his nerves steady. The situation was tense, one wrong move tonight and he could end up dead.

As Eric sat, he thought about River and Starr, and how both sisters could finally be reunited tonight after not seeing each other for several years. He thought about his uncle Pumpkin, and he knew he would miss his uncle dearly. And then Donald and Rah came to mind, and he knew their deaths were meaningless, and there was nothing he could do to bring them back.

He knew he had to move forward and bring down his cousin. Russell was a lunatic and he agreed with his deceased uncle that Russell was the devil.

Eric finally started the car and drove off.

Eric drove up to the barren warehouse and put the car in park. There were two guards outside gripping M-16 machine guns.

Fuck, this niggah think we're in Iraq, Eric said to himself.

He grabbed the cash, stepped out of the car, and slowly headed toward them. Both men stood erect when they noticed Eric approaching them gripping the bag that contained the cash.

One guard smiled, and commented, "Bitch must be that ill for you to bring your ass around here."

Eric just glared at him as the other man searched him for any weapons.

"That's the cash?"

Eric nodded.

"Open the bag and let me see," the man instructed.

Eric opened the duffle bag, allowing the thug to get a quick glance of the money.

"Ayyite," the thug said, satisfied that Eric was clean.

Eric zipped up the bag when he heard the same guard that commented before say, "Let me fuck her for you, E . . . she's definitely a pretty thang. Let me show her what a real man is like. She damn sure got some soft tits, though."

Eric glared at him and then suddenly struck him fast and hard across his jaw, drawing blood.

"Fuck you!" Eric exclaimed.

"Muthafucka!" the man shouted, trying to strike back, but he was held back by his partner.

"Chill, Rocky—let him be, that's still family to Yung Slim and he wants him alive," the thug said to his fuming partner.

"I'm gonna fuck you up, Eric!" Rocky screamed.

Eric smirked as he entered the building.

Eric made his way farther into the building, being cautious with every step he took. Eric walked into a vast open section of the building and was surrounded by a half dozen of Yung Slim's men. He looked ahead and saw River gagged and bound to a chair with Yung Slim standing over her holding a pistol in his hand.

"Damn, niggah, you actually came for this bitch," Yung Slim shouted.

"I got the money. I'm keeping my word," Eric said.

"You're willing to go all the way for this bitch. . . . Damn, you're a ride-or-die niggah fo' real. But let me show you how serious I am if you fuckin' cross me," Yung Slim proclaimed, pressing the gun to River's temple.

River squirmed and braced herself for the impact.

"Russell, no—c'mon, it ain't gotta be like this," Eric shouted.

"I know, but 'cuz of this bitch . . . it is like this," Yung Slim replied. "Yo, bring that niggah out."

Surprised, Eric watched them drag Critter out into the open. He was also bound and beaten badly.

"What the fuck is this?" Eric shouted, looking confused.

"This niggah here is a snake muthafucka! The whole time, he's been an informant, a fuckin' snitch to the NYPD. Come to find out, he tried to conduct business on his own, and got busted trying to purchase a kilo from undercover narcs. But instead of being a man about it and doing his time, he wanted to bring me down. Damn, Critter, I thought we were boys. You were good though, I'll give you that. I never expected for you to become a snitch," Yung Slim exclaimed, pressing the pistol to Critter's head.

"Russell, don't—please!" Critter cried out.

"You begging for your life now, after you tried to betray me. I made you a lieutenant in my organization and this is how you do me," Yung Slim said.

"Russell, it don't have to be this way, we can make things—"

Boom!

Yung Slim didn't even allow Eric to finish his sentence. He abruptly blew a hole in Critter's head, dropping him where he sat.

"You was sayin' somethin', E?" Yung Slim said. "I just made things right."

Eric was shocked and furious as he watched another friend of many years murdered in cold blood.

"Now, do you got somethin' to confess?" Yung Slim asked. "If so, now is the time."

"Nah," Eric dragged out.

"You sure, Eric? Say so now and I'll be easy on you and this bitch. But if the truth comes out—and eventually the truth will come out—it won't be pretty for you."

"You're a fuckin' monster. I'm disgusted to have the same blood running through my veins as you," Eric angrily stated.

"Niggah, whatever. Come clean wit' me, Eric—you a snitch, too?" Yung Slim asked, staring at Eric with contempt. "Tonight's your night to come clean and confess all your sins against me."

Eric's heart pounded rapidly. His nerves were edgy. He wanted nothing more than to kill Russell.

"I got your money. I came for her," Eric said, staring at River.

"Yeah, whatever," Yung Slim muttered as he pressed the gun to River's head again. "Now tell me, are you a snitch?"

"Russell, I said no!" Eric shouted.

"Somehow, I don't believe you. And you know why I don't believe you. . . ?" Yung Slim focused his attention on a doorway where Big Red loomed, and both Eric and River were shocked.

"Surprised to see me again?" Big Red asked, mocking Eric and River. "What I told you, niggah? I always get what I want, no matter the risks or the cost."

"See, me and Officer Gibson had a quick talk before your arrival, and he enlightened me on some shit about you, Eric."

"Fuck you!" Eric fumed.

"Nah, you the one fucked!" Yung Slim chided back. "I promised him River for information."

"I'm gonna fuck your little girlfriend a few times before I cut her throat," Red proclaimed.

Eric was furious. He stared at River as he squatted down near the duffle bag and slowly unzipped it. "Russell, I came wit' your money as promised," he said, holding up a small bundle of fifties and hundreds. "You gonna diss me for this pig, after he the one that set me up and caused all of this? You can't trust him."

"I thought I could trust you, cuz," Russell replied.

"It seems like you can't trust anyone anymore," Eric replied.

The situation was tense. Eric slowly reached his hand deeper into the bag and gripped a hidden .45 he had stashed under the money. He knew it was the only way to sneak the gun in without them finding it after the body search.

It was a standoff, and Eric knew that the chances of him and River leaving there alive were very slim. But he was going out with a fight. Eric knew the DEA had enough evidence now to convict his cousin. Critter's murder was caught on the wire, plus the kidnapping charge, among other counts they had against Yung Slim. Eric wondered why they didn't raid the place yet.

Eric stared at Critter, waiting for the right moment.

"You know, Eric, you're a disgrace to this family by cooperating with the DEA. Fuck is wrong wit' you?! Our family has never snitched, and your weak ass wanna be the first! Red, you can have that bitch," Yung Slim said.

"No!" Eric shouted, seeing Yung Slim finally lower the gun from River's head. He sprang into action and fired two rounds at his cousin, striking Yung Slim in the shoulder. Yung Slim fell back in shock.

Big Red pulled out his firearm, but Eric shot him twice in the chest. He quickly ran for River as Yung Slim's soldiers opened fire on him, barely missing him. He snatched up River swiftly, and took cover behind some empty steel drums. Eric's adrenaline was pumping as he quickly began untying River.

"Ohmygod . . . ohmygod . . . ohmygod," River huffed, terrified. She hugged Eric tightly, but Eric knew that this was no time to get sentimental. He gripped his gun and heard Yung Slim's goons coming their way.

But the loud crashing sound from afar, and the rough voices of men shouting, "DEA! DEA, everybody get down! DEA, put your guns down now!" distracted the thugs.

But unfortunately, Yung Slim and his thugs weren't going down that easily, and opened fire on the dozens of agents. Loud and intense gunfire erupted throughout the room, sounding like a small war.

Eric's main concern was getting River to safety. They bolted out the back exit, but were unaware that they were being followed.

Big Red took cover, still feeling the effects of two bullets penetrating his vest and pushing him back as if he'd gotten hit by a small car. He pulled out his police shield and tried to make a covert escape as he crept toward the nearest exit with his Glock gripped in his hand.

Eric and River made it out the back but were cut short by Yung Slim pointing a .45 at them.

"You set me up and bring DEA down on me, cousin! You supposed to be family?! You bitch-ass niggah," Yung Slim protested. He was bleeding from his shoulder and was furious.

"I have no more family—at least not wit' you, anyway," Eric countered, staring hostilely at his cousin. "All you do is bring destruction and death to everything around you. I got everything on tape, Russell, even Critter's murder."

"Fuck you, bitch!" Yung Slim shrieked and aimed his gat at Eric, but River ran in front of him and got hit first as a quick round penetrated her. She landed at Eric's feet. Eric promptly returned fire and shot his cousin in the head, dropping him to the ground dead.

"River, get up . . . please, you can't die on me now . . . please, please," Eric cried out, clutching River in his arms. "Why you do that for? Huh? It wasn't supposed to be like this. I found your sister, Starr. She's with the agents now. I found her for you. We still gotta make things right."

River stared up at Eric, bleeding and weak. She owed Eric everything, and she felt it was only right to take a bullet for him.

Quickly agents came into view and saw Eric gripping his woman in his arms and holding her tight. They immediately called for an emergency van. Her pulse was weak and her breathing shallow, but she was still alive.

The situation inside was finally under control, with agents taking everyone into custody. Three thugs lay dead in the gunfight, and two agents were seriously injured.

As they laid River on a gurney and were about ready to put her in the ambulance, Starr came running over.

"Is that my sister? River! River!" she screamed. "No! What happened? Eric, what happened to her?! River, it's me, Starr."

Eric gripped Starr in his arms, trying to calm her down.

"No! No! No!" Starr cried out, watching the medics work on her sister and load her into the ambulance. "I'm goin' wit' her!"

It was only right for Starr to be with her sister at such a critical moment. She finally got to hold River's hand as the ambulance rushed them away to Jamaica Hospital.

Eric stayed behind in tears, covered in blood. He stared at his dead cousin sprawled out on the ground and had no regrets for his actions. Agents Morris and Merchant walked over to him and wanted a full deposition from him about the night's action. Yung Slim was dead.

As Eric walked away with the agents he noticed Big Red in handcuffs and a small smile spread across Eric's face. Both men made quick eye contact. Red cursed Eric under his breath and was led away by two agents gripping both arms.

But it wasn't over for Eric.

Two black SUVs were parked near the warehouse and the faces on the men inside were not too pleasing. Rome and Reality stared at dozens of DEA agents surrounding the warehouse and knew it was too late for their revenge.

"This muthafucka!" Rome cursed, gripping a micro Uzi semiautomatic pistol. "What you think, Reality?"

"It was a setup," Reality replied, also gripping an Uzi. "DEA got to him first."

"Fuck it, we out," Rome said, instructing his driver to make a U-turn and head home. Yung Slim's reign was finally over. They watched the coroner load two body bags into the van.

Rome was upset that he hadn't pulled the trigger himself, but felt relieved that it was finally over between him and Yung Slim. The next day for him would be business as usual.

33

River was rushed into surgery in the emergency room at Jamaica Hospital; she had suffered a gunshot wound to the chest. Starr wasn't too far behind her, crying hysterically and cursing out every nurse or doctor who tried to pull her away from her sister as they rolled her down the corridor.

"Get the fuck off me! That's my sister! She needs me—that's my sister—get off me!" Starr shrieked, fighting off two nurses.

"Ma'am, please, you have to let the doctors work here, they're trying to help," one nurse said, trying to calm her down.

"No, she can't die! I haven't seen her in years. She can't die!" Starr cried out. "Get off me and help her! Fuckin' help her!! Help her!!"

Security quickly got involved and joined in with the nurses trying to contain and calm Starr down. She was little, but strong and feisty.

"Young lady, we're going to have to escort you outside if you don't calm down now!" one security guard said.

"Fuck you! Fuck you!" Starr screamed, trying to take a swing at the guard.

They quickly grabbed her, subduing her arms and legs, and were about to escort her outside.

Ms. Henderson was finishing up her tour when she heard all the commotion from down the hall. She heard a young lady screaming, cursing, and carrying on, and curiosity got the best of her. She started to walk toward the racket and was surprised to see Starr in the middle of it all.

It had been weeks since Starr ran away from the social workers who tried to take her away, and every day Starr had been on Ms. Henderson's mind. She was excited, but at the same time upset to see Starr acting in such an uncivilized way.

Ms. Henderson walked up to the scene, and called out, "Starr, what is going on with you?"

"Ms. Henderson, please help me! They shot my sister! They shot River," Starr cried out.

"Good God," Ms. Henderson uttered.

"Ms. Henderson, do you know this woman?" a guard asked.

"Yes, she's family," Ms. Henderson replied. "I'll take care of her."

Hearing that, the guards let go of Starr, and Starr immediately collapsed into Ms. Henderson's arms crying uncontrollably. "Please don't let her die on me, Ms. Henderson. Please don't."

"I'm here, chile . . . I'm here," Ms. Henderson consoled her.

A few hours later, the doctor came out looking exhausted. He removed his surgical mask as he approached Starr and Ms. Henderson sitting in the waiting area. His facial expression looked unemotional; both ladies didn't know if he was coming with good news or bad news.

Starr instantly stood up and gazed at the doctor in his wrinkled gown. The doctor let out a sigh, and then said, "She's alive."

Starr let out a quick cheer as she hugged Ms. Henderson. But Dr. Fermat wasn't finished.

"We were able to stop the bleeding, but she lost a tremendous amount of blood. Her heart rate was fading fast, and I thought we were about to lose her at one point. I had to authorize an emergency transfusion to get her heart rate moving again at a steady pace. She also has a ruptured lung, though I was able to save it. But she's in a coma, and I can't tell how long she'll be under. And if she does come through, she might have some brain damage, and may need months of physical therapy," he proclaimed.

Starr was teary-eyed but hugged Ms. Henderson. "She'll get better, right?"

"It's too soon to say. We're monitoring her vital signs closely. At this point, it takes patience and prayer," the doctor said.

"Thank you, Dr. Fermat," Ms. Henderson said.

He walked off, leaving the two alone.

"Oh, God . . . please help her . . . please let her come through this okay. Oh, God, I'm sorry . . . I won't be bad ever again if He brings my sister through this. I miss her so much," Starr prayed.

"Starr, everything now is in His hands. He'll get you through this," Ms. Henderson stated.

Starr felt so guilty. It had been years since she'd seen River, and unfortunately, they had to reunite now in a hospital where River was in a coma. She felt she had the worst luck in the world.

"Starr, have a seat. There's something I need to explain to you," Ms. Henderson gently stated.

Starr took a seat next to Ms. Henderson and clutched her warm hand. Ms. Henderson held Starr's pained gaze, staring into her teary eyes, and said, "Your father, Henry . . . well, he's my younger brother. You're my niece."

Starr was shocked. "What?"

"It's been so long since I've seen you and River, and that night they brought you into this hospital, I felt some kind of connection to you. But I wasn't sure until we started talking, and you said your name to me, and then you mentioned that you had an older sister named River. I was sure you were Henry's daughter. I haven't seen you since you were three."

"You know where my father is?"

"He's in North Carolina. He's been living there for over ten years," Ms. Henderson informed her. "After he left you and your mother he came to me crying one night, and explained everything that happened with him and his wife. I begged him to go back and get his children, but he was just too ashamed. Then one day he told me he was going to move back South, and he did, and never came back to New York."

Starr felt abandoned. She could never understand how her father could just leave and never come back for her and River. But she blamed her mother for everything.

"I went looking for you and River, but your mother Sheryl had moved y'all away from us. I knew what kind of woman she was, but when you explained to me the horror you and your sister endured, I felt so guilty. I felt that our family abandoned y'all. But the good Lord brought you back to me, yes, He did. It may have taken a few years, but He always delivers. And I wanted to adopt you, but you ran away from the social workers, and I felt so devastated, because I knew I should have told you about me sooner."

Starr was still teary-eyed as she continued to listen to Ms. Henderson. She wanted the pain to go away. She wanted to escape to a better place, of peace for the family.

"Ms. Henderson—" Starr began.

But Ms. Henderson interrupted her by saying, "Please, Starr . . . call me Aunt Diana. You're my family, and I promise you, I'll take care of you and your sister. Our family has been through so much, but as of tonight, no more." Ms. Henderson clutched Starr's hands tighter, closed her eyes, and began to pray. She got down on her knees, and began with, "O Lord, I come to You . . . we come to You for help. I pray for River, I pray for Starr . . . Please guide these young ladies, O Lord. I know You will bring us through hard times. . . . O Lord, we may fall, but with Your guidance I know we will get back up and rise again. . . . Lord, I pray for our family, I pray for River. I pray for Starr, and I pray for their mother, Sheryl. . . . I pray for her ways, her mistakes. O Lord, have the Spirit guide us,

34

Eric hugged River tightly, as they left the courthouse on Queens Boulevard on a breezy November afternoon six months later. They had both just finished testifying in court against Officer Gibson, a.k.a. Big Red. River and Eric held nothing back on the stand as the cop was indicted on numerous charges, from murder to drugs, extortion, and even conspiracy charges. Red was looking at twenty-five years to life.

Barnes and Bishop were on trial too, facing life in prison for numerous murders and other allegations against them. Eric became a witness for the DA and sang like a canary on the stand. He no longer cared about his or his family's reputation, or being labeled as a snitch since almost everyone close to him was dead. Eric even got bold enough to snitch to the feds about the Snowman, and with his cooperation, among other snitches and evidence, the Snowman was sitting in Riker's Island without bail, awaiting his trial date. And for his cooperation, Eric got full amnesty.

The media ate it up, and the trials of such notorious kingpins made headlines all over. Yung Slim's death even made front-page news. The press had a field day with the story for days when they found out it was a cousin who murdered Yung Slim.

The only men who seemed unaffected throughout the ordeal and the constant media coverage were Rome and Reality. For them, business continued as usual. They had over a dozen girls working the tracks night after night bringing in thousands and thousands of dollars a night. But unfortunately for Dynasty, she was murdered during the summer when an angry trick shot three rounds into her head, killing her instantly.

And Karen was gunned down by Reality as she sat parked in her brand-new BMW a few blocks from her office. Reality took pleasure in killing the crooked PO himself. It was payback for his son's mother and the others that she helped set up for Yung Slim. She was hit all over fifteen times, even in the face, necessitating a closed-casket funeral.

River was improving steadily over the months, but still needed a cane to move around, and still underwent physical therapy every week. But with Eric by her side, and Starr and Ms. Henderson back in her life, she was determined to get better and spend some quality time with her newfound family. They were by River's side constantly, and after the trial, they were planning to move down to North Carolina to become closer with their father. Eric was going too. He wanted to leave New York, especially Jamaica. He wanted his former home and neighborhood to be nothing but old memories. Some were good, but the majority were tragic and painful.

For Eric, being with River and her family was a new start for him. And he was willing to leave everything behind—the money, the game—and get an honest job in the South and start a regular family of his own.

It was late evening a few weeks before Christmas, and River, Starr, and Ms. Henderson walked into the North Hampton State Hospital in Upstate N.Y. Starr was very reluctant, but River was curious and just wanted answers, if she could get any.

A nurse guided Ms. Henderson through the corridors, with both girls following close behind. They had an hour's visit. They approached a room with a steel door, and the nurse pulled out her keys and slowly unlocked it.

When they walked into the bare room, they noticed a scrawny-looking woman balled up in the corner, shivering as if she was cold. The room was padded all around, with a small bed against the wall; it had an eerie feel to it, and had a strange odor.

Starr and River stared at their mother, Sheryl, and were speechless. Time and aging had not been good to her. She was so thin that her flesh looked as if it shriveled around her bones. Her fingers were long and gaunt, her hair was dirty and in disarray. The constant drug use, especially the abuse of heroin, had deranged Sheryl so much that she was no longer able to take care of herself. She wore an adult diaper, and mumbled incoherent statements and just stayed balled up in the corner with her knees pressed against her chest. It was hard to look at her.

"That can't be her," River muttered. For River, this was not the same woman who had tormented her years ago. She looked so weak and defenseless.

Starr stared at Sheryl with so much resentment, and thought karma must be real. Because of her mother, her life was hell. Starr had no words to say at first. The sight of her mother in such a horrible condition was too disturbing and appalling. She didn't know whether to smile or cringe.

"She's been here for two years," the nurse informed them. "We were trying to locate her family, but to no avail. Cops found her in a back alley one night, high and naked. She tried to attack one of the officers with a syringe."

Ms. Henderson was sad at the decline of her sister-in-law. She hugged her nieces tightly.

"I'll give you some time alone with her," the nurse said before she left the room.

"Sheryl," Ms. Henderson called out. "These are your daughters. Do you remember your daughters?"

Sheryl remained in the same position and glanced at the trio. Her mind was gone.

"I brought them here so you could see them again. You have two beautiful daughters, and they came to see you," Ms. Henderson said, approaching closer to Sheryl.

River was the next to approach. She came close to her mother and squatted down at eye level with her, peering at her mother's appalling features. Sheryl's hands shook as if she had Parkinson's disease. Ms. Henderson had brought the sisters so that they could pay their mother one last visit and forgive her. River reached out and gently took her mother's thin hand into hers. It was hard for River to forgive, but she wanted to close this chapter of her life and move on. She held on to her mother and then gave her a hug. "I forgive you, Mama. I do. I moved on. I've met someone, and he's great. We started off shaky, but I know everything will work out fine between us. We're gonna move with Daddy down South. I know you still love him, Mama, right? But Mama, why did you hurt us like that? I know it was the drugs. I know you wasn't yourself, and it's okay, I've learned to forgive you and move on. I still love you," River proclaimed. She then gave her mother a long hug.

For Starr it wasn't so easy. That anger, that contempt for her mother was still rooted in her heart. It was hard to forgive and forget. She felt reluctant to move forward. Ms. Henderson grabbed her hand and said a few encouraging words to her. Starr nodded and stepped forward.

Starr stood over her mother and she knew she needed to get what was hurting her off her chest. "I always hated you. Because of you, my life was hell. You made Daddy go away. You made men come into my room and forced me to have sex with them. I was only twelve, Mama, and you never once tried to protect me from them. Everything to you was always about money and sex . . . everything!" she shouted. "You were an evil woman. I was a prostitute, Mama. I always used what you told me. I sold my pussy for money, because you always told me that was the one thing that was gonna make me rich. I was raped, beaten, and did unthinkable things. I walked the streets every night tryin' to make my life rich. But you know what, Mama, I am rich. I have River back in my life, and now I found Aunt Diana, and she's been more of a mother to me than you ever were. We're leaving you, Mama. I always wanted you to burn in hell for all the sins you committed against me, River, and Daddy. But I look at you now and see you suffering in this place, alone, and I know you already lost everything. You probably don't even remember me. But I will not become you. I will not hate you. Because you and the trials and tribulations I endured living with you and on the streets made me stronger, and made me become a better person. So when the day comes, when I do have children, I will know how to love them and my husband with everything I have, and do the opposite of what you did to your family."

After her speech, Starr had tears streaming down her face as she gawked at her mother. She could no longer go on. Ms. Henderson walked over to her and hugged and consoled the tearful Starr and told her she did the right thing.

"I'm sorry. I'm sorry. I'm sorry. I'm sorry. I'm sorry," Sheryl meekly chanted continuously as she rocked back and forth, shaking and twitching, staring past Starr at the wall. It sounded like an apology, but a little incoherent. The girls didn't know if it was coming from her heart or if she was just chanting gibberish. But for River and Starr, it was good enough. They felt better for having confronted their past, and they were both able to move on.

They left with Ms. Henderson, and the door closed on their mentally disabled mother. The next road for them was I-95 toward North Carolina.

Eric stood outside the hospital next to a Ford Explorer. When the girls came out, he hugged River and then Starr, and asked how

Erick S. Gray

ERICK S. GRAY's climb to success in the literary genre has been fortunate, but also nothing but trials and tribulations for this talented, forty-four-year-old writer from Jamaica, Queens. Since his debut in 2003 with *Booty Call*, he's been consistent, with over sixteen books published, participating in many anthologies and novellas, and helping to cowrite the Streets of New York trilogy within the span of twenty years. His style of writing has been known to be raunchy, but also fruitful. His diversity in storytelling makes him one of the most prolific writers of the genre. His characters are memorable and true to life, and Mr. Gray has the drive to become an icon in a growing genre.